Mary Higgins Clark

ALL AROUND THE TOWN

I'LL BE SEEING YOU

ARROW

This edition published by Arrow in 1998
an imprint of The Ranodom House Group
20 Vauxhall Bridge Road, London SW1V 2SA

Copyright © Mary Higgins Clark 1998

The right of Mary Higgins Clark to be identified as
the author of this work has been asserted by her in
accordance with the Copyright Designs and Patents
Act 1988

All Around Town copyright © Mary Higgins Clark 1992
I'll Be Seeing You copyright © Mary Higgins Clark 1981

Papers used by Random House UK Ltd are natural
recyclable products made from wood grown in
sustainable forests. The manufacturing process
conform to the environment regulations of the
country of origin.

A catalogue record for this book is available from
the British Library

Printed in Australia by McPherson's Printing Pty Ltd

ISBN 0 099 27945 2

ALL AROUND THE TOWN

FOR MY NEWEST GRANDSON
JUSTIN LOUIS CLARK,
WITH LOVE AND JOY.

My sincere thanks and profound gratitude to Walter C. Young, M.D., Medical Director of the National Center for the treatment of Dissociative Disorders in Aurora, Colorado; Trish Keller Knode, A.T.R., L.P.C., art therapist; and Kay Adams, M.A., journal therapist, for the Center. Their guidance, assistance and encouragement have been infinitely invaluable in allowing me to tell this story.

Kudos and heartfelt thanks to my editor Michael V. Korda; his associate, senior editor Chuck Adams; my agent, Eugene H. Winick; Ina Winick, M.S.; and my publicist, Lisl Cade. And of course my terrific family and friends.

Bless you, my dears, one and all.

PART ONE

1

*T*EN MINUTES BEFORE it happened, four-year-old Laurie Kenyon was sitting cross-legged on the floor of the den rearranging the furniture in her dollhouse. She was tired of playing alone and wanted to go in the pool. From the dining room she could hear the voices of Mommy and the ladies who used to go to school with her in New York. They were talking and laughing while they ate lunch.

Mommy had told her that because Sarah, her big sister, was at a birthday party for other twelve-year-olds, Beth, who sometimes minded her at night, would come over to swim with Laurie. But the minute Beth arrived she started making phone calls.

Laurie pushed back the long blond hair that felt warm on her face. She had gone upstairs a long time ago and changed into her new pink bathing suit. Maybe if she reminded Beth again . . .

Beth was curled up on the couch, the phone stuck between her shoulder and ear. Laurie tugged on her arm. "I'm all ready."

Beth looked mad. "In a minute, honey," she said. "I'm having a very important discussion." Laurie heard her sigh into the phone. "I *hate* baby-sitting."

Laurie went to the window. A long car was slowly passing the house. Behind it was an open car filled with flowers, then a lot more cars with their lights on. Whenever she saw cars like that Laurie always used to say that a parade was coming, but Mommy said no, that they were funerals on the way to the cemetery. Even so, they made Laurie *think* of a parade, and she loved to run down the driveway and wave to the people in the cars. Sometimes they waved back.

Beth clicked down the receiver. Laurie was just about to ask her if they could go out and watch the rest of the cars go by when Beth picked up the phone again.

Beth was *mean,* Laurie told herself. She tiptoed out to the foyer and peeked into the dining room. Mommy and her friends were still talking and laughing. Mommy was saying, "Can you *believe* we graduated from the Villa thirty-two years ago?"

The lady next to her said, "Well, Marie, at least *you* can lie about it. You've got a four-year-old daughter. I've got a four-year-old *granddaughter!*"

"We still look pretty darn good," somebody else said, and they all laughed again.

They didn't even bother to look at Laurie. They were mean too. The pretty music box Mommy's friend had brought her was on the table. Laurie picked it up. It was only a few steps to the screen door. She opened it noiselessly, hurried across the porch and ran down the driveway to the road. There were still cars passing the house. She waved.

She watched until they were out of sight, then sighed, hoping that the company would go home soon. She wound up the music box and heard the tinkling sound of a piano and voices singing, " 'Eastside, westside . . .' "

"Little girl."

Laurie hadn't noticed the car pull over and stop. A woman was driving. The man sitting next to her got out, picked Laurie up, and before she knew what was happening she was squeezed be-

16

tween them in the front seat. Laurie was too surprised to say anything. The man was smiling at her, but it wasn't a nice smile. The woman's hair was hanging around her face, and she didn't wear lipstick. The man had a beard, and his arms had a lot of curly hair. Laurie was pressed against him so hard she could feel it.

The car began to move. Laurie clutched the music box. Now the voices were singing: " 'All around the town . . . Boys and girls together . . .' "

"Where are we going?" she asked. She remembered that she wasn't supposed to go out to the road alone. Mommy would be mad at her. She could feel tears in her eyes.

The woman looked so angry. The man said, "All around the town, little girl. All around the town."

2

*S*ARAH HURRIED ALONG the side of the road, carefully carrying a piece of birthday cake on a paper plate. Laurie loved chocolate filling, and Sarah wanted to make it up to her for not playing with her while Mommy had company.

She was a bony long-legged twelve-year-old, with wide gray eyes, carrot red hair that frizzed in dampness, milk-white skin and a splash of freckles across her nose. She looked like neither of her parents—her mother was petite, blond and blue eyed; her father's gray hair had originally been dark brown.

It worried Sarah that John and Marie Kenyon were so much

older than the other kids' parents. She was always afraid they might die before she grew up. Her mother had once explained to her, "We'd been married fifteen years and I'd given up hope of ever having a baby, but when I was thirty-seven I knew you were on the way. Like a gift. Then eight years later when Laurie was born—oh, Sarah, it was a miracle!

When she was in the second grade, Sarah remembered asking Sister Catherine which was better, a gift or a miracle?

"A miracle is the greatest gift a human being can receive," Sister Catherine had said. That afternoon, when Sarah suddenly began to cry in class, she fibbed and said it was because her stomach was sick.

Even though she knew Laurie was the favorite, Sarah still loved her parents fiercely. When she was ten she had made a bargain with God. If He wouldn't let Daddy or Mommy die before she was grown, she would clean up the kitchen every night, help to take care of Laurie and never chew gum again. She was keeping her side of the bargain, and so far God was listening to her.

An unconscious smile touching her lips, she turned the corner of Twin Oaks Road and stared. Two police cars were in her driveway, their lights flashing. A lot of neighbors were clustered outside, even the brand-new people from two houses down, whom they hadn't even really met. They all looked scared and sad, holding their kids tightly by the hand.

Sarah began to run. Maybe Mommy or Daddy was sick. Richie Johnson was standing on the lawn. He was in her class at Mount Carmel. Sarah asked Richie why everyone was there.

He looked sorry for her. Laurie was missing, he told her. Old Mrs. Whelan had seen a man take her into a car, but hadn't realized Laurie was being kidnapped . . .

3

*T*HEY WOULDN'T take her home.

They drove a long time and took her to a dirty house, way out in the woods somewhere. They slapped her if she cried. The man kept picking her up and hugging her. Then he would carry her upstairs. She tried to make him stop, but he laughed at her. They called her Lee. Their names were Bic and Opal. After a while she found ways to slip away from them, in her mind. Sometimes she just floated on the ceiling and watched what was happening to the little girl with the long blond hair. Sometimes she felt sorry for the little girl. Other times she made fun of her. Sometimes when they let her sleep alone she dreamt of other people, Mommy and Daddy and Sarah. But then she'd start to cry again and they'd hit her, so she made herself forget Mommy and Daddy and Sarah. *That's good,* a voice in her head told her. *Forget all about them.*

4

*A*T FIRST the police were at the house every day, and Laurie's picture was on the front page of the New Jersey and New York papers. Beyond tears, Sarah watched her mother and

19

father on "Good Morning, America," pleading with whoever took Laurie to bring her back.

Dozens of people phoned saying they'd seen Laurie, but none of the leads was useful. The police had hoped there'd be a demand for ransom, but there was none.

The summer dragged on. Sarah watched as her mother's face became haunted and bleak, as her father reached constantly for the nitroglycerin pills in his pocket. Every morning they went to the 7 A.M. mass and prayed for Laurie to be sent home. Frequently at night Sarah awoke to hear her mother's sobbing, her father's exhausted attempts to comfort her. "It was a miracle that Laurie was born. We'll count on another miracle to bring her back to us," she heard him say.

School started again. Sarah had always been a good student. Now she pored over the books, finding that she could blot out her own relentless sorrow by escaping into study. A natural athlete, she began taking golf and tennis lessons. Still she missed her little sister, with aching pain. She wondered if God was punishing her for the times she'd resented all the attention paid to Laurie. She hated herself for going to the birthday party that day and pushed aside the thought that Laurie was strictly forbidden to go out front alone. She promised that if God would send Laurie back to them she would always, *always* take care of her.

5

THE SUMMER PASSED. The wind began to blow through the cracks in the walls. Laurie was always cold. One day

Opal came back with long-sleeved shirts and overalls and a winter jacket. It wasn't pretty like the one Laurie used to wear. When it got warm again they gave her some other clothes, shorts and shirts and sandals. Another winter went by. Laurie watched the leaves on the big old tree in front of the house begin to bud and open, and then all the branches were filled with them.

Bic had an old typewriter in the bedroom. It made a loud clatter that Laurie could hear when she was cleaning up the kitchen or watching television. The clatter was a good sound. It meant that Bic wouldn't bother with her.

After a while, he'd come out of the bedroom holding a bunch of papers in his hand and start reading them aloud to Laurie and Opal. He always shouted and he always ended with the same words, "Hallelujah. Amen!" After he was finished, he and Opal would sing together. Practicing, they called it. Songs about God and going home.

Home. It was a word that her voices told Laurie not to think about anymore.

Laurie never saw anyone else. Only Bic and Opal. And when they went out, they locked her in the basement. It happened a lot. It was scary down there. The window was almost at the ceiling and had boards over it. The basement was filled with shadows, and sometimes they seemed to move around. Each time, Laurie tried to go to sleep right away on the mattress they left on the floor.

Bic and Opal almost never had company. If someone did come to the house, Laurie was put down in the basement with her leg chained to the pipe, so she couldn't go up the stairs and knock on the door. "And don't you dare call us," Bic warned her. "You'd get in big trouble, and, anyhow, we couldn't hear you."

After they'd been out they usually brought money home. Sometimes not much. Sometimes a lot. Quarters and dollar bills, mostly.

They let her go out in the backyard with them. They showed her how to weed the vegetable garden and gather the eggs from

21

the chicken coop. There was a newborn baby chick they told her she could keep as her pet. She played with it whenever she went outside. Sometimes when they locked her in the basement and went away they let her keep it with her.

Until the bad day when Bic killed it.

Early one morning they began to pack—just their clothes and the television set and Bic's typewriter. Bic and Opal were laughing and singing, "Ha-lay-loo-ya."

"A fifteen-thousand-watt station in Ohio!" Bic shouted, "Bible Belt, here we come!"

They drove for two hours. Then from the backseat where she was scrunched against the battered old suitcases, Laurie heard Opal say, "Let's go into a diner and get a decent meal. Nobody will pay any attention to her. Why should they?"

Bic said, "You're right." Then he looked quickly over his shoulder at Laurie. "Opal will order a sandwich and milk for you. Don't you talk to anybody, you hear?"

They went to a place with a long counter and tables and chairs. Laurie was so hungry that she could almost taste the bacon she could smell frying. But there was something else. She could remember being in a place like this with the other people. A sob that she couldn't force back rose in her throat. Bic gave her a push to follow Opal, and she began to cry. Cry so hard she couldn't get her breath. She could see the lady at the cash register staring at her. Bic grabbed her and hustled her out to the parking lot, Opal beside him.

Bic threw her in the backseat of the car, and he and Opal rushed to get in front. As Opal slammed her foot on the gas pedal, he reached for her. She tried to duck when the hairy hand swung forward and back across her face. But after the first blow she didn't feel any pain. She just felt sorry for the little girl who was crying so hard.

6

June 1976
Ridgewood, New Jersey

S*ARAH SAT* with her mother and father watching the program about missing children. The last segment was about Laurie. Pictures of her taken just before she disappeared. A computerized image that showed how she would probably look today, two years after she'd been kidnapped.

When the program ended, Marie Kenyon ran from the room screaming, "I want my baby. I want my baby."

Tears running down her face, Sarah listened to her father's agonized attempt to comfort her mother. "Maybe this program will be the instrument of a miracle," he said. He did not sound as if he believed it.

It was Sarah who answered the phone an hour later. Bill Conners, the police chief of Ridgewood, had always treated Sarah as an adult. "Your folks pretty upset after the program, honey?" he asked.

"Yes."

"I don't know whether to get their hopes up, but a call has come in that may be promising. A cashier in a diner in Harrisburg, Pennsylvania, is positive she saw Laurie this afternoon."

"This afternoon!" Sarah felt her breath stop.

"She'd been worried because the little girl suddenly became hysterical. But it was no tantrum. She was practically choking herself trying to stop crying. The Harrisburg police have Laurie's updated picture."

"Who was with her?"

"A man and woman. Hippie types. Unfortunately the description is pretty vague. The cashier's attention was on the kid, so she hardly got a glimpse of the couple."

He left it to Sarah to decide whether it was wise to tell her parents, to raise her parents' hopes. She made another bargain with God. "Let this be their miracle. Let the Harrisburg police find Laurie. I'll take care of her forever."

She hurried upstairs to offer her mother and father the new reason to hope.

7

*T*HE CAR STARTED to have trouble a little while after they left the diner. Every time they slowed down in traffic the engine sputtered and died. The third time it happened and cars had to pull out from behind them, Opal said, "Bic, when we break down for good and a cop comes along, you'd better be careful. He might start asking questions about her." She jerked her head toward Laurie.

Bic told her to look for a gas station and pull off the road. When they found one, he made Laurie lie down on the floor and piled garbage bags filled with old clothes over her before they drove in.

The car needed a lot of work; it wouldn't be ready till the next day. There was a motel next to the gas station. The attendant said it was cheap and pretty comfortable.

They drove over to the motel. Bic went inside the office and came back with the key. They drove around to the room and rushed Laurie inside. Then, after Bic drove the car back to the gas station, they watched television for the rest of the afternoon. Bic

24

brought in hamburgers for dinner. Laurie fell asleep just when the program came on about missing children. She woke up to hear Bic cursing. *Keep your eyes shut,* a voice warned her. *He's going to take it out on you.*

"The cashier got a good look at her," Opal was saying. "Suppose she's watching this. We'll have to get rid of her."

The next afternoon, Bic went to get the car by himself. When he came back he sat Laurie on the bed and held her arms against her. "What's my name?" he asked her.

"Bic."

He jerked his head at Opal. "What's her name?"

"Opal."

"I want you to forget that. I want you to forget us. Don't you ever talk about us. Do you understand, Lee?"

Laurie did not understand. *Say* yes, a voice whispered impatiently. *Nod your head and say* yes.

"Yes," she said softly and felt her head nodding.

"Remember the time I cut the head off the chicken?" Bic asked.

She shut her eyes. The chicken had flopped around the yard, blood spilling out from its neck. Then it had fallen on her feet. She had tried to scream as the blood sprayed over her, but no sound came out. She never went near the chickens after that. Sometimes she dreamed that the headless chicken was running after her.

"Remember?" Bic asked, tightening his grip on her arms.

"Yes."

"We have to go away. We're going to leave you where people will find you. If you ever tell anyone my name or Opal's name or the name we called you or where we lived or anything that we did together, I'm going to come with the chicken knife and cut your head off. Do you understand that?"

The knife. Long and sharp and streaked with blood from the chicken.

"Promise you won't tell anybody," Bic demanded.

25

"Promise, promise," she mumbled desperately.

They got in the car. Once more they made her lie on the floor. It was so hot. The garbage bags stuck to her skin.

When it was dark they stopped in front of a big building. Bic took her out of the car. "This is a school," he told her. "Tomorrow morning a lot of people will come, and other kids you can play with. Stay here and wait for them."

She shrank from his moist kiss, his fierce hug. "I'm crazy about you," he said, "but remember, if you say one word about us . . ." He lifted his arm, closed his fist as though he was holding a knife and made a slashing motion on her neck.

"I promise," she sobbed, "I promise."

Opal handed her a bag with cookies and a Coke. She watched them drive off. She knew that if she didn't stay right here they'd come back to hurt her. It was so dark. She could hear animals scurrying in the woods nearby.

Laurie shrank against the door of the building and wrapped her arms around her body. She'd been hot all day and now she was cold and she was so scared. Maybe the headless chicken was running around out there. She began to tremble.

Look at the 'fraidy cat. She slipped away to be part of the jeering voice that was laughing at the small figure huddled at the entrance to the school.

8

*P*OLICE CHIEF CONNERS phoned again in the morning. The lead looked promising, he said. A child who answered Laurie's description had been found when the caretaker arrived to open a school in a rural area near Pittsburgh. They were rushing Laurie's fingerprints there.

An hour later he phoned back. The prints were a perfect match. Laurie was coming home.

9

*J*OHN AND MARIE KENYON flew to Pittsburgh. Laurie had been taken to a hospital to be checked out. The next day on the noon edition of the TV news, Sarah watched as her mother and father left the hospital, Laurie between them. Sarah crouched in front of the set and gripped it with her hands. Laurie was taller. The waterfall of blond hair was shaggy. She was very thin. But it was more than that. Laurie had always been so friendly. Now even though she kept her head down, her eyes darted around as if she were looking for something she was afraid to find.

The reporters were bombarding them with questions. John Kenyon's voice was strained and tired as he said, "The doctors tell us Laurie is in good health, even though she is a touch underweight. Of course she's confused and frightened."

"Has she talked about the kidnappers?"

"She hasn't talked about anything. Please, we're so grateful for your interest and concern, but it would be a great kindness to allow our family to reunite quietly." Her father's voice was almost pleading.

"Is there any sign that she was molested?"

Sarah saw the shock on her mother's face. "Absolutely not!" she said. Her tone was appalled. "We believe that people who wanted a child took Laurie. We only hope they don't put another family through this nightmare."

Sarah needed to release the frantic energy that was churning inside her. She made Laurie's bed with the Cinderella sheets that Laurie loved. She arranged Laurie's favorite toys around her room, the twin dolls in their strollers, the dollhouse, the bear, her Peter Rabbit books. She folded Laurie's security blanket on the pillow.

Sarah bicycled to the store to buy cheese and pasta and chopped meat. Laurie loved lasagna. While Sarah was making it, she was constantly interrupted by phone calls. She managed to convince everyone to put off visiting for at least a few days.

They were due home at six o'clock. By five-thirty the lasagna was in the oven, the salad in the refrigerator, the table set for four again. Sarah went upstairs to change. She studied herself in the mirror. Would Laurie remember her? In the past two years she'd grown from five-four to five-seven. Her hair was short. It used to be shoulder-length. She used to be straight up and down. Now that she was fourteen her breasts had begun to fill out. She wore contact lenses instead of glasses.

That last night, before Laurie had been kidnapped, Sarah remembered that she had worn jeans and a long T-shirt to dinner. She still had the T-shirt in her closet. She put it on with jeans.

Crews with television cameras were in the driveway when the car pulled up. Groups of neighbors and friends waited in the background. Everyone began to cheer when the car door opened and John and Marie Kenyon led Laurie out.

Sarah ran to her little sister and dropped on her knees. "Laurie," she said softly. She stretched out her hands and watched as Laurie's hands fled to cover her face. She's afraid I'll hit her, Sarah thought.

It was she who picked Laurie up and took her inside the house as her parents once again spoke to the media.

Laurie did not show any sign that she remembered the house. She did not speak to them. At dinner she ate silently, her eyes looking down at the plate. When she had finished she got up, brought her plate to the sink and began to clear the table.

Marie stood up. "Darling, you don't have to—"

"Leave her alone, Mom," Sarah whispered. She helped Laurie clear, talking to her about what a big girl she was and how Laurie always used to help her with the dishes. Remember?

Afterwards they went into the den and Sarah turned on the television. Laurie pulled away trembling when Marie and John asked her to sit between them. "She's frightened," Sarah warned. "Pretend she isn't here."

Her mother's eyes filled with tears, but she managed to look absorbed in the program. Laurie sat cross-legged on the floor, choosing a spot where she could see but not be seen.

At nine o'clock when Marie suggested a nice warm bath and going to bed, Laurie panicked. She pressed her knees against her chest and buried her face in her hands. Sarah and her father exchanged glances.

"Poor little tyke," he said. "You don't have to go to bed now." Sarah saw in his eyes the same denial she had seen in her mother's. "It's just everything is so strange for you, isn't it?"

Marie was trying to hide the fact that she was weeping. "She's afraid of us," she murmured.

No, Sarah thought. She's afraid to go to bed. Why?

They left the television on. At quarter of ten, Laurie stretched out on the floor and fell asleep. It was Sarah who carried her up, changed her, tucked her into bed, slipped the security blanket between her arms and under her chin.

John and Marie tiptoed in and sat on either side of the small

29

white bed, absorbing the miracle that had been granted them. They did not notice when Sarah slipped from the room.

Laurie slept long and late. In the morning Sarah looked in on her, drinking in the blessed sight of the long hair spilling on the pillow, the small figure nestling the security blanket against her face. She repeated the promise she had made to God. "I will always take care of her."

Her mother and father were already up. Both looked exhausted but radiant with joy. "We kept going in to see if she was really there," Marie said. "Sarah, we were just saying we couldn't have made it through these two years without you."

Sarah helped her mother prepare Laurie's favorite breakfast, pancakes and bacon. Laurie pattered into the room a few minutes later, the nightgown that used to be ankle length now stopping at her calves, her security blanket trailing behind her.

She climbed on Marie's lap. "Mommy," she said, her tone injured. "Yesterday I wanted to go in the pool and Beth kept talking on the phone."

PART TWO

10

September 12, 1991
Ridgewood, New Jersey

DURING THE MASS, Sarah kept glancing sideways at Laurie. The sight of the two caskets at the steps of the sanctuary had clearly mesmerized her. She was staring at them, tearless now, seemingly unaware of the music, the prayers, the eulogy. Sarah had to put a hand under Laurie's elbow to remind her to stand or kneel.

At the end of the mass, as Monsignor Fisher blessed the coffins, Laurie whispered, "Mommy, Daddy, I'm sorry. I won't go out front alone again."

"Laurie," Sarah whispered.

Laurie looked at her with unseeing eyes, then turned and with a puzzled expression studied the crowded church. "So many people." Her voice sounded timid and young.

The closing hymn was "Amazing Grace."

With the rest of the congregation, a couple near the back of the church began to sing, softly at first, but he was used to leading the music. As always he got carried away, his pure baritone becoming louder, soaring above the others, swelling over the thinner voice of the soloist. People turned distracted, admiring.

33

" 'I once was lost but now am found . . .' "

Through the pain and grief, Laurie felt icy terror. The voice. Ringing through her head, through her being.

I am lost, she wailed silently. *I am lost.*

They were moving the caskets.

The wheels of the bier holding her mother's casket squealed. She heard the measured steps of the pallbearers.

Then the clattering of the typewriter.

" *'. . . was blind but now I see.'* "

"No! No!" Laurie shrieked as she crumpled into merciful darkness.

Several dozen of Laurie's classmates from Clinton College had attended the mass, along with a sprinkling of faculty. Allan Grant, Professor of English, was there and with shocked eyes watched Laurie collapse.

Grant was one of the most popular teachers at Clinton. Just turned forty, he had thick, somewhat unruly brown hair, liberally streaked with gray. Large dark brown eyes that expressed humor and intelligence were the best feature in his somewhat long face. His lanky body and casual dress completed an appearance that many young women undergraduates found irresistible.

Grant was genuinely interested in his students. Laurie had been in one of his classes every year since she entered Clinton. He knew her personal history and had been curious to see if there might be any observable aftereffects of her abduction. The only time he'd picked up anything had been in his creative writing class. Laurie was incapable of writing a personal memoir. On the other hand, her critiques of books, authors and plays were insightful and thought-provoking.

Three days ago she had been in his class when the word came for her to go to the office immediately. The class was ending and, sensing trouble, he had accompanied her. As they hurried across the campus, she'd told him that her mother and father were driving down to switch cars with her. She'd forgotten to have her convertible inspected and had returned to college in her mother's sedan. "They're probably just running late," she'd said, obviously trying to reassure herself. "My mother says I'm too much of a worrier about them. But she hasn't been that well and Dad is almost seventy-two."

Somberly the dean told them that there had been a multivehicle accident on Route 78.

Allan Grant drove Laurie to the hospital. Her sister, Sarah, was already there, her cloud of dark red hair framing a face dominated by large gray eyes that were filled with grief. Grant had met Sarah at a number of college functions and been impressed with the young assistant prosecutor's protective attitude toward Laurie.

One look at her sister's face was enough to make Laurie realize that her parents were dead. Over and over she kept moaning "my fault, my fault," seeming not to hear Sarah's tearful insistence that she must not blame herself.

Distressed, Grant watched as an usher carried Laurie from the nave of the church, Sarah beside him. The organist began to play the recessional hymn. The pallbearers, led by the monsignor, started to walk slowly down the aisle. In the row in front of him, Grant saw a man making his way to the end of the pew. "Please excuse me. I'm a doctor," he was saying, his voice low but authoritative.

Some instinct made Allan Grant slip into the aisle and follow him to the small room off the vestibule where Laurie had been taken. She was lying on two chairs that had been pushed together. Sarah, her face chalk white, was bending over her.

"Let me . . ." The doctor touched Sarah's arm.

Laurie stirred and moaned.

The doctor raised her eyelids, felt her pulse. "She's coming around but she must be taken home. She's in no condition to go to the cemetery."

"I know."

Allan saw how desperately Sarah was trying to keep her own composure. "Sarah," he said. She turned, seemingly aware of him for the first time. "Sarah, let me go back to the house with Laurie. She'll be okay with me."

"Oh, would you?" For an instant gratitude replaced the strain and grief in her expression. "Some of the neighbors are there preparing food, but Laurie trusts you so much. I'd be so relieved."

" *'I once was lost but now am found . . .'* "

A hand was coming at her holding the knife, the knife dripping with blood, slashing through the air. Her shirt and overalls were soaked with blood. She could feel the sticky warmth on her face. Something was flopping at her feet. The knife was coming . . .

Laurie opened her eyes. She was in bed in her own room. It was dark. What happened?

She remembered. The church. The caskets. The singing.

"Sarah!" she shrieked, "Sarah! Where are you?"

11

THEY WERE STAYING at the Wyndham Hotel on West Fifty-eighth Street in Manhattan. "Classy," he'd told her. "A lot of show business people go there. Right kind of place to start making connections."

He was silent on the drive from the funeral mass into New York. They were having lunch with the Reverend Rutland Garrison, pastor of the Church of the Airways, and the television program's executive producer. Garrison was ready to retire and in the process of choosing a successor. Every week a guest preacher was invited to co-host the program.

She watched as he discarded three different outfits before settling on a midnight blue suit, white shirt and bluish gray tie. "They want a preacher. They're gonna get a preacher. How do I look?"

"Perfect," she assured him. He did too. His hair was now silver even though he was only forty-five. He watched his weight carefully and had taught himself to stand very straight so that he always seemed to stand above people, even taller men. He'd practiced widening his eyes when he thundered a sermon until that had become his usual expression.

He vetoed her first choice of a red-and-white checked dress. "Not classy enough for this meeting. It's a little too Betty Crocker."

That was their private joke when they wanted to impress the congregations who came to hear him preach. But there was nothing joking about him now. She held up a black linen sheath with a matching jacket. "How's this?"

He nodded silently. "That will do." He frowned. "And remember . . ."

"I never call you Bic in front of anyone," she protested coaxingly. "Haven't for years." He had a feverish glitter in his eyes. Opal knew and feared that look. It had been three years since the last time he was brought in by local police for questioning because some little girl with blond hair had complained to her mother about him. He'd always managed to scorn the complainant into stammering apologies, but even so it had happened too often in too many different towns. When he got that look it meant he was losing control again.

Lee was the only child he'd ever kept. From the minute he spotted her with her mother in the shopping center, he'd been obsessed by her. He followed their car that first day and after that cruised past their house hoping to get a glimpse of the child. He and Opal had been doing a two-week stint, playing the guitar and singing at some crummy nightclub on Route 17 in New Jersey and staying in a motel twenty minutes from the Kenyon home. It was going to be their last time singing in a nightclub. Bic had started gospel singing at revivals and then preaching in upstate New York. The owner of a radio station in Bethlehem, Pennsylvania, heard him and asked him to start a religious program on his small station.

It had been bad luck that he'd insisted on driving past the house one last time on their way back to Pennsylvania. Lee was outside alone. He'd scooped her up, brought her with them, and for two years Opal lived in a state of perpetual fear and jealousy that she didn't dare let him see.

It had been fifteen years since they dumped her in the school-yard, but Bic had never gotten over her. He kept her picture hidden in his wallet, and sometimes Opal would find him staring at it, running his fingers over it. In these last years, as he became more and more successful, he worried that someday FBI agents would come up to him and tell him he was under arrest for kidnapping and child molestation. "Look at that girl in California who got her daddy put in prison because she started going to a psychiatrist and remembering things best forgotten," he would sometimes say.

They had just arrived in New York when Bic read the item in the *Times* about the Kenyons' fatal accident. Over Opal's beseeching protests, they'd gone to the funeral mass. "Opal," he had told her, "we look as different as day and night from those two guitar-playing hippies Lee remembers."

It was true that they looked totally different. They'd begun to change their appearance the morning after they got rid of Lee. Bic shaved his beard off and got a short haircut. She'd dyed her hair ash blond and fastened it in a neat bun. They'd both bought sensible clothes at JC Penney, the kind of stuff that made them blend in with everyone else, gave them the middle-American look. "Just in case anyone in that diner got a good look at us," he'd said. That was when he'd warned her never to refer to him as Bic in front of anyone and said that from now on, in public he'd call her by her real name, Carla. "Lee heard our names over and over again in those two years," he'd said. "From now on I'm the Reverend Bobby Hawkins to everyone we meet."

Even so she'd felt the fear in him when they hurried up the steps of the church. At the end of the mass as the organist began to play the first notes of "Amazing Grace," he'd whispered, "That's our song, Lee's and mine." His voice soared over all the others. They were in the seats at the end of the pew. When the usher carried Lee's limp body past them, Opal had to grab his hand to keep him from reaching out and touching her.

"I'll ask you again. Are you ready?" His voice was sarcastic. He was standing at the door of the suite.

"Yes." Opal reached for her purse, then walked over to him. She had to calm him down. The tension in him was something that shot through the room. She put her hands on the sides of his face. "Bic, honey. You gotta relax," she said soothingly. "You want to make a good impression, don't you?"

It was as though he hadn't heard a word she'd said. He murmured, "I still have the power to scare that little girl half to death, don't I?" Then he began sobbing, hard, dry, racking sobs. "God, how I love her."

12

DR. PETER CARPENTER was the Ridgewood psychiatrist Sarah called ten days after the funeral. Sarah had met him occasionally, liked him, and her inquiries justified her own impressions. Her boss, Ed Ryan, the Bergen County prosecutor, was Carpenter's most emphatic supporter. "He's a straight shooter. I'd trust any one of my family with him, and you know that for me that's saying a lot. Too many of those birds are yo-yos."

She asked for an immediate appointment. "My sister blames herself for our parents' accident," she told Carpenter. Sarah realized as she spoke that she was avoiding the word "death." It was still so unreal to her. Gripping the phone, she said, "There was a recurrent nightmare she's had over the years. It hasn't happened in ages, but now she's having it regularly again."

Dr. Carpenter vividly remembered Laurie's kidnapping. When she was abandoned by her abductors and returned home, he had discussed with colleagues the ramifications of her total memory loss. He was keenly interested in seeing the girl now, but he told Sarah, "I think it would be wise if I talk to you before I see Laurie. I have a free hour this afternoon."

As his wife often teased, Carpenter could have been the model for the kindly family doctor. Steel gray hair, pink complexion, rimless glasses, benign expression, trim body, looking his age, which was fifty-two.

His office was deliberately cozy: pale green walls, tieback draperies in tones of green and white, a mahogany desk with a cluster of small flowering plants, a roomy wine-colored leather armchair opposite his swivel chair, a matching couch facing away from the windows.

When Sarah was ushered in by his secretary, Carpenter studied the attractive young woman in the simple blue suit. Her lean, athletic body moved with ease. She wore no makeup, and a smattering of freckles was visible across her nose. Charcoal brown brows and lashes accentuated the sadness in her luminous gray eyes. Her hair was pulled severely back from her face and held by a narrow blue band. Behind the band a cloud of dark red waves floated, ending just below her ears.

Sarah found it easy to answer Dr. Carpenter's questions. "Yes. Laurie was different when she came back. Even then I was certain she must have been sexually abused. But my mother insisted on telling everyone that she was sure loving people who wanted a child had taken her. Mother needed to believe that. Fifteen years ago people didn't talk about that kind of abuse. But Laurie was so frightened to go to bed. She loved my father but would never sit on his lap again. She didn't want him to touch her. She was afraid of men in general."

"Surely she was examined when she was found?"

"Yes, at the hospital in Pennsylvania."

"Those records may still exist. I wish you'd arrange to send for them. What about that recurring dream?"

"She had it again last night. She was absolutely terrified. She calls it the knife dream. Ever since she came back to us, she's been afraid of sharp knives."

"How much personality change did you observe?"

"At first a great deal. Laurie was an outgoing sociable child before she was kidnapped. A little spoiled, I suppose, but very sweet. She had a play group and loved to visit back and forth with her friends. After she came back she would never stay overnight in anyone's house again. She always seemed a little distant with her peers.

"She chose to go to Clinton College because it's only an hour-and-a-half drive away and she came home many weekends."

Carpenter asked, "What about boyfriends?"

"As you'll see, she's a very beautiful young woman. She cer-

41

tainly got asked out plenty and in high school did go to the usual dances and games. She never seemed interested in anyone until Gregg Bennett, and that ended abruptly."

"Why?"

"We don't know. Gregg doesn't know. They went together all last year. He attends Clinton College as well and would often come home weekends with her. We liked him tremendously, and Laurie seemed so happy with him. They're both good athletes, especially fine golfers. Then one day last spring it was over. No explanations. Just over. She won't talk about it, won't talk to Gregg. He came to see us. He has no idea what caused the break. He's in England this semester, and I don't know that he's even heard about my parents."

"I'd like to see Laurie tomorrow at eleven."

The next morning Sarah drove Laurie to the appointment and promised to return in exactly fifty minutes. "I'll bring in some stuff for dinner," she told her. "We've got to perk up that appetite of yours."

Laurie nodded and followed Carpenter into his private office. With something like panic in her face, she refused to recline on the couch, choosing to sit across the desk from him. She waited silently, her expression sad and withdrawn.

Obvious profound depression, Carpenter thought. "I'd like to help you, Laurie."

"Can you bring back my mother and father?"

"I wish I could. Laurie, your parents are dead because a bus malfunctioned."

"They're dead because I didn't have my car inspected."

"You forgot."

"I didn't forget. I decided to break the appointment at the gas station. I said I'd go to the free inspection center at the Motor Vehicle Agency. That one I forgot, but I deliberately broke the first appointment. It's my fault."

"Why did you break the first appointment?" He watched closely as Laurie Kenyon considered the question.

"There was a reason but I don't know what it was."

"How much does it cost to have the car inspected at the gas station?"

"Twenty dollars."

"And it's free at the Motor Vehicle Agency. Isn't that a good enough reason?"

She seemed to be immersed in her own thoughts. Carpenter wondered if she had heard him. Then she whispered, "No," and shook her head.

"Then why do you think you broke the first appointment?"

Now he was sure she had not heard him. She was in a different place. He tried another tack. "Laurie, Sarah tells me that you've been having bad dreams again, or rather the same bad dream you *used* to have has come back."

Inside her mind, Laurie heard a loud wail. She pulled her legs against her chest and buried her head. The wailing wasn't just inside her. It was coming from her chest and throat and mouth.

13

THE MEETING with Preacher Rutland Garrison and the television producers was sobering.

They had eaten lunch in the private dining room of Worldwide Cable, the company that syndicated Garrison's program to an international audience. Over coffee, he made himself very clear. "I began the 'Church of the Airways' when ten-inch black-and-white TVs were luxuries," he said. "Over the years this ministry has given comfort, hope and faith to millions of people. It has raised a great deal of money for worthwhile charities. I intend to see that the right person continues my work after me."

Bic and Opal had nodded, their faces set in expressions of deference, respect and piety. The following Sunday they were introduced on the "Church of the Airways." Bic spoke for forty minutes.

He told of his wasted youth, his vain desire to be a rock star, of the voice the good Lord had given him and how he had abused it with vile secular songs. He spoke of the miracle of his conversion. Yea, verily, he understood the road to Damascus. He had traveled it in the footsteps of Paul. The Lord didn't say, "Saul, Saul, why persecuteth thou Me?" No, the question hurt even more. At least Saul thought he was acting in the name of the Lord when he tried to blot out Christianity. As he, Bobby, stood in that crowded dirty nightclub, singing those filthy lyrics, a voice filled his heart and soul, a voice that was so powerful and yet so sad, so angry and yet so forgiving. The voice asked, "Bobby, Bobby, why do you blaspheme me?"

Here he began to cry.

At the end of the sermon, Preacher Rutland Garrison put a fatherly arm around him. Bobby beckoned to Carla to join him. She came onto the set, her eyes moist, her lips quivering. He introduced her to the Worldwide audience.

They led the closing hymn together. " 'Bringing in the sheaves . . .' "

After the program the switchboard came alive with calls praising the Reverend Bobby Hawkins. He was invited to return in two weeks.

On the drive back to Georgia, Bic was silent for hours. Then he said, "Lee's at the college in Clinton, New Jersey. Maybe she'll go back. Maybe she won't. The Lord is warning me it's time to remind her of what will happen if she talks about us."

Bic was going to be chosen as Rutland Garrison's successor. Opal could sense it. Garrison had been taken in the same as all the others. But if Lee started remembering... "What are you going to do about her, Bic?"

"I got ideas, Opal. Ideas that came to me full blown while I was praying."

14

ON HER SECOND VISIT to Dr. Carpenter, Laurie told him that she was returning to college the next Monday. "It's better for me, better for Sarah," she said calmly. "She's so worried about me that she hasn't gone back to work, and work will be the best thing for her. And I'll have to study like crazy to make up for losing nearly three weeks."

Carpenter was not sure what he was seeing. There was something different about Laurie Kenyon, a brisk matter-of-fact attitude that was at total variance with the crushed, heartbroken girl he had seen a week earlier.

That day she had worn a gold cashmere jacket, beautifully cut black slacks, a gold, black and white silk blouse. Her hair had been loose around her shoulders. Today she had on jeans and a baggy sweater. Her hair was pulled back and held by a clip. She seemed totally composed.

"Have you had any more nightmares, Laurie?"

She shrugged. "I'm positively embarrassed remembering the way I carried on last week. Look, a lot of people have bad dreams and they don't go mewing around about them. Right?"

"Wrong," he said quietly. "Laurie, since you feel so much

stronger, why don't you stretch out on the couch and relax and let's talk?" Carefully he watched her reaction.

It was the same as last week. Absolute panic in her eyes. This time the panic was followed by a defiant expression that was almost a sneer. "There's no need to stretch out. I'm perfectly capable of talking sitting up. Not that there's much to talk about. Two things went wrong in my life. In both cases I'm to blame. I admit it."

"You blame yourself for being kidnapped when you were four?"

"Of course. I was forbidden to go out front alone. I mean really forbidden. My mother was so afraid that I'd forget and run into the road. There was a teenager who lived down the block, and he had a lead foot on the accelerator. The only time that I remember my mother really scolding me was when she caught me on the front lawn, alone, throwing a ball in the air. And you know I'm responsible for my parents' death."

It was not the time to explore that. "Laurie, I want to help you. Sarah told me that your parents believed that you were better off not to have psychological counseling after your abduction. That probably is part of the reason you're resisting talking to me now. Why don't you just close your eyes and rest and try to learn to feel comfortable with me? In other sessions we may be able to work together."

"You're so sure there will be other sessions?"

"I hope so. Will there be?"

"Only to please Sarah. I'll be coming home weekends, so they'll have to be on Saturdays."

"That can be arranged. You're coming home every weekend?"

"Yes."

"Is that because you want to be with Sarah?"

The question seemed to excite her. The matter-of-fact attitude disappeared. Laurie crossed her legs, lifted her chin, reached her hand back and opened the clip that held her hair in a ponytail.

Carpenter watched as the shining blond mass fell around her

face. A secretive smile played on her lips. "His wife comes home weekends," she said. "There's no use hanging around the college then."

15

*L*AURIE OPENED the door of her car. "Starting to feel like fall," she said.

The first leaves were falling from the trees. Last night the heat had gone on automatically. "Yes, it does," Sarah said. "Now look, if it's too much for you . . ."

"It won't be. You put all the creeps in prison, and I'll make up all the classes I missed and keep my cum laude. I still may even have a shot at magna. You left me in the dust with your summa. See you Friday night." She started to give Sarah a quick hug, then clung to her. "Sarah, don't you ever let me switch cars with you."

Sarah smoothed Laurie's hair. "Hey, I thought we'd agreed that Mom and Dad would get real upset about that kind of thinking. After you see Dr. Carpenter on Saturday, let's go for a round of golf."

Laurie attempted a smile. "Winner buys dinner."

"That's because you know you'll beat me."

Sarah waved vigorously until the car was no longer in sight, then turned back to the house. It was so quiet, so empty. The prevailing wisdom was to make no dramatic changes after a family death, but her instinct told her that she should start hunting immediately

47

for another place, perhaps a condo, and put the house on the market. Maybe she'd phone Dr. Carpenter and ask him about that.

She was already dressed for work. She picked up her briefcase and shoulder bag, which were on the table in the foyer. The delicate eighteenth-century table, inlaid with marble, and the mirror above it were antiques that had belonged to her grandmother. Where would they and all the other lovely pieces, all the first-edition volumes of classics that lined John Kenyon's library fit in a two-bedroom condo? Sarah pushed the thought away.

Instinctively she glanced in the mirror and was shocked at what she saw. Her complexion was dead white. There were deep circles under her eyes. Her face had always been thin, but now her cheeks were hollowed out. Her lips were ashen. She remembered her mother saying that last morning, "Sarah, why not wear a little makeup? Shadow would bring out your eyes . . ."

She dropped her shoulder bag and briefcase back on the table and went upstairs. From the vanity in her bathroom she took her seldom-used cosmetic case. The image of her mother in her shell-pink dressing gown, so naturally pretty, so endearingly maternal, telling her to put on eyeshadow brought at last the scalding tears she had forced back for Laurie's sake.

It was so good to get to her airless office with its chipped-paint walls, stacks of files, ringing telephone. Her coworkers in the prosecutor's office had come to the funeral home en masse. Her closest friends had been at the funeral, had phoned and stopped at the house these past few weeks.

Today they all seemed to understand that she wanted to get back to a semblance of normality. "Good to have you back." A quick hug. Then the welcome "Sarah, let me know when you have a minute . . ."

Lunch was a cheese on rye and black coffee from the courthouse cafeteria. By three o'clock Sarah had the satisfying feeling that she'd made a dent in responding to the urgent messages from plaintiffs, witnesses and attorneys.

At four o'clock, unable to wait any longer, she called Laurie's room at college. The phone was picked up immediately. "Hello."

"Laurie, it's me. How's it going?"

"So-so. I went to three classes, then cut the last one. I just felt so tired."

"No wonder. You haven't had a decent night's sleep. What are you doing tonight?"

"Going to bed. Got to clear out my brain."

"Okay. I'm going to work late. Be home around eight. Why don't I give you a call?"

"I'd like that."

Sarah stayed at the office until seven-fifteen, stopped at a diner and bought a hamburger to go. At eight-thirty she phoned Laurie.

The ringing at the other end continued. Maybe she's showering, maybe she's had some kind of reaction. Sarah held the receiver as the staccato sound buzzed and buzzed in her ear. Finally an impatient voice answered. "Laurie Kenyon's line."

"Is Laurie there?"

"No, and please, if the phone isn't answered in five or six rings, give me a break. I'm right across the hall and I've got a test to prepare for."

"I'm sorry. It's just that Laurie was planning to go to bed early."

"Well, she changed her plans. She went out a few minutes ago."

"Did she seem to be all right? I'm her sister and I'm a bit concerned."

"Oh, I didn't realize. I'm so sorry about what happened to your mother and father. I think Laurie was okay. She was all dressed up, like for a date."

Sarah called again at ten, at eleven, at twelve, at one. The last time, a sleepy Laurie answered. "I'm fine, Sarah. I went to bed right after dinner and have been asleep since then."

"Laurie, I rang so long the girl across the hall came over and picked up your phone. She told me you went out."

"Sarah, she's wrong. I swear to God I was right here." Laurie sounded frightened. "Why would I lie?"

I don't know, Sarah thought.

"Well, as long as you're okay. Get back to sleep," she said and replaced the receiver slowly.

16

DR. CARPENTER could sense the difference in Laurie's posture as she leaned back in the roomy leather chair. He did not suggest that she lie on the couch. The last thing he wanted was to have her lose this tentative trust in him that he sensed she was developing. He asked her how the week at college had been.

"Okay, I guess. People were awfully nice to me. I have so much catching up to do that I'm burning the midnight oil." She hesitated then stopped.

Carpenter waited then said mildly, "What is it, Laurie?"

"Last night when I got home, Sarah asked me if I'd heard from Gregg Bennett."

"Gregg Bennett?"

"I used to go out with him. My mother and father and Sarah liked him a lot."

"Do you like him?"

"I did, until . . ."

Again he waited.

Her eyes widened. "He wouldn't let go of me."

"You mean he was forcing himself on you?"

"No. He kissed me. And that was all right. I liked it. But then he pressed my arms with his hands."

"And that frightened you."

"I knew what was going to happen."

"What was going to happen?"

She was looking off into the distance. "We don't want to talk about that."

For ten minutes she was silent, then said sadly, "I could tell that Sarah didn't believe I hadn't been out the other night. She was worried."

Sarah had called him about that. "Maybe you were out," Dr. Carpenter suggested. "It would be good for you to be with friends."

"No. I don't care about dating now. I'm too busy."

"Any dreams?"

"The knife dream."

Two weeks ago she had become hysterical when she was asked about it. Today her voice was almost indifferent. "I have to get used to it. I'm going to keep having it until the knife catches up with me. It will, you know."

"Laurie, in therapy we call acting out an emotionally disturbing memory *abreaction*. I'd like you to abreact for me now. Show me what you see in the dream. I think you dread going to sleep because you're afraid you'll have the dream. Nobody can do without sleep. You don't have to talk. Just show me what is happening in the dream."

Laurie got up slowly, then raised her hand. Her mouth twisted into a cunning thin-lipped smile. She started walking around the desk toward him, her steps deliberate. Her hand jerked up and down as she swung an imaginary blade. Just before she reached him she stopped. Her posture changed. She stood, riveted to the spot, staring. Her hand tried to wipe away something from her face and hair. She looked down and jumped back terrified.

She collapsed on the floor, her hands over her face, then crouched against the wall, shivering and making hurting sounds like a wounded animal.

Ten minutes passed. Laurie quieted, dropped her hands and got up slowly.

"That's the knife dream," she said.

"Are you in the dream, Laurie?"

"Yes."

"Who are you, the one who has the knife or the one who is afraid?"

"Everybody. And in the end we all die together."

"Laurie, I'd like to talk to a psychiatrist I know who's had a great deal of experience with people who have suffered childhood trauma. Will you sign a release to let me discuss your case with him?"

"If you like. What difference can it make to me?"

17

*A*T SEVEN-THIRTY Monday morning, Dr. Justin Donnelly walked rapidly up Fifth Avenue from his Central Park South apartment to Lehman Hospital on Ninety-sixth Street. He constantly competed with himself to cover the two mile distance a minute or two faster each day. But short of actually jogging, he could not better his ten-minute record.

He was a big man who always looked as if he'd be at home in cowboy boots and a ten-gallon hat, not an inaccurate image. Donnelly had been raised on a sheep station in Australia. His curly black hair had a permanently tousled look. His black mustache was luxuriant, and when he smiled, it accentuated his strong white teeth. His intense blue eyes were framed by dark lashes and brows that women envied. Early in his psychiatric training he had decided to specialize in multiple personality disorders. A persuasive ground-breaker, Donnelly fought to establish a clinic for MPD in New South Wales. It quickly became a model facility. His papers, published in prominent medical journals, soon brought him international recognition. At thirty-five he was invited to set up a multiple personality disorder center at Lehman.

After two years in Manhattan, Justin considered himself a dyed-in-the-wool New Yorker. On his walks to and from the office he affectionately drank in the newly familiar sights: the horses and carriages arriving at the park, the glimpse of the zoo at Sixty-fifth Street, the doormen at the swank Fifth Avenue apartment buildings. Most of them greeted him by name. Now as he strode past, several remarked about the fine October weather.

It was going to be a busy day. Justin usually tried to keep the ten-to-eleven time slot free for staff consultations. This morning he'd made an exception. An urgent phone call Saturday from a New Jersey psychiatrist had piqued his interest. Dr. Peter Carpenter wanted to consult with him immediately about a patient who he suspected was an MPD and potentially suicidal. Justin had agreed to a ten o'clock meeting today.

He reached Ninety-sixth and Fifth in twenty-five minutes and consoled himself that the heavy pedestrian traffic had slowed his progress. The main entrance to the hospital was on Fifth Avenue. The MPD clinic was entered by a discreet private door on Ninety-sixth. Justin was almost invariably the first one there. His office was a small suite at the end of the corridor. The outer room, painted a soft ivory and simply furnished with his desk and swivel chair, two armchairs for visitors, bookcases and a row of files, was enlivened by colorful prints of sailboats in Sydney Harbor.

The inner room was where he treated patients. It was equipped with a sophisticated video camera and tape recorder.

His first patient was a forty-year-old woman from Ohio who had been in treatment for six years and was diagnosed as schizophrenic. It was only when an alert psychologist began to believe that the voices the woman kept hearing were those of alter personalities that she had come to him. She was making good progress.

Dr. Carpenter arrived promptly at ten. Courteously grateful to Justin for seeing him on such short notice, he immediately began to talk about Laurie.

Donnelly listened, took notes, interjected questions. Carpenter concluded, "I'm not an expert on MPD, but if ever there were signs of it, I've been seeing them. There's been a marked change in her voice and manner during her last two visits. She definitely is unaware of at least one specific incident when she left her room and was out for hours. I'm sure she's not lying when she claims to have been asleep at that time. She has a recurring nightmare of a knife slashing at her. Yet during abreaction at one point she was acting out holding the knife and doing the slashing. Then she switched to trying to avoid it. I've made a copy of her file."

Donnelly read down the pages swiftly, stopping to circle or check when something jumped out at him. The case fascinated him. A beloved child kidnapped at the age of four and abandoned by the kidnappers at age six, with total memory loss of the intervening two years! A recurring nightmare! A sister's perception that since her reunion with the family, Laurie had responded to stress with childlike anxiety. Tragic parental death for which Laurie blamed herself.

When he laid the file down, he said, "The records from the hospital in Pittsburgh where she was examined indicated probable sexual abuse over a long period of time and counseling was strongly recommended. I gather there was none."

"There was total denial on the part of the parents," Dr. Carpenter answered, "and therefore no therapy whatsoever."

54

"Typical of the pretend-it-didn't-happen thinking of fifteen years ago, plus the Kenyons were significantly older parents," Donnelly observed. "It would be a good idea if we could persuade Laurie to come here for evaluation, and I'd say the sooner the better."

"I have a feeling that will be very difficult. Sarah had to beg her to come to me."

"If she resists, I'd like to see the sister. She should watch for signs of aberrant behavior and of course she must not take any talk of suicide lightly."

The two psychiatrists walked to the door together. In the reception room a dark-haired teenaged girl was staring moodily out the window. Her arms were covered with bandages.

In a low voice, Donnelly said, "You have to take it seriously. The patients who have experienced trauma in their childhood are at high risk for self-harm."

18

*T*HAT EVENING when Sarah got home from work the mail was neatly stacked on the foyer table. After the funeral, Sophie, their longtime daily housekeeper, had proposed cutting down to two days a week. "You don't need me more than that anymore, Sarah, and I'm not getting any younger."

Monday was one of the days she came in. That was why the mail was sorted, the house smelled faintly of furniture polish, the draperies were drawn and the soft light of lamps and sconces gave a welcoming glow to the downstairs rooms.

This was the hardest part of the day for Sarah, coming into an empty house. Before the accident, if she was expected home, her mother and father would be waiting to have their predinner cocktail with her.

Sarah bit her lip and pushed aside the memory. The letter on top of the pile was from England. She ripped open the envelope, certain it was from Gregg Bennett. She read the letter quickly then again, slowly. Gregg had just learned about the accident. His expression of sympathy was profoundly moving. He wrote about his affection for John and Marie Kenyon, about the wonderful visits to their home, how rough it must be for her and Laurie now.

The final paragraph was disturbing: "Sarah, I tried to phone Laurie, and she sounded so despondent when she answered. Then she screamed something like, 'I won't, I won't,' and hung up on me. I'm terribly worried about her. She's so fragile. I know you're taking good care of her, but be very careful. I'll be back at Clinton in January and would like to see you. My love to you, and kiss that girl for me, please. Gregg."

Her hands trembling, Sarah carried the mail into the library. Tomorrow she'd call Dr. Carpenter and read this to him. She knew he had given Laurie antidepressants, but was she taking them? The answering machine was blinking. Dr. Carpenter had called and left his home number.

When she reached him, she told him about Gregg's letter then listened, shocked and frightened, to his careful explanation of why he had seen Dr. Justin Donnelly in New York and why it was imperative that Sarah see him as soon as possible. He gave her the number of Donnelly's service. Her voice low and strained, she had to repeat her phone number twice to the operator.

Sophie had roasted a chicken, prepared a salad. Sarah's throat closed as she picked at the food. She had just made coffee when Dr. Donnelly returned her call. His day was full, but he could see her at six tomorrow evening. She hung up, reread Gregg's letter and, with a frantic sense of urgency, dialed Laurie. There was no answer. She tried every half hour until finally at eleven o'clock she heard the receiver being picked up. Laurie's "Hello" was cheerful enough. They chatted for a few minutes, then Laurie said, "How's this for a pain? After dinner I propped myself up on the bed to research this damn paper and fell asleep. Now I've got to burn the midnight oil."

19

*A*T ELEVEN O'CLOCK on Monday evening, Professor Allan Grant stretched out on his bed and switched on the night table lamp. The long bedroom window was partially open, but the room was not cool enough for his taste. Karen, his wife, used to teasingly tell him that in a previous incarnation he must have been a polar bear. Karen hated a cold bedroom. Not that she was around much to joke about it anymore, he thought as he threw back the blanket and swung his feet onto the carpet.

For the last three years, Karen had been working at a travel agency in the Madison Arms Hotel in Manhattan. At first she'd stayed overnight in New York only occasionally. Then more and more often she'd phone in late afternoon. "Sweetie, we're so busy, and I've got stacks of paperwork. Can you fend for yourself?"

He'd fended for himself for thirty-four years before he'd met her six years ago on a tour of Italy. Getting back in the habit wasn't that hard. Karen now had an apartment in the hotel and usually stayed there most of the week. She did come home weekends.

Grant padded across the room and cranked the window wide open. The curtains billowed in, followed by an eminently satisfying blast of chilly air. He hurried toward the bed but hesitated and turned in the direction of the hallway. It was no use. He was not sleepy. Another bizarre letter had come in his office mail today. Who the hell was Leona? He had no students by that name, had never had.

The house was a comfortable-size ranch model. Allan had bought it before he and Karen were married. For a time she'd seemed interested in decorating it and replacing shabby or dull furniture, but now it was beginning to look as it had in his bachelor days.

Scratching his head and yanking up pajama bottoms, which always seemed to settle around his hips, Grant walked down the hallway past the guest bedrooms, across the center hall, past the kitchen, living and dining rooms, and into the den. He turned on the overhead lights. After rummaging successfully for the key to the top drawer of his desk, he opened it, got out the letters and began to reread them.

The first one had come two weeks ago: "Darling Allan, I'm reliving now the glorious hours we spent together last night. It's hard to believe that we haven't always been madly in love, but maybe it's because no other time counts for us, does it? Do you know how hard it is for me not to shout from the rooftops that I'm crazy about you? I know you feel the same way. We have to hide what we are to each other. I understand that. Just keep on loving me and wanting me the way you do now. Leona."

All the letters were in the same vein. One arrived every other day, each talking about wild love scenes with him in his office or this house.

He'd had enough informal workshops here that any number of students knew the layout. Some of the letters referred to the shabby brown leather chair in the den. But never once had he had a student alone in the house. He wasn't that much of a fool.

Grant studied the letters carefully. They were obviously typed on an old machine. The *o* and the *w* were broken. He'd gone through his student files, but no one used a machine like that. He also did not recognize the scrawled signature.

Once again he agonized about whether to show them to Karen and to the administration. It would be hard to predict how Karen would react. He didn't want to upset her. Neither did he want her to decide to give up her job and stay home. Maybe he would have wanted that a few years ago, but not now. He had a big decision to make.

The administration. He'd bring the Dean of Student Affairs in on this the minute he found out who was sending them. The trouble was he simply didn't have a clue, and if anyone believed they contained an iota of truth, he could kiss his future at this college goodbye.

He read the letters once more, searching for a writing style, phrases or expressions that might bring one of his students to mind. Nothing. Finally he replaced them in the drawer, locked it, stretched and realized that he was dead tired. And chilly. It was one thing to sleep in a cold room under warm blankets, another to be in the path of a direct draft when you're sitting there in cotton pajamas. Where the heck was the draft coming from?

Karen always closed the draperies when she was home but he never bothered. He realized that the sliding glass door from the den to the patio was open a few inches. The door was heavy and slow to move on the track. He probably hadn't closed it completely the last time he went out. The lock was a pain in the neck too. Half the time it didn't catch. He walked over, shoved the door closed, snapped the lock and without bothering to see if it had caught, turned out the light and went back to bed.

He hunched under the covers in the now satisfyingly cold bedroom, closed his eyes and promptly fell asleep. In his wildest dreams he could not have imagined that half an hour ago a slender figure with long blond hair had been curled up in his brown leather chair and had only slipped away at the sound of his approaching footsteps.

20

*F*IFTY-EIGHT-YEAR-OLD private investigator Daniel O'Toole was known in New Jersey as Danny the Spouse Hunter. Under his hard-drinking, hail-fellow-well-met exterior, he was a remarkably thorough worker and quietly discreet in compiling information.

Danny was used to people using false names when they hired him to check on possibly erring husbands or wives. It didn't bother him. As long as he received his retainer and follow-up bills were paid promptly, his clients could call themselves anything they pleased.

Even so it was a bit surprising when a woman identifying herself as Jane Graves phoned his Hackensack office Tuesday morning, hinting at a possible insurance claim and engaging him to investigate the activities of the Kenyon sisters. Was the older sister working at her job? Was the younger sister back in college, completing her studies? Did she come home often? How were they reacting to the death of their parents? Were there any signs of breakdown? Very important, was either young woman seeing a psychiatrist?

Danny sensed something fishy. He had met Sarah Kenyon a few times in court. The accident that killed the parents had been caused by a speeding chartered bus with failed brakes. It was entirely possible that there was a suit pending against the bus company, but insurance companies usually had their own investigators. Still a job was a job, and because of the recession the divorce business was lousy. Breaking up was really hard to do when money was tight.

Taking a gamble, Danny doubled his usual retainer and was told the check would be in the mail immediately. He was instructed to send his reports and further bills to a private post office box in New York.

Smiling broadly, Danny replaced the receiver.

21

*S*ARAH DROVE into New York after work on Tuesday evening. She was on time for the six o'clock appointment with Dr. Justin Donnelly, but when she entered his reception area he was hurrying out of his office.

With a quick apology he explained that he had an emergency and asked her to wait. She had an impression of height and breadth, dark hair and keen blue eyes—then he was gone.

The receptionist had obviously gone home. The phones were quiet. After ten minutes of scanning a news magazine and registering nothing, Sarah put it down and sat quietly absorbed in her own thoughts.

It was after seven o'clock when Dr. Donnelly returned. "I'm very sorry," he said simply as he brought her into his office.

Sarah smiled faintly, trying to ignore her hunger pangs and the unmistakable beginning of a headache. It had been a long time since noon when she'd gulped a ham on rye and coffee.

The doctor indicated the chair across from his desk. She sat there, aware that he was studying her, and got to the point immediately.

"Dr. Donnelly, I had my secretary go to the library and copy material on multiple personality disorder. I'd only known about it vaguely, but what I read today frightens me."

He waited.

"If what I understand is accurate, a primary cause is childhood trauma, particularly sexual abuse over a prolonged period. Isn't that right?"

"Yes."

"Laurie certainly had the trauma of being kidnapped and held captive away from home for two years when she was a small child. The doctors who examined her when she was found believe she was abused."

"Is it okay if I call you Sarah?" he asked.

"Of course."

"All right then, Sarah. If Laurie has become a multiple personality, it probably started back at the time of her abduction. Assuming she was abused, she must have been so frightened, so terrified, that one small human being couldn't absorb everything that was happening. At that point, there was a shattering. Psychologically Laurie, the child as you knew her, withdrew from the pain and fear and alter personalities came to help her. The memory of those years is locked away in them. It would seem that the other personalities have not been apparent until now. From what I understand, after Laurie came home at age six she gradually returned to pretty much her old self except for a recurring nightmare. Now, in the death of your parents, she's experienced another terrible trauma, and Dr. Carpenter has seen distinct personality changes in her during her recent sessions with him. The reason he came to me so quickly is that he's afraid she might be suicidal."

"He didn't tell me that." Sarah felt her mouth go dry. "Laurie's been depressed, of course, but . . . Oh God, surely you don't think that's possible?" She bit her lip to keep it from quivering.

"Sarah, can you persuade Laurie to see me?"

She shook her head. "It's a job to make her see Dr. Carpenter. My parents were wonderful human beings but they had no use for psychiatry. Mother used to quote one of her college teachers. According to him there are three types of people: the ones who go for therapy when they're under stress; the ones who talk out their troubles with a friend or a cabdriver or bartender; the ones who hug their problems to themselves. The teacher claimed that the rate of recovery is exactly the same in all three types. Laurie grew up listening to that."

Justin Donnelly smiled. "I'm not sure that opinion isn't shared by quite a lot of people."

"I know Laurie needs professional help," Sarah said. "The problem is she doesn't want to open up to Dr. Carpenter. It's as though she's afraid of what he might find out about her."

"Then at least for now it's important to work around her. I've reread her file and made some notes."

At eight o'clock, observing Sarah's drawn, tired face, Dr. Donnelly said, "I think we'd better stop here. Sarah, listen for any reference to suicide, no matter how offhand it might seem, and report it to Dr. Carpenter and me. I'm going to be perfectly honest. I'd like to stay involved in Laurie's case. My work is research into multiple personality disorder and it's not often we catch a patient at the beginning of the emergence of alter personalities. I'll be discussing Laurie with Dr. Carpenter after her next several sessions with him. Unless there's a radical change, I have a hunch that we'll get more information from you than from Laurie. Be very observant."

Sarah hesitated then asked, "Doctor, isn't it a fact that until Laurie unlocks those lost years, she'll never really be well?"

"Think of it this way, Sarah. My mother broke her nail down to the quick once and an infection developed. A few days later the whole finger was swollen and throbbing. She kept doctoring it herself because she was afraid to have it lanced. When she finally went to the emergency room she had a red streak up her arm and was on the verge of blood poisoning. You see, she had ignored the warning signs because she didn't want the immediate pain of treatment."

"And Laurie is exhibiting warning signs of psychological infection?"

"Yes."

They walked together through the long corridor to the front door. The security guard let them out. There was no wind but the October evening had an unmistakable bite in the air. Sarah started to say good night.

"Is your car nearby?" Donnelly asked.

"Miracle of miracles, I found a parking spot right down the block."

He walked her to it. "Keep in touch."

What a nice guy, Sarah thought as she drove away. She tried to analyze her own feelings. If anything she was more worried now about Laurie than she had been before she saw Dr. Donnelly, but at least now she had a sense of solid help available to her.

She drove across Ninety-sixth Street past Madison and Park avenues, heading for the FDR Drive. At Lexington Avenue she impulsively turned right and headed downtown. She was famished, and Nicola's was only a dozen blocks away.

Ten minutes later she was being ushered to a small table. "Gee, it's great to see you again, Sarah," Lou, Nicola's longtime waiter, told her.

The restaurant was always cheery, and the delectable sight of steaming pasta being carried from the kitchen lifted Sarah's spirits. "I know what I want, Lou."

"Asparagus vinaigrette, linguine with white clam sauce, Pellegrino, a glass of wine," he rattled off.

"You've got it."

She reached into the bread basket for a warm crusty roll. Ten minutes later, just after the asparagus was served, the small table to her left was taken. She heard a familiar voice say, "Perfect, Lou. Thanks. I'm starving."

Sarah glanced up quickly and found herself looking into the surprised then obviously pleased face of Dr. Justin Donnelly.

22

SEVENTY-EIGHT-YEAR-OLD Rutland Garrison had known from the time he was a boy that he was called to the ministry. In 1947 he had been inspired to recognize the potential reach of television and persuaded the Dumont station in New York to allocate time on Sunday mornings for a "Church of the Airways" religious hour. He had been preaching the Lord's word ever since.

Now his heart was quite simply wearing out and his doctor had warned him to retire immediately. "You've done enough in your lifetime for a dozen men, Reverend Garrison," he'd said. "You've built a Bible college, a hospital, nursing homes, retirement communities. Now be good to yourself."

Garrison knew more than anyone how vast sums could be diverted from worthy causes to greedy pockets. He did not intend that his ministry fall into the hands of anyone of that ilk.

He also knew that by its very nature a television ministry needed a man in the pulpit who could not only inspire and lead his flock but also preach a rousing good sermon.

"We must choose a man with showmanship but not a showman," Garrison cautioned the members of the Church of the Airways Council. Nevertheless in late October, after Reverend Bobby Hawkins's third appearance as guest preacher, the council voted to invite him to accept the pulpit.

Garrison had the power of veto over council decisions. "I am not sure of that man," he told the members angrily. "There's something about him that troubles me. There's no need to rush into a commitment."

"He has a messianic quality," one of them protested.

"The Messiah Himself was the one who warned us to beware of false prophets." Rutland Garrison saw from the tolerant but somewhat irritated expressions on the faces of the men around him that they all believed his objections were based solely on his unwillingness to retire. He got up. "Do what you want," he said wearily. "I'm going home."

That night Reverend Rutland Garrison died in his sleep.

23

*B*IC HAD BEEN edgy since the last time he'd preached in New York. "That old man has it in for me, Opal," he told her. "Jealous because of all the calls and letters they're getting about me. I called one of those council members to see why I haven't heard from them again and that's the reason."

"Maybe it's better if we stay here in Georgia, Bic," Opal suggested. She turned away from his scornful glance. She was at the dining room table, surrounded by stacks of envelopes.

"How were the donations this week?"

"Very good." Every Thursday on his local program and when he spoke at meetings, Bic made appeals for different overseas charities. Opal and he were the only ones allowed to touch the donations.

"They're not good compared to what the 'Church of the Airways' takes in whenever I speak."

On October 28 a call came from New York. When Bic hung up the phone he stared at Opal, his face and eyes luminescent. "Garrison died last night. I'm invited to become the pastor of the Church of the Airways. They want us to move permanently to New York as soon as possible. They want us to stay at the Wyndham until we select a residence."

Opal started to run to him, then stopped. The look on his face warned her to leave him alone. He went into his study and closed the door. A few minutes later she heard the faint sounds of music and knew that once again he had taken out Lee's music box. She tiptoed over to the door and listened as high-pitched voices sang, "All around the town . . . Boys and girls together . . ."

24

*I*T WAS so hard to keep Sarah from realizing how afraid she was. Laurie stopped telling Sarah and Dr. Carpenter when she had the knife dream. There was no use talking about it. Nobody, not even Sarah, could understand that the knife was getting closer and closer.

Dr. Carpenter wanted to help her, but she had to be so careful. Sometimes the hour with him went by so swiftly, and Laurie knew she had told him things she didn't remember talking about.

She was always so tired. Even though almost every night she stayed in her room and studied, she was always struggling to keep up with assignments. Sometimes she'd find them finished on her desk and not remember having done them.

She was getting so many loud thoughts that pounded in her head like people shouting in an echo chamber. One of the voices told her she was a wimp and stupid and caused trouble for everyone and to shut her mouth around Dr. Carpenter. Other times a little kid kept crying inside Laurie's mind. Sometimes the child cried very softly, sometimes she sobbed and wailed. Another voice, lower and sultry, talked like a porno queen.

Weekends were so hard. The house was so big, so quiet. She never wanted to be alone in it. She was glad Sarah had listed it with a real estate agency.

The only time Laurie felt like herself was when she and Sarah played golf at the club and had brunch or dinner with friends. Those days made her think of playing golf with Gregg. She missed him in an aching, hurting way but was so afraid of him now, the fear blotted out all the love. She dreaded the thought that he'd be coming back to Clinton in January.

25

*J*USTIN DONNELLY had already gathered from his meeting with Dr. Carpenter that Sarah Kenyon was a remarkably strong young woman, but he had not been prepared for the impact she had on him when he met her. That first evening in his office she'd sat across the desk from him, lovely and poised, only the pain in her eyes hinting at the grief and anxiety she was experiencing. Her quietly expensive dark blue tweed suit had made him remember that wearing subdued colors was once considered an appropriate gesture for someone in mourning.

He'd been impressed that her immediate response to the possibility of her sister suffering from multiple personality disorder had been to gather information about it even before she saw him. He'd admired her intelligent understanding of Laurie's psychological vulnerability.

When he'd left Sarah at her car, it had been on the tip of Justin's tongue to suggest dinner. Then he'd walked into Nicola's and found her there. She'd looked pleased to see him, and it felt easy and natural to suggest that he join her and free up the last small table for the couple who came in just behind him.

It was Sarah who had set the tone of the conversation. Smiling, she passed him the basket of rolls. "I imagine you had the same kind of lunch on the run I did," she'd told him. "I'm starting to work on a murder case and I've been talking to witnesses all day."

She'd talked about her job as an assistant prosecutor, then skillfully turned the conversation to him. She knew he was Australian. Over osso bucco Justin told her about his family and growing up on a sheep station. "My paternal great-grandfather came over from Britain in chains. Of course for generations that wasn't mentioned. Now it's a matter of pride to have an ancestor who was a guest of the Crown in the penal colony. My maternal grandmother was born in England, and the family moved to Australia when she was three months old. All her life Granny kept sighing how she missed England. She was there twice in eighty years. That's the other kind of Aussie mind-set."

It was only as they sipped cappuccino that the talk turned to his decision to specialize in the treatment of multiple personality disorder patients.

After that evening, Justin spoke to Dr. Carpenter and Sarah at least once a week. Dr. Carpenter reported that Laurie was increasingly uncooperative. "She's dissembling," he told Justin. "On the surface she agrees that she should not feel responsible for her parents' death, but I don't believe her. She talks about them as though it's a safe subject. Tender memories only. When she becomes emotional she talks and cries like a small child. She continues to refuse to take the MMPI or Rorschach tests."

Sarah reported that she saw no indication of suicidal depression. "Laurie hates going to Dr. Carpenter on Saturdays," she told him. "Says it's a waste of money and it's perfectly normal to be very sad when your parents die. She does brighten up when we go to the club. A couple of her midterm marks were pretty bad, so she told me to call her by eight o'clock if I want to talk to her in the evening. After that she wants to be able to study without interruption. I think she doesn't want me checking up on her."

Dr. Justin Donnelly did not tell Sarah that both he and Dr. Carpenter sensed that in Laurie's behavior they were witnessing a calm before the storm. Instead he continued to urge her to keep a careful watch on Laurie. Whenever he hung up he realized he was starting to look forward to Sarah's calls in a highly unprofessional way.

26

*I*N THE OFFICE, the murder case Sarah was prosecuting was a particularly vicious one in which a twenty-seven-year-old woman, Maureen Mays, had been strangled by a nineteen-year-old youth who forced his way into her car in the parking lot of the railroad station.

It was a welcome change to plunge into final preparation as the trial date drew near. With intense concentration, she pored over the statements of the witnesses who had seen the defendant lurking in the station. If only they had done something about it, Sarah thought. They all had the feeling that he was up to no good. She knew that the physical evidence of the victim's desperate attempt to save herself from her attacker would make a strong impression on the jury.

The trial began December second, no longer open and shut, as a hearty, likable sixty-year-old defense attorney, Conner Marcus, attempted to tear apart Sarah's case. Under his skillful questioning, witnesses admitted that it had been dark in the parking area, that they did not know if the defendant had opened the door to the car or if Mays had opened it to allow him in.

But when it was Sarah's turn on redirect examination, all of the witnesses firmly declared that when James Parker came on to Maureen Mays in the train station, she had clearly rebuffed him.

The combination of the viciousness of the crime and the showmanship of Marcus caused the media to descend in droves. Spectators' benches filled. Courtroom junkies placed bets on the outcome.

Sarah was in the rhythm that in the past five years had become second nature to her. She ate, drank and slept the matter of State v. James Parker. Laurie began going back to college on Saturdays after she saw Dr. Carpenter. "You're busy and it's good for me to get involved too," she told Sarah.

"How's it going with Dr. Carpenter?"

"I'm starting to blame the bus driver for the accident."

"That's good news." On her next weekly call to Dr. Donnelly, Sarah said, "I only wish I could believe her."

Thanksgiving was spent with cousins in Connecticut. It wasn't as bad as Sarah had feared. At Christmas she and Laurie flew to Florida and went on a five-day Caribbean cruise. Swimming in the outside pool on the Lido deck made Christmas with all its attendant memories seem far away. Still Sarah found herself longing for the holiday court recess to be over so that she could get back to the trial.

Laurie spent much of the cruise in the cabin, reading. She had signed on for Allan Grant's class in Victorian women writers and wanted to do some advance study. She had brought along their mother's old portable typewriter, supposedly to make notes. But Sarah knew she was also writing letters on it, letters she would rip from the machine and cover if Sarah entered the cabin. Had Laurie become interested in someone? Sarah wondered. Why be so secretive about it?

She's twenty-one, Sarah told herself sternly. Mind your own business.

27

ON CHRISTMAS EVE, Professor Allan Grant had an unpleasant scene with his wife, Karen. He'd forgotten to hide the key to his desk drawer and she'd found the letters. Karen demanded to know why he'd kept them from her; why he had not turned them over to the administration if, as he claimed, they were all ridiculous fabrications.

Patiently and then not so patiently, he explained. "Karen, I saw no reason to upset you. As far as the administration is concerned, I can't even be sure that a student is sending them, although I

72

certainly suspect it. What is the dean going to do except just what you're doing right now, wonder how much truth there is in them?"

The week between Christmas and New Year's Day the letters stopped coming. "More proof that they're probably from a student," he told Karen. "Now I *wish* I'd get one. A postmark would be a big help."

Karen wanted him to spend New Year's Eve in New York. They'd been invited to a party at the Rainbow Room.

"You know I hate big parties," he told her. "The Larkins invited us to their place." Walter Larkin was the Dean of Student Affairs.

On New Year's Eve it snowed heavily. Karen called from her office. "Darling, turn the radio on. The trains and buses are all delayed. What do you think I should do?"

Allan knew what he was supposed to answer. "Don't get stuck in Penn Station or on the highway in a bus. Why don't you stay in town?"

"Are you sure you don't mind?"

He didn't mind.

Allan Grant had entered marriage with the definite idea that it was a lifetime commitment. His father had walked out on his mother when Allan was a baby and he'd vowed he'd never do that to any woman.

Karen was obviously very happy with their arrangement. She liked living in New York during the week and spending weekends with him. At first it had worked pretty well. Allan Grant was used to living alone and enjoyed his own company. But now he was experiencing growing dissatisfaction. Karen was one of the prettiest women he'd ever seen. She wore clothes like a fashion model. Unlike him, she had a good business sense, which was why she handled all their finances. But her physical attraction for him had long since died. Her amusing hardheaded common sense had become predictable.

What did they really have in common? Allan asked himself yet again as he dressed to go to the dean's home. Then he put the nagging question aside. Tonight he'd just enjoy the evening with good friends. He knew everyone who would be there and they were all attractive, interesting people.

Especially Vera West, the newest member of the faculty.

28

IN EARLY JANUARY, the campus of Clinton College had been a crystal palace. A heavy storm inspired students to create imaginative snow sculptures. The below-freezing temperature preserved them in pristine beauty, until the arrival of an unseasonably warm rain.

Now the remaining snow clung to soggy brown grass. The remnants of the sculptures seemed grotesque in their half-melted state. The frivolous postexam euphoria was over and business as usual began in the classrooms.

Laurie walked quickly across the campus to Professor Allan Grant's office. Her hands were clenched in the pockets of the ski jacket she was wearing over jeans and a sweater. Her tawny blond hair was pulled back and clipped in a ponytail. In preparation for the conference she had started to dab on eyeshadow and lipliner, then scrubbed them off.

Don't try to kid yourself. You're ugly.

The loud thoughts were coming more and more often. Laurie quickened her steps as though somehow she might be able to outrun them. *Laurie, everything is your fault. What happened when you were little is your fault.*

74

Laurie hoped she hadn't done badly in the first test on Victorian authors. She'd always gotten good marks till this year, but now it was like being on a roller coaster. Sometimes she'd get an A or B+ on a paper. Other times the material was so unfamiliar that she knew she must not have been paying attention in class. Later she'd find notes she didn't remember taking.

Then she saw him. Gregg. He was walking across the driveway between two dormitories. When he'd gotten back from England last week he'd called her. She'd shouted at him to leave her alone and slammed down the phone.

He hadn't spotted her yet. She ran the remaining distance to the building.

Mercifully the corridor was empty. She leaned her head against the wall for an instant, grateful for the coolness.

'Fraidy cat.

I'm not a 'fraidy cat, she thought defiantly. Straightening her shoulders, she managed a casual smile for the student emerging from Allan Grant's office.

She knocked on the partly open door. A pleasant warmth and a sense of brightness permeated her at his welcoming, "Come on in, Laurie." He was always so kind to her.

Grant's tiny office was painted a sunny yellow. Crammed bookshelves lined the wall to the right of the window. A long table held reference books and student papers. The top of his desk was tidy, holding only a phone, a plant and a fishbowl in which a solitary goldfish swam aimlessly.

Grant motioned toward the chair opposite his desk. "Sit down, Laurie." He was wearing a dark blue sweater over a white turtleneck shirt. Laurie had the fleeting thought that the effect was almost clerical.

He was holding her last paper in his hand, the one she'd written on Emily Dickinson. "You didn't like it?" she asked apprehensively.

"I thought it was terrific. It's just I don't see why you changed your mind about old Em."

He liked it. Laurie smiled in relief. But what did he mean about changing her mind?

"Last term when you wrote about Emily Dickinson, you made a strong case for her life as a recluse, saying that her genius could only be fully expressed by removing herself from contact with the many. Now your thesis is that she was a neurotic filled with fear, that her poetry would have reached greater heights if she hadn't suppressed her emotions. You conclude, 'A lusty affair with her mentor and idol, Charles Wadsworth, would have done her a lot of good.' "

Grant smiled. "I've sometimes wondered the same thing, but what made you change your mind?"

What indeed? Laurie found an answer. "Maybe my mind works like yours. Maybe I started to wonder what would have happened if she had found a physical outlet for her emotions instead of being afraid of them."

Grant nodded. "Okay. These couple of sentences in the margin . . . You wrote them?"

It didn't even look like her writing, but the blue cover had her name on it. She nodded.

There was something about Professor Grant that was different. The expression on his face was thoughtful, even troubled. Was he just trying to be nice to her? Maybe the paper was lousy after all.

The goldfish was swimming slowly, indifferently. "What happened to the others?" she asked.

"Some joker overfed them. They all died. Laurie, there is something I want to talk to you about . . ."

"I'd rather die from overeating than being smashed in a car, wouldn't you? At least you don't bleed. Oh, I'm sorry. What did you want to talk about?"

Allan Grant shook his head. "Nothing that won't keep. It isn't getting much better, is it?"

She knew what he meant.

"Sometimes I can honestly agree with the doctor that if there was any fault, it was with the bus with faulty brakes that was going much too fast. Other times, no."

The loud voice in her head shouted: *You robbed your mother and father of the rest of their lives just as you robbed them of two years when you waved at that funeral procession.*

She didn't want to cry in front of Professor Grant. He'd been so nice, but people got sick of always having to bolster you up. She stood up. "I . . . I have to go. Is there anything else?"

With troubled eyes, Allan Grant watched Laurie leave. It was too soon to be sure, but the term paper he was holding had given him the first solid clue as to the identity of the mysterious letter writer who signed herself "Leona."

There was a sensual theme in the paper that was totally unlike Laurie's usual style but similiar to the tone of the letters. It seemed to him that he recognized some unusually extravagant phrases as well. That wasn't proof, but at least it gave him a place to start looking.

Laurie Kenyon was the last person he'd have dreamt could be the writer of those letters. Her attitude toward him had been consistently that of a respectful student toward a teacher whom she admired and liked.

As Grant reached for his jacket, he decided he would say nothing to either Karen or the administration about his suspicions. Some of those letters were downright salacious. It would be embarrassing for any innocent person to be questioned about them, particularly a kid living through the kind of tragedy Laurie was. He turned out the light and started home.

From behind a row of evergreens, Leona watched him go, her nails digging into her palms.

Last night she had hidden outside his house again. As usual he'd left the draperies open, and she'd watched him for three hours. He'd heated a pizza around nine and brought it and a beer to his den. He'd stretched out in that old leather chair, kicked off his shoes and rested his feet on the ottoman.

He was reading a biography of George Bernard Shaw. It was so endearing the way Allan would run his hand through his hair unconsciously. He did it in class occasionally as well. When he finished the beer he looked at the empty glass, shrugged, then went into the kitchen and came back with a fresh one.

At eleven he watched the news then turned out the light and left the den. She knew he was going to bed. He always left the window open, but the bedroom draperies were drawn. Most nights she simply went away after he turned out the light, but one night she'd pulled at the handle of the sliding glass door and discovered that the lock didn't catch. Now some nights she went inside and curled up in his chair and pretended that in a minute he'd call her. "Hey, darling, come to bed. I'm lonesome."

Once or twice she'd waited till she was sure he was asleep and tiptoed in to look at him. Last night she was cold and very tired and went home after he turned out the den light.

Cold and very tired.

Cold.

Laurie rubbed her hands together. It had gotten so dark all of a sudden. She hadn't noticed how dark it was when she left Professor Grant's office a minute ago.

29

"*R*IDGEWOOD IS ONE of the finest towns in New Jersey," Betsy Lyons explained to the quietly dressed woman who was going over pictures of real estate properties with her. "Of course it is in the upscale price bracket, but even so, with market conditions as they are, there are some excellent buys around."

Opal nodded thoughtfully. It was the third time she had visited Lyons Realty. Her story was that her husband was being transferred to New York and she was doing preliminary househunting in New Jersey, Connecticut and Westchester.

"Let her get to trust you," Bic had instructed. "All these real estate agents are taught to keep an eye on prospective buyers so they don't get light-fingered when they're being shown around houses. Right off, tell whoever sees you that you're looking in different locations, then, after a visit or two, that you like New Jersey best. First time you go in, say you didn't want to go as high as Ridgewood prices. Then drop hints that you think it's a nice town and you really could afford it. Finally get her to show you Lee's house on one of the Fridays we come out. Distract her and then . . ."

It was early Friday afternoon. The plan was in motion. Opal had won Betsy Lyons's confidence. It was time to see the Kenyon place. The housekeeper was in on Monday and Friday mornings. She would be gone by now. The older sister was busy in court, involved in a highly publicized trial. Opal would be alone inside Lee's home with someone who would be off guard.

Betsy Lyons was an attractive woman in her early sixties. She loved her job and was good at it. She frequently bragged that she

79

could spot a phony a mile away. "Listen, I don't waste my time," she would tell new agents. "Time is money. Don't think because people obviously can't afford the houses they want to see that you should automatically steer them away. Daddy might be sitting in the background with a bundle of cash he made in his 7-Eleven. On the other hand, don't assume because people look as though they can pay steep prices that they're really serious. Some of the wives just want to get inside pricey houses to see the decorating. *And never take your eyes off any of them.*"

The thing that Betsy Lyons liked about Carla Hawkins was that she was so on the level. Straight off, she'd put her cards on the table. She was looking in other locations. She didn't gush at every house she saw. Neither did she point out what was wrong with it. Some people did that whether or not they had any plans to buy. "The baths are too small." Sure, honey. You're used to a Jacuzzi in the bedroom.

Mrs. Hawkins asked intelligent questions about the houses that sparked mild interest in her. There was obviously money there. A good real estate agent learned to spot expensive clothes. The bottom line was that Betsy Lyons had a feeling that this could turn into a big sale.

"This is a particularly charming place," she said, pointing to the picture of an all-brick ranch house. "Nine rooms, only four years old, in mint condition, a fortune in landscaping and on a cul-de-sac."

Opal pretended interest, poring over the specifics listed under the picture. "That would be interesting," she said slowly, "but let's keep looking. Oh, what's this?" She had finally come to the page with the picture of the Kenyon home.

"Now if you want a really beautiful, roomy, comfortable house, this is a buy," Lyons said enthusiastically. "Over an acre of property, a swimming pool, four large bedrooms, each with its own bath; a living room, dining room, breakfast room, den and library on the main floor. Eight thousand square feet, crown molding, wainscoting, parquet floors, butler's pantry."

"Let's see both of these this morning," Opal suggested. "That's about as much as I'm up to with this ankle."

Bic had fastened an Ace bandage on her left ankle. "You tell that agent you sprained it," he told her. "Then when you say you must have dropped a glove up in one of the bedrooms she won't mind leaving you in the kitchen."

"I'll check about the ranch," Lyons said. "They have young children and want us to call ahead. I can go in the Kenyon place any weekday without notice."

They stopped at the ranch house first. Opal remembered to ask all the right questions. Finally they were on their way to the Kenyon home. Mentally she reviewed Bic's instructions.

"Rotten weather, isn't it," Lyons said as she drove through the quiet streets of Ridgewood. "But it's nice to think that spring is on the way. The Kenyon property is alive with flowering trees in the spring. Dogwood. Cherry blossoms. Mrs. Kenyon loved gardening and there are three blooms a year. Whoever gets this place will be lucky."

"Why is it being sold?" It seemed to Opal that it would be unnatural not to ask the question. She hated driving down this road. It reminded her of those two years. She remembered how her heart pounded when they turned at the pink corner house. That house was painted white now.

Lyons knew there was no use trying to hide the truth. Problem was, some people steered clear of a hard-luck house. Better to say it right out than let them nose around and find out for themselves was her motto. "There are just two sisters living here now," she said. "The parents were killed in an automobile accident last September. A bus slammed into them on Route 78." Skillfully she attempted to make Opal concentrate on the fact that the accident had taken place on Route 78 and not in the house.

They were turning into the driveway. Bic had told Opal to be sure to notice everything. He was real curious about the kind of place where Lee lived. They got out of the car, and Lyons fished for the key to the lock.

"This is the central foyer," she said as she opened the door. "See what I mean about a well-kept place? Isn't this beautiful?"

Be quiet, Opal wanted to tell her as they walked around the first floor. The living room was to the left. Archway. Big windows. Upholstery predominantly blue. Dark polished floor with a large Oriental and a contrasting small rug in front of the fireplace. Opal felt a nervous impulse to laugh. They had taken Lee from this place to that dumpy farm. Wonder she didn't crack up on the spot.

In the library, portraits lined the walls. "Those are the Kenyons," Betsy Lyons pointed out. "Handsome couple, weren't they? And those are watercolors of the girls when they were little. From the time Laurie was born, Sarah was always such a little mother to her. I don't know if, being in Georgia, you would have known about it but . . ."

As she heard the story of the disappearance seventeen years earlier, Opal felt her heart begin to race. On an end table there was a picture of Lee with an older girl. Lee was wearing the pink bathing suit she'd had on when they picked her up. With the cluster of framed photos in this room, it was crazy that her eye fell on that one. Bic was right. There was a reason why God had sent them here to be on guard against Lee now.

She chose to fake a sneeze, pull her handkerchief from her coat pocket and drop a glove in Lee's bedroom. Even if Betsy Lyons hadn't told her, it was easy to figure which one was Lee's. The sister's room was loaded with law books over the desk.

Opal followed Lyons down the stairs, then asked to see the kitchen again. "I love this kitchen," she sighed. "This house is a dream." At least that was honest, she thought with some amusement. "Now I'd really better be going. My ankle is telling me to stop walking." She sat on one of the tall stools in front of the island counter.

"Of course." Betsy Lyons could smell a potential sale warming up.

Opal reached in her coat pocket for her gloves, then frowned.

"I know I had both of them when we came in." She fished in the other pocket, brought out her handkerchief. "Oh, I know. I bet when I sneezed, I pulled out my glove with the hankie. That was in the bedroom with the blue carpet." She began to slide from the stool.

"You wait right there," Betsy Lyons ordered. "I'll run up and look for it."

"Oh, would you?"

Opal waited until a faint padding on the staircase assured her that Lyons was on her way to the second floor. Then she jumped from the stool and raced to the row of blue-handled knives attached to the wall next to the stove. She grabbed the largest one, a long carving knife, and dropped it in her oversize shoulder bag.

She was back on the stool, slightly bent over, her hand rubbing her ankle, when Betsy Lyons returned to the kitchen, a triumphant smile on her face, the missing glove clutched in her fingers.

30

*T*HE FIRST PART of the week had passed in a blur. Sarah worked through Thursday night, poring over her closing statement.

She read intently, clipping, inserting, preparing three-by-five cards with the highlights of the points she wanted to hammer at the jury. The morning light began to filter into the bedroom. At seven-fifteen, Sarah read her closing paragraph. "Ladies and gentlemen, Mr. Marcus is a skilled and experienced defense attorney. He hammered away at each of the witnesses who had been in the station that night. Admittedly it was not broad daylight but neither was it so dark they could not see James Parker's face. Every one of them had seen him approach and be rebuffed by Maureen Mays in the railroad station. Every one of them told you, without hesitation, that James Parker is the person who got into Maureen's car that night. . . .

"I would say, ladies and gentlemen, the evidence has shown to you beyond any reasonable doubt that James Parker murdered this fine young woman and forever robbed her husband, mother, father and siblings of her love and support.

"There is nothing any of us can do to bring her back, but what you, the jury, can do is to bring her murderer to justice."

She had covered all the points. The solid mass of evidence was undeniable. Still Conner Marcus was the best criminal attorney she'd ever been up against. And juries were unpredictable.

Sarah got up and stretched. The adrenaline that always pulsed through her body during a trial would reach fever pitch when she began her final arguments. She was counting on that.

She went into the bathroom and turned on the shower. It was a temptation to linger under the cascade of hot water. Her shoulders especially seemed to be tied up in knots. Instead she turned off the hot water and twisted the cold-water tap completely to the right. Grimacing, she endured the icy blast.

She toweled dry quickly, pulled on a long, thick terry-cloth robe, stuck her feet in slippers and ran downstairs to make coffee. While she waited for it to seep through the coffee maker, she did stretching exercises and looked around the kitchen. Betsy Lyons, the real estate agent, seemed to think that she had a hot prospect for the house. Sarah realized she was still ambivalent about selling it. She had told Lyons she absolutely would not lower the price.

The coffee was ready. She dug out her favorite mug, the one her squad of detectives gave her when she was the assistant prosecutor in charge of the sex-crimes unit. It was inscribed "For Sarah, who made sex so interesting." Her mother had not been amused.

She carried the coffee upstairs and sipped while she dabbed on a touch of lipstick, blusher and eyeshadow. That had become a morning ritual, a loving tribute to her mother. Mom, if you don't mind I'll look tailored today, she thought. But she knew Marie would have approved of the blue-and-gray tweed suit.

Her hair. A cloud of curls . . . no, a mass of frizz. Impatiently she brushed it. "The sun will come out tomorrow . . ." she sang softly. All I need is a red dress with a white collar and a dopey-looking dog.

She checked her briefcase. All her notes for the closing argument were there. This is it, she thought. She was almost at the bottom of the stairs when she heard the kitchen door open. "It's me, Sarah," Sophie called. Footsteps padded across the kitchen. "I have to go to the dentist, so I thought I'd come a bit early. Oh, you look nice."

"Thanks. You didn't have to come so early. After ten years, don't you think you should just take some time off when you need it?" They smiled at each other.

The prospect of the house being sold distressed Sophie, and she'd said as much.

"Unless, of course, you girls get an apartment near here so I can look after you," she'd told Sarah.

This morning she looked troubled. "Sarah, you know the good set of knives next to the stove?"

Sarah was buttoning her coat. "Yes."

"Did you take one of them out for anything?"

"No."

"I just noticed the biggest carving knife is missing. It's the queerest thing."

"Oh, it's got to be around somewhere."

"Well, I can't tell you where."

Sarah felt suddenly uneasy. "When was the last time you saw it?"

"I'm not sure. I missed it on Monday and began looking around. It isn't in the kitchen, I'll tell you that. How long it's been gone, I have no idea." Sophie hesitated. "I don't suppose Laurie would have had any use for it at school?"

Sophie knew about the knife dream. "I hardly think so." Sarah swallowed over the sudden constriction in her throat. "Got to run." As she opened the door, she said, "If, by any chance, you come across that knife, leave a message for me at the office, will you? Just a simple 'I found it.' Okay?"

She saw the compassion in Sophie's face. She thinks Laurie took it, Sarah thought. My God!

Frantically she ran to the phone and dialed Laurie's number. A sleepy voice. Laurie had picked up on the first ring.

"Sarah? Sure. I'm fine. In fact I got a couple of my marks back. They're good. Let's celebrate somehow."

Relieved, Sarah hung up and rushed outside to the garage. A four-car garage with only her car in it. Laurie always left hers in the driveway. The other empty spaces were a constant reminder of the accident.

As she pulled out, she decided that for the moment Laurie sounded okay. Tonight she'd call Dr. Carpenter and Dr. Donnelly and tell them about the knife. But now she had to put it out of her mind. It wasn't fair to Maureen Mays or her family to do less than her best in court today. But why in the name of God would Laurie take the carving knife?

31

"*S*ARAH'S JURY is still out," Laurie told Dr. Carpenter as she sat across from him in his office. "I envy her. She's so committed to what she does, to being a prosecutor, that she can block out everything she doesn't want to think about."

Carpenter waited. The temperature had changed. Laurie was different. It was the first time he had seen her express hostility toward Sarah. There was pent-up anger flashing in her eyes. Something had happened between her and Sarah. "I've been reading about that case," he said mildly.

"I'll bet you have. Sarah the prosecutor. But she's not as subtle as she thinks she is."

Again he waited. "I no sooner got home last night than she came in. All apologies. Sorry she hadn't been home to welcome me. Big sister. I said, 'Look, Sarah, at some point even I have to take care of myself. I'm twenty-one, not four.' "

"Four?"

"That's the age I was when she should have stayed home from her damn party. I wouldn't have been kidnapped if she'd stayed home."

"You've always blamed yourself for being kidnapped, Laurie."

"Oh, me too. But big sister had a hand in it. I bet she hates me."

Dr. Carpenter had intended as one of his goals to wean Laurie away from dependence on her sister, but this was something new. It was like being with a totally different patient. "Why would she hate you?"

"She has no time for a life of her own. You should have *her* as a patient. Boy, that would be something to hear! All her life being big sister. I read her old diary this morning. She's been keeping one since she was a little kid. She wrote a lot about me being kidnapped and then coming back and that she thought I was different. I guess I really chilled her out." There was satisfaction in Laurie's tone.

"Do you make it a habit to go through Sarah's diaries?"

The look Laurie gave him was pure pity. "You're the one who wants to know what everyone is thinking. What makes you better?"

It was the way she was sitting, the belligerent posture, knees pressed together, hands grasping the arms of the chair, head thrust forward, features rigid. Where was the soft, troubled young face, the hesitant Jackie Onassis voice?

"That's a good question, but I don't have any one-sentence answer to it. Why are you annoyed at Sarah?"

"The knife. Sarah thinks I sneaked a carving knife out of the kitchen."

"Why would she think that?"

"Only because it's missing. I sure as hell didn't take it. Sophie, our housekeeper, started the whole thing. I mean I don't mind admitting that a lot of things fall in my camp, but not this one, Doc."

"Did Sarah accuse you or just ask you about the knife? There's a big difference, you know."

"Buddy, I know an accusation when I hear one."

"I had the feeling that you were afraid of knives. Was I wrong, Laurie?"

"I wish you'd call me Kate."

"Kate? Any reason?"

"Kate sounds better than Laurie—more mature. Anyhow, my middle name is Katherine."

"That could be very positive. Putting away of childish things. Is that the way you feel now, that you're putting away childish things?"

"No. I just don't want to be afraid of knives."

"I was under the strong impression that you were desperately afraid of them."

"Oh no. Not me. Laurie is afraid of everything. A knife is her 'worst-case scenario.' You know, Doctor, there are some people who bring grief and pain to the rest of the universe. Our gal Laurie, for example."

Dr. Peter Carpenter realized that he now knew that Kate was the name of one of Laurie Kenyon's alter personalities.

32

ON SATURDAY MORNING they parked near Dr. Carpenter's office. Bic had deliberately rented the same color late-model Buick that Laurie drove. Only the interior was a different shade of leather. "If anyone happens to question my opening this door, I'll point to the other car," he explained, then answered her unspoken question. "We have observed that Lee never locks her car. Her tote bag filled with textbooks is always on the floor of the front seat. I'll just slip in that knife right at the bottom. Doesn't matter when she finds it. The point is that she's sure to come across it soon. Just a little reminder for her of what happens if she starts thinking on us with her head doctor. And now do what you must do, Opal."

Lee always left Dr. Carpenter's office at exactly five of twelve. At six of twelve Opal casually opened the door of the private entrance to his upstairs office. A narrow foyer with a flight of stairs led to his suite. She glanced around as though she'd made a mistake and meant to use the main door of the professional building at the corner of Ridgewood Avenue. There was no one on the stairs. Quickly she unwrapped the small package she was holding, dropped its contents in the center of the foyer and left. Bic was already in the rented car.

"A blind person couldn't miss it," Opal told him.

"Nobody was paying any attention to you," he assured her. "Now we'll just wait here a minute and see what happens."

Laurie stamped down the stairs. She was going directly back to college. Who the hell needed to be sitting having her head taken apart? Who needed to be fussed over by long-suffering Sarah? That was something else. It was time she concentrated on those trust funds and knew exactly how much money she was worth. Plenty. And when the house sold, she didn't want any talk of other people investing it for her. She was sick of having to deal with the wimp who said "Yes, Sarah; no, Sarah; whatever you say, Sarah."

She was at the bottom of the stairs. Her boot touched something soft, something squishy. She looked down.

The lifeless eye of a chicken stared up at her. Straggly feathers clung to its skull. The severed neck was crusted with dried blood.

Outside, Bic and Opal heard the first screams. Bic smiled. "Sound familiar?" He turned the key in the ignition, then whispered, "But now I should be comforting her."

33

THE JURY was filing in when Sarah's secretary hurried into the courtroom. Word had spread that a verdict had been reached, and there was a scramble for seats. Sarah's heart pounded as the judge asked, "Mr. Foreman, has the jury agreed upon a verdict?"

"Yes we have, your Honor."

This is it, Sarah thought as she stood at the prosecution table, facing the bench. She felt a tug on her arm and turned to see her secretary, Janet. "Not now," she said firmly, surprised that Janet would interrupt when a verdict was being rendered.

"Sarah, I'm sorry. A Dr. Carpenter has taken your sister to the emergency room of Hackensack Medical Center. She's in shock."

Sarah gripped the pen she was holding until her knuckles turned white. The judge was looking at her, clearly annoyed. She whispered, "Tell him I'll be there in a few minutes."

"On the charge of murder what is your verdict, guilty or not guilty?"

"Guilty, your Honor."

A cry of "not fair!" went up from the family and friends of James Parker. The Judge rapped his gavel, warned against further outbursts, ascertained that the verdict was unanimous and began to poll the jury.

Bail was revoked for James Parker. A sentencing date was set and he was led away in handcuffs. Court was adjourned. Sarah had no time to relish her victory. Janet was in the corridor holding her coat and shoulder bag. "Now you can go right to your car."

Dr. Carpenter was waiting for her in the emergency room. Briefly he explained what had happened. "Laurie had just left my office. As she approached the outside door on the ground floor, she began to scream. By the time we reached her, she had fainted. She was in deep shock but she's coming around now."

"What caused it?" The concerned kindness of the doctor brought hot tears to the back of Sarah's eyes. There was something about Carpenter that reminded her of her father. She longed for him to be with her now.

"Apparently she stepped on the head of a dead chicken, became hysterical then went into shock."

"The head of a chicken! In the lobby of your office!"

"Yes. I have a deeply disturbed patient who is involved in a cult and this is the sort of thing he would do. Does Laurie have an inordinate fear of chickens or mice or any animals?"

"No. Except she never eats chicken. She loathes the taste of it."

A nurse came out of the curtained-off area. "You can go in."

Laurie was lying quietly. Her eyes were closed. Sarah touched her hand. "Laurie."

Slowly she opened her eyes. It seemed to be an effort, and Sarah realized that she must be heavily sedated. Her voice was weak but crystal clear as she said, "Sarah, I'll kill myself before I see that doctor again."

34

*A*LLAN WAS in the kitchen eating a sandwich.

"Sweetie, I'm sorry I didn't get down last night, but it was really important to prepare my pitch for the Wharton account." Karen threw her arms around his neck.

He pecked at her cheek and stepped back from her embrace. "That's okay. Want some lunch?"

"You should have waited. I'd have taken care of that."

"You could have been another hour."

"You never care about food." Karen Grant poured Chianti from the decanter and handed a glass to Allan. She clinked her glass against his. "Cheers, darling."

"Cheers," he said unsmilingly.

"Hey, Professor, something's wrong."

"What's wrong is that as of about an hour ago, I became certain that Laurie Kenyon is the mysterious Leona, the one writing those letters."

Karen gasped. "You're absolutely sure?"

"Yes, I was grading papers. The one she turned in had a note attached that her computer went on the blink and she had to finish it on the old portable typewriter she keeps as a backup. There's no question it's the same one the letters were written on—including the one that came yesterday." He reached in his pocket and handed it to Karen.

It read: "Allan, my dearest, I'll never forget tonight. I love to watch you sleep. I love to see the way you turn and scrunch up when you're getting more comfortable, the way you pull up the covers. Why do you let the room get so cold? I shut the window a little. Did you notice, darling? I'll bet not. In some ways you could be the prototype for the absentminded professor. But only in some ways. Don't ever permit me to be absent from your mind. Always remember. If your wife doesn't want you enough to be with you all the time, I do. My love to you. Leona."

Karen reread the letter slowly. "Good Lord, Allan, do you think that girl actually came in here?"

"I don't think so. She certainly fantasizes all those trysts in my office. She's fantasizing this too."

"I'm not sure about that. Come on."

He followed her into the bedroom. Karen stood in front of the long window. She reached for the crank and turned it. The window opened outward noiselessly. She easily stepped over the low sill onto the ground then turned to him. Her hair blew in her face as a draft of cold air sent the curtain whirling. "Easy to get in, easy to get out," she said as she stepped back into the room. "Allan, maybe she is fantasizing, but she could have been here. You sleep like a dead man. From now on you can't leave that window open so wide."

"This has gone far enough. I'm damned if I'll change my sleeping habits. I've got to talk to Sarah Kenyon. I'm terribly sorry for Laurie, but Sarah has got to get her whatever help she needs."

He reached Sarah's answering machine and left a brief message: "It really is very important that I talk to you."

At two-thirty Sarah returned the call. Karen listened as Allan's voice changed from cool to solicitous. "Sarah, what's the matter?

Laurie? Has anything happened to her?" He waited. "Oh God, that's lousy. Sarah, don't cry. I know how tough this has been for you. She'll be okay. Give it some time. No, I just wanted to see how you thought she was doing. Sure. Talk to you soon. 'Bye."

He replaced the receiver and turned to Karen. "Laurie's in the hospital. She had some sort of shock reaction on her way out of the shrink's office. I guess she's okay now, but they wanted her to stay overnight. Her sister is about at the end of her rope."

"Will Laurie come back to school?"

"She's determined to be here on Monday for classes." He shrugged helplessly. "Karen, I couldn't lay these letters on Sarah Kenyon now."

"You will turn them over to the office?"

"Of course. I'm sure Dean Larkin will have one of the psychologists speak to Laurie. I know she goes to a psychiatrist in Ridgewood, but maybe she needs counseling here as well. The poor kid."

35

*L*AURIE WAS propped up in bed reading the Bergen *Record* when Sarah arrived at the hospital late Sunday morning. Her greeting to Sarah was cheerful. "Hi. You brought the clothes. Terrific. I'll get dressed and let's go to the club for brunch."

It was what she had said she wanted to do when she'd phoned an hour earlier. "Are you sure it won't be too much for you?" Sarah asked anxiously. "You were pretty sick yesterday."

"It may be too much for *you*. Oh, Sarah, why don't you move and not leave a forwarding address? Honest to God, I'm such a damn nuisance to you." Her smile was both apologetic and rueful as Sarah bent down and hugged her.

Sarah had come in not knowing what to expect. But this was the real Laurie, sorry if she put anyone out, ready to have fun. "You look better than you have in ages," she said sincerely.

"They gave me something, and I slept like a rock."

"It's a mild sleeping pill. Dr. Carpenter has ordered that and an antidepressant for you."

Laurie stiffened. "Sarah, I wouldn't let him give me any pills, and he's been trying. You know I hate those things. But I will do *this:* I'll start the pills. But no more therapy, ever."

"You *will* have to check with Dr. Carpenter about any reaction to the medication."

"Over the phone. That I don't mind."

"And Laurie, you know Dr. Carpenter consulted with a psychiatrist, Dr. Donnelly, in New York about you. If you won't see him, will you allow me to talk to him?"

"Oh, Sarah, I wish you wouldn't, but okay, if it makes you happy." Laurie jumped out of bed. "Let's get out of this place."

In the club friends invited them to join their table. Laurie ate well and was in good spirits. Looking at her, Sarah found it hard to believe that only yesterday she herself had been near despair. She winced thinking of how she had been crying on the phone with that nice Professor Grant.

When they left the club, Sarah did not drive directly home. Instead she went in the opposite direction.

Laurie raised an eyebrow. "Where?"

"About ten minutes from the house. Glen Rock. They're about to open up some condominiums that are supposed to be great. I thought we'd take a look."

"Sarah, maybe we should just rent for a while. I mean, suppose you decide to go with a law firm in New York? You've had offers.

Anyplace we live should be tied to you, not me. If I do give a shot at pro golf I'll be following the sun."

"I'm not going with a private firm. Laurie, when I sit with the families of these victims and I see their grief and anger, I know that I can't work on the other side looking for one damn loophole in the law to set them free. I can sleep a lot better prosecuting murderers than defending them."

There was a model with three levels that they both liked. "Nice layout," Sarah commented. "Dearly as I love the house, those up-to-date bathrooms are something else." She told the agent who was showing them around, "We seem to have serious interest in our home. When we know we have a sale we'll be back."

She linked her arm companionably with Laurie's as they walked to the car. It was a clear, cold day and the light wind had a bite. Even so there was a sense that spring was only six weeks away. "Nice grounds," Sarah commented. "And just think. We wouldn't have to worry about having them tended. Happy thought, isn't it?"

"Dad loved puttering outside and Mom was happiest on her knees in the garden. Wonder how we both missed it?" Laurie's tone was affectionate and amused.

Was she beginning to be able to talk about their parents without instantly being reduced to raw pain and self-recrimination? Please God, Sarah thought prayerfully. They reached the parking lot. It was busy with prospective buyers coming and going. Word of mouth about the new section of the Fox Hedge condos had been excellent. Laurie spoke hurriedly, "Sarah, let me say just one thing. When we get home, I don't want to talk about yesterday. The house has gotten to be a place where you study me with such a worried expression, where you ask questions that are not as casual as they seem. From now on, don't grill me about how I sleep, what I eat, do I date, that kind of thing. Let *me* tell you what I want to talk about. You do the same with me. Okay?"

"Okay," Sarah said matter-of-factly. You *have* been treating her like a little kid who has to tell Mommy everything, she told herself. Maybe it's a good sign that she's starting to resent it. But what happened yesterday?

It was as though Laurie could read her mind. "Sarah, I don't know what made me faint yesterday. I do know that it's a terrible ordeal to have Dr. Carpenter keep after me with leading questions that are nothing but traps. It's like trying to lock all the doors and windows when an intruder is breaking in."

"He's not an intruder. He's a healer. But you're not ready for him. Agreed on everything."

"Good."

Sarah drove past the security guards at the gate, noticing how all arriving cars were stopped and checked. Laurie had obviously taken that in as well. She said, "Sarah, let's put a deposit on that corner unit. I'd love to live here. With that gate and those guards, we'd be safe. I want to feel safe. And that's what scares me so much. I never do."

They were on the road. The car began to pick up momentum. Sarah had to ask the question that was torturing her. "Is that why you took the knife? Was it necessary for you to have it in order to feel safe? Laurie, I can understand that. Just as long as you don't let yourself get so depressed that you'd . . . hurt yourself. I'm so sorry to ask, but that's what scares me."

Laurie sighed. "Sarah, I have no intention of committing suicide. I know that's what you're getting at. I do wish you could believe me. On my oath, I did *not* take that knife!"

That night, back at college, in order to repack her tote bag Laurie dumped its contents on her bed. Textbooks, spiral pads, and loose-leaf binders tumbled out. The very last object was the one that had been concealed at the bottom of the deep carryall. It was the missing carving knife from the set on the kitchen wall.

Laurie backed away from the bed. "No! No! No!" She sank to

her knees and buried her face in her hands. "I didn't take it Sare-wuh," she sobbed. "Daddy said I mustn't play with knives."

A jeering voice crashed through her mind. *Oh, shut up, kid. You know why you have it. Why not take the hint and stick it in your throat. God, I need a cigarette.*

36

*G*REGG BENNETT told himself that he didn't give a damn. Being honest, what he really meant was that he *shouldn't* give a damn. There were plenty of attractive women on this campus. He'd be meeting plenty more in California. He'd have his degree in June and be on his way to Stanford to study for his MBA.

At twenty-five Gregg was and felt considerably older than his fellow students. He still looked back in bewilderment at the nine-teen-year-old dope who had quit college after his freshman year to become an entrepreneur. Not that the experience had hurt. Even getting his ears pinned back had been a long-range blessing. If nothing else he found out exactly how much he didn't know. He'd also learned that international finance was the career for him.

He'd been back from England a month and the January blahs had by now caught up with him. At least he'd been able to get in some skiing at Camelback over the weekend. The powder snow had made the runs great.

Gregg lived in a studio apartment over the garage of a private home two miles from the campus. It was a nice setup that suited him well. He had no desire to share a place with three or four other guys and end up with constant partying. This place was clean and airy; the pullout couch was comfortable for both sitting and sleeping; he could prepare simple meals in the kitchenette.

When he first arrived at Clinton, he'd noticed Laurie around the campus. Who wouldn't? But they'd never been in a class together. Then, a year and a half ago they'd sat next to each other in the auditorium at a showing of *Cinema Paradiso*. The picture had been terrific. As the lights went on, she turned to him and asked, "Wasn't that wonderful?"

That was the beginning. If a girl that attractive gave him the signal that she wanted him to come on to her, Gregg was more than willing to make the next move. But there was something about Laurie that held him back. He'd known instinctively that he'd get nowhere if he tried anything too quickly; as a result, their relationship had developed more as a friendship. She was so darn sweet. Not sugar sweet—she could be bitingly funny and she could be strong-willed. On their third date he told her that it was obvious she'd been a spoiled kid. They'd gone golfing and the starter had overbooked. They had to wait an extra hour for tee-off time. She'd been sore.

"I bet you never had to wait. I bet Mommy and Daddy called you their little princess," he had told her. She'd laughed and said, actually they had. Over dinner that night she told him about having been abducted. "The last thing I remember was standing in front of my house in a pink bathing suit and someone picking me up. The next thing, I woke up in my own bed. The only problem is that was two years later."

"I'm sorry I said you were spoiled," he'd told her. "You deserved to be."

She'd laughed. "I was spoiled before and after. You hit the nail on the head."

Gregg knew that to Laurie he was a trusted friend. It wasn't that simple for him. You don't spend a lot of time with a girl who looks like Laurie, he thought, with that marvelous ripple of blond hair, those midnight blue eyes and perfect features, without wanting to spend all the time you'll ever have with her. But then when she started inviting him home some weekends, he'd been sure she had begun to fall in love too.

Then suddenly it came to an end one Sunday morning last May. He remembered it clearly. He had slept late, and Laurie took it into her head to stop by after church with bagels and cream cheese and smoked salmon. She rapped on the door, then when he didn't hear, yelled, "I know you're in there."

He grabbed a robe, opened the door and just looked at her. She was wearing a linen dress and sandals and looking cool and fresh as the morning itself. She came in, put on the coffee, set out the bagels and told him not to bother making up the bed. She was driving home and could only stay a few minutes. After she left, he could sack out all day if he wanted.

When she was leaving, she put her arms around his neck and kissed him lightly, telling him he needed a shave. "But I still like your looks," she'd teased. "Nice nose, strong chin, cute cowlick." She'd kissed him again, then turned to go. That was when it had happened. Impulsively Gregg followed her to the door, put his hands on her arms, swooped her up and hugged her. She went crazy. Sobbing. Kicking her legs to push him away. He dropped her, angrily asked her what the hell was the matter. Did she think he was Jack the Ripper? She ran out of the apartment and never even spoke to him again except to tell him to leave her alone.

He would have liked to do just that. The only problem was that over last summer, working an internship in New York, and during the fall term, studying at the Banking Institute in London, he'd never gotten her out of his mind. Now that he was back, she was still adamant about refusing to see him.

On Monday evening Gregg wandered over to the cafeteria at the student center. He knew Laurie sometimes dropped by there. He deliberately joined a group that included some of the people from her residence. "It makes sense," one of them was saying at the other end of the table. "Laurie goes out about nine o'clock a lot of weeknights. His wife stays in New York during the week. I tried kidding Laurie about it, but she just ignored me. Obviously she was meeting someone but she sure wasn't talking about it."

Gregg's ears pricked up. Casually he moved his chair to hear better.

"Anyhow, Margy works afternoons in the administration office. She picks up a lot of dirt and knew something was up when Sexy Allan came in looking worried."

"I don't think Grant is sexy. I think he's just a very nice guy." The objection came from a dark-haired student with an air of common sense about her.

The gossiper waved aside the objection. "*You* may not think he's sexy, but a lot of people do. Anyhow, Laurie certainly does. I hear she's been sending him a bunch of love letters and signing them 'Leona.' He turned the letters over to the administration and claims that everything in them is fantasy. Maybe he's afraid if she's writing to him about their little romance she might be blabbing to other people too. I guess he's making a preemptive strike before anything gets back to his wife."

"What did she write?"

"What *didn't* she write? According to the letters, they were making out in his office, his house, you name it."

"No kidding!"

"Well, his wife's away a lot. These things happen. Remember how at her parents' funeral, he went racing down the aisle after her when she fainted?"

Gregg Bennett did not bother to pick up the chair that he knocked over as he strode from the cafeteria.

37

WHEN LAURIE CHECKED her mailbox on Tuesday, she found a note asking her to phone the Dean of Student Affairs for an appointment at her earliest convenience. What's that about? she wondered. When she made the call, the dean's secretary asked if she was free to come in at three o'clock that day.

At the end of the ski season last year, she'd bought a blue-and-white ski jacket on sale. It had hung in her closet unused this winter. Why not, she thought as she reached for it. Perfect for this weather, it's pretty and I might as well get some use out of it. She matched it with blue jeans and a white turtleneck sweater.

At the last minute she twisted her hair into a chignon. Might as well look like the sophisticated senior about to leave the halls of learning for the great world outside. Maybe when she was out of the college atmosphere and among working adults she'd lose this crazy feeling of being a scared kid.

It was another cold, clear day, the kind that made her take deep breaths and throw back her shoulders. It was such a relief to know that Saturday morning she wouldn't be sitting in that damn office with Dr. Carpenter trying to look kindly but always probing, always digging.

She waved to a group of students from her residence then wondered if they were looking at her in a funny kind of way. Don't be silly, she told herself.

The knife. How had it gotten to the bottom of her tote bag? She certainly hadn't put it there. But would Sarah believe her? "Look, Sarah, the stupid thing was stuck between my books. Here it is. Problem solved."

And Sarah would reasonably ask, "How did it get in your bag?" Then she'd probably suggest talking to Dr. Carpenter again.

The knife was in the back of the closet now, hidden in the sleeve of an old jacket. The elastic cuff would keep it from falling. Should she simply throw it away, let the mystery go unsolved? But Dad valued that set of knives and always said they could cut anything clean as a whistle. Laurie hated the thought of something being cut clean as a whistle.

As she walked across the campus to the administration building she mulled over the best way to place the knife back in the house. Hide it in a kitchen cupboard? But Sarah had said that Sophie had looked everywhere in the kitchen for it.

An idea came to her that seemed simple and foolproof: Sophie was always looking for things to polish. Sometimes she'd take the knives down and do them when she was going over the silver flatware. That was it, Laurie thought! I'll sneak the knife into the silver chest in the dining room, way to the back so it won't be seen easily. Even if Sophie had looked there, she might think she'd missed it. The point was Sarah would know that was at least a good possibility.

The solution brought relief until inside her head a derisive voice shouted, *Very clever, Laurie, but how do you explain the knife to yourself? Do you think it jumped into your bag?* The mocking laugh made her curl her fingers into fists.

"Shut up!" she whispered fiercely. "Go away and leave me alone."

Dean Larkin was not alone. Dr. Iovino, the Director of the Counseling Center, was with him. Laurie stiffened when she saw him. A voice in her mind shouted, *Be careful. Another shrink. What are they trying to pull now?*

Dean Larkin invited her to sit down, asked her how she was feeling, how her classes were going, reminded her that everyone was aware of the terrible tragedy in her family and that he wanted her always to understand that the entire faculty had the deepest concern for her well-being.

Then he said he'd excuse himself. Dr. Iovino wanted to have a little talk with her.

The dean closed the door behind him. Dr. Iovino smiled and said, "Don't look scared, Laurie. I just wanted to talk to you about Professor Grant. What do you think of him?"

That was easy. "I think he's wonderful," Laurie said. "He's a great teacher and he's been a good friend."

"A good friend."

"Of course."

"Laurie, it's not uncommon for students to develop a certain attachment to a faculty member. In a case like yours, where you especially needed compassion and kindness, it would be unusual if in loneliness and grief you didn't misinterpret that kind of relationship. Fantasize about it. What you daydreamed it *might* be, became in your mind what it *is*. That's very understandable."

"What are you *talking* about?" Laurie realized that she sounded like her mother the time she became annoyed at a waiter who had suggested he'd like to phone Laurie for a date.

The psychologist handed her a stack of letters. "Laurie, did you write these letters?"

She skimmed them, her eyes widening. "These are signed by someone named Leona. What in the world gave you the idea I wrote them?"

"Laurie, you have a typewriter, don't you?"

"I write my assignments on a computer."

"But you do *have* a typewriter?"

"Yes, I do. My mother's old portable."

"Do you keep it here?

"Yes. As a backup. Every once in a while, the computer has gone down when I had an assignment due."

"You turned in this term paper last week?"

She glanced at it. "Yes, I did."

"Notice that the *o* and *w* are broken wherever they appear on these pages. Now check that against the broken *o* and *w* that regularly appear in the letters to Professor Grant. They were typed on the same machine."

Laurie stared at Dr. Iovino. His face became superimposed with the face of Dr. Carpenter. *Inquisitors! Bastards!*

Dr. Iovino, heavyset, his manner one of all-is-well-don't-worry, said, "Laurie, comparing the signature 'Leona' with the written addenda to your term paper shows a great similarity in the handwriting."

The voice shouted: *He's not only a shrink. He's a handwriting expert now.*

Laurie stood up. "Dr. Iovino, as a matter of fact, I've let a number of people use that typewriter. I feel this conversation is nothing short of insulting. I am shocked that Professor Grant leapt to the conclusion that I wrote this trash. I'm shocked that you would send for me to discuss it. My sister is a prosecutor. I've seen her in court. She would make mincemeat of the kind of 'evidence' that you purport connects me with these disgusting outpourings."

She picked up the letters and threw them across the desk. "I expect a written apology, and if this has leaked out just as everything that happens in this office seems to leak out, I demand a public apology and retraction of this stupid accusation. As for Professor Grant, I considered him a good friend, an understanding friend at this very difficult time in my life. Clearly I was wrong. Clearly the students who call him 'Sexy Allan' and gossip about his flirtatious attitude are right. I intend to tell him that myself, immediately." She turned and walked rapidly from the room.

She was due in Allan Grant's class at 3:45. It was now 3:30. With any luck she'd catch him in the hallway. It was too late to go to his office.

She was waiting when he strode down the corridor. His cheery greetings to other students as he made his way to the classroom ended when he spotted her. "Hi, Laurie." He sounded nervous.

"Professor Grant, where did you get the preposterous idea that I wrote those letters to you?"

"Laurie, I know what a tough time you've been having and . . ."

"And you thought you'd make it easier by telling Dean Larkin that I was fantasizing sleeping with you? Are you crazy?"

"Laurie, don't be upset. Look, we're getting an audience. Why don't you see me in my office after class?"

"So we can strip for each other and I can see your gorgeous body and satisfy my lust for it?" Laurie did not care that people were stopping and listening to their exchange. "You are disgusting. You are going to regret this." She spat out the words. "As God is my witness, you are going to regret this."

She broke through the crowd of stunned students and ran back to the dorm. She locked the door, fell on the bed and listened to the voices that were now shouting at her.

One said, *Well at least you stood up for yourself for a change.*

The other screamed, *How could Allan have betrayed me? He was warned not to show those letters to anyone. You bet he's going to regret it. It's a good thing you have the knife. Kiss-and-Tell will never have to worry about hearing from us again.*

38

BIC AND OPAL flew to Georgia directly after the Sunday program. That night there was a farewell banquet for them.

On Tuesday morning they started driving to New York. In the trunk were Bic's typewriter, their luggage and a can of gasoline carefully wrapped in towels. No other personal possessions would be forwarded. "When we pick a house, we'll get ourselves a state-of-the-art entertainment center," Bic decreed. Till then they would live in the suite at the Wyndham.

As they drove, Bic explained his reasoning to Opal. "That case I told you, where a grown-up woman remembered something her daddy did and Daddy's in prison now. She had vivid memories of what happened in her house and in the van. Now suppose the Lord tests us by allowing Lee to start remembering little bits of our life with her. Suppose she talks about the farmhouse, the way the rooms are laid out, the short steps to the upstairs? Suppose somehow they find it and start going back to see who rented it those years? That house is visible proof that she was under our protection. Other than that, well, Lee's a troubled woman. No one ever saw her with us 'cept that cashier who couldn't describe us. So we got to get rid of the house. The Lord has dictated that."

It was dark when they drove through Bethlehem and arrived in Elmville. Even so they were able to see that little had changed in the fifteen years since they'd left. The shabby diner off the highway, the one gas station, the row of frame houses whose porch lights revealed peeling paint and sagging steps.

Bic avoided Main Street and drove a circuitous route the five miles to the farm. As they neared it, he turned off the headlights. "Don't want anyone to happen to get a look at this car," he said. "Not likely of course. There's never anyone on this road."

"Suppose a cop comes along?" Opal was worried. "Suppose he asks why you don't have lights on?"

Bic sighed. "Opal, you have no faith. The Lord is caring for us. Besides, the only places this road leads to are swamps and the farm." But when they reached the farmhouse, he did drive the car behind a clump of trees.

There was no sign of life. "Curious?" Bic asked. "Want to take a peek?"

"I just want to get out of here."

"Come with me, Opal." It was a command.

Opal felt herself sliding on the ice-crusted ground and reached for Bic's arm.

There was no sign that anyone was living in the house. It was totally dark. Windowpanes were broken. Bic turned the door handle. The door was locked, but when he pressed his shoulder against it, it squeaked open.

Bic set down the gasoline can and took a pencil-thin flashlight from his pocket. He directed the beam of light around the room. "Looks pretty much the same," he observed. "They sure didn't refurnish. That's the very rocking chair where I used to sit with Lee on my lap. Sweet, sweet child."

"Bic, I want to get out of here. It's cold and this place always gave me the creeps. That whole two years I was always so worried someone would come along and see her."

"No one did. And now if this place exists in her memory that's the only place it will exist. Opal, I'm going to sprinkle this gasoline around. Then we'll go outside and you can light the match."

They were in the car and moving rapidly away when the first flames shot above the tree line. Ten minutes later they were back on the highway. They had not encountered another car in their half-hour visit to Elmville.

39

*O*N *MONDAY* Sarah had been interviewed by *The New York Times* and the Bergen *Record* about the Parker conviction. "I realize that he has a right to argue that the victim was the enticer, but in this case, it makes my blood boil."

"Are you sorry you didn't ask for the death penalty?"

"If I'd thought I could have made it stick, I would have asked for it. Parker stalked Mays. He cornered her. He killed her. Tell me that isn't cold-blooded, premeditated murder."

In the office, her boss, the Bergen County prosecutor, led the congratulations. "Conner Marcus is one of the two or three best criminal defense attorneys in this country, Sarah. You did a hell of a job. You could make yourself a bundle if you wanted to switch to the other side of the courtroom."

"Defend them? No way!"

Tuesday morning the phone rang as Sarah settled at her desk. Betsy Lyons, the real estate agent, was bubbling with news. There was another potential buyer seriously interested in the house. Problem was the woman was pregnant and anxious to get settled before the new baby arrived. How soon would the house be available if they decided to buy?

"As fast as they want it," Sarah said. Making that commitment felt as if she were taking a weight off her shoulders. Furniture or anything else she and Laurie decided to keep could be stored.

Tom Byers, a thirty-year-old attorney who was making a name for himself in the patent infringement field, poked his head in. "Sarah, congratulations. Can I buy you a drink tonight?"

"Sure." She liked Tom a lot. It would be fun to have a drink with him. But he'd never be special, she thought, as Justin Donnelly's face popped into her mind.

It was seven-thirty when she unlocked the front door of the house. Tom had suggested going on to dinner, but she'd taken a rain check. The unwinding process that always followed an intense trial had been taking place all afternoon, and as she told Tom, "My bones are starting to ache."

She changed immediately to pajamas and a matching robe, stuck her feet in slippers and looked in the refrigerator. Bless Sophie, she thought. There was a small pot roast already cooked.

Vegetables, potatoes and gravy were in individual plastic-wrapped dishes waiting to be heated.

She was just about to carry the dinner tray into the den when Allan Grant phoned. Sarah's cheerful greeting died on her lips as she heard him say, "Sarah, I started to tell you this the other day. I know now that it wasn't fair not to warn both you and Laurie before I went to the administration."

"Warn about what?"

As she listened, Sarah felt her knees go weak. Holding the receiver with one hand, she pulled out a kitchen chair and sat down. The typewriter. The letters Laurie had been writing on the cruise and the way she'd been so secretive about them. When Allan told her about his confrontation with Laurie, Sarah closed her eyes and wished she could close her ears instead. Allan concluded, "Sarah, she needs help, a lot of help. I know she's seeing a psychiatrist, but . . ."

Sarah did not tell Allan Grant that Laurie had refused to continue seeing Dr. Carpenter. "I . . . I can't tell you how sorry I am, Professor Grant," she said. "You've been so kind to Laurie, and this is very difficult for you. I'll call her. I'll somehow find whatever help she needs." Her voice broke. "Goodbye. Thank you."

There was no way she could put off talking to Laurie, but what was the best approach to take? She dialed Justin Donnelly's home number. There was no answer.

She reached Dr. Carpenter. His questions were brief. "Laurie adamantly denies writing the letters? I see. No, she's not lying. She's blocking. Sarah, call her, reassure her of your support, suggest she come home. I don't think it's wise for her to be around Professor Grant. We've got to get her in to see Dr. Donnelly. I knew that at the Saturday session."

The dinner was forgotten. Sarah dialed Laurie's room. There was no answer. She tried every half hour until midnight. Finally she phoned Susan Grimes, the student who roomed across the hall from Laurie.

Susan's sleepy voice became instantly alert when Sarah identified herself. Yes, she knew what had happened. Of course she'd look in on Laurie.

While she waited, Sarah realized she was praying. Don't let her have done anything to herself. Please God, not that. She heard the sound of the receiver being picked up.

"I looked in. Laurie's fast asleep. I can tell; she's breathing evenly. Do you want me to wake her up?"

Relief flooded through Sarah. "I'll bet she took a sleeping pill. No, don't disturb her and please forgive me for bothering you."

Exhausted, Sarah went up to bed and fell asleep instantly, secure in the knowledge that at least she didn't have to worry about Laurie anymore tonight. She'd call her first thing in the morning.

40

THAT REALLY PUTS the icing on a perfect day, Allan Grant thought as he replaced the receiver after his call to Sarah. She'd sounded heartsick. Why wouldn't she? Her mother and father dead five months, her kid sister well into a nervous breakdown.

Allan went into the kitchen. One corner of the largest cabinet held the liquor supply. Except for a beer or two at night, he was not a solitary drinker, but now he poured a generous amount of vodka in a tumbler and reached for the ice cubes. He hadn't bothered much with lunch, and the vodka burned his throat and stomach. He'd better get something to eat.

There were only leftovers in the refrigerator. Grimacing, he dismissed them as potential dinner material, opened the freezer and reached for a frozen pizza.

While it heated, Allan sipped the drink and continued to debate with himself how badly he had botched the business with Laurie Kenyon. Both Dean Larkin and Dr. Iovino had been impressed by Laurie's adamant denials. As the dean pointed out, "Allan, Miss Kenyon is quite right when she says that it's a typewriter anyone in her residence might have used, and that a similarity in handwriting style is hardly proof that she is the author of those letters."

So now they feel that I've started something that may embarrass the college, Allan thought. Great. How do I deal with her in class until the end of the term? Is there any chance at all that I'm wrong?

As he took the pizza from the oven, he said aloud, "There's no chance that I'm wrong. Laurie wrote those letters."

Karen phoned at eight. "Darling, I've been thinking about you. How did it go?"

"Not well, I'm afraid." They talked for twenty minutes. When they finally hung up, Allan felt a lot better.

At ten-thirty the phone rang again. "I'm really okay," he said. "But, God—it's so good to finally have it out on the table. I'm going to take a sleeping pill now and go to bed. See you tomorrow." He added, "I love you."

He put the radio on the SLEEP button, tuned the dial to CBS and promptly fell asleep.

Allan Grant never heard the soft footsteps, never sensed the figure bending over him, never woke up as the knife slid through the flesh over his heart. A moment later, the sound of the flapping curtains muffled the choking gasps that escaped him as he died.

41

IT WAS the knife dream again, but this time it was different. The knife wasn't coming at her. She was holding it and moving it up and down, up and down. Laurie sat bolt upright in bed, clamping her hand over her mouth to keep from shrieking. Her hand felt sticky. Why? She looked down. Why was she still wearing jeans and her jacket? Why were they so stained?

Her left hand was touching something hard. She closed her fingers around it and a quick stab of pain raced through her hand. Warm, wet blood trickled from her palm.

She threw back the bedclothes. The carving knife was half-hidden under the pillow. Smears of dried blood covered the sheets. What had happened? When did she cut herself? Had she been bleeding that much? Not from that cut. Why had she taken the knife from the closet? Was she still dreaming? Was this part of the dream?

Don't waste a minute, a voice shouted. *Wash your hands. Wash the knife. Hide it in the closet. Do as I tell you. Hurry up. Take off your watch. The band is filthy. The bracelet in your pocket. Wash that too.*

Wash the knife. Blindly she ran into the bathroom, turned on the taps in the tub, held the knife under the gushing water.

Put it in the closet. She raced back into the bedroom. *Throw your watch in the drawer. Get those clothes off. Strip the bed. Throw everything in the tub.*

Laurie stumbled into the bathroom, flipped the handle to the shower setting and dropped the bedding into the tub. As she stripped, she flung her clothes into the water. She stared as it turned red.

She stepped into the tub. The sheets billowed around her feet.

113

Frantically she scrubbed the stickiness from her hands and face. The cut on her palm continued to bleed even when she wrapped a washcloth around it. For long minutes she stood, eyes closed, the water cascading over her hair and face and body, shivering even as the bathroom filled with steam.

Finally she stepped out, wrapped her hair in a towel, pulled on her long terry-cloth robe and plugged the drain. She washed her clothes and the bedding until the water ran clear.

She bundled everything into a laundry bag, dressed and went down to the dryer in the basement. She waited while the dryer spun and whirled. When it clicked off, she folded the sheets and her clothing neatly and brought them back to her room.

Now remake the bed and get out of here. Be at your first class and stay calm. You're really in a mess this time. The phone's ringing. Don't answer it. It's probably Sarah.

On the walk across the campus, she met several other students, one of whom rushed to assure her that she had a real sexual harassment case, a kind of reverse one, but she ought to press it against Professor Grant. What a nerve he had to accuse her that way.

She nodded in an absent way, wondering who the little kid was who kept crying so hard, a muffled kind of crying like her head was buried in a pillow. The image came to her of a small child with long blond hair lying on a bed in a cold room. Yes, she was the one who was crying.

Laurie did not notice when the other students left her to go to their own classes. She was unaware of the stares as they glanced back at her. She did not hear one of them say, "She is really weird."

Automatically she entered the building, took the elevator to the third floor. She started down the corridor. As she passed the classroom where Allan Grant was scheduled to teach, she poked her head in the doorway. A dozen students were gathered in a circle waiting for him. "You're wasting your time," she told them. "Sexy Allan is dead as a doornail."

PART THREE

42

*W*HEN SARAH COULD not reach Laurie in her room Wednesday morning, she called Susan Grimes again. "Please leave a note on Laurie's door to call me at the office. It's very important."

At eleven o'clock Laurie phoned from the police station.

Total numbness took over Sarah's emotions. She took precious minutes to phone Dr. Carpenter, told him what had happened, and asked him to contact Dr. Donnelly. Then she grabbed her coat and purse and rushed to the car. The hour-and-a-half-long drive to Clinton was hell.

Laurie's halting, stunned voice saying, "Sarah, Professor Grant has been found murdered. They think I did it. They arrested me and brought me to the police station. They said I could make one call."

Her only question to Laurie, "How did he die?" She'd known the answer before Laurie told her. Allan Grant had been stabbed. Oh God, merciful God, why?

Sarah arrived at the police station and was told that Laurie was being interrogated. Sarah demanded to see her.

117

The desk lieutenant knew Sarah was an assistant prosecutor. He looked at her sympathetically. "Miss Kenyon, you know that the only one allowed in while she's being questioned is her lawyer."

"I'm her lawyer," Sarah said.

"You can't—"

"As of this minute, I've quit my job. You can listen while I call in my resignation."

The interrogation room was small. A video camera was filming Laurie, who was seated on a rickety wooden chair, staring into the lens. Two detectives were with her. When she saw Sarah, Laurie rushed into her arms. "Sarah, this is crazy. I'm so sorry about Professor Grant. He was so good to me. I was so angry yesterday because of those letters that he thought I'd written. Sarah, tell them to find whoever wrote them. That's the crazy person who must have killed him." She began to sob.

Sarah pressed Laurie's head against her shoulder, instinctively rocking her, vaguely realizing it was the way their mother used to comfort them when they were little.

"Sit down, Laurie," the younger detective said firmly. "She's signed a Miranda warning," he told Sarah.

Sarah eased Laurie back onto the chair. "I'm staying right here with you. I don't want you to answer any more questions now."

Laurie buried her face in her hands. Her hair fell forward.

"Miss Kenyon, may I speak with you? I'm Frank Reeves." Sarah realized that the older detective looked familiar. He had testified in one of her trials. He drew her to the side. "I'm afraid it's an open-and-shut case. She threatened Professor Grant yesterday. This morning, before his body was discovered, she announced to a roomful of students that he was dead. There was a knife that is almost certainly the murder weapon hidden in her room. She tried to wash her clothing and bedding, but there are faint bloodstains on them. The lab report will clinch it."

"Sare-wuh."

Sarah spun around. It was Laurie but it wasn't Laurie in the chair. Her expression was different, childlike. The voice was that of a three-year-old. *Sare-wuh.* That's how the toddler Laurie used to pronounce her name. "Sare-wuh, I want my teddy."

Sarah held Laurie's hand as she was arraigned on the complaint. The judge set bail at one hundred fifty thousand dollars. She promised Laurie, "I'll have you out of here in a few hours." Beyond pain, she watched a handcuffed, uncomprehending Laurie led away.

Gregg Bennett came into the courthouse as she was filling out forms for the bondsman. "Sarah."

She glanced up. He looked as shocked and heartsick as she felt. She had not seen him for months; Laurie had once seemed so happy with this nice young man.

"Sarah, Laurie would never willfully hurt anyone. Something must have snapped in her."

"I know. Insanity will be her defense. Insanity at the time of the killing." As she said the words, Sarah thought of all the defense attorneys whom she had defeated in court who had tried that strategy. It seldom worked. The best it usually did was to create enough doubt to keep the accused from the death sentence.

She realized that Gregg had put his hand on her shoulder. "You look as though you could use some coffee," he told her. "Still take it black?"

"Yes."

He returned carrying two steaming Styrofoam cups as she completed the last page of the application; then he waited with her while it was processed. He's such a nice guy, Sarah thought. Why didn't Laurie fall in love with him? Why a married man? Had she chosen Allan Grant as a father substitute? As the shock wore off, she thought of Professor Grant, of how he'd rushed to be with

119

Laurie when she fainted. Was there any chance he had led her on in subtle ways? Led her on, at a time when she was emotionally bereft? Sarah realized that possible defenses were forming in her mind.

At quarter-past six, Laurie was freed on bond. She came out of the jail accompanied by a uniformed matron. When she saw them, her knees began to buckle. Gregg rushed to catch her. Laurie moaned as he grabbed her. Then she began to shriek, "Sarah, Sarah, don't let him hurt me."

43

*A*T ELEVEN O'CLOCK Wednesday morning the phone rang in the Global Travel Agency in the Madison Arms Hotel on East Seventy-sixth Street in Manhattan.

Karen Grant was on her way out the door. She hesitated, then called over her shoulder, "If it's for me say I'll be back in ten minutes. I have to get this settled before I do anything else."

Connie Santini, the office secretary, picked up the receiver. "Global Travel Agency, good morning," she said, then listened. "Karen just stepped out. She'll be back in a few minutes." Connie's tone was brisk.

Anne Webster, owner of the agency, was standing at the file cabinet. She turned. The twenty-two-year-old Santini was a good secretary but sounded too abrupt on the telephone for Anne's taste. "Always get a name immediately," Anne would preach. "If it's a business call, always ask if someone else can help."

"Yes, I'm sure she'll be back right away," Connie was saying. "Is something wrong?"

Anne hurried over to Karen's desk, picked up the extension and nodded to Connie to hang up. "This is Anne Webster. May I help you?"

Any number of times in her sixty-nine years Anne had received bad news over the phone about a relative or friend. When this caller identified himself as Dean Larkin of Clinton College, she knew with icy certainty that something was wrong with Allan Grant. "I'm Karen's employer and friend," she told the dean. "Karen is right across the lobby in the jeweler's. I can get her for you."

She listened as Larkin hesitantly said, "Perhaps it would be wise if I tell you. I'd drive in but I'm so afraid Karen might hear about it on the radio or a reporter might phone her before I can get there . . ."

A horrified Anne Webster then heard the terrible news of Allan Grant's murder. "I'll take care of it, she said. Tears were welling in her eyes as she hung up the receiver and told the secretary what had happened. "One of Allan's students has been writing love letters to him. He turned them over to the administration. Yesterday the student made a terrible scene and threatened him. This morning when Allan was late for class, this student told everyone he was dead. They found him in bed, stabbed through the heart. Oh, poor Karen."

"She's coming," Connie said. Through the glass wall that separated the travel agency from the lobby, they could see Karen approaching. Her step was springy. A smile was playing on her lips. Her dark hair was swirling around her collar. Her Nippon suit, red with pearl buttons, enhanced her model-size figure. Obviously the errand had been a success.

Webster bit her lip nervously. How should she begin to break the news? Say there'd been an accident and wait until they were in Clinton to say more? Oh God, she prayed, give me the strength I'll need.

The door was opening. "They apologized," Karen said triumphantly. "Admitted it was their fault." Then her smile faded. "Anne, what's wrong?"

"Allan is dead." Webster could not believe she had blurted out those words.

"Allan? Dead?" Karen Grant's tone was questioning, uncomprehending. Then she repeated, "Allan. Dead."

Webster and Santini saw her complexion fade to an ashen pallor and rushed to her. Each taking an arm, they eased her into a chair. "How?" Karen asked, her voice a monotone. "The car? The brakes have been getting soft. I warned him. He's not good at taking care of things like that."

"Oh, Karen." Anne Webster put her arms around the trembling shoulders of the younger woman.

It was Connie Santini who gave what details they knew, who called the garage and told them to have Karen's car brought around immediately, who collected coats and gloves and purses. She offered to go with them and drive. It was Karen who vetoed the suggestion. The office needed to be covered.

Karen insisted on driving. "You don't know the roads, Anne." On the way down, she was tearless. She talked about Allan as though he were still alive. "He's the nicest guy in the whole world . . . He's so good . . . He's the smartest man I've ever known . . . I remember . . ."

Webster was grateful that the traffic was light. It was as though Karen were on automatic pilot. They were passing Newark Airport, going onto Route 78.

"I met Allan on a trip," Karen said. "I was leading a group to Italy. He joined it at the last minute. That was six years ago. It was over the holidays, and his mother had died that year. He told me that he realized he had no place to go for Christmas and he didn't want to stay around the college. By the time we got back to Newark Airport we were engaged. I called him my Mr. Chips."

It was a few minutes past noon when they arrived in Clinton.

Karen began to sob as she saw the cordoned area around her home. "Up till this minute I thought it was a bad dream," she whispered.

A policeman stopped them at the driveway, then quickly stepped aside to let the car pass through. Cameras flashed as they got out of the car. Anne put a comforting arm around Karen as they hurried the few steps to the front door.

The house was filled with police. They were in the living room, the kitchen, the hallway that led to the bedrooms. Karen started down the hallway. "I want to see my husband," she said.

A gray-haired man stopped her, led her into the living room. "I'm Detective Reeves," he said. "I'm very sorry, Mrs. Grant. We've taken him away. You can see him later."

Karen began to tremble. "That girl who killed him. Where is she?"

"She's under arrest."

"Why did she do this to my husband? He was so kind to her."

"She claims she's innocent, Mrs. Grant, but we found a knife that may be the murder weapon in her room."

At last the dam broke. Anne Webster had known that it would. Karen Grant let out a strangled cry that was half laugh, half sob, and became hysterical.

44

BIC TURNED ON the noon news as they were eating lunch in his office in the television studio on West Sixty-first Street. The breaking story was headlined: FATAL ATTRACTION MURDER AT CLINTON COLLEGE.

Opal gasped and Bic turned white as the picture of the child, Laurie, flashed on the screen. "As a four-year-old, Laurie Kenyon was the victim of an abduction. Today, at twenty-one, Kenyon is accused of stabbing to death a popular professor to whom she is alleged to have written dozens of love letters. Allan Grant was found in bed . . ."

A picture of a house flashed on the screen. The area around it was roped off. There was a shot of an open window. "It is believed that Laurie Kenyon entered and left Allan Grant's bedroom by this window." Squad cars lined the streets.

A student, her eyes popping with excitement, was interviewed. "Laurie was yelling at Professor Grant about having sex with him. I think he was trying to break off with her and she went crazy."

When the segment was over, Bic said, "Turn that off, Opal."

She obeyed.

"She gave herself to another man," Bic said. "She was creeping into his bed at night."

Opal didn't know what to do or say. Bic was trembling. His face was sweaty. He took off his jacket and rolled up his sleeves, then held out his arms. The lush curly hair on them was now steel gray. "Remember how scared she'd be when I held my arms out to her?" he asked. "But Lee knew I loved her. She's haunted me all these years. You've witnessed that, Opal. And while I suffered these last months, seeing her, being near enough to touch her, worrying that she'd talk about me to that doctor, threaten all I've worked for, she was writing filth to someone else."

His eyes were enormously wide, brilliantly bright, firing darts of lightning. Opal gave him the answer that was expected of her. "Lee should be punished, Bic."

"She will be. If the eye offends, pluck it out. If the hand offends, cut it off. Lee is clearly under Satan's influence. It is my duty to

124

send her to the healing forgiveness of the Lord by compelling her to turn the blade upon herself."

45

S*ARAH DROVE UP* the Garden State Parkway, Laurie beside her, sleeping. The matron had promised to call Dr. Carpenter and tell him they were on the way home. Gregg had thrust Laurie into Sarah's arms, protesting, "Laurie, Laurie, I'd never hurt you. I love you." Then, shaking his head, he'd said to Sarah, "I don't understand."

"I'll call you," Sarah told him hurriedly. She knew his phone number was in Laurie's address book. Last year Laurie had called Gregg regularly.

When she reached Ridgewood and turned into their street, she was dismayed to see three vans parked in front of the house. A crowd of reporters with cameras and microphones were clustered there, blocking the driveway. Sarah leaned on the horn. They let her pass but ran beside the car until it stopped at the porch steps. Laurie stirred, opened her eyes, looked around. "Sarah, why are these people here?"

To Sarah's relief, the front door opened. Dr. Carpenter and Sophie rushed down the steps. Carpenter pushed his way through the reporters, opened the passenger door and put his arm around Laurie. Cameras flashed and questions were shouted at Laurie as he and Sophie half carried her up the steps into the house.

Sarah knew she had to make a statement. She got out of the car and waited as the microphones were thrust at her. Forcing herself to appear calm and confident, she listened to the questions: "Is this a fatal attraction murder? . . . Will you plea bargain? . . . Is it true you quit your job to defend Laurie? . . . Do you believe she's guilty?"

Sarah chose to answer the last query. "My sister is legally and morally innocent of any crime and we will prove that in court." She turned and pushed her way through the inquisitors.

Sophie was holding open the door. Laurie was lying on the couch in the den, Dr. Carpenter beside her. "I've given her a strong sedative," he whispered to Sarah. "Get her upstairs and into bed immediately. I've left a message for Dr. Donnelly. He's expected back from Australia today."

It was like dressing a doll, Sarah thought as she and Sophie pulled the sweater over Laurie's head and slipped the nightgown in its place. Laurie did not open her eyes nor seem to be aware of them. "I'll get another blanket," Sophie said quietly. "Her hands and feet are ice cold."

The first mewing sound came as Sarah was turning on the nightlight. It was a heartbroken weeping that Laurie was trying to muffle in the pillow.

"She's crying in her sleep," Sophie said. "The poor child."

That was it. If she were not looking at Laurie, Sarah would have thought the sound was coming from a frightened child. "Ask Dr. Carpenter to come up."

Her instinct was to put her arms around Laurie and comfort her, but she forced herself to wait until the doctor was in the room. He stood beside her in the dim light and studied Laurie. Then, as the sobs faded and Laurie's grip on the pillow relaxed, she began to whisper. They bent over to hear. "I want my daddy. I want my mommy. I want Sare-wuh. I want to go home."

46

*T*HOMASINA PERKINS LIVED in a small four-room row house in Harrisburg, Pennsylvania. Now seventy-two, she was a cheerful presence whose one fault was that she loved to talk about the most exciting event of her life—her involvement in the Laurie Kenyon case. She had been the cashier who had called the police when Laurie became hysterical in the diner.

Her greatest regret was that she hadn't gotten a good look at the couple and couldn't remember what name the woman had called the man when they rushed Laurie out of the diner. Sometimes Thomasina would dream about them, especially the man, but he never had a face, just longish hair, a beard and powerful arms with a heavy growth of curly hair.

Thomasina heard about Laurie Kenyon's arrest on the six o'clock television news. That poor family, she thought sadly. All that trouble. The Kenyons had been so grateful to her. She had appeared with them on "Good Morning, America" after Laurie returned home. That day John Kenyon had quietly given her a check for five thousand dollars.

Thomasina had hoped that the Kenyons would keep in touch with her. For a while she wrote regularly to them, long newsy letters describing how everyone who came into the diner wanted to hear about the case and how they'd get tears in their eyes when Thomasina described how frightened Laurie looked and how pitifully she had been crying.

Then one day she received a letter from John Kenyon. He thanked her again for her kindness but said maybe it would be better if she didn't write to them anymore. The letters upset his

127

wife so much. They were all trying to put the memory of that terrible time behind them.

Thomasina had been intensely disappointed. She wanted so much to be invited to visit them and to be able to tell new stories about Laurie. But even though she continued to send Christmas cards every year, they never responded again.

Then she'd sent a sympathy note to Sarah and Laurie when she read about the accident in September and received a lovely note from Sarah saying her mother and father always felt that Thomasina was God's way of answering their prayers and thanking her for the fifteen happy years their family had enjoyed since Laurie's return. Thomasina framed the note and made sure any visitors became aware of it.

Thomasina loved to watch television, especially on Sunday morning. She was deeply religious, and the "Church of the Airways" was her favorite program. She'd been devoted to Reverend Rutland Garrison and was heartbroken when he died.

Reverend Bobby Hawkins was so different. Thomasina wasn't sure about him. He gave her a funny feeling. However, there was something mesmerizing about watching him and Carla together. She couldn't take her eyes off them. And he certainly was a powerful preacher.

Now Thomasina fervently wished that it was Sunday morning so that when Reverend Bobby told everyone to put their hands on the television and ask for a personal miracle, she could ask that Laurie's arrest would turn out to be a mistake. But it was Wednesday, not Sunday, and she'd have to wait the whole rest of the week.

At nine o'clock the phone rang. It was the producer of the local television show "Good Morning, Harrisburg." He apologized for the late call and asked if Thomasina would consider being on the program in the morning to talk about Laurie.

Thomasina was thrilled. "I was looking over the files of the Kenyon case, Miss Perkins," the producer said. "Boy, what a pity you couldn't remember the name of that guy who was with Laurie in the diner."

"I know," Thomasina acknowledged. "It's like it still rattles somewhere in my brain, but he's probably either dead or living in South America by now anyhow. What good would it do?"

"It would do a lot of good," the producer said. "Your testimony is the only eyewitness proof that Laurie may have been abused by her abductors. They'll need a lot more evidence than that to create sympathy for her in court. We'll talk about it tomorrow on the program."

When she put down the phone, Thomasina sprang up and rushed into the bedroom. She reached for her best blue silk dress with the matching jacket and examined it carefully. No stains, thank heaven. She laid out her good corset, her Sunday oxfords, the pair of Alicia Pantihose from JC Penney she'd been saving for a special occasion. Since she'd stopped working she hadn't bothered putting pin curls in her hair at night, but now she carefully set every one of the thinning strands.

Just as she was about to get into bed, Reverend Bobby's advice to pray for a miracle flashed into her mind.

Thomasina's niece had given her lavender stationery for Christmas. She got it out and searched for the new Bic pen she'd bought at the supermarket. Settling at the dinette table she wrote a long letter to Reverend Bobby Hawkins telling him all about her involvement with Laurie Kenyon. She explained that years ago she had refused to undergo hypnosis to help her remember the name the woman had called the man. She'd always believed that to go under hypnosis meant that you were putting your soul in the power of another, and that it would be displeasing to God. What did Reverend Bobby think? She'd be guided by him. Please write soon.

She wrote a second letter to Sarah, explaining what she was doing.

As an afterthought, she enclosed an offering of two dollars in Reverend Bobby Hawkins's envelope.

47

*D*R. *JUSTIN DONNELLY* had gone home to Australia for Christmas vacation, with plans to stay a month. It was summer there and for those four weeks he visited his family, saw his friends, caught up with his old colleagues and reveled in the chance to unwind.

He also spent a great deal of time with Pamela Crabtree. Two years ago, when he'd left for the United States, they'd been close to making a commitment but agreed neither was ready. Pamela had her own career as a neurologist and was developing a considerable reputation in Sydney.

Over the holiday season they dined together, sailed together, went to the theater together. But as much as he'd always looked forward to being with Pamela, as much as he admired her and enjoyed her company, Justin sensed a vague feeling of dissatisfaction. Perhaps there were more than professional conflicts holding them back.

Justin's gnawing sense of unease gradually centered on the realization that he was thinking more and more of Sarah Kenyon. He'd only seen her that one time in October, yet he missed their weekly conversations. He wished he hadn't been so reluctant to suggest that they have dinner together again.

Shortly before he returned to New York, Pamela and he talked it through and agreed that whatever had been between them was over. With a vast sense of relief, Justin Donnelly boarded the plane to New York, arriving exhausted from the long trip at noon on Wednesday. When he got to the apartment he fell into bed and slept until ten o'clock, then checked his messages.

Five minutes later he was on the phone to Sarah. The sound of her voice, tired and strained, tore at his gut. Dismayed, he listened as she told him what had happened. "You must get Laurie in to see me," he told her. "Tomorrow I've got to sort out things in the clinic. Friday morning at ten?"

"She won't want to come."

"She has to."

"I know." There was a pause, then Sarah said, "I'm so glad you're back, Dr. Donnelly."

So am I, Justin thought as he replaced the receiver. He knew Sarah had not yet fully absorbed the ordeal she was facing. Laurie had committed murder in one of her altered states, and that might put the persona who was Laurie Kenyon already beyond his help.

48

*B*RENDON MOODY returned to Teaneck, New Jersey, late Wednesday night from a week of fishing with his buddies in Florida. His wife, Betty, was waiting up for him. She told him about Laurie Kenyon's arrest.

Laurie Kenyon! Brendon had been a detective with the Bergen County prosecutor's office seventeen years ago when four-year-old Laurie disappeared. Until his retirement, he'd been on the homicide squad there and knew Sarah very well. Shaking his head, he turned on the eleven o'clock news. The campus murder was the main story. The segment included shots of Allan Grant's home, Grant's widow being escorted into the house, Laurie and Sarah emerging from the police station, Sarah making a statement in front of the Kenyons' Ridgewood house.

131

With growing dismay, Brendon watched and listened. When the report was over, he snapped off the set. "That's a tough one," he said.

Thirty years ago, when Brendon was courting Betty, her father had said derisively, "That little bantam thinks he's the cock of the walk." There was an element of truth in the remark. Betty always felt that when Brendon was upset or angry, a certain electricity went through him. His chin went up; his thinning gray hair became tousled; his cheeks became flushed; his eyes behind rimless glasses seemed magnified.

At sixty Brendon had lost none of the feisty energy that had made him the top investigator in the prosecutor's office. In three days they were supposed to visit Betty's sister in Charleston. Knowing that she was giving him carte blanche to beg off from the trip, she said, "Isn't there something you can do?" Brendon was now a licensed private investigator, taking only cases that interested him.

Brendon's smile was both grim and relieved. "You bet there is. Sarah needs to have someone down on that campus gathering and sifting every possible tidbit of information she can get. This looks like an open-and-shut case. Bets, you've heard me say it a thousand times and I'll say it again. When you go in with that attitude the only thing you can hope for is a few years off the sentence. You gotta go in believing your client is as innocent as the babe in the manger. That's how you find extenuating circumstances. Sarah Kenyon is a hell of a nice woman and a hell of a good lawyer. I always predicted she'd have a gavel in her hand someday. But she needs help now. Real help. Tomorrow I go see her and sign on."

"If she'll have you," Betty suggested mildly.

"She'll have me. And Bets, you know how you hate the cold. Why don't you go down to Charleston and visit Jane on your own?"

Betty untied her robe and got into bed. "I might just as well. From now on, knowing you, you'll be eating, sleeping and dreaming this case."

49

"CARLA, describe Lee's bedroom in detail to me."

Opal was holding the coffeepot, about to pour coffee for Bic. She paused then carefully tilted the spigot over his cup. "Why?"

"I have many times warned you not to question my requests." The voice was gentle, but Opal shivered.

"I'm sorry. You just surprised me." She looked across the table, trying to smile. "You look so handsome in that velvet jacket, Bobby. Now let's see. Like I told you, her room and her sister's room are on the right side of the staircase. The real estate agent said that the Kenyons turned smaller rooms into baths, so the four bedrooms each have a bath. Lee's room has a double bed with a velvet headboard, a dresser, desk, a standing bookcase, night tables and a slipper chair. It's very feminine, blue-and-white flowered pattern on the spread and headboard and draperies. Two nice-sized closets, cross ventilation, pale blue carpet."

She could tell he was not yet satisfied and narrowed her eyes in concentration. "Oh yes, there are family pictures on her desk and a telephone on the night table."

"Is there a picture of Lee as a child in the pink bathing suit she was wearing when she joined us?"

"I think so."

"You think so?"

"I'm sure there is."

"You're forgetting something, Carla. Last time we discussed this, you told me that there was a stack of family albums on the bottom shelf of the bookcase and it looked as though Lee might have been going through them or perhaps was rearranging them. There appeared to be a great many loose pictures of Lee and her sister as young children."

"Yes. That's right." Opal sipped her coffee nervously. A few minutes ago she'd been telling herself that everything would be all right. She'd been reveling in the luxury of the pretty sitting room of their hotel suite, enjoying the feel of her new brushed-velvet Dior robe. She looked up and her gaze met Bic's stare. His eyes were flashing, messianic. With a sinking heart she knew he was going to demand something dangerous of her.

50

*A*T *QUARTER* of twelve on Thursday Laurie awakened from her sedated sleep. She opened her eyes and looked around the familiar room. A bewildering cacophony of thoughts shouted through her mind. Somewhere a child was crying. Two women in her head were screaming at each other. One of them was yelling, *I was mad at him but I loved him and I didn't want that to happen.*

The other was saying, *I told you to stay home that night. You fool. Look what you've done to her.*

I didn't tell everybody that he was dead. You're the fool.

Laurie pressed both hands to her ears. Oh God, had she dreamt it all? Was Allan Grant really dead? Could anyone believe that she had hurt him? The police station. That cell. Those cameras taking her picture. It hadn't happened to her, had it? Where was Sarah? She got out of bed and ran to the door. "Sarah! Sarah!"

"She'll be back soon." It was Sophie's familiar voice, reassuring, soothing. Sophie was coming up the stairs. "How do you feel?"

134

Relief flowed through Laurie. The voices in her head stopped quarreling. "Oh, Sophie. I'm glad you're here. Where's Sarah?"

"She had to go to her office. She'll be back in a couple of hours. I have a nice lunch all fixed for you, consommé and tuna salad just the way you like it."

"Just the consommé, Sophie. I'll be down in ten minutes."

She went into the bathroom and turned on the shower. Yesterday she had washed sheets and clothes while she showered. What a strange thing to do. She adjusted the shower head until the hot water was a needle-sharp waterfall massaging the knotted muscles in her neck and shoulders. The groggy headache brought on by the sedatives began to clear and the enormity of what had happened started to sink in. Allan Grant, that lovely, warm human being had been murdered with the missing knife.

Sarah asked me if I had taken the knife, Laurie thought as she turned off the taps and stepped from the shower. She wrapped one of the giant bath towels around her body. Then I found the knife in my tote bag. Somebody must have taken it from my room, the same person who wrote those disgusting letters.

She wondered why she didn't feel more emotion for Allan Grant. He had been so kind to her. When she opened the closet door, trying to decide what to wear, she thought she understood. The shelves of sweaters. Mother had been with her when she bought most of them.

Mother, whose joy was to give and give. Daddy's mock dismay when they arrived home with the packages. "I'm subsidizing the entire retail business."

Laurie wiped tears from her eyes as she dressed in jeans and a pullover. After you've lost two people like them, you haven't much grief left for anyone else.

She stood in front of the mirror, brushing her hair. It really needed a trim. But she couldn't make an appointment today. People would be staring at her, whispering about her. But I didn't do anything, she protested to her reflection in the mirror. Again a sharp, focused memory of Mother. How many times had she said, "Oh, Laurie, you look so like me when I was your age."

But Mother had never had that anxious, frightened look in her eyes. Mother's lips always curved in a smile. Mother made people happy. She didn't cause trouble and pain for everyone.

Hey, why should you take all the blame, a voice sneered. *Karen Grant didn't want Allan. She kept making excuses to stay in New York. He was lonesome. He had pizza for dinner half the time. He needed me. It was just that he didn't know it yet. I hate Karen. I wish she was dead.*

Laurie went over to the desk.

Minutes later, Sophie knocked and called in a worried voice, "Laurie, lunch is ready. Are you all right?"

"Will you please leave me alone? The damn consommé won't evaporate will it?" Irritated, she finished folding the letter she'd just written and inserted it in an envelope.

The mailman came around twelve-thirty. She watched from the window until he started up the walk, then hurried downstairs and opened the door as he reached the porch.

"I'll take it and here's one for you."

As Laurie closed the door, Sophie rushed from the kitchen. "Laurie, Sarah doesn't want you to go out."

"I'm not going out, silly. I just picked up the mail." Laurie put her hand on Sophie's arm. "Sophie, you'll stay with me until Sarah comes back, won't you? I don't want to be alone here."

51

EARLY WEDNESDAY evening a pale but composed Karen Grant drove back to New York with her partner, Anne Webster. "I'm better off in the city," she said. "I couldn't bear to stay in the house."

Webster offered to stay overnight, but Karen refused. "You look more exhausted than I am. I'm going to take a sleeping pill and go right to bed."

She slept long and deeply. It was nearly eleven when she awakened on Thursday morning. The three top floors of the hotel were residential apartments. In the three years she'd had her apartment, Karen had gradually added touches of her own: Oriental scatter rugs in tones of cardinal red, ivory and blue that transformed the bland off-white hotel carpeting; antique lamps; silk pillows; Lalique figurines; original paintings by promising new artists.

The effect was charming and luxurious and personal. Yet Karen loved the amenities of hotel living, especially the room service and maid service. She also loved the closet full of designer clothes, the Charles Jourdan and Ferragamo shoes, the Hermès scarves, the Gucci handbags. It was such a satisfying feeling to know that the uniformed desk clerks were always watching to see what she'd be wearing when she stepped off the elevator.

She got up and went into the bathroom. The thick terry-cloth robe that enveloped her from neck to toe was on the hook there. She pulled the belt tightly around her waist and studied herself in the mirror. Eyes still swollen a bit. Seeing Allan on that slab in the morgue had been awful. In one rush she'd thought of all the marvelous times they'd had together, of the way she used to thrill

137

to the sound of his footsteps coming down the hall. The tears had been genuine. There would be more weeping when she looked at his face for the last time. Which reminded her, she'd have to make the necessary arrangements. Not now, however; now she wanted breakfast.

On the telephone, she pressed 4 for room service. Lilly was taking orders. "I'm so sorry, Mrs. Grant," she said. "We're all just shocked."

"Thank you." Karen ordered her usual: fresh juice, fruit compote, coffee, hard roll. "Oh, and send all the morning papers."

"Of course."

She was sipping the first cup of coffee when there was a discreet knock on the door. She flew to open it. Edwin was there, his handsome patrician features set in an expression of solicitous concern. "Oh, my dear," he sighed.

His arms closed around her, and Karen laid her face against the soft cashmere jacket she had given him for Christmas. Then she clasped her hands around his neck, careful not to dishevel his precisely combed dark blond hair.

52

*J*USTIN DONNELLY met Laurie on Friday morning. He had seen newspaper pictures of her but still was not prepared for her striking good looks. Breathtaking blue eyes, shoulder-length golden blond hair that made him think of an illustration of a princess in a fairy tale. She was dressed simply in dark blue slacks, a white high-necked silk blouse and a blue-and-white jacket. There was an innate elegance despite the palpable fear he could sense emanating from her.

Sarah was sitting near her sister, but a little in back of her. Laurie had refused to come into the office alone. "I promised Sarah I'd talk to you, but I cannot do it without her."

Perhaps it was Sarah's reassuring presence, but even so, Justin was surprised to hear Laurie's direct question. "Dr. Donnelly, do you think I killed Professor Allan Grant?"

"Do you think I have reason to believe that?"

"I would guess that everyone has good reason to suspect me. I quite simply did not and would not kill any human being. The fact that Allan Grant could possibly link me to the sort of anonymous trash he'd received was humiliating. But we don't kill because someone misreads a nasty situation."

"*We,* Laurie?"

Was it embarrassment or guilt that flickered in her expression for a fleeting moment? When she did not answer, Justin said, "Laurie, Sarah has talked with you about the serious charges against you. Do you understand what they are?"

"Certainly. They're absurd, but I haven't listened to my father and Sarah talk about the cases she was prosecuting or the sentences the defendants got without knowing what this can mean."

"It would be pretty reasonable to be frightened of what's ahead for you, Laurie."

Her head went down. Her hair fell forward, shielding her face. Her shoulders rounded. She clasped her hands in her lap and drew up her feet so that they did not touch the floor but dangled above it. The soft weeping that Sarah had heard several times in the last few days began again. Instinctively, Sarah reached out to comfort Laurie, but Justin Donnelly shook his head. "You're so scared, aren't you, Laurie," he commented kindly.

She shook her head from side to side.

"You're not scared?"

Her head bobbed up and down. Then between sobs she said, "Not Laurie."

"You're not Laurie. Will you tell me your name?"

"Debbie."

"Debbie. What a pretty name. How old are you, Debbie?"

"I'm four."

Dear God, Sarah thought as she listened to Dr. Donnelly talking to Laurie as though he were speaking to a little child. He is right. Something terrible must have happened to her in those two years she was gone. Poor Mother, always determined to believe that some child-hungry couple took her and loved her. I knew there was a difference when she came home. If she had had help back then, would we be here now? Suppose Laurie has a totally separate personality that wrote those letters and then killed Allan Grant? Should I let him get to it? Suppose she confesses? What was Donnelly asking Laurie now?

"Debbie, you're very tired aren't you?"

"Yes."

"Would you like to go to your room and rest? I'll bet you have a pretty bedroom."

"No! No! No!"

"That's all right. You can stay right here. Why don't you nap sitting in that chair, and if Laurie's around will you ask her to come back and talk to me?"

Her breathing became even. A moment later she lifted her head. Her shoulders straightened. Her feet touched the floor and she brushed her hair back. "Of course I'm frightened," Laurie told Justin Donnelly, "but since I had nothing to do with Allan's death, I know I can count on Sarah to find the truth." She turned, smiled at Sarah and then looked directly at the doctor again. "If I were Sarah, I'd wish I'd stayed an only child. But here I am, and she's always been there for me. She's always understood."

"Understood what, Laurie?"

She shrugged. "I don't know."

"I think you do."

"I really don't."

Justin knew it was time to tell Laurie what Sarah already knew. Something terrible had happened during the two years that she had been missing, something so overwhelming that as a little child she could not handle it alone. Others came to help her, maybe one or two, maybe more, and she had become in effect a multiple personality. When she was returned home, the loving environment had made it unnecessary for the alter personalities to come forward except perhaps very occasionally. The death of her parents had been so painful that the alters were needed again.

Laurie listened quietly. "What kind of treatment are you talking about?"

"Hypnosis. I'd like to videotape you during the sessions."

"Suppose I confess that some part of me . . . some person, if you will—*did* kill Allan Grant? What then?"

It was Sarah's turn to answer. "Laurie, I'm very much afraid that as it stands a jury will almost inevitably convict you. Our only hope is to prove extenuating circumstances or that you were incapable of knowing the nature of the crime."

"I see. So it is possible that I killed Allan, that I wrote those letters? Not just possible. Probable. Sarah, have there been other people who claimed multiple personality as a defense against a murder charge?"

"Yes."

"How many of them got off?"

Sarah did not answer.

"How many of them, Sarah?" Laurie persisted. "One? Two? None? That's it, isn't it? Not one of them got off. Oh my God. Well, let's go ahead. We might as well know the truth even though it's very clear the truth won't set me free."

She seemed to be fighting back tears, then her voice became

strident, angry. "Just one thing, Doctor. Sarah stays with me. I will *not* be alone with you in a room with a closed door and I will not lie on that couch. Got it?"

"Laurie, I'll do anything I can to make this easier for you. You're a very nice person who's had a very bad break."

She laughed, a jeering laugh. "What's nice about that stupid wimp? She's never done anything but cause trouble since the day she was born."

"Laurie," Sarah protested.

"I think Laurie's gone away again," Justin said calmly. "Am I right?"

"You're right. I've got my hands full with her."

"What is your name?"

"Kate."

"How old are you, Kate?"

"Thirty-three. Listen, I didn't mean to come out. I just wanted to warn you. Don't think you're going to hypnotize Laurie and get her to talk about those two years. You're wasting your time. See you."

There was a pause. Then Laurie sighed wearily. "Would it be all right if we stopped talking now? I have such a headache."

53

*O*N FRIDAY morning, Betsy Lyons received a firm offer of five hundred and seventy-five thousand dollars for the Kenyon home from the couple who wanted to move in quickly because the wife was expecting a baby. She called Sarah but could not reach her until the afternoon. To her dismay, Sarah told her the house was off the market. Sarah was sympathetic but firm. "I'm terribly sorry, Mrs. Lyons. First of all I wouldn't entertain an offer that low, but anyhow there is no way I can worry about moving at this time. I know how much work you've put into this sale, but you do understand."

Betsy Lyons did understand. On the other hand the real estate business was desperately slow and she was counting on the commission.

"I'm sorry," Sarah repeated, "but I can't see planning to leave this house before fall at the earliest. Now I do have someone here. I'll talk to you another time."

She was in the library with Brendon Moody. "I had decided it would be a good idea if Laurie and I moved to a condominium," she explained to the detective, "but under the circumstances . . ."

"Absolutely," Brendon agreed. "You're better to take the place off the market. Once this case comes to trial, you'll have reporters posing as potential buyers just to get a look inside."

"I never thought of that," Sarah confessed. Wearily she pushed back a strand of hair that had fallen on her forehead. "Brendon, I can't tell you how glad I am that you want to take on this investigation." She had just finished telling him everything, including what had happened during the session with Laurie at Justin Donnelly's office.

Moody had been taking notes. His high forehead puckered in concentration, his rimless glasses magnifying his snapping brown eyes, his precise bow tie and conservative dark brown suit gave him the air of a meticulous auditor. It was an image that Sarah knew was both accurate and dependable. When he was conducting an investigation, Brendon Moody missed nothing.

She waited while he reread his notes carefully. It was a familiar procedure. That was the way they had worked together in the prosecutor's office. She heard Sophie going up the stairs. Good. She was checking on Laurie again.

Sarah thought back for a moment to the drive home from

Dr. Donnelly's office. Laurie had been deeply despondent, saying, "Sarah, I wish I had been in my car when that bus hit it. Mom and Dad would still be alive. You'd be working at the job you love. I'm a pariah, a jinx."

"No, you're not," Sarah had told her. "You were a four-year-old kid who had the hard luck to get kidnapped and be treated God only knows how badly. You're a twenty-one-year-old who's in a hell of a mess through no fault of her own, so stop blaming yourself!"

Then it was Sarah's turn to cry. Blinding tears obscured her vision. Frantically she wiped them away, trying to focus on the heavy Route 17 traffic.

Now she reflected that in a way her outburst might have been a blessing in disguise. A shocked, contrite Laurie had said, "Sarah, I'm so damn selfish. Tell me what you want me to do."

She'd answered, "Do exactly what Dr. Donnelly asks. Keep a journal. That will help him. Stop fighting him. Cooperate with the hypnosis."

"All right, I think I have everything," Moody said briskly, breaking Sarah's reverie. "I have to agree. The *physical aspects* are pretty cut and dried."

It gave Sarah a lift to hear him accentuate "physical aspects." Clearly he understood where the defense was heading.

"You're going for stress, diminished mental capacity?" he asked.

"Yes." She waited.

"What kind of fellow was this Grant guy? He was married. Why wasn't his wife home that night?"

"She works for a travel agency in New York and apparently stays in the city during the week."

"Don't they have travel agencies in New Jersey?"

"I would think so."

"Any chance that the professor was the kind who compensated for the absence of his wife by leading on his students?"

"We're on the same wavelength." Suddenly the library, with its cheery mahogany bookcases, family pictures, paintings, blue Oriental rug, butter-soft leather couches and chairs, assumed the electric atmosphere of the stuffy cubicle that had been her domain in the prosecutor's office. Her father's antique English desk became the battered, shabby relic she'd worked at for nearly five years. "There's a recent case where a defendant was convicted of raping a twelve-year-old," she told Moody.

"I would hope so," he said.

"The legal issue was that the victim is chronologically twenty-seven years old. She suffers from multiple personality disorder and convinced a jury that she'd been violated when she was in her twelve-year-old persona and not capable of giving informed consent. He was found guilty of statutory rape of a person who was found to be mentally defective. The verdict was overturned on appeal, but the point is, a jury believed the testimony of a woman with multiple personality disorder."

Moody leaned forward with the swiftness of a hound catching its first scent of the prey. "You're talking about turning it around."

"Yes. Allan Grant was particularly solicitous of Laurie. When she fainted in church at the funeral mass, he rushed to be with her. He offered to take her home and stay with her. Looking back, I wonder if that wasn't pretty unusual concern." She sighed. "At least it's a starting point. We don't have much else."

"It's a good starting point," Moody said decisively. "I've got a few things to clear up, then I'll get down to Clinton and start digging."

The phone rang again. "Sophie will get it," Sarah said. "Bless her. She's moved in with us. Says we can't be alone. Now let's settle the terms . . ."

"Oh, we'll talk about that later."

"No, we won't," she said firmly. "I know you, Brendon Moody."

Sophie tapped on the door, then opened it. "I'm sorry to interrupt, Sarah, but that real estate agent is on the phone again and she says it's very important."

Sarah picked up the receiver, greeted Betsy Lyons, then listened. Finally she said slowly, "I suppose I owe this to you, Mrs. Lyons. But I have to be clear. That woman cannot keep looking at the house. We'll be out on Monday morning and you can bring her in between ten o'clock and one o'clock, but that is it."

When Sarah hung up she explained to Brendon Moody. "There's a prospective buyer who's been hemming and hawing about this place. Apparently she's pretty much decided on it at full price. She wants one more walk through and then indicates she'll be willing to wait to occupy it until it's available. She'll be here on Monday."

54

*T*HE FUNERAL SERVICE for Professor Allan Grant was held on Saturday morning at St. Luke's Episcopal Church near the Clinton campus. Faculty members and students crowded together to pay their final respects to the popular teacher. The rector's homily spoke of Allan's intellect, warmth and generosity. "He was an outstanding educator ... That smile would brighten the darkest day ... He made people feel good about themselves ... He could sense when someone was having a tough time. Somehow he found a way to help."

Brendon Moody was at the service in the capacity of observer, not mourner. He was especially interested in studying Allan

Grant's widow, who was wearing a deceptively simple black suit with a string of pearls. Somewhat to his surprise, Brendon had developed over the years a reasonably accurate sense of fashion. On a faculty salary, even with her travel agent job thrown in, Karen Grant would find it pretty tough to buy designer clothes. Did either she or Grant have family money? It was raw and windy out and she had not elected to wear a coat into church. That meant she must have left one in the car. The cemetery would be a damn cold place on a day like this.

She was weeping as she followed the casket from the church. Good-looking woman, Brendon thought. He was surprised to see the president of the college and his wife accompany Karen Grant into the first limousine. No family member? No close friend? Brendon decided to continue to pay his respects. He'd go to the burial service.

His question about Karen's coat was answered there. She emerged from the limousine wearing a full-length Blackglama mink.

55

THE CHURCH of the Airways had a twelve-member council that met on the first Saturday of the month. Not all of the members approved of the rapid changes the Reverend Bobby Hawkins was instituting on the religious hour. The Well of Miracles particularly was anathema to the senior member of the council.

Viewers were invited to write in explaining their need for a

147

miracle. The letters were placed in the well, and just before the final hymn, Reverend Hawkins extended his hands over it and emotionally prayed that the requests be granted. Sometimes he invited a member of the studio congregation who was in need of a miracle to come up for a special blessing.

"Rutland Garrison must be spinning in his grave," the senior member told Bic at the monthly council meeting.

Bic eyed him coldly. "Have the donations increased substantially?"

"Yes, but—"

"But *what?* More money for the hospital and the retirement home, more for the South American orphanages that have always been my personal charity, more of the faithful voicing their needs to the Lord."

He looked around the table from one member to the other. "When I accepted this ministry I said that I must steer it into wider waters. I've studied the records. In the past several years donations have been steadily decreasing. Isn't that true?"

There was no answer.

"Isn't that true?" he thundered.

Heads nodded.

"Very well. Then I suggest that he who is not with me is against me and ought to resign from this august body. The meeting is adjourned."

He strode from the conference room and down the corridor into his private office where Opal was going through the Well of Miracles mail. Her system was to glance at the requests and separate any unusual ones for Bic to possibly read aloud on the program. The letters were then dropped in one pile to be placed in the Well of Miracles. The donations were in another pile for Bic to tabulate.

Opal dreaded having to show him one letter she had put aside.

"They're seeing the light, Carla," he informed her. "They're coming to understand that my way is the Lord's way."

"Bic," she said timidly.

He frowned. "In this office you must never—"

"I know. I'm sorry. It's just . . . Read this." She thrust Thomasina Perkins' rambling letter into his outstretched hand.

56

*A*FTER THE FUNERAL, Karen and the faculty members went to the home of the president of the college where a buffet luncheon was waiting. Dean Walter Larkin told Karen that he could not forgive himself for not realizing how sick Laurie Kenyon was. "Dr. Iovino, the Director of the Counseling Center, feels the same way."

"What has happened is a tragedy, and there's no use trying to place blame on ourselves or others," Karen said quietly. "I ought to have persuaded Allan to show those letters to the administration even before he was sure Laurie was writing them. Allan himself ought not to have left that bedroom window wide open. I should hate that girl, but all I can remember is how sorry Allan felt for her."

Walter Larkin had always thought that Karen was something of a cold fish but now he wondered if he'd been unfair. The tears in her eyes and her quivering lip certainly weren't faked.

At breakfast the next morning, he commented on that to his wife, Louise. "Oh, don't be such a romantic, Walter," she told him crisply. "Karen was bored stiff with campus life and faculty teas. She'd have been gone long ago if Allan hadn't been so generous with her. Look at the clothes she wears! You know what I think? Allan was finally waking up to the truth about the woman he was married to. I bet he wouldn't have put up with it much longer. That poor Kenyon girl gave Karen a one-way, first-class ticket to New York."

57

*O*PAL APPEARED at the real estate office promptly at ten o'clock on Monday morning. Betsy Lyons was waiting for her. "Mrs. Hawkins," she said, "I'm afraid that this will be the only time I can bring you to the Kenyon house, so please, try to make a note of anything you want to see or ask about."

It was the opening Opal needed. Bic had told her to try to pump the real estate agent for any information about the case. "That family has so much tragedy." She sighed. "How is that poor girl?"

Betsy Lyons was relieved to see that Carla Hawkins did not seem to be linking the house to the shocking headlines of Laurie Kenyon's arrest on the murder charge. She rewarded her by being less closemouthed than usual. "As you can imagine, the whole town is buzzing. Everyone feels so sorry for them. My husband is a lawyer, and he says they'll have to go with a diminished capacity defense but it will be hard to prove. Laurie Kenyon never acted odd or crazy in all the years I've known her. Now we'd better be on our way."

Opal was quiet on the drive to the house. Suppose leaving this picture of Lee backfired and gave her a flash of memory? But even if it did, it would remind her of Bic's threat.

Bic had been pretty scary that day. He'd encouraged Lee to really love that silly chicken. Lee's eyes, usually downcast and sad, would brighten when she went in the backyard. She'd rush over to the chicken, put her arms around it and hug it. Bic had taken the butcher knife from the kitchen drawer and winked at Opal. "Watch this performance," he'd said.

He'd run outside, slashing the knife back and forth in front of Lee. She'd been terrified and hugged the chicken tighter. Then he'd reached down and grabbed it by the neck. It began to squawk, and Lee in an unusual show of courage tried to pull it from Bic. He'd slapped her so hard she fell backwards, then as she scrambled to her feet, he'd lifted his arm and swung it in an arc, cutting that chicken's head off in one blow.

Opal had felt her own blood go cold as he threw the body of the chicken at Lee's feet where it flapped around spattering her with blood. Then Bic had held up the head of the dead creature and pointed the knife at Lee's throat, chopping the air with it, his eyes fearsome and glittering. In a terrible voice, he'd sworn that that's what would happen to her if she ever talked about them. Bic was right. A reminder of that day would shut Lee up or drive her completely crazy.

Betsy Lyons was not displeased by her passenger's silence. It was her experience that when people were about to commit themselves to a purchase, they tended to become serious and introspective. It was a worry that Carla Hawkins had not brought her husband to see the house at least once though. As she steered the car into the Kenyon driveway, Betsy asked about that.

"My husband is leaving the decision entirely up to me," Opal said calmly. "He trusts my judgment. I know exactly what will make him happy."

"That's a compliment to you," Betsy assured her with fervent haste.

151

Lyons was about to insert the key in the lock when the door opened. Opal was dismayed to see the stocky figure in the dark skirt and cardigan who was introduced as the housekeeper, Sophie Perosky. If the woman trailed around the house with them, Opal might not be able to plant the picture.

But Sophie stayed in the kitchen, and planting the photo was easier than Opal expected. In every room, she stood by the windows to observe the view. "My husband asked me to be sure that we're not too near any other houses," she explained. In Lee's room, she spotted a spiral notebook on the desk. The cover was partially raised and the tip of a pen could be seen protruding from under it. "What are the exact dimensions of this room?" she asked as she leaned over the desk to look out the window.

As she had expected, Betsy Lyons fished in her briefcase for the house plan. Opal glanced down swiftly and flipped open the notebook. Just the first three or four pages had writing on them. The words "Dr. Donnelly wants me . . ." jumped out at her. Lee must be keeping a journal. With all her being, Opal wished she could read the entry.

It took only an instant to take the picture from her pocket and slip it about twenty pages back in the book. It was the photo Bic had taken of Lee that first day, just after they reached the farm. Lee had been standing in front of the big tree, shivering in her pink bathing suit, crying, hugging herself tightly.

Bic had cut Lee's head from the picture and stapled the fragment to the bottom. Now the picture showed Lee's face, eyes puffy with tears, hair tangled, staring up at her own decapitated body.

"You really do have a great deal of privacy from the other houses," Opal commented as Betsy Lyons announced that the room was twelve by eighteen feet, really a wonderful size for a bedroom.

58

JUSTIN DONNELLY had arranged his schedule so that he could see Laurie every morning, Monday to Friday, at ten o'clock. He'd also set up appointments for her with the art and journal therapists. On Friday he had given her a half-dozen books on multiple personality disorder.

"Laurie," he'd said, "I want you to read these and understand that most of the patients with your problem are women who were abused as children. They blocked out what happened to them just as you're blocking it out. I think that the personalities who helped you to cope those two years you were missing were just about dormant until you lost your parents. Now they've come back in full force. When you read these books, you're going to see that alter personalities are often trying to help you, not hurt you. That's why I hope you'll do your best to consciously let me talk to them."

On Monday morning he had his video camera set up in his office. He knew that if Sarah decided to use any of the tapes at the trial, he had to be extremely careful not to look as though he was putting words in Laurie's mouth.

When Sarah and Laurie came in, he showed them the camera, explained that he was going to record the sessions and told Laurie, "After a while I'll play them back for you." Then he hypnotized her for the first time. Clinging to Sarah's hand, Laurie obediently riveted her attention on him, listened as he urged her to relax, closed her eyes, visibly settled back, let her hand slip from her sister's.

"How do you feel, Laurie?"

"Sad."

"Why are you sad, Laurie?"

"I'm always sad." Her voice was higher, hesitant, with a trace of a lisp.

Sarah watched as Laurie's hair fell forward, as her features seemed to become fluid and change until a childlike expression came over them. She listened as Justin Donnelly said, "I think I'm talking to Debbie. Am I right?"

He was rewarded by a shy nod.

"Why are you sad, Debbie?"

"Sometimes I do bad things."

"Like what, Debbie?"

"Leave that kid alone! She doesn't know what she's talking about."

Sarah bit her lip. The angry voice she'd heard on Friday. Justin Donnelly did not seem perturbed. "Kate, is that you?"

"You know it's me."

"Kate, I don't want to hurt Laurie or Debbie. They've been hurt enough. If you want to help them, why don't you trust me?"

An angry, bitter laugh preceded the statement that chilled Sarah. "We can't trust any man. Look at Allan Grant. He acted so nice to Laurie, and look at the fix he put her in. Good riddance to him, I say."

"You don't mean that you're glad he's dead?"

"I wish he'd never been born."

"Do you want to talk about that, Kate?"

"No, I don't."

"Would you write about it in your journal?"

"I was going to write this morning but that stupid kid had the book. She can't spell worth a damn."

"Do you remember what you were going to write about?"

A derisive laugh. "It's what I'm *not* going to write that would interest you."

. . .

154

On the way home in the car, Laurie was again visibly exhausted. Sophie had lunch waiting, and after Laurie picked at it she decided to lie down.

Sarah settled at the desk and went through her messages. The grand jury would consider the complaint against Laurie on Monday the seventeenth. That was only two weeks away. If the prosecutor was convening the jury that fast, he must be convinced he had a very strong case already. As indeed he did.

A stack of mail had piled up on her desk. She scanned the envelopes, not bothering to open any until she came to the one with the carefully printed return address in the corner. Thomasina Perkins! She was the cashier who long ago had spotted Laurie in the restaurant. Sarah could remember how her father's heartfelt gratitude to the woman had eroded when her frequent letters arrived, filled with increasingly lurid memories of the trauma Laurie exhibited in the restaurant. But there was no doubt Thomasina Perkins meant well. She had written a very kind note in September. This was probably another expression of sympathy. Sarah slit the envelope and read the single sheet of paper. In it, Perkins had given her phone number. Sarah dialed rapidly.

Thomasina picked up on the first ring. She was thrilled to realize it was Sarah calling. "Oh, wait till I tell you my news," she bubbled. "Reverend Bobby Hawkins phoned me himself. He doesn't believe in hypnosis. He invited me to be a guest on next Sunday's program. He's going to pray over me so that God will whisper in my ear the name of that terrible man who kidnapped Laurie."

59

R*EVEREND BOBBY HAWKINS* skillfully turned the Thomasina Perkins problem into a potential advantage. A trusted staff member was instantly sent to Harrisburg to check on her. It was a reasonable thing to do. The Reverend Hawkins and the council needed to be sure there was no investigative reporter putting her up to writing the letter. Bic also wanted details of Thomasina's health, particularly her hearing and vision.

The results of the probe were gratifying. Thomasina wore trifocals and had been operated on for cataracts. Her description of the two people she'd seen with Laurie had been vague from the beginning.

"She clearly doesn't recognize us on the TV screen and won't in person," Bic told Opal as he read the report. She'll be an inspiration to our congregation."

The following Sunday morning, a delighted Thomasina, her hands clasped together in the attitude of prayer, gazed worshipfully up into Bic's face. He laid his hands on her shoulders. "Years ago, this good woman brought about a miracle when the Lord gifted her with the ability to see that a child was in need. But the Lord did not grant Thomasina the ability to remember the name of the villainous man who was accompanying Laurie Kenyon. Now Lee is in need again. Thomasina, I command you to listen and remember the name that has been drifting in your unconscious all these years."

Thomasina could hardly contain herself. Here she was, a celebrity on international television; there was no way she could fail to obey Reverend Bobby's command. She strained her ears. The organ was playing softly. From somewhere she heard a whisper: "Jim . . . Jim . . . Jim . . ."

Thomasina straightened her shoulders, threw out her arms and cried, "The name I have been seeking is Jim!"

60

S*ARAH HAD TOLD* Justin Donnelly about Thomasina Perkins and the reason for her appearance on the "Church of the Airways" program. At ten o'clock on Sunday morning Donnelly turned on the television set and at the last minute decided to tape the program.

Thomasina did not appear until the hour was almost over. Then, incredulously, Donnelly witnessed the Reverend Bobby's histrionics and Perkins' revelation that "Jim" was the abductor's name. That guy claims he can bring on miracles and he couldn't even get Laurie's name straight, Donnelly thought in disgust as he snapped off the set. He referred to her as *Lee.* Nevertheless he carefully labeled the video cassette and put it in his briefcase.

Sarah phoned a few minutes later. "I don't like to call you at home," she apologized, "but I have to ask. What did you think? Is there any chance that Miss Perkins was right about the name?"

"No," Donnelly said flatly. He heard her sigh.

"I'm still going to ask the Harrisburg police to run 'Jim' through the computers," she told him. "There might be a file on a child abuser by that name who was active seventeen years ago."

"I'm afraid you're wasting your time. The Perkins woman was taking a wild guess. After all, she had Almighty God on the line, didn't she? How's Laurie doing?"

"Pretty well." She sounded cautious.

"Did she watch the program?"

"No, she refuses to listen to any kind of gospel music. Besides, I'm trying to keep her mind off all this. We're going to play a round of golf. It's fairly pleasant out considering it's February."

"I always meant to try golf. That should be relaxing for both of you. Has Laurie been writing in the journal?"

"She's upstairs scribbling away now."

"Good. See you tomorrow." Donnelly hung up and decided that the best way to shake his feeling of restlessness was to take a long walk. He realized that for the first time since he'd lived in New York, the prospect of a totally unstructured Sunday was not appealing to him.

61

*T*HOMASINA HAD HOPED that after the "Church of the Airways" program the Reverend Bobby Hawkins and his lovely wife, Carla, might invite her to lunch at a nice place like the Tavern on the Green and maybe suggest that they drive her around New York to see the sights. Thomasina hadn't been to New York in thirty years.

But something happened. The minute the cameras were turned off, Carla whispered something to Reverend Bobby and they both looked upset. The upshot of it was that they sort of brushed Thomasina off with a hurried goodbye and thank you and keep praying. Then an escort brought her to the car that would take her to the airport.

On the ride, Thomasina tried to console herself with the glory of her appearance on the program, of the new stories she'd have to tell. Maybe "Good Morning, Harrisburg" would want her back to talk about the miracle.

Thomasina sighed. She was tired. She'd barely closed her eyes last night for the excitement and now her head ached and she wanted a cup of tea.

She arrived at the airport with nearly two hours to wait for her plane and went into one of the cafeterias. Orange juice, oatmeal, bacon, eggs, a Danish and a pot of tea restored her usual good nature. It had been a very exciting experience. The Reverend Bobby seemed so Godlike that she'd shivered when he prayed over her.

She pushed back her empty plate, poured a second cup of tea and, while she sipped it, thought of the miracle. God had spoken directly to her, saying, "Jim, Jim."

Not for the world would she contradict anything the Almighty told her, but as Thomasina dipped the paper napkin in her water glass and scrubbed away at a spot of bacon grease on her good blue dress she was ashamed of the guilty thought that imposed itself in her mind: That just isn't the name I remember hearing.

62

*O*N MONDAY MORNING, ten days after her husband's funeral, Karen Grant entered the travel agency, a heavy stack of mail in her arms.

Anne Webster and Connie Santini were already there. They had been discussing once again the fact that Karen had not invited them to join her at the reception even though they clearly heard the college president tell her to be sure to include any close friends who had attended the service.

Anne Webster still puzzled over the omission. "I'm certain it was just that Karen was so upset."

Connie had other ideas. She was sure Karen didn't want any of the faculty asking them about the travel agency. It would have been just like Anne to artlessly say that business had been terrible for several years. Connie would have bet her bottom dollar that at Clinton College, Karen had given the impression that Global Travel was on a level with Perillo Tours.

The discussion ended with Karen's arrival. She greeted them briefly and said, "The dean had someone pick up the mail at the house. There's an awful pile. Most of it sympathy cards, I suppose. I hate to read them, but I guess I can't avoid it."

With an exaggerated sigh, she settled at her desk and reached for a letter opener. Minutes later she gasped, "Oh, my God."

Connie and Anne jumped up and rushed to her. "What is it? What's wrong?"

"Call the police in Clinton," Karen snapped. Her face was the color of chalk. "It's a letter from Laurie Kenyon, signing herself 'Leona' again. Now that crazy girl is threatening to kill *me!*"

63

*T*HE MONDAY MORNING SESSION with Laurie was unproductive. She'd been quiet and depressed. She told

Justin about playing golf. "I was terrible, Dr. Donnelly. I just couldn't concentrate. So many loud thoughts." But he couldn't get her to discuss the loud thoughts. None of the alters would talk to him either.

When Laurie went into art therapy, Sarah told Donnelly that she had begun to prepare her for the grand jury hearing. "I think everything is really starting to sink in," she explained. "Then last night I caught her going through some photo albums she keeps in her room." Sarah's eyes began to fill with tears that she hastily blinked away. "I told her it wasn't a great idea to look at pictures of Mom and Dad just now."

They left at noon. At two o'clock, Sarah phoned. In the background, Justin Donnelly could hear Laurie screaming.

Her voice trembling, Sarah said, "Laurie's hysterical. She must have been going through the albums again. There's a picture she's torn to bits."

Now Donnelly could make out what Laurie was shrieking. "I promise I won't tell. I promise I won't tell."

"Give me directions to your house," he snapped. "And then get two Valiums into her."

Sophie let him in.

"They're in Laurie's room, Doctor." She led the way upstairs. Sarah was sitting on the bed, holding a sedated Laurie.

"I made her take the Valiums," Sarah told him. "She quieted down, but now she's almost out of it." She released Laurie and eased her head onto the pillow.

Justin bent over Laurie and began to examine her. Her pulse was erratic, her breathing shallow, her pupils dilated, her skin cold to the touch. "She's in shock," he said quietly. "Do you know what brought it on?"

"No. She seemed to be all right after we got home. She said she was going to write in her journal. Then I heard her screaming. I think she must have started going through the album because she tore up a picture. There are pieces of it all over her desk."

"I want those pieces collected," Justin said. "Try not to miss any of them." He began to tap Laurie's face. "Laurie, it's Dr. Donnelly. I want you to talk to me. Tell me your full name."

She did not respond. Donnelly's fingers tapped her face with greater force. "Tell me your name," he said insistently. Finally Laurie opened her eyes. As they focused on him, they took on a surprised expression followed by one of relief.

"Dr. Donnelly," she murmured. "When did you come?"

Sarah felt herself go limp. The last hour had been agony. The sedative had calmed Laurie's hysteria, but then her total withdrawal was even more frightening. Sarah had been terrified that Laurie was slipping so far away she would not make it back.

Sophie was standing in the doorway. "Would a cup of tea be good for her?" she asked softly.

Justin heard. He looked over his shoulder. "Please."

Sarah went over to the desk. The picture was virtually shredded. In those few moments from the time Laurie started shrieking till Sarah and Sophie reached her, she had managed to reduce it to minuscule pieces. It would be a miracle if it could be put together.

"I don't want to stay here," Laurie said.

Sarah whirled around. Laurie was sitting up, hugging herself. "I can't stay here. Please."

"Okay," Justin said calmly. "Let's go downstairs. We could all use a cup of tea." He supported Laurie as she got to her feet. They were halfway down the stairs, Sarah behind them, when the chimes rang in the foyer signaling someone was at the front door.

Sophie bustled to answer it. Two uniformed policemen were on the porch. They were carrying a warrant for Laurie's arrest. By contacting the widow of Allan Grant with a threatening letter, she had violated the terms of her bail and it had been revoked.

. . .

That evening, Sarah sat in Justin Donnelly's office in the clinic. "If you hadn't been there, Laurie would be in a jail cell right now," she told him. "I can't tell you how grateful I am."

It was true. When Laurie was brought before the judge, Donnelly had convinced him that she was under intense psychological stress and required hospitalization in a secured facility. The judge had amended his order, to permit inpatient hospitalization. On the drive from New Jersey to New York, she had been in a trance-like sleep.

Justin chose his words carefully. "I'm glad to have her here. She needs to be watched and monitored constantly right now."

"To keep her from sending threatening letters?"

"And to keep her from harming herself."

Sarah got up. "I've taken enough of your time for one day, Doctor. I'll be back first thing in the morning."

It was nearly nine o'clock. "There's a place around the corner where the menu is good and the service is fast," Donnelly told her. "Why don't you grab a quick bite with me and then I'll send for a car to take you home?"

Sarah had already phoned Sophie to tell her that Laurie was checked into the hospital and to be sure to keep her own plans for the evening. The thought of something to eat and a cup of coffee with Justin Donnelly instead of going home to the empty house was comforting. "I'd like that," she said simply.

Laurie was standing at the window of her room. She liked the room. It wasn't large, so she could see all of it in one glance. She felt safe in it. The outside window didn't open. She had tried it. There was an interior window that looked out on the hallway and the nurses' station. It had a drape but she'd left it partially open. She didn't ever want to be in the dark again.

What had happened today? The last thing she remembered was sitting at the desk writing. She'd turned the page and then . . .

And then it all went blank until I saw Dr. Donnelly bending over me, she thought. Then we were going down the stairs and the police came.

The police said she had written a letter to Allan Grant's wife. Why would I write to her? Laurie wondered. They said I threatened her. That's silly, she thought. When would I have written the letter? When would I have mailed it?

If Karen Grant had received a threatening letter in the last few days it was proof that somebody else must have sent it. She couldn't wait to point that out to Sarah.

Laurie leaned her forehead against the window. It felt so cool. She was tired now and would go to bed. A few people were on the sidewalk, hurrying down the block, their heads down. You could tell it was chilly out.

She saw a man and a woman cross the street in front of the clinic. Was that Sarah and the doctor? She couldn't be sure.

She turned, crossed the room and got into bed, pulling the covers around her. Her eyes were so heavy. It was good to drift away. It would be so good never to have to wake up again.

64

ON TUESDAY MORNING, Brendon Moody drove to the Clinton College campus. His plan was to canvas the residents of the building where Laurie had her studio apartment. After Allan Grant's funeral, he'd given it the once-over. Five years old, it had been erected to serve the needs of upperclassmen. The rooms were good-sized and included a kitchenette and private bath. It was popular housing for students like Laurie who could afford to pay the surcharge for privacy.

Laurie's apartment had been thoroughly searched and then released by lab technicians from the prosecutor's office. Brendon made it his first stop.

It was totally disheveled. The bed was stripped. The door of the closet was ajar and the clothing looked as though it had been examined and replaced haphazardly on the hangers. The drawers of the dresser were partially open. The contents of the desk were strewn on its surface.

Moody knew that the investigators had taken the typewriter on which the letters to Allan Grant had been written and the rest of the stationery. He knew that the bed sheets and Laurie's blood-stained clothing and watchband and bracelet had been confiscated.

What then was he looking for?

If asked the question, Brendon Moody would have said "Nothing," and meant that he had no particular agenda in mind. He looked around, getting a feel for the premises.

It was obvious that in its normal condition the room was quite attractive. Tie-back, floor-length ivory curtains, an ivory dust ruffle on the bed, framed prints of Monet and Manet, paintings on the walls, a half-dozen golf trophies on a shelf over the bookcase. She had not stuck pictures of classmates and friends in the mirror frame over the dresser, the way so many students did. There was only a single family picture on the desk. Brendon studied the photograph. The Kenyons. He'd known the parents. This shot must have been taken in the pool area behind their house. The family had obviously been happy and content together.

Put yourself in Laurie's place, Moody thought. The family is destroyed. You blame yourself. You're vulnerable and latch onto a guy who's kind to you, who's both an attractive man and old enough to be a sort of father figure, and then he rejects you. And you explode.

Open and shut. Brendon prowled around, examining, evaluating. He stood over the tub in the bathroom. Traces of blood had been found in it. Laurie had been smart enough to wash the sheets and her clothing here, bring them down to the dryer, then fold and put them away. She'd tried to clean the watchband too. Brendon knew what the prosecutor could do with that evidence. Try to prove panic and confusion when the killer had systematically attempted to destroy evidence.

As Brendon was about to leave the room, he looked around one more time. He had found absolutely nothing, not one shred of evidence that could be used to help Laurie. Why did he have the nagging sense that somehow, someway, he was missing something?

65

SARAH HAD a sleepless night. The day kept replaying in her mind: Laurie's bloodcurdling screams; the torn picture; the policemen at the door; Laurie being taken out in handcuffs; Justin swearing he'd get her released in his custody as they followed the squad car to Clinton. It was dawn when Sarah finally slept, an uneasy, troubled sleep in which she dreamt of courtrooms and guilty verdicts.

She woke up at eight o'clock, showered, put on a tan cashmere shirt, matching slacks and dark brown ankle boots and went downstairs. Sophie was already in the kitchen. Coffee was brewing. In the breakfast area, a flowered pitcher held freshly squeezed orange juice. A compote of cut-up oranges, grapefruit, apples and cantaloupe was attractively arranged in a Tiffany bowl. An English toast rack was positioned next to the toaster.

Everything looks so normal, Sarah thought. It's just as though Mom and Dad and Laurie will come downstairs any minute. She pointed to the toast rack. "Sophie, remember how Dad used to call that thing a toast *cooler.* He was right."

Sophie nodded. Her round, unlined face showing distress, she poured juice into Sarah's glass. "I was worried last night—not being here when you got back. Was Laurie really willing to go into the hospital?"

"She did seem to understand that it was the clinic or jail." Wearily Sarah rubbed her forehead. "Something happened yesterday. I don't know what it was, but Laurie said she'll never spend another night in her bedroom. Sophie, if that woman who came back to see the house the other day wants it, I'm going to sell."

She did not hear the expected protest. Instead Sophie sighed. "I think maybe you're right. This isn't a happy home anymore. Maybe it's too much to expect it to be after what happened in September."

It was both a relief and a blow to realize that Sophie agreed with her. Sarah finished the juice, swallowing over the large lump in her throat. "I'll skip everything except the coffee." A thought struck her. "Do you think you found most of the pieces of that picture Laurie tore up yesterday?"

Sophie's lips creased in a triumphant smile. "Better than that. I put it together." She produced it. "See, I assembled it on the sheet of paper and then, when I was sure it was right, I glued it. Only trouble is the pieces were so small that the glue ran all over them. It's kind of hard to tell much about it."

"Why it's just a picture of Laurie when she was a kid," Sarah said. "That certainly can't be what caused her to get so upset." She studied it, then shrugged helplessly. "I'll put it in my briefcase right now. Doctor Donnelly wants to see it."

With troubled eyes, Sophie watched Sarah push back her chair. She'd so hoped that pasting the picture together would somehow be helpful and show what had brought on Laurie's hysterical outburst. She remembered something and fished inside the pocket of her apron. It wasn't there. Of course it wasn't. The staple that she'd removed from one of the scraps of the picture was in the pocket of the housedress she'd been wearing yesterday. It certainly couldn't be important, she decided as she poured coffee into Sarah's cup.

66

ON TUESDAY MORNING, while listening to the eight o'clock CBS news, Bic and Opal heard about Laurie Kenyon's threatening letter to Karen Grant, the revoking of her bail and her confinement in the locked facility of a clinic for multiple personality disorder.

Nervously Opal asked, "Bic, do you think they'll get her to talk in that place?"

"Intense efforts will be made to have her recall her childhood," he said. "We must know what is going on. Carla, call that real estate woman."

Betsy Lyons caught Sarah as she was about to leave for New York. "Sarah," she bubbled, "have I got good news for you! Mrs. Hawkins phoned. She's crazy about the house, wants to close on it as soon as possible and is willing to give you up to a year to live in it. She only asks to be able to come in occasionally with her decorator, at your convenience. Sarah, remember I told you that in this market you might have to come down from seven hundred fifty thousand? My dear, she didn't bicker about the price at all and is paying cash."

"I guess it's meant to be," Sarah said quietly. "I'm glad people who want the house that much are going to have it. You can tell them they can move in by August. The condominium should be ready then. I don't care if they come in with their decorator. Laurie will be staying in the hospital, and if I'm home I'll be working in the library."

Betsy called Carla Hawkins. "Congratulations. It's all set. Sarah is perfectly willing for you to bring in your decorator. She says if she's home she'll be working in the library." Betsy's tone became confidential. "You know, she's going to defend her sister at the trial. Poor darling, she'll have her hands full."

Bic had picked up the extension and listened to the conversation. After a final, "Congratulations again. I'm sure you'll be so happy in that beautiful house," Lyons said goodbye.

Smiling, Bic replaced the receiver. "I'm sure we'll be very happy together," he said and went to the desk. "My special phone book, Carla. Where is it?"

She hurried over. "Right here, Bic, in this drawer." She handed it to him. "Bic, what interior decorator do you want me to get?"

He sighed, "Oh, Carla." Thumbing through the book, he found the name he was looking for and dialed a number in Kentucky.

67

*S*ARAH REMEMBERED that Laurie had gone into the clinic with only the clothes she was wearing. Grateful that she wasn't already on her way to New York, she went to Laurie's room and with Sophie's help packed a bag.

At the clinic the bag's contents were examined, and a nurse quietly removed a leather belt and laced sneakers. "Just a precaution," she said.

"You all think that she's suicidal," Sarah told Justin a few minutes later, then looked away from the understanding in his eyes. She knew she could bear anything except sympathy. I can't lose it, she warned herself, again swallowing over the constriction in her throat.

"Sarah, I told you yesterday that Laurie is fragile and depressed. But there is one thing I can promise you—and this is our great hope—she doesn't want you hurt anymore. She'll do anything to prevent that."

"Does she realize that the worst way she could hurt me would be to harm herself?"

"Yes, I do think she knows that. And I believe she is starting to trust me. She knows that I convinced the judge to let her come here instead of going to jail. Were you able to figure out what it was she tore up yesterday?"

"Sophie managed to put it together." Sarah removed the reconstructed photograph from her bag and showed it to him. "I don't understand why this picture would upset her," she said. "It's similar to a lot of others in the album and around the house."

Justin Donnelly studied it. "With all the cracks and glue, it's hard to tell much. I'll have the nurse bring her in."

Laurie was wearing some of the clothes Sarah had brought, jeans and a blue sweater that accentuated her cornflower blue eyes. Her hair was loose. She wore no makeup and looked to be about sixteen. Seeing Sarah, she ran to her and the sisters embraced. As Sarah smoothed down Laurie's hair, she thought, When we come to trial, this is the way she's got to look. Young. Vulnerable.

The thought helped her to get a grip on herself. She realized that when she concentrated on defending Laurie, her own emotions were safely harnessed.

Laurie sat in one of the armchairs. Clearly she had no intention of going near the couch. She made that apparent immediately.

"I'll bet you thought you'd coax her into lying down." It was the strident voice again.

"I think it's Kate who's talking, isn't it?" Justin asked pleasantly.

The look of a sixteen-year-old had vanished. Laurie's face had hardened. No, firmed, Sarah thought. She seems older.

"Yes, it's Kate. And I want to thank you for keeping the wimp out of jail yesterday. That really would have done her in. I tried to stop her from writing that crazy letter to Allan's wife the other day, but she wouldn't listen and see what happened."

"Laurie wrote the letter?" Justin asked.

"No, Leona wrote it. The wimp would have written a letter of condolence. That would have been just as bad. I swear I can't stand her, and as for those other two! One of them always mooning about Allan Grant, the other, the little kid, always crying. If she doesn't shut up soon, I'll throttle her."

Sarah could not take her eyes from Laurie. This alter personality who called herself Kate dwelt inside Laurie, directed or tried to direct Laurie's actions. If she came out on the witness stand with that arrogance and bullying attitude, no jury would ever acquit Laurie.

Justin said, "You know, I haven't turned on the video camera yet. You came out awfully fast this morning. Is it okay if I turn it on now?"

An annoyed shrug. "Go ahead. You will anyhow."

"Kate, Laurie got awfully upset yesterday, didn't she."

"You should know. You were there."

"I was there after she got upset. I just wondered if you could tell me what caused it?"

"That discussion is forbidden."

Donnelly did not seem fazed. "All right, so we won't discuss it. Could you show me what Laurie was doing when she got upset."

"No way, pal." She turned her head. "Oh shut up that sniffling."

"Is Debbie crying?" Justin asked.

"Who else?"

"I don't know. How many of you are there?"

"Not many. Some of the others went away after Laurie was back home. Just as well. It was getting crowded. I said, *shut up*."

"Kate, maybe if I spoke to Debbie, I could find out what's bothering her."

"Go ahead. I can't do a thing with her."

"Debbie, please don't be afraid. I promise nothing will hurt you. Talk to me again, won't you?" Justin Donnelly's voice was gentle, coaxing.

The changeover happened in an instant. The hair falling forward, the features smoothed out, the mouth puckered, lips quivering, the hands clasped in her lap, the dangling legs. Tears began to gush down her cheeks.

"Hi, Debbie," Justin said. "You've been crying a lot today, haven't you."

She nodded vigorously.

"Did something happen to you yesterday?"

She nodded assent.

"Debbie, you *know* I like you. You know I keep you safe. Do you think you can trust me?"

A tentative nod.

"Then can you tell me what scared you?"

She shook her head from side to side.

"You can't tell me. Then maybe you can show me. Were you writing in the journal?"

"No. Laurie was writing." The voice was soft, childlike and sad.

"Laurie was writing, but you could tell what she was writing, couldn't you?"

"Not everything, I just started to learn how to read."

"All right. Show me what Laurie was doing."

She picked up an imaginary pen, made the motion of opening a book and began to write in the air. She hesitated, held up the pen as though thinking, looked around and then her hand reached down to turn another page.

Her eyes widened. Her mouth opened in a silent scream. She jumped up, threw the book away from her and began a tearing motion, both hands working vigorously, her face contorted in horror.

Abruptly she stopped, dropped her hands and shouted, "Debbie, get back inside! Listen, Doctor, I may be sick of that little kid, but I take care of her. You burn that picture, do you hear me? Just don't make her look at it again."

Kate had taken charge.

At the end of the session, an attendant came for Laurie. "Can you come back later?" Laurie begged Sarah as she was leaving.

"Yes. Whatever time Dr. Donnelly says is okay."

When Laurie was gone, Justin handed the picture to Sarah. "Can you see anything about this that might frighten her?"

Sarah studied it. "You can't see much with all those cracks and that glue drying over it. You can tell she looks cold, the way she's hugging herself. She's wearing that same bathing suit in the picture

173

with me that we have in the library. It was taken a few days before she was kidnapped. In fact that's the bathing suit she was wearing when she disappeared. Do you think that might have triggered the fear?"

"Very possibly." Dr. Donnelly put the picture in the file. "We'll keep her busy today. She'll be in art therapy this morning and a journal-writing session this afternoon. She still refuses to take any of the standardized tests. I'll be available to see her between and around other patients. I hope the time will come when she's willing to talk to me without you. I think that may happen."

Sarah stood up. "What time shall I come back?"

"Right after she has dinner. Six o'clock work out for you?"

"Of course." As she left, Sarah was calculating the time. It was now nearly noon. With luck she'd be home by one. She'd have to be on her way back by four-thirty to avoid the worst of the commuter traffic. That still gave her three-and-a-half hours at her desk.

Justin walked her to the door of the reception area, then watched her go. Her slim back was straight, her tote bag over her shoulder, her head high. Chin up, he thought, good girl. Then as he watched her walk down the corridor he saw her shove both hands in her pockets as though seeking warmth from a chill only she could feel.

PART FOUR

68

THE GRAND JURY convened on February 17 and did not take long to indict Laurie for the purposeful and knowing murder of Allan Grant. A trial date was set for October fifth.

The next day Sarah met Brendon Moody in Solari's, the popular restaurant around the corner from the Bergen County courthouse. As lawyers and judges came in, they all stopped to speak to Sarah. She should be eating with them, joking with them, Brendon thought, not meeting them this way.

Sarah had spent the morning in the courthouse library researching insanity and diminished mental capacity defenses. Brendon could see the worry in her eyes, the way the smile faded as soon as anyone who greeted her turned away. She looked pale, and there were hollows in her cheeks. He was glad that she had ordered a decent lunch and commented on that.

"Everything tastes like sawdust, but there's no way I can let myself get sick at this stage of the game," Sarah said wryly. "How about you, Brendon? How's the food around the campus?"

"Predictable." Brendon took an appreciative bite of his cheeseburger. "I'm not getting very far, Sarah." He pulled out his notes. "The best and maybe the most dangerous witness is Susan Grimes, who lives across the hall from Laurie. She's the one you called a couple of times. Since October she's noticed Laurie going out regularly between eight and nine o'clock at night and not coming back till eleven or later. She said Laurie looked different on those occasions, pretty sexy, lots of makeup, hair kind of wild, jeans tucked into high-heeled boots—not her usual style at all. She was sure Laurie was meeting some guy."

"Is there any indication that she was ever actually *with* Allan Grant?"

"You can pinpoint specific dates from some of the letters she wrote to him, and they don't hold up," Moody said bluntly. He pulled out his notepad. "On November sixteenth, Laurie wrote that she loved being in Allan's arms the night before. The night before was Friday, November fifteenth, and Allan and Karen Grant were at a faculty party together. Same kind of fantasizing for December second, twelfth, fourteenth, January sixth and eleventh. I could go on right up to January twenty-eighth. The point is, I hoped to prove that Allan Grant had been leading her on. We know she was hanging around his house, but we haven't a shred of evidence that he was aware of it. In fact everything points the other way."

"Then you're saying that all this was in Laurie's mind, that we can't even suggest that Grant might have been taking advantage of her despondency?"

"There's someone else I want to talk to, a teacher who's been away on sick leave. Her name's Vera West. I'm picking up some rumors about her and Grant."

The pleasant background hum of voices and laughter and dishes being placed on tables, all the familiar sounds that had been part of her workday world seemed suddenly intrusive and foreign to Sarah. She knew what Brendon Moody was saying. If Laurie had fantasized all the encounters with Allan Grant, if in his wife's absence Allan had begun a romance with another woman and Laurie had learned about it, it gave more credence to the prosecutor's contention that she had killed him in a jealous rage.

"When will you question Vera West?" she asked.

"Soon, I hope."

Sarah swallowed the rest of her coffee and signaled for the check. "I'd better get back. I'm going to meet the people who are buying our house. Guess what? This Mrs. Hawkins who's been coming out is none other than the wife of the Reverend Bobby Hawkins."

"Who's that?" Brendon asked.

"The hot new preacher on the 'Church of the Airways' program. That's the one Miss Perkins was on when she came up with the name 'Jim' as the man Laurie was with in the diner years ago."

"Oh, that guy. What a faker. How come he's buying your house? That's quite a coincidence with him being involved with the Perkins woman."

"Not really. His wife had been looking at the house before all this happened. The Perkins woman wrote to him, not the other way round. Have we gotten any feedback yet from the Harrisburg police on 'Jim'?"

Brendon Moody was hoping Sarah would not ask him about that. Choosing his words carefully, he said, "Sarah, as a matter of fact we just did. There's a Jim Brown from Harrisburg who's a known child molester. He has a record a mile long. He was in the area when Laurie was spotted in the diner. Miss Perkins was shown his picture at that time but couldn't identify him. They wanted to bring him in for questioning. After Laurie was found, he disappeared without a trace."

"He never showed up again?"

"He died in prison six years ago in Seattle."

"What was the offense?"

"Kidnapping and assault of a five-year-old girl. She testified at his trial about the two months she was with him. I've read the testimony. Bright little kid. Came out with some pretty harrowing stuff. It was all over the papers at the time."

"Which means that even if he was Laurie's abductor it won't do us any good. If Laurie has a breakthrough and remembers him and is able to describe what he did to her, the prosecutor would bring the Seattle newspapers into court and claim that she'd just parroted that case."

"We don't know that this guy had anything to do with Laurie at all," Moody said briskly. "But, yes, if he did, no matter what Laurie remembers about him, it will sound as if she's lying."

Neither one of them spoke the thought that was in their minds. The way it was going, they might have to ask the prosecutor to consider plea-bargaining for Laurie. If that proved necessary, it would mean that by the end of the summer Laurie would be in prison.

69

*B*IC AND OPAL drove with Betsy Lyons to the Kenyon home. For this meeting they had both dressed conservatively. Bic was wearing a gray pin-striped suit with a white shirt and bluish gray tie. His topcoat was dark gray, and he carried gray kidskin gloves.

Opal's hair had just been lightened and shaped at Elizabeth Arden's. Her gray wool dress had a velvet collar and cuffs. Over it she wore a black fitted coat with a narrow sable collar. Her shoes and bag, purchased at Gucci, were black lizard.

Bic was sitting next to Lyons in the front seat of her car. As she chatted, indicating various points of interest in the town, Lyons kept glancing sideways at Bic. She'd been startled when another agent had asked, "Betsy, do you know who that guy *is?*"

She knew he was in television. She certainly hadn't realized he had his own program. She decided that the Reverend Hawkins was a terribly attractive and charismatic man. He was talking about moving to the New York area.

"When I was called to the Church of the Airways ministry, I knew that we'd want to have a home nearby. I'm just not a city person. Carla has had the undesirable job of scouting for us. And she has kept coming back to this town and this house."

Praise the Lord, Betsy Lyons thought.

"My one hesitation," the preacher was saying in his courteous, gentle voice, "is that I was so afraid that Carla was letting herself in for a disappointment. I honestly thought that the house might be taken off the market permanently."

So did I, Betsy Lyons thought, shivering at the prospect. "The girls will be happier in a smaller place," she confided. "Look, this is the street. You drive down Lincoln Avenue and pass all these lovely homes, then the road bends here and it's Twin Oaks Road."

As they turned onto Twin Oaks Road, she rattled off the names of the neighbors. "He owns the Williams Bank. The Kimballs live in the Tudor. She's Courtney Meier, the actress."

In the backseat, Opal clutched her gloves nervously. It seemed to her that every time they came to Ridgewood it was as though they were skating on thin ice and insistently, consistently testing it, pushing nearer and nearer the breaking point.

Sarah was waiting for them. Attractive, Opal decided, as for the first time she got a close look at her. The kind who gets better looking as she gets older. Bic would have passed her by when she was a little kid. Opal wished Lee hadn't had golden hair down to her waist. She wished Lee hadn't been standing by the road that day.

Mutton dressed as lamb, Sarah thought as she extended her hand to Opal. Then she wondered why in the name of God that old Irish expression, a favorite of her grandmother's, had jumped into her mind at this moment. Mrs. Hawkins was a well-dressed, fashionably coiffed woman in her mid-forties. It was the small lips and tiny chin that gave her a weak, almost furtive expression. Or maybe it was that the Reverend Bobby Hawkins had such a magnetic presence. He seemed to fill the room, to absorb all the energy in it. He spoke immediately about Laurie.

"I don't know if you're aware that we prayed on our holy hour that memory of the name of your sister's abductor would be returned to a Miss Thomasina Perkins."

"I saw the program," Sarah told him.

"Have you looked into the name, Jim, to see if there is any possible connection? The Lord works in strange ways, sometimes directly, sometimes indirectly."

"There is nothing we're not checking in my sister's defense," Sarah said with closure in her voice.

He took the hint. "This is a beautiful room," he said, looking around the library. "My wife kept saying how happy I'd be working here with the bookcases and those big windows. I like to be always in the light. Now I don't want to take any more of your time. If we can just go through the house with Mrs. Lyons one last time, then my lawyer can contact your lawyer about passing papers . . ."

Betsy Lyons took the couple upstairs, and Sarah returned to work, filing the notes she had made in the law library. Suddenly she realized she'd better get started for New York.

The Hawkinses and Betsy Lyons looked in to say they were leaving. Reverend Hawkins explained that he would like to bring his architect in as soon as possible but certainly didn't want to have him going over the library while Sarah was working. What would be a good time?

"Tomorrow or the next day between nine and twelve, or late afternoon," Sarah told him.

"Tomorrow morning, then."

When Sarah returned from the clinic and went into the library the next afternoon, she had no way of knowing that from now on every word spoken in that room would be turning on sophisticated voice-activated equipment and that all her conversations would be transmitted to a tape recorder hidden in the wall of the guest-room closet.

70

IN MID-MARCH, Karen Grant drove to Clinton for what she hoped would be the last time. In the weeks since Allan's death, she had spent Saturdays going through the house, weeding out the accumulation of six years of marriage, selecting the pieces of furniture she wanted in the New York apartment, arranging for a used-furniture dealer to pick up the rest. She had sold Allan's car and put the house in the hands of a real estate agent. Today there was going to be a memorial service for Allan in the chapel on campus.

Tomorrow she was leaving for four days in St. Thomas. It

would be good to get away, she thought as she drove swiftly down the New Jersey Turnpike. The travel business perks were wonderful. She'd been invited to Frenchman's Reef, one of her favorite places.

Edwin would be going too. Her pulse quickened and unconsciously she smiled. By fall they wouldn't have to sneak around anymore.

The memorial service was like the funeral. It was overwhelming to hear Allan eulogized. Karen heard herself sobbing. Louise Larkin, seated next to her, put an arm around her. "If only he'd listened to me," Karen whispered to Louise. "I warned him that girl was dangerous."

There was a reception afterwards at the Larkin home. Karen had always admired this house. It was over one hundred years old and had been beautifully restored. It reminded her of the houses in Cooperstown where so many of her high school friends lived. She had grown up in a trailer park and could still remember when one of the kids in school asked derisively if her folks were going to have a sketch of their mobile home on their Christmas card.

The Larkins had invited not only faculty members and administrative staff but a dozen or so students. Some of them offered fervent condolences, some paused to tell a favorite story about Allan. Karen's eyes moistened as she told people that she missed Allan more and more each day.

Across the room, forty-year-old Vera West, newest member of the faculty, nursed a glass of white wine. Her round, pleasant face was framed by short, naturally wavy brown hair. Tinted glasses concealed her hazel eyes. She did not need the glasses for vision. She was afraid that the expression in her eyes was too revealing. She sipped her wine, trying not to remember that at a faculty party a few months ago Allan, not his wife, had been across the room. Vera had hoped that the sick leave would give her the time she needed to get a grip on her emotions—emotions no one must suspect her of having. As she pushed back the single strand of hair that always managed to fall on her forehead, she thought of the verse written by a nineteenth-century poet: "Sorrow which is never spoken is the heaviest load to bear."

Louise Larkin joined her. "It's so good to have you back, Vera. We've missed you. How are you feeling?" Larkin's eyes were inquisitive.

"Much better, thank you."

"Mononucleosis is so debilitating."

"Yes, it is." After Allan's funeral, Vera had fled to her cottage in Cape Cod. Mono was the excuse she'd used when she phoned the dean.

"Karen really looks quite marvelous for someone who's had such a devastating loss, don't you think, Vera?"

Vera raised the glass to her lips, sipped, then said calmly, "Karen's a beautiful woman."

"I mean, you've lost so much weight, and your face is so drawn. I swear, if I were a stranger and had to make a guess between the two of you, I'd pick you as the mourner." Louise Larkin squeezed Vera's hand and smiled sympathetically.

71

*L*AURIE AWAKENED to the faint murmur of voices in the corridor. It was a comforting sound, one she'd been hearing for three months now. February. March. April. It was the beginning of May. Outside, before coming here, whether on the street, on the campus, or even at home, she had begun to feel as though she was free-falling, unable to stop her descent. Here in the clinic, she felt suspended in time. Her plunge had been slowed. She was grateful for the reprieve even though she knew that in the end no one could save her.

She sat up slowly and hugged her legs. This was one of the best moments of the day, when she'd awaken to know the knife dream hadn't wrenched her awake during the night, that whatever stalked her was being held at bay.

It was the sort of thing that they wanted her to write in the journal. She reached over to the night table for the spiral notebook and pen. She had time to jot down a few thoughts before dressing and going to breakfast. She propped up the pillows, pulled herself up and opened the book.

There were pages of writing in it that hadn't been there last night. Over and over a childish hand had written, "I want my mommy. I want to go home."

Later that morning as she and Sarah sat across the desk from Justin Donnelly, Laurie carefully studied the doctor as he read the journal. He was such a big man, she thought, with those broad shoulders, those strong features, that mass of dark hair. She liked his eyes. They were intensely dark blue. She normally didn't like mustaches, but his seemed so right, especially above those even white teeth. She liked his hands too. Wide but with long fingers. Tanned but no hint of fuzz on them. Funny, she could think a mustache looked great on Dr. Donnelly, but she hated fuzz on a man's hands or arms. She heard herself saying that.

Donnelly looked up. "Laurie?"

She shrugged. "I don't know why I said that."

"Would you repeat it?"

"I said I hate fuzz on a man's hands or arms."

"Why do you think that just occurred to you?"

"She's not going to answer that."

Sarah had come to recognize Kate's voice immediately.

Justin wasn't fazed. "Come on, Kate," he said good-humoredly. "You can't keep getting away with bullying Laurie. She wants to talk to me. Or Debbie does. I think it was Debbie writing in the book last night. It looks like her handwriting."

"Well it certainly isn't mine." Over the past three months the tone had become less strident. A certain wary understanding had been struck between Justin and the alter personality, Kate.

"May I speak to Debbie now?"

"Oh, all right. But don't get her crying again. I'm sick of that kid's sniffling."

"Kate, you're a bluff," Justin said. "You protect Debbie and Laurie and we both know it. But you've got to let me help you. It's too big a job for you."

The hair falling forward was the usual signal. It wrenched Sarah's heart to hear the frightened child who called herself Debbie. Was this the way it was for Laurie those two years she was away, weeping, terrified, longing for the people she loved?

"Hi, Debbie," Justin said. "How's the big girl today?"

"Better, thank you."

"Debbie, I'm so glad you started writing in the journal again. Do you know why you wrote this last night?"

"I knew the book was empty. I shook it first."

"You shook the book? What did you expect to find?"

"I don't know."

"What were you afraid to find, Debbie?"

"More pictures," she whispered. "I have to go now. They're looking for me."

"Who? Who is looking for you?"

But she was gone.

A lazy laugh. Laurie had crossed her legs, slumped a little in the chair. In a deliberately provocative gesture, she ran her hand through her hair.

"There she goes, trying to hide, hoping they won't find her."

Sarah stiffened. This was Leona, the alter personality who wrote the letters to Allan Grant. This was the scorned woman who had killed him. She'd only come out twice before in these months.

"Hi, Leona." Justin leaned across the desk, his manner that of offering flattering attention to an attractive woman. "I've been hoping you'd pay us a visit."

"Well, a girl's got to live. You can't keep moping around forever. Got a cigarette?"

"Sure." He reached in the drawer, held out the pack, lit the cigarette for her. "Have you been moping around, Leona?"

She shrugged. "Oh, you know how it is. I was pretty crazy about Professor Kiss-and-Tell."

"Allan Grant?"

"Yes, but listen, it's over, right? I'm sorry for him, but these things happen."

"What things?"

"I mean him giving me away to the shrink and the dean at school."

"You were angry at him for that, weren't you."

"You bet I was. So was Laurie, but for different reasons. She really put on a class-A performance when she buttonholed him in the hall."

I'll have to plea bargain, Sarah thought. If this personality got on the stand, displaying not a shred of remorse about Allan Grant's death . . .

"You know that Allan's dead . . ."

"Oh, I'm used to that now. What a shock though."

"Do you know how he died?"

"Sure I do. Our kitchen knife." The bravado crumbled. "I sure wish to God I'd left it in my room when I dropped in on him that night. I really was crazy about him, you know."

72

IN THE THREE months between the beginning of February and the end of April, Brendon Moody had made frequent visits to Clinton College. He had become a familiar figure, chatting with students in the Rathskeller or the student center, talking to the faculty, falling in step with residents of Laurie's dormitory.

At the end of that time he had learned little that would be useful in Laurie's defense, although there were a few things he'd come up with that might possibly lighten her sentence. For the first three years of college she'd been an exemplary student, popular with both faculty and fellow students. "Well liked, but, if you know what I mean, not close," a student from the third floor of her apartment building volunteered. "It's just natural after a while for friends to talk pretty openly about their dates or their families or what's on their minds. Laurie never did that. She was with the crowd and agreeable, but if anyone teased her about Gregg Bennett, who obviously was crazy about her, she'd laugh it off. There was always something very private about her."

Brendon Moody had looked thoroughly into Gregg Bennett's background. Family money. Bright. Had quit college to become an entrepreneur, gotten his ears pinned back and returned for his degree. Carried a double major with honors in both. Graduating in May. Would be starting Stanford next September in the master's program. The kind of guy you'd want your daughter to bring home to meet the family, Brendon thought, and then reminded himself they'd said the same thing about serial killer Ted Bundy.

All the students were in agreement that the change in Laurie after her parents' death was dramatic. Moody. Withdrawn. Complained of headaches. Skipped classes. Assignments late. "Sometimes she'd pass me right by and not even say hello, or she'd look at me as though she'd never seen me before," one junior explained.

Brendon did not tell anyone about Laurie's multiple personality disorder. Sarah was saving that for the trial and did not want a plethora of publicity on the subject.

A significant number of students had noticed Laurie regularly going out alone at night and returning late. They'd commented on it among themselves, trying to guess whom she was meeting. A few had started to put two and two together because of the way Laurie frequently arrived at Allan Grant's classes early and lingered to talk with him afterwards.

The dean's wife, Louise Larkin, enjoyed talking with Moody. It was from her that he got the hint that Allan Grant had become interested in one of the new teachers in the English department. Following Mrs. Larkin's lead, he spoke to Vera West, but she stonewalled him.

"Allan Grant was a good friend to everybody," West said when Brendon talked with her. She ignored any implication in his questions.

Start sifting again, Brendon thought grimly. The problem was that the school year would be over soon, and a lot of the seniors who knew Laurie Kenyon well would be graduating. People like Gregg Bennett.

With that thought in mind, Brendon called Bennett and asked if they could get together again for a cup of coffee. Gregg was on his way out for the weekend, however, so they agreed to meet on Monday. As always, Bennett asked how Laurie was doing.

"From what her sister tells me, she's coming along pretty well," Brendon told him.

"Remind Sarah to call me if there's anything I can do."

Another unproductive week, Brendon thought as he drove home. To his disgust, he learned that his wife was having a Tupperware party at their home that evening. "I'll grab something at Solari's," he said, planting an irritated kiss on the top of her forehead. "How you let yourself get roped into that nonsense, I can't fathom."

"Have fun, dear. It will do you good to catch up with the regulars."

That night Brendon got his long-awaited break. He was sitting at the bar, talking with some of the old crowd from the prosecutor's office. The talk led to Sarah and Laurie Kenyon. The general feeling was that Sarah would be better off to plea bargain. "If they drop the charge to aggravated manslaughter, Laurie might get between fifteen and thirty, probably serve one third . . . be out by the time she's twenty-six or -seven."

"Judge Armon has been assigned, and he doesn't cut deals," one of the other assistant prosecutors said. "Anyhow, the fatal attraction killers aren't popular with any judge at sentencing time."

"I'd hate to see a good-looking kid like Laurie Kenyon locked up with some of those tough babes," another commented.

Bill Owens, a private investigator for an insurance company, was standing next to Brendon Moody. He waited till the subject was changed. Then he said, "Brendon, it can't get around that I tipped you off."

Moody's head did not turn, but his eyes darted to the side. "What's up?"

"You know Danny O'Toole?"

"Danny the Spouse Hunter? Sure. Who's he been spying on lately?"

"That's the point. He was a little drunk here the other night, and as usual, something came up about the Kenyon case. Listen to this. After the parents were killed, Danny was hired to investigate the sisters. Something about an insurance claim. When the younger one was arrested, the job ended."

"Sounds fishy," Moody said. "I'll get right on it. And thanks."

191

73

"*THE PEOPLE* who bought our house are getting on Sarah's nerves," Laurie volunteered to Dr. Donnelly.

Justin was surprised. "I hadn't realized that."

"Yes, Sarah said they're around too much. They'll be taking over the house in August and asked permission to do some planting."

"Have you ever watched them on television, Laurie?"

She shook her head. "I don't like that kind of program."

Justin waited. On his desk he had the report from the art therapist. Little by little a pattern was forming in Laurie's sketches. The last half dozen had been collages, and in each she had included two specific scenes: one showed a rocking chair with a thick, deep cushion, and next to it a stick figure of a woman, the other, a thick-trunked tree with wide, heavy branches in front of a windowless house.

Justin pointed to those illustrations on each of the papers. "Remember doing these?"

Laurie looked at them indifferently. "Sure. I'm not much of an artist, am I?"

"You'll do. Laurie, look at that rocking chair. Can you describe it?"

He saw her start to slip away. Her eyes widened. Her body became tense. But he did not want one of the alter personalities to block him. "Laurie, try."

"I have a headache," she whispered.

"Laurie, you trust me. You've just remembered something, haven't you? Don't be afraid. For Sarah's sake, tell me about it, let it out."

She pointed to the rocking chair, then clamped her lips together and squeezed her arms against her sides.

"Laurie, show me. If you can't talk about it, show me what happened."

"I will." The lisping, childlike voice.

"Good girl, Debbie." Justin waited.

She hooked her feet under his desk and tilted back the chair. Her arms crushed against her sides as though held in place by an outside force. She brought down the chair onto the floor with a thud and tilted it back again. Her face was contorted in fear. " 'Amazing grace, how sweet the sound,' " she sang in a frail, little-girl voice.

The chair thudded and tilted in perfect imitation of a rocker. With her body arched and arms immobile, she was miming a young child being held on a lap. Justin glanced down at the top drawing. That was it. The cushion looked like a lap. A small child held by someone and singing as she was being rocked. Back and forth. Back and forth.

" '. . . And grace will lead me home.' " The chair stopped. Her eyes closed again. Her breathing became quick, painful gasps. She stood and went up on her toes as though she was being lifted. "Time to go upstairs," she said in a deep voice.

74

"*HERE THEY COME* again," Sophie observed tartly as the familiar dark blue Cadillac pulled up into the driveway.

Sarah and Brendon Moody were in the kitchen waiting for the coffee to perk. "Oh God," Sarah said, her tone irritated. "It's my fault for letting it happen," she said to Brendon. "Tell you what. Sophie, bring the coffee into the library when it's ready and tell them I'm in a meeting. I'm just not in the mood to be prayed over."

Brendon scurried behind her and closed the library door as the chimes sounded through the house. "I'm glad you didn't give them a key," he said.

Sarah smiled. "I'm not that crazy. The thing is that there are so many things in this house that I can't use, and they're willing and anxious to buy them. I've been having appraisals. They're bringing in experts to have their own appraisals, and it's beginning to feel as though I have star boarders."

"Why not get it over with at once?" Brendon asked.

"Mostly my fault. I tell them what I'm willing to sell, then I take a look at all the stuff in this house and realize no way am I going to fit it into a condo, and so I tell them all this other stuff is available too. Or they come to me and ask about that painting or that table or that lamp. And so it goes." Sarah pushed back her hair. The day was warm and humid, and her hair had frizzed into a cloud resembling dark autumn leaves around her face.

"That's something else," she added as she sat down at the desk. "Dad never went for air-conditioning, and they intend to put in a new system. They'd like to be able to move on it as soon as we close, and that means engineers and whatever now."

Keep your mouth shut, Brendon told himself as he settled in the leather chair opposite the desk. He knew that the Hawkinses had paid top dollar for the house, and if they were buying the furniture Sarah could not use, it meant she didn't have to try to find buyers or store it. Laurie's hospitalization was costing a fortune, and the student insurance policy she carried was covering only a small portion of it. To say nothing of the costs of preparing a defense, and Sarah not working, he thought.

"You've had a chance to go over your insurance policies?" he asked.

194

"Yes. Brendon, I don't get it. There is no outstanding or questionable claim. My father kept his records straight. His insurance went to Mother, and then, in the event of her predeceasing him, to us. Since he outlived her by a few minutes, it came directly to us. Unfortunately everything except the house is tied up in trusts, which would have made a lot of sense if all this hadn't happened. We get payouts of fifty thousand dollars each for five years for a total of a quarter of a million each, and there's no way we can invade the principal of those trusts."

"What about the bus company?" Brendon asked. "Have you filed suit against them?"

"Of course," Sarah said. "But why would they have us checked? We weren't involved in the accident."

"Oh, hell," Brendon said, "I was hoping to get somewhere with this angle. I'll get the investigator drunk and pump him, but that's probably what it's about. Just the bus company. How's Laurie?"

Sarah considered. "She's better in a lot of ways. I think she's coming to terms with losing Dad and Mom. Dr. Donnelly is wonderful."

"Any memory of Allan Grant's death?"

"Nothing. However, she is starting to let things out about what happened to her those years she was away. Just bits and pieces. Justin, I mean Dr. Donnelly, is sure that she was molested in that time. But even showing her the videotapes of her therapy sessions when her alter personalities come out isn't helping her to have a real breakthrough." Sarah's voice lost its calm tone and became desperate. "Brendon, it's May. In three months I have found nothing to use as a defense for her. She seems to have three alter personalities. Kate, who is kind of a protector, almost like a cross nanny. Calls Laurie a wimp and gets angry at her, but then tries to shield her. She keeps blocking memory. Leona is a sexpot. That personality did have a fatal attraction for Allan Grant. Just last week she told Dr. Donnelly that she's so sorry she brought the knife with her that night."

195

"Sweet Jesus," Brendon muttered.

"The last personality is Debbie, a four-year-old kid. She cries all the time." Sarah raised her hands, then let them fall. "Brendon, that's it."

"Will she ever remember what happened?"

"Possibly, but no one can predict how long it will take. She does trust Justin. She understands that she can end up in prison. But she can't seem to make the breakthrough." Sarah looked at him. "Brendon, don't suggest I plea bargain."

"I have no intention of suggesting that," Brendon growled. "At least not yet."

Sophie entered the library, carrying a tray of coffee. "I left them alone upstairs," she said. "That's all right, isn't it?"

"Of course," Sarah said. "After all, Sophie, he's a preacher. Surely he's not stuffing trinkets in his pockets."

"Today they're having a big debate about combining your bathroom and Laurie's and putting in a Jacuzzi. I thought clergymen lived simply." She banged the tray on the desk.

"Not necessarily," Brendon commented. He dropped three lumps of sugar in the coffee and stirred it vigorously. "Sarah, Gregg Bennett honestly doesn't know what triggered Laurie's reaction to him last year. I think he's still pretty crazy about her. The evening before Grant died, some of the students were discussing Laurie's crush on the professor and Gregg overheard them. Stormed out of the student center."

"Jealous?" Sarah asked quickly.

Brendon shrugged. "If he was, it doesn't seem to have any bearing on Allan Grant's death unless . . ."

"Unless Laurie gets her memory back."

There was a tap on the door. Sarah raised her eyes. "Prepare yourself to be blessed," she murmured, then called, "come in."

Bic and Opal, their faces set in solicitous smiles, stood in the doorway. They were dressed casually. Bic had taken off his jacket, and his shortsleeved T-shirt revealed muscular arms covered with

196

soft graying hair. Opal wore slacks and a cotton blouse. "Not to disturb, just to see how it's going," she said.

Sarah introduced Brendon Moody to them. He grunted a greeting.

"And how is that little girl?" Bic asked. "You don't know how many people we have praying on her."

75

JUSTIN DONNELLY did not want to admit to Sarah that he now believed Laurie would not recover significant memory in time for the trial. With two members of his staff, Pat and Kathie, the art and journal therapists, he reviewed the tapes of his therapy sessions with Laurie. "Notice how the alter personalities trust me now and are willing to talk, but they all stonewall me when I try to go back to the night of January twenty-eighth or the years of Laurie's abduction. Let's discuss the three alter personalities again.

"Kate is thirty-three, which makes her fairly close to Sarah's age. I think she was created by Laurie to be a protector, which is how Laurie sees Sarah. Totally unlike Sarah, Kate is usually annoyed at Laurie, calls her a wimp, gets disgusted with her for getting in trouble. I think that shows Laurie's feeling that she deserves to have Sarah angry at her.

"Debbie, the four-year-old child, wants to talk but is too frightened or maybe just doesn't understand what happened. I suspect she is pretty much as Laurie was at that age. Sometimes she shows flashes of humor. Sarah Kenyon said that Laurie was a precociously funny child before she was kidnapped.

"Leona is a pretty sexy lady. There's no question she was crazy about Allan Grant and jealous of his wife. There's no question that she was so angry about what she perceived as his betrayal of her that she might have been capable of killing him, but now she talks about him with a kind of affection, the way you might talk about an old lover. The fight's over. The anger's faded and you remember the good parts."

They were in the staff room adjacent to Justin's office. The late spring sun was streaming in the windows. From where he sat, Justin could look over at the solarium. Several of the patients were there, enjoying the sunshine. As he watched, Laurie walked into the solarium, arm in arm with Sarah.

Pat, the art therapist, was holding several new drawings. "Have you got the snapshot that Laurie tore up at home?" she asked.

"Right here." Justin riffled through the file.

The therapist studied the photograph, compared it with some of Laurie's sketches, then laid them side by side. "Okay, see this." She pointed to a stick figure. "And this. And this. What do you make of it?"

"She's starting to put a playsuit or a bathing suit on the stick figure," Justin commented.

"Right. Now notice how in these three, the figure has long hair. In these two, look at the difference. Very short hair. She's drawn a face of sorts that gives me the impression of a boy's face. The arms are folded the way they are in the picture that's glued together. I think there's a possibility that she's recreating that image of herself but changing it to a boy. I wish to God the print wasn't so mutilated. She sure did a terrific job of shredding it."

Kathie, the journal therapist, was holding Laurie's latest composition. "This is the handwriting of her alternate Kate. But notice how different it is from the way it was in February. It's more and more like Laurie's penmanship. And listen to what it says. 'I'm getting so tired. Laurie will be strong enough to accept what has to be. She'd like to walk in Central Park. She'd like to take the golf clubs, drive to the club and tee off. It would have been fun for her to be on the golf circuit. Was it less than a year ago they called her the best young woman golfer in New Jersey? Maybe prison isn't much different than here. Maybe it's secure like this place. Maybe the knife dream will stay far away in prison. Nobody can sneak into prison with guards around. They can't come with knives in the night. They check all the incoming mail in prison. That means that pictures can't walk into books by themselves.' " The journal therapist handed the composition to Justin. "Doctor, this may be a sign that Kate is accepting guilt and punishment for Laurie."

Justin stared out the window. Sarah and Laurie were sitting side by side. Whatever Sarah was saying, Laurie was laughing. They could have been two very attractive young women on their terrace at home or at a country club.

The art therapist had followed his gaze. "I was talking to Sarah yesterday. I think she's going on sheer nerve now. The day the prison door closes behind Laurie, you may have a new patient, Dr. Donnelly."

Justin stood up. "They're due in my office in ten minutes. Pat, I think you're right. She's drawing different versions of the torn snapshot. Do you know anyone who might be able to take it apart, clean off all that glue, reassemble it and blow it up so we can get a better look?"

She nodded. "I can try."

He turned to Kathie. "Do you think that if Laurie or Kate realizes the effect her imprisonment will have on Sarah that she'll be less resigned to an automatic conviction?"

"Possibly."

"Okay. And there's something else I'm going to do. I'm going to talk to Gregg Bennett, Laurie's ex-boyfriend, and try to find out all the circumstances of the day she became so frightened of him."

199

76

AS *BRENDON MOODY* slid onto a bar stool at Solari's next to Danny the Spouse Hunter, he noted that Danny's cherubic face was beginning to sag at the jawline. Broken capillaries on his nose and cheeks were tributes to his appreciation of dry Manhattans.

Dan greeted Moody with his usual exuberance. "Ah, there you are, Brendon. A sight for sore eyes."

Brendon grunted a greeting, resisting the urge to tell Dan what he could do with his acquired brogue. Then, reminding himself of the reason he was here and of Danny's fondness for dry Manhattans and the Mets, he ordered a round and asked Danny how he figured the team would do this season.

"Brilliant. A pennant," Danny crowed happily. "The lads have it together, by jingo."

I knew you when you could speak English, Brendon thought, but said, "Grand. Grand."

An hour later as Brendon nursed his first drink, Danny finished his third. It was time. Brendon directed the conversation to Laurie Kenyon. "I've been on the case," he said in a confidential whisper.

Danny's eyes narrowed. "So I've heard. Poor girl went bonkers, did she not?"

"Looks it," Brendon acknowledged. "Guess she went nuts after the parents were killed. Too bad she didn't get regular professional counseling then."

Danny glanced around. "Ah, but she did," he whispered. "And forget where you heard it. I hate to think they'd keep you in the dark."

Brendon looked shocked. "You mean she was seeing some shrink?"

"Right over in Ridgewood."

"How do you know, Danny?"

"Between the two of us?"

"Of course."

"Right after the parents died my services were engaged just to do a background check on the sisters and their activities."

"No kidding. Insurance company, I suppose. Something about a claim against the bus company?"

"Now, Brendon Moody, you know the client-investigator relationship is strictly confidential."

"Of course it is. But that bus was going too fast; the brakes were bad. The Kenyons never had a chance. Naturally an insurance company would be pretty nervous and want to get a line on the potential plaintiffs. Who else would be checking on them?"

Danny remained stubbornly silent. Brendon signaled the bartender, who shook his head. "I'll drive my good friend home," Brendon promised. He knew it was time to change the subject. An hour later, after he hoisted Danny into the passenger seat of his car, he started talking about the Kenyons again. As he pulled up in the driveway of Danny's modest split level he hit pay dirt.

"Brendon, me lad, you're a good friend," Danny said, his voice thick and slow. "Don't think I don't know but that you've been pumping me. Between you and me and the lamppost, I don't know who hired me. All very mysterious. A woman it was. Called herself Jane Graves. Never did meet her. Called every week to get a progress report. Had it sent to a private mail drop in New York City. You know who I think it might be? The widow of the late professor. Wasn't the poor dingbat Kenyon girl writing mash notes to him? And didn't the demand for my services end the day after the murder?"

Danny pushed open the car door and staggered out. "A grand good night to ye, and next time ask me straight. It won't cost you so many drinks."

77

*T*HE "ARCHITECT" Bic had brought to the Kenyon home on one of his early visits was an ex-convict from Kentucky. It was he who wired the library and telephone with sophisticated, voice-activated equipment, and concealed a recorder in the guest bedroom above the study.

As Bic and Opal roamed upstairs with measuring tapes, fabrics and paint samples, it was an easy matter for them to change the cassettes. The minute they were in the car, Bic began playing the tapes and he continued to listen to them over and over in their Wyndham Hotel suite.

Sarah had begun to have regular evening telephone conversations with Justin Donnelly, and these were gold mines of information. At first Opal had to make a concerted effort to conceal her sullen annoyance at Bic's absolute passion for any news of Lee. But as the weeks went by she was torn between fear of discovery and fascination at the talk about Laurie's flashes of recall. Sarah's discussion with the doctor about the rocking chair memory especially gratified Bic.

"The little darlin'," he sighed. "Remember how pretty she was and how nice she could sing. We taught her well." He shook his head. "My, my." Then he frowned. "But, she's starting to talk."

Bic had opened the hotel windows, allowing the warm May air to fill the room, the faint breeze rippling the curtains. He was letting his hair grow a little longer, and today it was disheveled. He was wearing only old slacks and a T-shirt, which exposed the thick curly hair on his arms that Opal called her favorite pillow. She stared at him, worshipping him with her eyes.

"What are you thinking, Opal?" he asked.

"You'll say I'm crazy."

"Try me."

"It just occurred to me that right at this minute, with your hair mussed and you in your T-shirt and your jacket off, all you need is that gold earring you used to wear and the Reverend Hawkins would disappear. You'd be Bic the nightclub singer again."

Bic stared at her for a long minute. I shouldn't have told him that, she thought aghast. He won't want to think that's possible. But then he said, "Opal, the Lord directed you to that revelation. I was thinking on the old farmhouse in Pennsylvania and that rocking chair where I used to sit with that sweet baby in my arms, and a plan was forming. Now you've completed it."

"What is it?"

The benevolent expression faded. "No questions. You know that. Never any questions. This is between me and the Blessed Lord."

"I'm sorry, Bobby." She deliberately addressed him that way, knowing it would mollify him.

"That's all right. One thing I am learning from all that listening is that I don't wear short sleeves around those people. The business of fuzzy arm hair is coming up pretty regular. And did you notice something else?"

She waited.

Bic smiled coldly. "This whole situation may be starting a little romantic brush fire. Listen to the way that doctor and Sarah talk to each other. Tone of voice, warmer and warmer. He's more and more concerned about her. It will be nice for her to have someone for comfort after Lee joins the heavenly choir."

78

K*AREN GRANT* glanced up from her desk and smiled brightly. The small, balding man with the wrinkled forehead looked vaguely familiar. She invited him to sit down. He presented his card, and she understood why she had recognized him. He was the investigator working for the Kenyons, and he'd been at the funeral. Louise Larkin had told her that he had been questioning people on the campus.

"Mrs. Grant, if this isn't a good time, just say so." Moody glanced around the office.

"Absolutely fine," she assured him. "It's a quiet morning."

"I gather the travel business in general is pretty quiet these days," Moody said casually. "At least that's what my friends tell me."

"Oh, like everything else, it's gotten leaner and meaner. Can I sell you a trip?"

Sharp lady, Brendon thought, and just as attractive up close as across a grave site. Karen Grant was wearing a turquoise linen suit and matching blouse. The blue-green color brought out the green in her eyes. That oufit didn't come from K Mart, Brendon decided. Neither did the crescent of jade and diamonds on her lapel. "Not today," he said. "If I may I'd like to ask a few questions about your late husband."

The smile faded. "It's very hard to talk about Allan," she said. "Louise Larkin told me about you. You're working on Laurie Kenyon's defense. Mr. Moody, I'm terribly sorry for Laurie, but she did take my husband's life and she threatened mine."

"She doesn't remember anything about it. She's a very sick girl," Brendon said quietly. "It's my job to try to help a jury to understand that. I've been going over copies of the letters she, or someone, sent to Professor Grant. How long were you aware that he was receiving them?"

"At first, Allan didn't show them to me. I guess he was afraid I'd be upset."

"Upset?"

"Well, they were patently ludicrous. I mean some of the 're-membrances' were of nights when Allan and I were together. It was obvious they were all fantasy, but even so, they were certainly unpleasant. I happened to see the letters in his desk drawer and I asked about them."

"How well did you know Laurie?"

"Not well. She's a marvelous golfer, and I'd seen write-ups about her in the papers. I met her parents at some college affairs, that sort of thing. I felt terribly sorry for her after they died. I know Allan thought that she was heading for a breakdown."

"You were in New York the night he died?"

"I was at the airport meeting a client."

"When did you last speak to your husband?"

"I called him at about eight o'clock that night. He was terribly upset. He told me about the scene with Laurie Kenyon. He felt he hadn't handled the situation properly. He thought he should have sat down with Sarah and Laurie before having Laurie called in by the dean. He said that he honestly believed she had no recollection of writing those letters. She was so angry and shocked when she was accused."

"You do realize that if you testify to that on the witness stand it could be helpful to Laurie."

Now tears welled in Karen Grant's eyes. "My husband was the nicest, kindest human being I've ever known. He of all people would not want me to hurt that girl."

Moody's eyes narrowed. "Mrs. Grant, was there any point when you had a few doubts about whether or not your husband was falling in love with Laurie?"

She looked astonished. "That's ridiculous. She's twenty or twenty-one. Allan was forty."

"It's been known to happen. I certainly wouldn't blame you if you wanted to be sure, say maybe have it checked out."

"I don't know what you're talking about."

"I mean possibly hire a private investigator like myself . . ."

The tears dried. Karen Grant was visibly angry. "Mr. Moody, I wouldn't have insulted my husband like that. And you're insulting me." She stood up. "I don't think we have anything more to say to each other."

Moody rose slowly. "Mrs. Grant, please forgive me. Try to understand that my job is to find some reason for Laurie's actions. You said that Professor Grant thought Laurie was nearing a breakdown. If there was something going on between them, if he then betrayed her to the administration and she then snapped . . ."

"Mr. Moody. Do not try to defend the girl who murdered my husband by ruining his reputation. Allan was a private man and intensely embarrassed by student crushes. You cannot change that fact to save his murderer."

As he nodded apologetically, Brendon Moody's glance was sweeping the office. Attractively furnished with a red leather settee and chairs. Framed posters of exotic travel scenes on walls. Fresh flowers on Karen Grant's desk and on the coffee table by the couch. Her desk, however, was clear of paperwork, and the phone had not rung since he'd been in the office. "Mrs. Grant, I'd like to leave on a happier note. My daughter is an American Airlines hostess. Loves the job. Says the travel business gets into your blood. I hope you feel that way and your job is helping you to adjust to the loss of your husband."

He thought she seemed slightly mollified. "I'd be lost without it."

There was no sign of anyone else. "How many people work here?" he asked casually.

"My secretary is on an errand. Anne Webster, the owner, is out ill today."

"Then you're in charge?"

"Anne is retiring soon. I'll be taking over completely."

"I see. Well, I've taken enough of your time."

Moody did not leave the hotel immediately. Instead he sat in the lobby and observed the travel agency. Two hours later not a single person had entered it. Through the glass wall he could see that Karen did not pick up the phone even once. Putting down the newspaper he had used to disguise his presence, he moseyed over to the bell captain's desk and began to chat with him.

79

GREGG BENNETT drove up the Turnpike to the exit for the Lincoln Tunnel. It was a warm, hazy day, more like July than the last week in May. He rode with the top down on his new Mustang convertible, a graduation gift from his grandfather. The gift made him uncomfortable. "Granpa, I'm twenty-five, old enough to earn the money for my own cars," he'd protested. Then his mother pulled him aside.

"For heaven's sake, Gregg, don't be such a stiff-neck. Granpa is so proud that you've been accepted at Stanford that he's busting his buttons."

In truth, Gregg preferred the ten-year-old secondhand Ford he'd driven at Clinton. He could still see himself throwing the golf bags in the trunk, Laurie getting in beside him, teasing him about his game.

Laurie.

He turned the car onto the Route 3 approach to the tunnel. As usual traffic was backed up, and he glanced at the clock on the dashboard. Three-forty. It was okay. He'd left plenty of time to get to the clinic. He hoped he looked all right. He had debated about what to wear, then chosen a tan linen jacket, open-neck shirt, chinos and loafers. Laurie wouldn't know him if he got too gussied up. His mouth went dry at the thought that after all these months he would be seeing her again.

Sarah was waiting for him in the reception area. He kissed her cheek. It was obvious to him that she'd been going through hell. Deep circles underlined her eyes. Her dark brows and lashes made her skin seem transparent. She immediately brought him in to meet Laurie's doctor.

Donnelly was gravely honest. "Someday Laurie may be able to tell us about those years she was missing and about Allan Grant's death, but as it stands now, she can't tell us in time to prepare her defense. What we're trying to do is to in effect go around her, to recreate a scene in which she had a dissociative reaction and see if we can learn what set her off. You've told Sarah and Detective Moody about the episode in your apartment a year ago—we'd like to recreate it.

"Laurie's agreeable to the experiment. We're going to videotape you with her. We need you to describe in her presence, what you were doing, what you were saying, where you were in relation to each other. Please, for her sake don't edit or hide anything. I mean anything."

Gregg nodded.

Dr. Donnelly picked up the phone. "Will you bring Laurie in, please?"

Gregg didn't know what to expect. Certainly it wasn't the attractive Laurie dressed in a short cotton skirt and T-shirt, a narrow belt cinching her slender waist, sandals on her feet. She stiffened when she saw him. Some instinct made Gregg decide not to get up. He waved at her casually. "Hi, Laurie."

She watched him warily as she took a seat next to Sarah, then nodded but said nothing.

Justin turned on the camera. "Gregg, Laurie came to visit you about a year ago and for some unknown reason, she panicked. Tell us about it."

Gregg had gone over that morning so often in his mind that there was no hesitation. "It was Sunday. I slept late. At ten o'clock Laurie rang the bell and woke me up."

"Describe where you live," Justin cut in.

"A rented studio over a garage a couple of miles from the campus. Compact kitchen, countertop with stools, convertible sofa bed, bookcases, dresser, two closets, decent-sized john. Actually it's not bad as these things go."

Sarah watched Laurie close her eyes as though remembering.

"All right," Justin said. "Did you expect Laurie to drop in?"

"No. She was going home for the day. Actually she had invited me to go with her, but I had a term paper due. She'd been to the nine o'clock mass, then stopped at the bakery. When I opened the door, she said something like, 'Coffee for a hot bagel? Fair trade?' "

"What was her attitude?"

"Relaxed. Laughing. We'd played golf on Saturday and it had been a close round. She'd beaten me by only a stroke. Sunday morning she was wearing a white linen dress and looked terrific."

"Did you kiss her?"

Gregg glanced at Laurie. "On the cheek. I'd get signals from her. Occasionally she could be pretty responsive when I'd start to kiss her, but I was always careful. It was like you could scare her away. When I kissed her or put my arm around her, I'd do it slowly and casually and see if she'd tense up. If she did, I quit right away."

"Didn't you find that pretty frustrating?" Justin asked quickly.

209

"Sure. But I think I always knew there was something in Laurie that was afraid, and that I would have to wait for her to trust me." Gregg looked directly at Laurie. "I'd never hurt her. I'd kill before I let anyone else hurt her."

Laurie was staring at him, no longer avoiding his gaze. It was she who spoke next. "I sat next to Gregg at the counter. We had two cups of coffee and split the third bagel. We were talking about when we could get in another round of golf. I felt so happy that day. It was such a beautiful morning and everything felt so fresh and clean." Her voice faltered as she said "clean."

Gregg stood up. "Laurie said she had to be on her way. She kissed me and started to leave."

"There was no sign of fear or panic at that point?" Justin interjected.

"None."

"Laurie, I want you to stand near Gregg just as you did that day. Pretend you're about to leave his apartment."

Hesitantly Laurie stood up. "Like this," she whispered. She reached out for an imaginary doorknob, her back to Gregg. "And he . . ."

"And I started to pick her up . . ." Gregg said. "I mean jokingly. I wanted to kiss her again."

"Show me how," Justin commanded.

"Like this." Gregg stood behind Laurie, pressed his hands against her arms and started to raise her.

Her body stiffened. She began to whimper. Instantly Gregg released her.

"Laurie, tell me why you're afraid," Justin said swiftly.

The whimper changed into stifled, childlike weeping, but she did not answer.

"Debbie, you're the one crying," Justin said. "Tell me why."

She pointed down and to the right. A frail, small voice sobbed, "He's going to take me there."

Gregg looked shocked and puzzled. "Wait a minute," he said. "If we were in my apartment, she'd be pointing to the sofabed."

"Describe it," Justin snapped.

"I'd just gotten up, so it was still open and unmade."

"Debbie, why were you afraid when you thought Gregg was taking you to the bed? What might happen to you there? Tell us."

She had dropped her face in her hands. The soft childlike crying continued. "I can't."

"Why not, Debbie? We love you."

She looked up and ran to Sarah. "Sare-wuh, I don't know what happened," she whispered. "Whenever we got to the bed, I floated away."

80

*V*ERA WEST was counting the days until the term ended. She was finding it increasingly difficult to keep up the calm façade that she knew was absolutely necessary. Now as she walked across the campus in the late afternoon, her leather zipbag bulging with final term papers clasped in her arms, she found herself praying that she would reach the sanctuary of her rented cottage before she began to cry.

She loved the cottage. It was on a wooded cul-de-sac and at one time had been the home of the gardener of the large manor house nearby. She had taken the job in the English Department at Clinton because after going back to school for her doctorate at age thirty-seven and receiving it at forty, she'd felt restless, ready for a change from Boston.

Clinton was the kind of jewellike smaller college she loved. A theater buff, she also enjoyed the nearness to New York.

Along the way, a few men had been interested in her. At times she wistfully wished she could find someone who would seem special but had decided she was destined to follow in the footsteps of her unmarried aunts.

Then she'd met Allan Grant.

Until it was too late, it never occurred to Vera that she was falling in love with him. He was another faculty member, a very nice human being, a teacher whose intellect she admired, whose popularity she understood.

It had begun in October. One night Allan's car wouldn't start, and she'd offered him a ride home from a Kissinger lecture in the auditorium. He'd invited her in for a nightcap and she'd accepted. It hadn't occurred to her that his wife wasn't there.

His house was a surprise. Expensively furnished. Surprisingly so, considering what she knew to be his salary. But there was no sense of an effort having been made to pull it together. It looked as though it could stand a good cleaning. She knew that Karen, his wife, worked in Manhattan but didn't realize that she had an apartment there.

"Hi, Dr. West."

"What—oh, hello." Vera tried to smile as she passed a group of students. From the air of buoyancy about them it was obvious that the term was nearly over. None of these students would be dreading the emptiness of the summer, the emptiness of the future.

That first evening at Allan's home, she'd offered to get the ice while he prepared a scotch and soda for them. In the freezer individual packages of pizza, lasagna, chicken-pot pies and God knows what else were piled together. Good heavens, she'd wondered, is that the way this poor guy eats?

Two nights later, Allan dropped off a book at her place. She'd just roasted a chicken, and the inviting aroma filled the cottage. When he commented on it, she impulsively invited him to dinner.

Allan was in the habit of taking a long predinner walk. He began to stop by occasionally, and then more often on the nights

212

Karen was in New York. He would phone, ask if she wanted company and if so, what could he bring? Calling himself the man who came to dinner, he'd arrive with wine or a wedge of cheese or some fruit. He always left by eight or eight-thirty. His manner toward her was always attentive, but no different than if the room had been filled with people.

Even so, Vera began to lie awake at night wondering how long it would be before people started to gossip about them. Without asking, she was sure that he did not tell his wife about their time together.

Allan showed her the "Leona" letters as soon as they began to arrive. "I'm not going to let Karen see these," he said. "They'd only upset her."

"Surely she wouldn't put any stock in them."

"No, but underneath that sophisticated veneer, Karen is pretty insecure, and she does depend on me more than she realizes." A few weeks later he told her that Karen had found the letters. "Just what I expected. She's upset and worried."

At the time, Vera had thought that Karen sent some pretty mixed signals. Worried about her husband but away so much. Foolish lady.

At first, Allan seemed to deliberately avoid any kind of personal discussion. Then gradually he began to talk about growing up. "My dad split when I was eight months old. My mother and grandmother . . . what a pair. They did anything to make a dollar." He'd laughed. "I mean just *about* anything. My grandmother had a big old house in Ithaca. She rented rooms to old people. I always said I was raised in a nursing home. Four or five of them were retired teachers, so I had a lot of help with my homework. My mother worked in the local department store. They saved every penny they could for my education and invested it wisely. I swear they were disappointed when I won a full scholarship to Yale. They were both good cooks. I can still remember how great it was to get home on a cold afternoon after I finished my paper route, open the door, feel that blast of warmth and breathe in all the good smells from the kitchen."

Allan had told her all that a week before he died. Then he'd said, "Vera, that's the way I feel when I come here. Warmth and a sense of coming home to someone I want to be with and who I hope wants me." He'd put his arm around her. "Can you be patient with me? I've got to work something out."

The night he died, Allan had been with her for the last time. He'd been depressed and upset. "I should have spoken to Laurie and her sister first. I jumped the gun by going to the dean. Now the dean has as much as said that my manner with these kids is too friendly. He flat out asked me if Karen and I were having problems, if there was any reason she was away so much." At the door that night, he'd kissed her slowly and said, "It's going to change. I love and need you very much."

Some instinct had warned her to tell him to stay with her. If only she'd listened to it and to hell with the gossips. But she let him go. A little after ten-thirty she'd phoned him. He sounded remarkably cheerful. He'd spoken to Karen and it was all out on the table. He had taken a sleeping pill. Again he had said, "I love you," the last words she would ever hear from him.

Too restless to go to bed herself, Vera had watched the eleven o'clock news and started tidying up the living room, fluffing pillows, straightening magazines. In the wing chair she'd noticed something gleaming. The ignition key to Allan's car. It must have slipped out of his pocket.

She was filled with unreasoning worry about him. The key was an excuse to call again. She dialed his number, letting the phone ring and ring. There was no answer. The sleeping pill must really have taken effect, she'd reassured herself.

Today, suddenly reminded again of her loneliness, Vera hurried, head down, along her cobblestone walk, Allan's face filling her mind. Her arms ached for him. She reached the steps. *"Allan. Allan. Allan."*

214

Vera didn't realize she'd spoken his name aloud until she looked up into the keen eyes of Brendon Moody, who was waiting for her on the porch.

81

SEATED AT a corner table in Villa Cesare in Hillsdale, a few miles from Ridgewood, Sarah wondered why in heaven's name she had let herself get talked into having dinner with the Reverend Bobby and Carla Hawkins.

The couple had shown up at her door five minutes after she returned from New York. They'd been just driving around, they explained, getting to know their new neighborhood, and she'd passed them on Lincoln Avenue.

"You looked as though you needed a little help," the Reverend Bobby said. "I just felt the Lord telling me to turn around, drop by and say hello."

When she'd reached home at seven o'clock after leaving the clinic and saying goodbye to Gregg Bennett, Sarah had realized she was tired and hungry. Sophie was out, and the minute Sarah opened the door of the empty house she knew she didn't want to stay there.

Villa Cesare was a longtime favorite restaurant, a great place to eat. Clams casino, shrimp scampi, a glass of white wine, cappuccino; that always-friendly, welcoming atmosphere, she thought. She was walking out the door when the Hawkinses arrived; somehow they ended up joining her.

As she nodded to familiar faces at other tables, Sarah told herself, these are caring people and I'll accept any prayers I can get. Lost in her thoughts, she suddenly realized that Reverend Hawkins was asking about Laurie.

"It's all a matter of time," she explained. "Justin—I mean Dr. Donnelly—doesn't have any doubt that eventually Laurie will let down her defenses and talk about the night Professor Grant died, but it seems as though that memory is entwined with her fear of whatever happened to her in the past. The doctor feels that at some point she'll achieve a spontaneous breakthrough. Pray God she does."

"Amen," Bobby and Carla said in unison.

Sarah realized her guard was down. She was talking about Laurie too much. These people were, after all, strangers whose only connection to her was that they had bought the house.

The house. Safe ground. "Mother planned the landscaping so we'd always have color," she said as she selected a crusty roll. "The tulips were marvelous. You saw them. The azaleas will be out in a week or so. They're my favorites. Ours are great, but the D'Andreas' are spectacular. They're in the corner house."

Opal smiled brightly. "Which house is that? The one with green shutters or the white one that used to be pink?"

"The one that used to be pink. God, my father hated it when the old owners painted it that color. I remember he said he was going to go to the town hall and petition to have his taxes lowered."

Opal felt Bic's eyes glaring at her. The enormity of her mistake almost made her gasp. Why had the pink corner house popped into her mind now? How many years since it had been painted?

But fortunately Sarah Kenyon did not seem to notice the slip. She began talking about the condominium and how well it was coming along. "It will be ready by August first," she said. "So we'll be on target to vacate the house for you. You've been very kind to wait so long to occupy it."

216

"Is there any chance that Laurie may get home?" Bic asked casually as the waiter served him veal piccata.

"Pray for that, Reverend Hawkins," Sarah told him. "Dr. Donnelly has said she is absolutely no threat to anyone. He wants a psychiatrist appointed by the prosecutor's office to examine her and agree that she should become an outpatient. He believes that in order to cooperate in her defense, Laurie must overcome the feeling that she needs to be behind locked doors in order to feel safe."

"There is nothing I want more than to see your little sister at home in Ridgewood," Bic said as he patted Sarah's hand.

That night when Sarah settled in bed, she had the nagging feeling that something she should have noticed had escaped her attention.

It must have been something Laurie said, she decided as she drifted off to sleep.

82

JUSTIN DONNELLY walked from the clinic to his Central Park South apartment, so engrossed in his own meditation today that for once he did not drink in the changing panorama of New York. At seven o'clock, the sun was still forty minutes from setting. The hazy warmth had brought out a steady stream of people, strolling along Fifth Avenue, browsing through the bookstands on the sidewalk flanking the park or appraising the amateurish art.

The pungent smell of souvlaki that wafted to his nostrils as the weary vendors pushed their carts to overnight shelters, the sight of the patient horses as they stood fastened to festively decorated carriages at the corner of Fifth and Central Park South, the line of limousines in front of the Plaza Hotel—all these things escaped him. Justin's thoughts were totally on Laurie Kenyon.

She was by far the most interesting patient he'd ever encountered. It was common for women who had been molested as small children to feel that they had somehow invited or caused the abuse. Most of them at some point came to understand they had been powerless to prevent what had happened to them. Laurie Kenyon was resisting that knowledge.

But there was progress. He'd stopped in to see her before he left the clinic. Dinner was over, and she was sitting in the solarium. She'd been quiet and pensive. "Gregg was awfully nice to have come today," she'd volunteered and then added, "I know he'd never hurt me."

Justin had taken a chance. "He did more than not hurt you, Laurie. He helped you to see that by jokingly picking you up, he triggered a memory that, if you let it out, will help you to get well. The rest is up to you."

She'd said, "I know it is. I'll try. I promise. You know, Doctor, what I'd like to do more than anything in the world?" She hadn't waited for an answer. "I'd like to fly to Scotland and play golf at St. Andrews. Does that seem crazy to you?"

"It sounds terrific to me."

"But of course it will never happen."

"Not unless you help yourself."

As Justin turned in to his building, he wondered if he'd pushed her too far. He wondered if calling the psychiatrist appointed by the prosecutor's office and asking him to reevaluate Laurie for the purpose of reinstating bail was a mistake.

A few minutes later he was sitting on the terrace of his apartment, sipping his favorite Australian Chardonnay, when the phone rang. It was the clinic. The head nurse apologized for calling. "It's Miss Kenyon. She says she must speak to you at once."

"Laurie!"

"Not Laurie, Doctor. Her alter Kate. She wants to tell you something terribly important."

"Put her on!"

The strident voice said, "Dr. Donnelly, listen, you ought to know. There's a kid who wants to talk to you something fierce, but Laurie's afraid to let him."

"Who is the kid, Kate?" Justin asked quickly. I'm right, he thought. Laurie does have another alter who hasn't surfaced yet.

"I don't know his name. He won't tell me what it is. But he's nine or ten and smart and took a hell of a lot for Laurie. He's tired of shutting his mouth. Keep working on her. You're wearing her down. He came within inches of talking to you today."

The receiver clicked in Justin's ear.

83

ON JUNE 15 the Reverend Bobby Hawkins received a phone call from Liz Pierce of *People* magazine requesting an interview. She'd been assigned to do a feature on him for a September issue, she said.

Bic protested, then said that he was flattered and pleased. "It will be a joy to spread the word of my ministry," he assured Pierce.

But when he hung up the phone, the warmth disappeared from his voice. "Opal, if I refuse, that reporter might think I was hiding something. At least this way I can influence what she writes."

84

B*RENDON MOODY* looked compassionately at Sarah. The mid-June day was sticky, but she still had not turned on the window air conditioner in the library. She was wearing a dark blue linen jacket with a white collar and a white skirt. It was only eight-thirty, but she was already dressed to go to New York. Four months of this, Brendon thought, eating, drinking, breathing a defense that's going nowhere; spending the day in a psychiatric clinic and being grateful her sister is there instead of in the Hunterdon County jail. And he was about to shoot down her last hope for a viable defense.

Sophie knocked and without waiting for a response opened the door and came in carrying a tray with cups of coffee, rolls and orange juice. "Mr. Moody," she said, "I hope you can make Sarah swallow this roll. She's at the point where she eats nothing and is becoming skin and bones."

"Oh, Sophie," Sarah protested.

"Don't, 'oh, Sophie,' me—it's the truth." Sophie put the tray down on the desk, her face puckered with worry. "Is the miracle man going to show up today?" she asked. "I swear, Sarah, you should charge those people rent."

"They should charge me rent," Sarah said. "They've owned this house since March."

"And the agreement was that you'd move out in August."

"They don't bother me. In fact they've been very nice to me."

"Well, I've been watching them on TV every Sunday lately, and let me tell you, they are some pair. As far as I'm concerned that man is taking the name of the Lord in vain what with promising miracles in return for cash and talking as though God drops in to chat with him every day."

"Sophie," Sarah protested.

"All right, all right, you're busy." Shaking her head, Sophie marched from the library, her heavy footsteps signaling her disapproval.

Sarah handed Brendon a coffee cup. "As we were saying, or did we get around to saying anything?"

Brendon took the coffee, added three heaping teaspoons of sugar and stirred noisily. "I wish I had good news," he said, "but I don't. Our best hope was that Allan Grant was taking advantage of Laurie's depression and grief and then drove her over the edge by giving her letters to the administration. Well, Sarah, if he was taking advantage of her, we'll never be able to prove it. His marriage was rotten. I could sense that and I've followed up on the wife. She's a piece of goods. According to the hotel staff, she's had quite a variety of different male friends. For the past year or so, however, she's stuck to the same one and seems pretty crazy about him. Name is Edwin Rand. He's one of those polished, good-looking types who's lived off women all his life. About forty or forty-five. A travel writer who doesn't make enough money to live on but gets invited to resorts all over the world. He's made an art of the freebie."

"Did Allan Grant know about him?" Sarah asked.

"Can't be sure. When Karen was at home they seemed okay together."

"But suppose he did know and was hurt and rejected and turned to Laurie, who was crazy about him?"

Sarah seemed to come alive as she spoke. Poor kid, Brendon thought, grabbing at anything that would be the basis for a defense.

"It doesn't wash," he said flatly. "Allan had been seeing a member of the faculty, Vera West. West broke down when she told me that the last time she spoke to him was at about ten-thirty the night he died. He was in good spirits and said that he was relieved because it was all out on the table."

"Meaning?"

"She took it to mean that he'd told his wife he wanted a divorce."

Brendon looked away from the despair in Sarah's eyes. "Actually, you could make a prima facie case against the wife," he told her. "Allan Grant's mother left him a trust fund. He got in the neighborhood of $100,000 a year income from it. Couldn't touch the principal—and that's close to a million and a half and still growing—until he was sixty. The mother obviously realized he had no money sense.

"From what I hear, Karen Grant was treating that income as her personal allowance. In the event of a divorce, that trust was not community property. Whatever she makes at the travel agency wouldn't support her pricey apartment and designer clothers. The writer boyfriend would have been history. With Allan's death, however, she got it all.

"The only problem," Brendon concluded, "is that Karen Grant certainly didn't borrow the knife, kill her husband and then return the knife to Laurie afterwards."

Sarah didn't notice that her coffee was barely lukewarm. Sipping it helped to release the tightened muscles in her neck and throat.

"I've heard from the Hunterdon County prosecutor's office," she told him. "The psychiatrist they sent to examine Laurie re-

222

viewed the tapes of her therapy sessions. They accept the possibility that she suffers from multiple personality disorder."

She ran her hand over her forehead as though trying to brush away a headache. "In return for Laurie's pleading guilty to manslaughter, they won't press for the maximum penalty. She'd probably be out in five years, maybe less. But if we go to court, the charge will be purposeful and knowing murder. There's a good chance they could make it stick."

85

"*I*T'S BEEN a month since Kate phoned to tell me that there's another alter personality, a nine- or ten-year-old boy, who wants to talk to me," Justin Donnelly told Sarah. "As you know, since then, Kate disclaims any knowledge of that personality."

Sarah nodded. "I know." It was time to tell Justin Donnelly that she and Brendon Moody had agreed that it was in Laurie's best interest that they accept the offer of a plea bargain. "I've reached a decision," she began.

Justin listened, his eyes never leaving Sarah's face. If I were an artist, he thought, I would sketch that face and caption it "Grief."

"So you see," Sarah concluded, "the psychiatrists for the state do believe that Laurie was abused as a child and there is substantial indication of multiple personality disorder. They know the jury is going to sympathize with her, and it's unlikely she'd be convicted of murder. But the penalty for aggravated manslaughter

223

is also a possible thirty years. On the other hand, if she pleads guilty to second-degree manslaughter, intentionally killing in the heat of passion with reasonable provocation, at worst she could be sentenced to a maximum of ten years. It would be up to the judge if she got a mandatory five years without parole. He could also give her as little as a five-year flat term with no parole ineligibility stipulation, and she could be out in a year or two. I don't have the right to gamble with nearly thirty years of Laurie's life."

"How can she plead guilty to a crime she doesn't remember committing?" Justin asked.

"It's legal. Her statement will be something to the effect that while she has no memory of the crime, she and her lawyer, having reviewed the evidence, are satisfied that she committed it."

"How long can you hold off?"

Sarah's voice became unsteady. "What would be the point? I think if anything, taking the pressure off Laurie to remember might in the long run be beneficial to her. Let it go."

"No, Sarah." Justin pushed back his chair and walked over to the window, then was sorry he had. Across the garden, Laurie was standing in the solarium, her hands resting on the glass wall, looking out. Even from where he was, he could sense the feeling of a trapped bird longing to fly. He turned to Sarah. "Give me a little longer. How soon do you think the judge will allow her to go home?"

"Next week."

"All right. Are you busy tonight?"

"Well, let's see." Sarah spoke rapidly, obviously trying to rein in her emotions. "If I go home, one of two things will happen. The Hawkinses will come bursting in to deposit more of their possessions and want to take me to dinner. Or else Sophie, whom I love dearly, will be there, sorting through my parents' closets and relieving me of the job I've put off—giving away their clothes. The third alternative is that I'll try to figure out a brilliant defense for Laurie."

"Surely you have friends who ask you out."

"I have lots of friends," Sarah said. "Good friends, cousins too, terrific people who want to help. But, you see, at the end of the day I can't start explaining to everyone what's going on. I can't stand listening to the empty promises that something will turn up, that it's all going to be just fine. I can't bear to hear that none of this would have happened if Laurie hadn't been kidnapped all those years ago. I know that. That knowledge is driving me mad. Oh yes, I also don't want to hear that after all Dad was in his seventies and Mother had that operation a few years ago and the prognosis wasn't great and maybe it was a blessing they went together. You see, I do accept that. *But I don't want to hear it.*"

Justin knew that one comforting word would reduce Sarah to tears. He didn't want that to happen. Laurie would be joining them momentarily. "I was going to suggest that you have dinner with me tonight," he said mildly. "Here's something I want you to see now."

From Laurie's file, he pulled out an eight-by-ten photograph. Faint lines crisscrossed back and forth over it.

"This is an enlargement of the picture Laurie tore up the day she was admitted here," he explained. "The man who reconstructed it did a good job. Tell me what you see in it."

Sarah looked down at the photograph, and her eyes widened. "The way this was before, I didn't see that Laurie was crying. That tree. That dilapidated house. And what's that, a barn behind it? There's nothing like that in Ridgewood. Where was this taken?"

Then she frowned. "Oh, wait a minute. Laurie went to a nursery school three afternoons a week. They used to take the kids on excursions to parks and lakes. There are farmhouses like this around Harriman State Park. But why would this picture have upset her the way it did?"

"I'm going to try to find out," Justin said, switching on the video camera as Laurie opened the door.

. . .

Laurie forced herself to look at the picture. "The chicken coop behind the farmhouse," she whispered. "Bad things happen there."

"What bad things, Laurie?" Justin asked.

"Don't talk, you jerk. He'll find out and you know what he'll do to you."

Sarah dug her nails into her palms. This was a voice she had never heard before, a young, strong, boyish voice. Laurie was frowning. Even though her face seemed to have lost its contours, her mouth was set in a determined line. One hand was smacking the other.

"Hi," Justin said casually. "You're new. What's your name?"

"Get back inside, you!" It was Leona's catlike tone. "Listen, Doctor, I know that bossy Kate has been trying to go around me. It won't happen."

"Leona, why are you always the troublemaker?" Justin demanded.

Sarah realized he was trying a new tactic. His voice was belligerent.

"Because people are always pulling things on me. I trusted Allan and he made a fool of me. I trusted you when you told us to keep a journal, and you stuck that picture in it."

Laurie's hair was tumbling over her face. She was brushing it back with an unconsciously seductive gesture.

"That's impossible. You didn't find this picture in your journal, Leona."

"I certainly did. Just the way I found that damn knife in my tote bag. I was so nice when I went to Allan's for the showdown and he looked so peaceful I didn't even wake him up, and now people are blaming me because he's dead."

Sarah held her breath. Don't react, she told herself. Don't distract her.

226

"Did you try to wake him up?" Justin might have been commenting on the weather.

"No. I was going to show him. I mean there's no way I can escape. The kitchen knife that was missing. Sarah. Sophie. Dr. Carpenter. Everybody wants to know why I took it. I did *not* take the knife. Then Allan makes a fool of me. You know what I decided to do?" She did not wait for an answer. "I was going to show that guy. Kill myself right in front of him. Let him be sorry for what he did to me. No use going on living. Nothing's ever going to be good for me."

"You went to his house and the big window was open?"

"No. I don't go in windows. The terrace door to the study. The lock doesn't catch. He was already in bed. I went into his room. For Pete's sake, have you got a cigarette?"

"Of course." Donnelly waited until Leona had settled back, the lit cigarette between her fingers, before he asked, "What was Allan doing when you went in?"

Her lips curved in a smile. "He was snoring. Can you believe it? My big scene wasted. He's curled up in bed like a little kid, arms all wrapped around the pillow, hair sort of tousled, and he's snoring." Her voice softened and became hesitant. "My daddy used to snore. Mommy used to say that was the only thing about him she'd change. He could wake up the dead when he started snoring."

Yes, Sarah thought, yes.

"And you had the knife?"

"Oh, that. I put my tote bag down on the floor by the bed. I had the knife in my hand by then. I laid the knife on top of the bag. I was so tired. And you know what I thought?"

"Tell me."

The voice changed completely, became that of four-year-old Debbie. "I thought of all the times I wouldn't let my daddy hold me or kiss me after I came back from the house with the chicken coop and I laid down on the bed next to Allan and he never knew, he just kept on snoring."

"Then what happened, Debbie?"

Oh please, God, Sarah thought.

"Then I got scared, afraid he'd wake up and be mad at me and tell the dean on me again, so I got up and tiptoed out. And he never even knew I was there."

She giggled happily like a little girl who had played a trick and gotten away with it.

Justin took Sarah to dinner at Neary's Restaurant on East Fifty-seventh Street.

"I'm a regular here," he told her, as a beaming Jimmy Neary rushed to greet them. Justin introduced Sarah. "Here's someone you've got to fatten up, Jimmy."

At the table he said, "I think you've had a tough enough day. Want to hear about Australia?"

Sarah wouldn't have believed that she could eat every bite of a sliced steak sandwich and french fries. When Justin had ordered a bottle of Chianti, she'd protested. "Hey, you can walk home. I've got to drive."

"I know. It's only nine o'clock. We're going to take a long walk back to my place and have coffee there."

New York on a summer evening, Sarah thought as they sat on his small terrace, sipping espresso. The lights on the trees surrounding the Tavern on the Green, the lush foliage, the horses and carriages, the strollers and joggers. All this was a world away from locked rooms and prison bars.

"Let's talk about it," she said. "Is there any chance that what Laurie, or rather Debbie, told us today—about lying down with Allan Grant and then leaving him sleeping—is true?"

"As far as Debbie knows it's probably true."

"You mean that Leona might have taken over when Debbie started to leave?"

"Leona or an alter personality we haven't met so far."

"I see. I thought Laurie remembered something when she saw that picture. What could it be?"

"I believe there probably was a chicken coop wherever Laurie was kept during those two years. That picture reminded her of something that happened there. As time goes on we may be able to learn what it was."

"But time is running out." Sarah did not know she was going to cry until she felt the tears gushing down her cheeks. She held her hands over her mouth, trying to stifle racking sobs.

Justin put his arms around her. "Let it out, Sarah," he said tenderly.

86

*I*T WAS Brendon Moody's theory that if you waited long enough you'd get a break. His break came on June 25, from an unexpected source. Don Fraser, a junior at Clinton, was arrested for selling drugs. Realizing he'd been caught red-handed, he hinted that in exchange for leniency, he could tell them something about Laurie Kenyon's whereabouts the night she killed Allan Grant.

The prosecutor guaranteed nothing but said he'd do what he could. Dealing drugs within a thousand feet of a high school could mean a mandatory three-year sentence. Since the place where Fraser was picked up was just at the edge of the thousand-foot zone, the prosecutor agreed that he would not press for the within-school-zone offense if Fraser came up with something significant.

"And I want immunity from prosecution for what I'm telling you," Fraser insisted.

"You'd have made a good lawyer," the prosecutor told him sourly. "I'll say it again. You give us something helpful, and we'll help you. That's as far as I'll go right now. Take it or leave it."

"All right. All right. I happened to be on the corner of North Church and Maple the night of January twenty-eighth," Fraser began.

"Happened to be! What time was that?"

"Ten after eleven."

"All right. What happened then?"

"I'd been talking to a couple of friends. They'd left and I'd been waiting for someone else who never showed up. It was cold, so I figured I'd take off and go back to the dorm."

"This is ten after eleven."

"Yes." Fraser picked his words carefully. "All of a sudden this chick comes out of nowhere. I knew it was Laurie Kenyon. Everybody knows who she is. She was always getting her picture in the paper because of golf and then when her folks died."

"How was she dressed?"

"Ski jacket. Jeans."

"Was there any sign of blood on her?"

"No. Not a bit."

"Did you talk to her?"

"She came over to me. The way she was acting, I thought she was going to try to pick me up. There was something real sexy about her."

"Back up a minute. North Church and Maple is about ten blocks from the Grant home, isn't it?"

"About that. Anyhow she came up to me and said she needed a cigarette."

"What did you do?"

"Now this doesn't get used against me?"

"No. What did you do?"

"I thought she meant grass, so I pulled some out."

"And then?"

"She got mad. She said she didn't like that stuff and wanted a real cigarette. I had some with me and told her I'd sell her a pack."

"You didn't offer her one?"

"Hey, why should I?"

"Did she buy cigarettes from you?"

"No. She went to reach for her purse and then said something funny. She said, 'Damn it. I'll have to go back. That stupid kid forgot to bring it.' "

"What kid? Forgot to bring what?"

"I don't know what kid. I'm sure she was talking about her purse. She said to wait twenty minutes. She'd be back."

"Did you wait?"

"I figured why not? Maybe my other friend would show up too."

"You stood there."

"No. I didn't want to be seen. I got off the sidewalk and stood between two bushes on the lawn of the corner house."

"How long before Laurie got back?"

"Maybe fifteen minutes. But she never stopped. She was running like hell."

"This is very important. Was she carrying her bag?"

"She was hanging onto something with both hands, so I guess so."

87

BIC AND OPAL listened with rapt attention to the tape of Sarah's conversation with Brendon Moody about the testimony of the student drug dealer. "It's consistent with what Laurie told us," Sarah explained to Moody. "Debbie, the child alter, remembers leaving Allan Grant. None of Laurie's personalities will talk about what happened after she went back."

Bic remarked ominously, "Sneaking out of a man's house—going back and committing murder—terrible."

Opal tried to stifle her jealousy, comforting herself with the knowledge that it wasn't going to go on much longer. Sarah Kenyon would be out of the house in a matter of weeks, and Bic wouldn't have access to the condominium.

Bic was replaying the last part of the tape. "The judge is going to allow Lee to leave the clinic on July eighth. That's next Wednesday," he said. "We're going to pay a visit to Ridgewood to welcome Lee home."

"Bic, you don't mean to face her."

"I know what I mean, Opal. We'll both be conservatively dressed. We won't talk about prayer or God, much as it hurts me not to bring the Lord into our every activity. The point is, we must befriend her. Then, just in case she does get too much memory back, we'll be all mixed up in her mind. We won't stay long. We'll apologize for intruding and take our leave. Now try this on and let's see how cute you look."

He handed her a box. She opened it and took out a wig. She went to the mirror, put it on and adjusted it, then turned for him to see. "My Lord, it's just perfect," he observed.

The phone rang. Opal picked it up.

It was Rodney Harper from station WLIS in Bethlehem.

"You remember me?" he asked. "I was the station manager when you broadcast from here all those years ago. Proud to say I own the place now."

Opal motioned for Bic to pick up the extension as she said, "Rodney Harper. Of course I remember you."

"Been meaning to congratulate you on all your success. You folks have sure gone a long way. Reason I called today is that a woman from *People* magazine was in here talking to me about you."

Opal and Bic exchanged glances. "What did she ask?"

"Oh just about what kind of folks you were. I said Bobby was the best damn preacher we ever had in these parts. Then she wanted to know if I had a picture of you from those days."

Opal saw the sudden alarm on Bic's face and knew it mirrored her own. "And did you?"

"I'm sorry to say we can't find one. We moved the station to a new facility about ten years ago and got rid of a heap of stuff. I guess your pictures got caught in the throwaway bags."

"Oh that doesn't matter," Opal said as she felt her stomach muscles begin to relax. "Wait a minute. Bobby's on the line and wants to say hello."

Bic cut in with a robust greeting. "Rodney, my friend, it's a treat to hear your voice. I'll never forget you gave us our first big break. If we hadn't been in Bethlehem on your station and getting known, I don't know we'd be on the 'Church of the Airways' today. Even so, if you do come across some old picture, I'd appreciate if you just tore it up. Looked too darn much like a hippie in those days, and it kind of doesn't go with preaching to the older folks in the 'Church of the Airways.' "

"Sure, Bobby. Just one thing I hope you won't mind. I did take that reporter from *People* to see the farmhouse where you lived those two years you were with us. Son of a gun. I missed the fact it had burned down. Kids or some bum, I suppose, broke in and got careless with matches."

Bic rounded his thumb and first finger, then winked at Opal.

"These things happen, but I'm real sorry to hear that. Carla and I loved that snug little place."

"Well, they took a couple of pictures of the property. I heard the reporter say she wasn't sure if she'd even use them in the article, but at least the chicken coop was still standing and that was proof enough for anyone that you came from humble beginnings."

88

KAREN GRANT reached her desk at nine o'clock and sighed with relief that Anne Webster wasn't already in the office. Karen was having a hard time hiding her anger at the agency's retiring owner. Webster did not want to complete the sale of the agency to Karen until mid-August. She had been invited on an inaugural flight of New World Airlines to Australia and didn't intend to miss it. Karen had been hoping to go on that one. Edwin had been invited too, and they'd planned to enjoy it together.

Karen had told Anne that there was really no need for her to come in to the office anymore. Business was slow and Karen could handle it herself. After all, Anne was almost seventy, and the trip from Bronxville to the city was taxing. But Anne was proving unexpectedly stubborn about hanging on and was making a crusade of taking regular clients out to lunch and assuring them that Karen would take just as good care of them as she had.

Of course there was a reason for that. For three years Webster would get a percentage of the profits, and there was no question that even though the travel business had been abysmal for nearly two years, the mood was changing and people were starting to do more traveling.

As soon as Anne was totally out of the way, Edwin could use her office. But they'd wait until the late fall to move in together. It would look better for Karen to testify as the grieving widow at Laurie Kenyon's trial. Except for Anne hanging around and that damn detective dropping in so much, Karen was blissfully happy. She was so crazy about Edwin. Allan's trust fund was now in her name. One hundred thousand or better a year for the next twenty years, and in the meantime those stocks were increasing in value. In a way she wasn't sorry not to get the principal now. She might not always be crazy about Edwin, and if anything, his tastes were more expensive than hers.

She loved jewelry. It was hard to pass the L. Crown boutique in the lobby without looking in the showcase. It used to be that when she bought something that caught her eye she'd worry that one day Allan would come out of his dreamworld and ask to see the bankbook. He believed she was putting the bulk of the trust fund money in a savings account. Now she didn't have that worry, and between Allan's life insurance and the trust fund, he'd left her in great shape. When that damn house in Clinton sold, she was going to treat herself to an emerald necklace. Trouble was, a lot of people were squeamish about buying a house where someone had been murdered. She'd already reduced the selling price twice.

This morning she was debating about what to give Edwin for his birthday. Well, she still had two weeks to make up her mind.

The door opened. Karen forced a welcoming smile as Anne Webster came in. Now I'll hear how she didn't sleep well last night but got her usual nap on the train, she thought.

"Good morning, Karen. My, don't you look lovely. Is that another new dress?"

"Yes, I just got it yesterday." Karen couldn't resist telling the designer's name. "It's a Scaasi."

"It looks it." Anne sighed and brushed back a strand of gray hair that had escaped from the braid that circled the top of her head. "My, I'm feeling my age this morning. Awake half the night and then, as usual, dead asleep on the train. I was sitting next to Ed Anderson, my next-door neighbor. He always calls me the sleeping beauty and says that someday I'll wake up in the freight yard."

Karen laughed with her. My God, how many times more do I have to hear the sleeping beauty story? she thought. Only three weeks, she promised herself. The day we close the deal, Anne Webster will be history.

On the other hand . . . This time she gave Anne a genuinely warm smile. "You *are* a sleeping beauty!"

They chuckled together.

89

*B*RENDON MOODY was watching when, at quarter of ten, Connie Santini, the secretary, came in and Karen Grant left the travel agency office. Something was bothering him about Anne Webster's account of the evening she had spent with Karen Grant at Newark Airport. He had talked to Webster a week ago, and today he wanted to talk to her again. He walked over to the agency. As he opened the door, he attempted to plaster on his face the smile of a casual visitor. "Good morning, Mrs. Webster. I was passing this way and thought I'd drop by. You're looking well. It's good to see you again. I was afraid that by now you'd be retired."

"How nice of you to remember, Mr. Moody. No, I decided to wait and have the closing in mid-August. Frankly right now business is really picking up and I sometimes wonder if I should have held off selling. But then when I get up in the morning and rush for a train and leave my husband reading the papers over coffee, I say, enough's enough."

"Well, you and Karen Grant certainly know how to give custom service," Moody commented as he sank into a chair. "Remember you told me that the night Professor Grant died, you and Karen were at Newark Airport? Not too many travel agents will personally go to the airport to meet even the very best client."

Anne Webster looked pleased at the compliment. "The lady we met is quite elderly," she said. "She loves to travel and usually has a contingent of friends and relatives with her, at her expense. Last year we booked her and eight others at full first-class fare on a round-the-world cruise. The night we met her, she had cut short a trip and returned alone because she wasn't feeling well. Her chauffeur happened to be away, so we volunteered to pick her up at the airport. It's little enough to do to keep her happy. Karen drove and I sat in back talking to her."

"The plane arrived at nine-thirty, as I remember," Brendon said casually.

"No. It was supposed to arrive at nine-thirty. We got to the ariport at nine. The flight had been delayed in London. They said it would get in at ten, so we went to the VIP Lounge."

Brendon consulted his notes. "Then, according to your statement, it did arrive at ten."

Anne Webster looked embarrassed. "I was wrong. I thought about it later and realized it was nearly twelve-thirty."

"Twelve-thirty!"

"Yes. When we reached the lounge they said that the computers were down and there would be that long a delay. But Karen and I were watching a film on the TV in the lounge, so the time passed very quickly."

237

"I'll bet it did." The secretary laughed. "Now Mrs. Webster, you know you probably slept through the whole thing."

"I certainly did not," Anne Webster said indignantly. "They had *Spartacus* on. That was my favorite movie years ago, and now they've restored the footage that had been cut out. I never closed an eye."

Moody let it go. "Karen Grant has a friend Edwin who's a travel writer, doesn't she?" He did not miss the expression on the secretary's face, the tightened lips. She was the one he wanted to question when she was alone.

"Mr. Moody, a woman in business meets many men. She may have lunch or dinner with them, and it does offend me that in this day and age anyone can read anything improper in their meetings." Anne Webster was adamant. "Karen Grant is an attractive, hardworking young woman. She was married to a brilliant professor who understood her need to carve out her own life. He had an independent income and was extremely generous to her. She always talked about Allan in the most glowing terms. Her relationships with other men were totally on the up-and-up."

Connie Santini's desk was behind and to the right of Webster's. Catching Brendon's glance, she raised her eyes to heaven in the classic expression of total disbelief.

90

THE JULY 8 staff meeting at the clinic was almost over. There was only one patient left to discuss—Laurie Kenyon.

As Justin Donnelly well knew, her case was the one that had engrossed everyone.

"We're making breakthroughs," he said. "Maybe even significant breakthroughs to what happened to her in those missing two years. The problem is that we don't have enough time. Laurie will go home this afternoon and will be an outpatient from now on. In a few weeks she'll go to court and plead guilty to manslaughter. The deadline from the prosecutor on the plea offer to manslaughter expires then."

The room was quiet. In addition to Dr. Donnelly, there were four others at the conference table: two psychiatrists, the art therapist, and the journal therapist. Kathie, the journal therapist, shook her head. "Doctor, it doesn't matter which alter personality writes in the journal, not one of them admits killing Allan Grant."

"I know that," Justin said. "I've asked Laurie to let us take her to Grant's house in Clinton to act out what happened that night. She certainly gave us a vivid picture of being in that rocking chair on someone's lap during abreaction, but she's stonewalling me on doing the same thing with Grant's death."

"Which suggests that neither she nor her alters want to remember what happened there?"

"Possibly."

"Doctor, her recent drawings have been much more detailed when she does the stick figure of a woman. Look at these." Pat, the art therapist, passed some of them around. "Now they really look as though the figure of the woman is wearing a pendant of some sort. Will she talk about that?"

"No. All she says is that's it's clear she's no artist."

When Laurie came to Justin's office an hour later, she was wearing a pale pink linen jacket and pleated white skirt. Sarah was with her and acknowledged Justin's compliment on the outfit with quiet pleasure. "It caught my eye when I was shopping last night," she explained, "and this is an important day."

"Freedom," Laurie said quietly, "brief, frightening, but still welcome."

Then Laurie unexpectedly said, "Maybe it's about time I tried your couch, Doctor."

Justin tried to sound offhand. "Be my guest. Any reason why today?"

She kicked off her shoes and stretched out. "Maybe it's just that I'm so comfortable with you two, and I feel like my old self in this new outfit, plus it will be nice to see the house again before we move." She hesitated. "Sarah tells me that after I plead guilty I'll have about six weeks before sentencing. The prosecutor has agreed to consent before the judge to my remaining free on bail till the sentence. I know that the minute I'm sentenced I have to go to prison, so I'm going to have a wonderful time for those six weeks. We're going to play golf and we're going to fix up the condominium so I'll be able to think about it while I'm away."

"I hope you're not going to forget to come in for your sessions with me, Laurie."

"Oh no. We'll come in every day. It's just that there's so much I want to do. I'm dying to drive again. I used to love driving. Gregg has a new convertible. I'm going golfing with him next week." She smiled. "It's nice to look forward to going out with him and not be afraid that he'll hurt me. That's why I'm able to lie down. I know you won't hurt me either."

"No, I won't," Justin said. "Are you in love with Gregg, Laurie?"

She shook her head. "That's too strong. I'm too mixed up to love anybody, at least the way you mean. But the first step is just enjoying being with someone, isn't it?"

"Yes, it is. Laurie, could I speak to Kate?"

"If you want." She sounded indifferent.

For weeks now, Justin had not had to hypnotize Laurie to summon the alter personalities. Now Laurie sat up, thrust back her

240

shoulders, narrowed her eyes. "What is it this time, Doctor?" It was Kate's voice they were hearing.

"Kate, I'm a bit troubled," Justin said. "I want Laurie to make her peace with herself and with everything that happened, but not until the whole truth has come out. She's burying it deeper, isn't she?"

"Doctor, I am getting thoroughly sick of you! Can't you get it straight? She's willing to take her medicine. She swore she'd never sleep in the house again, but now she's looking forward to going back to it. She knows that her parents' death was a terrible accident and not her fault. That guy in the service station where she had the appointment to have her car checked had hairy arms. It wasn't her fault he scared the bejesus out of her. She really understands that. Aren't you ever satisfied?"

"Hey, Kate, all along you've known the reason Laurie broke that appointment to have her car inspected, yet you never told me. Why are you telling me now?"

Sarah thought of Sam, the attendant at the service station in town. She'd just filled the car with gas there yesterday. Sam had started work at the end of last summer. He was a big guy with thick arms. Yesterday he'd been wearing a short-sleeved shirt, and she'd noticed that even the backs of his hands were covered by a mass of thick curly hair.

Kate shrugged. "I'm telling you because I'm tired of keeping secrets. Besides, the wimp will be safe in prison."

"Safe from what? Safe from whom?" Justin asked urgently. "Kate, don't do this to her. Tell us what you know."

"I know that while she's out they can get to her. She can't escape and she knows it too. If she doesn't go to prison soon, they'll make it happen."

"Who threatened her? Kate, please." Justin was cajoling, pleading.

She shook her head. "Doctor, I'm tired of telling you that I don't know everything and the kid who does isn't going to talk to you. He's the smart one. You wear me out."

Sarah watched as the aggressive look faded from Laurie's features, as she slipped down and stretched out again on the couch, as her eyes closed and her breathing became even again.

"Kate isn't going to be around much longer," Justin whispered to Sarah. "For some reason she'll feel her job is done. Sarah, look at these." He held out Laurie's drawings. "See this stick figure. Do you make anything of this necklace she's wearing?"

Sarah frowned. "It looks familiar. I feel as though I've seen it."

"Compare these two," Justin said. "They're the most detailed of the batch. You see how the center seems to be oval-shaped and set in a square with brilliants. Does that mean anything to you?"

"I wonder . . ." Sarah said. "My mother had some nice pieces of jewelry. They're all in the safe-deposit box. One of them is a pendant. It has small diamonds all around the center stone—what is it—an aquamarine . . . no, it's not that. I can see it . . . it's—"

"*Don't say that word.* That's a forbidden word." The command was spoken in a young, alarmed but sturdy boyish voice. Laurie was sitting up, staring intently at Sarah.

"What's a forbidden word?" Justin asked.

"Don't say it." The boyish voice coming from Laurie's lips was part pleading, part commanding.

"You're the little boy who came to talk to us last month," Justin said. "We still don't know your name."

"It's not allowed to say names."

"Well, maybe it's forbidden for you, but Sarah can. Sarah, do you remember the stone that was in the center of your mother's pendant?"

"It was an opal," Sarah said quietly.

"What does *opal* mean to you?" Justin demanded, turning to Laurie.

On the couch, Laurie shook her head. Her expression became her own. She looked puzzled. "Did I drop off? I'm suddenly so sleepy. What did you ask me? Opal? Well, that's a gemstone, of course. Sarah, didn't Mama have a pretty opal pendant?"

91

AS ALWAYS, Opal felt the tension building inside her as they passed the sign that read ENTERING RIDGEWOOD. We look totally different, she assured herself, smoothing down the skirt of her navy-and-white print dress, a conservatively cut outfit with a V neck, long sleeves and a narrow belt. With it she wore navy shoes and a matching purse. Her only jewelry was a single strand of pearls and her wedding ring. She'd had her hair trimmed and colored a few hours ago. Now every ash blond strand was coiffed sleekly against her head. Large, blue-tinted sunglasses covered her eyes and subtly redefined the contours of her face.

"You look real classy, Carla," Bic had said approvingly before they left the Wyndham. "Don't worry. There isn't a snowball's chance in hell that Lee will recognize you. And what do you think of me?"

He was dressed in a crisp, white, long-sleeved shirt, a tan, single-breasted summer suit, and a tan-and-white tie with flecks of brown. His hair was now completely silver. Even though he'd let it grow a little longer, he had it combed back so that there was no suggestion of the wavy curls that he'd been so proud of in the early days. He'd also shaved the hair from the backs of his hands. He was very much the image of a distinguished clergyman.

Their car turned into Twin Oaks Road. "That used to be the pink house," Bic said sarcastically as he pointed. "Try not to refer to it again, and don't call the little girl Lee. Call her Laurie when you speak to her, which shouldn't be much at all."

Opal wanted to remind Bic that he was the one who had referred to her as Lee on the program, but she didn't dare. Instead she went over the few words she would exchange with Laurie when they came face to face with her.

243

There were three cars in the driveway. One they recognized as belonging to the housekeeper. The second, a BMW, was Sarah's. But the third, an Oldsmobile with New York plates—whose car was that?

"There's someone visiting," Bic said. "That might be the Lord's way of providing us with a witness who can testify that Lee met us, should the need arise."

It was just five o'clock. The afternoon sun's slanting rays brightened sections of the deep green lawn and glistened through the brilliant blue hydrangeas that bordered the sides of the house.

Bic pulled into the driveway. "We'll just stay a minute even if they encourage us to linger."

It was the last thing on Sarah's mind to encourage the Hawkinses to linger. She and Laurie and Justin were sitting in the den, and a smiling Sophie, having embraced Laurie for a full minute, was making tea.

While Laurie was packing her bags, Justin had surprised Sarah by suggesting he accompany them.

"I think it might be wise for me to be with you when Laurie gets home," he explained. "I don't necessarily anticipate an adverse reaction, but she hasn't been there in five months, and a lot of memories are going to come flooding in. We can swing by my apartment building in your car, I'll pick up mine and follow you out."

"And you also want to be there to see if you can catch any breakthroughs," Sarah had added.

"That too."

"Actually, I'd be glad if you'd come. I think I'm as frightened as Laurie is of this homecoming."

Unconsciously Sarah had stretched out her hand, and Justin had taken it. "Sarah, when Laurie begins serving that sentence, I want you to promise that you'll get some counseling yourself. Don't worry. Not from me. I'm sure you don't want that. But it's going to be rough."

For an instant, feeling the warmth of his hand closing over hers, Sarah had felt less afraid of everything—of Laurie's reaction to being at home, of the day in court next week when she would stand next to Laurie and hear her plead guilty to manslaughter.

When the doorbell rang, Sarah was especially grateful to have Justin there. Laurie, who had happily showed the doctor around the house, suddenly looked alarmed. "I don't want to see anyone."

Sophie muttered, "Ten to one it's that pair."

Sarah bit her lip in exasperation. God, these people were getting to be omnipresent. She could hear Reverend Hawkins explaining to Sophie that they had been looking for a box containing important papers and realized it had been mistakenly included in the things they'd shipped to New Jersey. "If I could just run down to the basement and get it, we'd be so grateful," he said.

"It's the people who bought the house," Sarah explained to Justin and Laurie. "Don't worry. I'm not going to invite them to so much as sit down, but I suppose I should speak to them. I'm sure they've noticed my car."

"I don't think you'll have to bother going to them," Justin said as footsteps came across the foyer. A moment later, Bic was standing in the doorway, Opal behind him.

"Sarah, my dear, my apologies. Some business records my accountant needs desperately. And, is this Laurie?"

Laurie had been sitting next to Sarah on the sofa. She stood up. "Sarah has told me about you and Mrs. Hawkins."

Bic did not leave the doorway. "We are delighted to meet you, Laurie. Your sister is a wonderful girl and talks about you a great deal."

"A wonderful girl," Opal echoed, "and we're so happy to be buying this lovely house."

Bic turned to look at Justin. "Reverend and Mrs. Hawkins, Dr. Donnelly," Sarah murmured.

To her relief, after an acknowledgment of the introduction,

Hawkins said, "We will not intrude on your reunion. If we may we'll just go down and get the material we need and let ourselves out the side door. Good day one and all."

In that minute or two, Sarah realized that the Hawkinses had managed to spoil the temporary happiness of Laurie's homecoming. Laurie fell silent and did not respond when Justin talked breezily about growing up in Australia on a sheep station.

Sarah was grateful when Justin accepted the invitation to dinner. "Sophie has cooked enough for an army," she said.

Laurie clearly wanted Justin to stay as well. "I feel better that you're here, Dr. Donnelly."

Dinner was unexpectedly pleasant. The chill that the Hawkinses had brought to the house vanished as they ate Sophie's delicious dinner of pheasant and wild rice. Justin and Sarah sipped wine, Laurie had Perrier. As they were finishing coffee, Laurie quietly excused herself. When she came back downstairs, she was carrying a small bag. "Doctor," she said, "I can't help it. I have to go back with you and sleep in the clinic. Sarah, I'm so sorry, but I know something terrible is going to happen to me in this house and I just don't want it to be tonight."

92

WHEN BRENDON MOODY phoned Sarah the next morning, he could hear the sounds of doors opening and closing, of furniture being moved. "We're getting out of here," Sarah told him. "It's not good for Laurie to be in this house. The condo isn't quite ready, but they can complete the finishing touches sometime later." She told him how Laurie had returned to the clinic the night before.

"I'm going to pick her up late this afternoon," she said, "and when I do, we'll go straight to the condo. She can help me put it together. The activity might be good for her."

"Just don't give the Hawkinses a key to your new place," Brendon said sourly.

"I don't intend to. Those two set my teeth on edge. But remember . . ."

"I know. They paid top dollar. They let you stay after the closing. How did you ever get a mover that fast?"

"It took a lot of doing."

"Let me come over and help. I can at least pack books or pictures."

The moving was well under way when Brendon arrived. Sarah, her hair held back by a bandana, and dressed in a pair of khaki shorts and a cotton blouse, was busily tagging the furniture the Hawkinses had purchased.

"I won't get everything out today," she told Brendon, "but turnabout is fair play. I'm supposed to have the use of this place till August twenty-fifth. I'll feel free to come in and out and sort the things I'm not sure of now."

Sophie was in the kitchen. "Never thought I'd see the day I'd be glad to leave this house," she told Brendon. "The nerve of those two Hawkins people. They asked if I'd help them get settled when they move in for good. The answer is no."

Brendon felt his antennae going up. "What don't you like about them, Sophie? You've heard Sarah say that they've done her a big favor."

Sophie snorted. Her round, usually pleasant face grimaced in disgust. "There's something about them. Mark my words. How

247

many times do you have to study rooms and closets to decide if you're going to enlarge them or cut them up? Too much talk as far as I'm concerned. I swear these last months their car has been on radar to this place. And all those boxes they left in the basement. Pick up one of them. They're light as a feather. I bet they're not half-full. But that hasn't stopped them from delivering another and another. Just an excuse for dropping in, is what I call it. What do you want to bet, the Reverend uses Laurie's story on one of his programs?"

"Sophie, you're a very clever woman," Brendon said softly. "You may have hit the nail on the head."

Sarah entrusted Brendon with packing the contents of her desk, including the deep drawer that contained all of Laurie's files. "I need them in the same order," she told him. "I just keep going through them hoping and hoping that something will jump out at me."

Brendon noticed the top file was marked "Chicken." "What's this?"

"I told you that the photograph of Laurie Dr. Donnelly had restored and enlarged had a chicken coop in the background and that something about it terrified Laurie."

Moody nodded. "Yes, you did."

"That's been nagging me particularly, and I've just realized why. Last winter Laurie was seeing Dr. Carpenter, a Ridgewood psychiatrist. A few days before Allan Grant died, she was leaving Carpenter's office and went into shock. What seems to have set her off is that she stepped on the head of a chicken in the lobby of his private entrance."

Moody's head tilted up in the position of a bird dog picking up a scent. "Sarah, are you telling me that the severed head of a chicken just *happened* to be on the floor at the entrance to a psychiatrist's office?"

"Dr. Carpenter had been treating a very disturbed man who would come by unexpectedly and who the police thought was involved in cult worship. Moody, it never occurred to me or Dr. Carpenter at the time that this could be in any way connected to Laurie. Now I wonder."

"I don't know what I think," he told her. "But I do know that some woman had Danny O'Toole reporting on your activities. Danny knew that Laurie had been seeing a psychiatrist in Ridgewood. He mentioned it to me. That means whoever was paying him knew it too."

"Brendon, is it possible that someone who knew the effect it would have on Laurie actually *planted* that chicken head?"

"I don't know. But I'll tell you this much. I felt in my bones that the idea of an insurance company hiring Danny didn't ring true. Danny thought his client was Allan Grant's wife. I never quite bought that."

He could see that Sarah was trembling with fatigue and emotion. "Take it easy," he said. "Tomorrow I'll drop in on Danny O'Toole, and I can promise you, Sarah, before I get finished we'll both know who ordered that report on you and Laurie."

93

*O*N THE DRIVE back to the clinic the night before, Laurie had been very quiet. The night nurse reported to Justin the next morning that she had slept fitfully and had talked aloud in her sleep.

"Did you hear what she said?" Justin asked.

"A word here or there, Doctor. I went in several times. She kept mumbling something about the tie that binds."

"The tie that binds?" Justin frowned. "Wait a minute. That's a phrase from a hymn. Let's see. He hummed a few notes. Here it is. 'Blest be the tie that binds . . .' "

When Laurie came in later for the therapy session, she looked calm but tired. "Doctor, Sarah just phoned. She won't be here till late this afternoon. Guess what? We're moving into the condo today. Isn't that terrific?"

"Hey, that's fast." Smart of Sarah, Justin thought. That house has too many memories now. He still wasn't sure what had changed Laurie so drastically yesterday. It had happened when the Hawkins couple stopped in. But they'd barely stayed a minute. Was it the fact that they were strangers and therefore represented some sort of threat to Laurie?

"What I like about the condo is that there's a security guard at the gate," Laurie said. "If anyone rings the bell, there's a television monitor so you'll never make a mistake and let a stranger in."

"Laurie, yesterday you said that something terrible was going to happen to you in the house. Let's talk about that."

"I don't want to talk about it, Doctor. I'm not going to stay there anymore."

"All right. Last night, in your sleep, you were apparently quite a chatterbox."

She looked amused. "Was I? Daddy used to say that if there was something I didn't get out during the day, I'd manage to have my say at night."

"The nurse couldn't understand a lot of it, but she did hear you say 'the tie that binds.' Do you remember what you were dreaming when you said that?"

The doctor watched as Laurie's lips became ashen, her eyelids drooped, her hands folded, her legs dangled. " 'Blest be the tie that binds . . .' " The childlike voice, true and clear, sang the words then faded into silence.

"Debbie, it's you, isn't it? Tell me about the song. When did you learn it?"

She resumed singing. " 'Our hearts in Christian love . . .' "

Abruptly she clamped her mouth shut. "Chill out and leave her alone, mister," a boyish voice ordered. "If you must know, she learned that one in the chicken coop."

94

THIS TIME Brendon Moody did not ply Danny the Spouse Hunter with liquor. Instead, he went to Danny's Hackensack office at 9 A.M., determined to get him at his most sober. Whatever condition that may be, Brendon thought as he sat across the shabby desk from him.

"Danny," he said. "I'm not going to mince words. You may have heard Laurie Kenyon is home."

"I heard."

"Anyone contact you to run a check on her again?"

Danny looked pained. "Brendon, you know perfectly well that the client-investigator relationship is as sacred as the confessional."

Brendon slammed his fist on the desk. "Not in this case. And not in any case where a person may be in jeopardy thanks to the good offices of the investigator."

Danny's florid complexion paled. "What's that supposed to mean?"

"It means that someone who knew Laurie's schedule may have deliberately tried to frighten her by putting the severed head of a chicken where she'd be sure to find it. It means that I'm damn sure no insurance company hired you and I don't believe Allan Grant's widow did either.

"Danny, I have three questions for you, and I want them answered. First, who paid you and how were you paid? Second, where did you send the information you gathered on the Kenyon sisters? Third, where is the copy of that information? After you've answered the questions, give a copy of your report to me."

The two men exchanged glares for a moment. Then Danny got up, took out a key, unlocked the file and riffled through the folders. He pulled out one and handed it to Brendon. "All the answers are in here," he said. "I was called by a woman who introduced herself as Jane Graves and said she represented one of the possible defendants in the Kenyon accident case. Wanted an investigation of the sisters. As I told you, that began right after the parents' funeral and continued until Laurie Kenyon was arrested for the murder of Allan Grant. I sent the reports to a private mail drop in New York City, enclosing my bill. The original retainer as well as all further bills were paid by a cashier's check from a bank in Chicago."

"A cashier's check," Brendon snorted. "A private mail drop. And you didn't think that was fishy?"

"When you're chasing spouses the way I do, you find the one who retains you often goes to great lengths to avoid being identified," Danny retorted. "You can make a copy of that file on my Xerox machine. And remember, you didn't get it from me."

The next day, Brendon Moody stopped by the condo. Sarah was there with Sophie, but Laurie had gone into New York. "She drove herself. She really wanted to. Isn't that great?"

"She's not nervous?"

"She locks the car doors at all times. She'll park next door to the clinic. She has a carphone now. That makes her feel safe."

"It's always best to be cautious," Brendon said, then decided to change the subject. "Incidentally, I like this place."

"So do I. It will be great when we get it in shape, which shouldn't take too long. I want Laurie to be able to enjoy it, really enjoy it before . . ." Sarah did not finish the sentence. Instead she said, "With all these levels, we do get our exercise. But this top floor makes a terrific study, don't you think? The bedrooms are the next floor down, then the living room, dining room, kitchen are entry level and the rec room opens out to the back."

It was clear to Brendon that Sarah welcomed the work involved in moving to take her mind off Laurie's problems. Unfortunately, there were some things Sarah had to know. He laid the file on her desk. "Take a look at this."

She began to read, her eyes widening in astonishment. "My God, it's our lives down to our every movement. *Who* would want this kind of information about us? Why would *anyone* want it?" She looked up at Moody.

"I intend to find out who it is if I have to blast open the records of that bank in Chicago," Moody said grimly.

"Brendon, if we can prove Laurie was under extraordinary duress from someone who knew how to terrify her, I'm sure the judge will be swayed."

Brendon Moody turned away from the look of naked hope on Sarah's face. He decided not to tell her that on gut instinct alone he was beginning to circle around Karen Grant. There are a number of things rotten in Denmark, he thought, and at least one of them has to do with that lady. Whatever it was, he was determined to find the answer.

95

THE PRIVATE postal box in New York had been rented under the name J. Graves. Rental payments had been made in cash. The clerk in charge of the boxes, a small man with slicked-back hair and an unpressed suit, had absolutely no memory of whoever made the pickups. "That box changed hands three times since February," he told Moody. "I'm paid to sort mail, not run Club Med."

Moody knew that this kind of mail drop was retained by purveyors of porno literature and get-rich-quick schemes, none of whom wanted to leave a paper trail that might lead back to them. His next call was to the Citizen's Bank in Chicago. He was keeping his fingers crossed on that one. In some banks it was possible to walk in, plunk down money and buy a cashier's check. Other institutions would only issue that kind of check for depositors. Muttering a prayer, he dialed the number.

The bank manager told Moody that it was bank policy that cashier's checks could only be sold to depositors who withdrew the funds from their savings or checking accounts. Bingo, Brendon thought. Then, predictably, the manager told him that without a subpoena no information would be forthcoming about any depositors or accounts. "I'll get the subpoena, don't worry," Moody told the manager grimly.

He dialed Sarah.

"I have a friend from law school who practices in Chicago," she said. "I'll get him to request the court for the subpoena. It will take a couple of weeks, but at least we're *doing* something."

"Don't get too excited about it yet," Moody cautioned. "I do have one theory. Karen Grant certainly had the money to hire

254

Danny. We know that in her own personality Laurie liked and trusted Professor Grant. Suppose she told him something about things that frightened her and he discussed them with his wife."

"You mean Karen Grant may have believed there was something between Allen and Laurie and tried to scare Laurie off?"

"It's the only explanation I can come up with, and I could be all wet. But Sarah, I'll tell you this: That woman is a cold-blooded phony."

96

O*N JULY 24,* with Sarah at her side, Laurie pled guilty to manslaughter in the death of Professor Allan Grant.

The press rows of the courtroom were packed with reporters from television and radio networks, newspapers and magazines. Karen Grant, in a black sheath and gold jewelry, was seated behind the prosecutor. From the visitors' section, students from Clinton and the usual contingent of courtroom junkies watched the proceedings, hanging on every word.

Justin Donnelly, Gregg Bennett and Brendon Moody sat in the first row behind Laurie and Sarah. Justin felt an overwhelming sense of helplessness as the clerk called, "All rise for the Court," and the judge strode in from his chambers. Laurie was wearing a pale blue linen suit that accentuated her delicate beauty. She looked more like eighteen than twenty-two as she answered the judge's questions in a low but steady voice. Sarah was the one who seemed the more fragile of the two, Justin thought. Her dark red hair flamed against her pearl gray jacket. The jacket hung loosely on her, and he wondered how much weight she had lost since this nightmare had begun.

There was an air of pervasive sadness throughout the courtroom as Laurie calmly answered the judge's questions. Yes, she understood what her plea meant. Yes, she had carefully reviewed the evidence. Yes, she and her lawyer were satisfied that she had killed Allan Grant in a fit of anger and passion after he turned her letters over to the school administration. She finished by saying, "I am satisfied from the evidence that I committed this crime. I don't remember anything about it but I know I must be guilty. I'm so terribly sorry. He was so good to me. I was hurt and angry when he turned those letters in to the administration, but that was because I didn't remember writing them either. I'd like to apologize to Professor Grant's friends and students and fellow members of the faculty. They lost a wonderful human being because of me. There's no way I can ever make that up to them." She turned to look at Karen Grant. "I'm so very, very sorry. If it were possible I would gladly give my life to bring your husband back."

The judge set the sentencing date for August 31. Sarah closed her eyes. Everything was moving too fast. She had lost her parents less than a year ago, and now her sister was to be taken away from her too.

A sheriff's officer led them to a side exit to escape the media. They drove away quickly, Gregg at the wheel, Moody beside him, Justin in the backseat with Laurie and Sarah. They were heading for Route 202 when Laurie said, "I want to go to Professor Grant's house."

"Laurie, you've been adamant about not going there. Why now?" Sarah asked.

Laurie pressed her head with her hands. "When I was in court before the judge, the loud thoughts were pounding like tom-toms. A little boy was shouting that I was a liar."

Gregg made an illegal U-turn. "I know where it is."

The realtor's multiple-listing sign was on the lawn. The white ranch-style house had a closed and shuttered look. The grass was in need of cutting. Weeds were sprouting around the foundation shrubbery. "I want to go in," Laurie said.

"There's a phone number for the real estate agent," Moody pointed out. "We could call and find out about getting the key."

"The lock doesn't catch on the sliding glass door to the den," Laurie said. She chuckled. "I should know. I opened it often enough."

Chilled, Sarah realized that the sultry laugh belonged to Leona.

They followed silently as she led them around the side of the house onto the flagstone patio. Sarah noticed the privacy screen of tall evergreens that shielded the patio from the side road. In her letters to Allan Grant, Leona had written about watching him through this door. No wonder she had not been noticed by passersby.

"At first it seems to be locked, but if you just jiggle it a little . . ." The door slid open, and Leona stepped inside.

The room smelled musty. There was still some furniture scattered haphazardly in it. Sarah watched as Leona pointed to an old leather chair with an ottoman in front of it. "That was his favorite chair. He'd sit there for a couple of hours. I used to love to watch him. Sometimes after he went to bed, I'd curl up in it."

"Leona," Justin said. "You came back for your pocketbook the night Allan Grant died. Debbie told us you had left him sleeping, and your tote bag and the knife were on the floor beside him. Show us what happened."

She nodded and began to walk with careful, silent footsteps to the hallway that led to the bedroom. Then she stopped. "It's so quiet. He isn't snoring anymore. Maybe he's awake." On tiptoe she led the way to the door of the bedroom, then stopped.

"The door was open?" Justin asked.

"Yes."

"Was there a light on?"

257

"The night-light in the bathroom. Oh no!"

She stumbled to the center of the room and gazed down. Immediately her stance changed. "Look at him. He's dead. They're going to blame Laurie again." The young boyish voice that came from Laurie's throat was shocked. "Got to get her out of here."

The boy again, Justin thought. I must get to him. He's the key to all this.

Sarah watched horrified as Laurie, who was not Laurie, her feet wide apart, her features somehow reassembled with fuller cheeks and narrowed lips, closed her eyes, bent down and with both hands made a yanking gesture.

She's taking the knife from the body, Sarah thought. Oh dear God. Justin, Brendon and Gregg were standing in a line with her like spectators at a surrealistic play. The empty room suddenly seemed to be furnished by Allan Grant's deathbed. The carpet had been cleaned, but Sarah could imagine it spattered with blood as it had been that night.

Now the boy alter personality was reaching for something on the carpet. Her tote bag, Sarah thought. He's hiding the knife in it.

"Got to get her out of here," the frightened young voice said again. The feet that were not really Laurie's feet rushed to the window, stopped. The body that was not her body turned. The eyes that were not her eyes swept the room. She bent down as though picking up something and mimed shoving it in a pocket.

That's why the bracelet was found with Laurie's jeans, Sarah thought.

The window was being cranked open. Still clutching the imaginary bag, the boy alter stepped over the low sill into the backyard.

Justin whispered, "Follow him out."

It was Leona who was waiting for them. "That night the kid didn't have to open the window," she said matter-of-factly. "It was already open when I went back. That's why the room had gotten so cold. I hope you brought cigarettes, Doctor."

97

BIC AND OPAL did not attend Laurie's court appearance. For Bic the temptation had been great, but he realized that he would undoubtedly be recognized by the media. "As a minister of the Lord and family friend it would be appropriate for me to be present," he said, "but Sarah is refusing all our invitations to share dinner or to visit with Lee."

They spent a lot of time in the New Jersey house now. Opal hated it. It upset her to see how often Bic would go into the bedroom that had been Lee's. The room's only piece of furniture was a decrepit rocking chair similar to the one they'd had on the farm. He'd sit in it for hours, rocking back and forth, fondling the faded pink bathing suit. Sometimes he'd sing hymns. Other days he'd listen to Lee's music box playing the same tinkling song over and over again.

" 'All around the town . . . Boys and girls together . . .' "

Liz Pierce, the *People* magazine reporter, had been in touch with Bic and Opal several times, checking on facts and dates. "You were in upstate New York and that's where you found your calling. You were preaching on the radio station in Bethlehem, Pennsylvania, then in Marietta, Ohio; Louisville, Kentucky; Atlanta, Georgia, and finally New York. That's right, isn't it?"

It always chilled Opal that Pierce had the dates in Bethlehem so accurately. But at least no one there had ever seen Lee. There wasn't a person who wouldn't swear that they'd lived alone. It would be all right, she told herself.

The same day Lee pled guilty to manslaughter, Pierce called to arrange for more photographs. They'd been chosen as the *People* magazine cover story for the August 31 issue.

98

*B*RENDON MOODY had driven to the Hunterdon County courthouse in his own car. He'd planned to go home from there, but after what he'd witnessed in Allan Grant's bedroom he wanted a chance to talk quietly to Dr. Justin Donnelly. That was why when Sarah suggested he join them for lunch at the condo, Brendon readily accepted.

He got his opening when Sarah asked Donnelly to start a fire in the barbecue. Moody followed him onto the patio. In a low voice, he asked, "Is there any chance that Laurie or the alter personalities were telling the truth, that she'd left Allan Grant alive and came back to find him dead?"

"I'm afraid it's more probable that an alter personality we haven't met is the one who took Grant's life."

"Do you think there is any possibility at all that she is totally innocent?"

Donnelly carefully arranged the charcoal briquettes in the barbecue and reached for the lighter fluid. "Possibility? I suppose anything is possible. You observed two of Laurie's alter personalities today, Leona and the boy. There may be a dozen more who haven't surfaced yet, and I'm not sure that they ever will."

"I still have a gut feeling—" Brendon clamped his lips together as Sarah came out to the patio from the kitchen.

99

"*THANK YOU* for going to the courthouse with us Friday, Dr. Donnelly," Laurie told Justin. She was lying on the couch; she seemed calm, almost tranquil. Only the way she clasped her hands together hinted at inner turmoil.

"I wanted to be with you and Sarah, Laurie."

"You know, when I was making the statement I was more worried about Sarah than myself. She's suffering so much."

"I know she is."

"This morning at about six o'clock I heard her crying and went into her room. Funny, all these years she's been the one to come to me. You know what she was doing?"

"No."

"Sitting up in bed making a list of more people she'd ask to write to the judge for me. She's been hoping that I'll only have to serve two years before I'm eligible for parole, but now she's worried that Judge Armon might give me five years without parole. I hope you'll stay in touch with Sarah when I'm in prison. She's going to need you."

"I intend to stay in touch with Sarah."

"Gregg is terrific, isn't he, Doctor."

"Yes, he is."

"I don't want to go to prison," Laurie burst out. "I want to stay home. I want to be with Sarah and Gregg. *I don't want to go to prison.*"

She sat bolt upright, swung her feet down onto the floor and clenched her hands into fists. Her face hardened. "Listen, Doctor, you can't let her get those ideas. Laurie's got to be locked up."

"Why, Kate, why?" Justin asked urgently.

She did not answer.

"Kate, remember a couple of weeks ago, you told me the boy was ready to talk to me. He came out yesterday in the Grants' house. Were he and Leona telling the truth about what happened? Is there someone else I should talk to?"

In an instant Laurie's face changed again. The features became smooth, the eyes narrowed. "You shouldn't be asking so many questions about me." The boyish voice was polite but determined.

"Hi," Justin said easily. "I was glad to see you again yesterday. You took very good care of Laurie the night the professor died. You're very smart for a nine-year-old. But I'm grown up. I think I could help you take care of Laurie. Isn't it about time you trusted me?"

"You don't take care of her."

"Why do you say that?"

"You let her tell people she killed Dr. Grant, and she didn't do it. What kind of friend are you?"

"Maybe someone else who hasn't talked to me yet did it?"

"There are just four of us, Kate and Leona and Debbie and me, and none of us killed anyone. That's why I kept trying to make Laurie stop talking to the judge yesterday."

100

*B*RENDON MOODY could not let go of his gut reaction to Karen Grant. The last week of July, as he impatiently waited for the subpoena to be issued by the Chicago court, he wandered around the lobby of the Madison Arms Hotel. It was obvious that Anne Webster had finally retired from the agency. Her desk had been replaced by a handsome cherrywood table, and in general the decor of the agency had become more sophisticated. Moody decided it was time to pay another visit to Karen Grant's ex-partner, this time at her home in Bronxville.

Anne was quick to let Brendon know that she had been deeply offended by Karen's attitude. "She kept after me to move up the sale. The ink wasn't dry on the contract when she told me that it was not necessary for me to come into the office at all, that she would handle everything. Then immediately she replaced my things with new furniture for that boyfriend of hers. When I think of how I used to stick up for her when people made remarks about her, let me tell you, I feel like a fool. Some grieving widow!"

"Mrs. Webster," Moody said, "this is very important. I think there is a chance that Laurie Kenyon is not guilty of Allan Grant's murder. But she'll go to prison next month unless we can prove that someone else did kill him. Will you please go over that evening again, the one you spent at the airport with Karen Grant? Tell me every detail, no matter how unimportant it seems. Start with the drive out."

"We left for the airport at eight o'clock. Karen had been talking to her husband. She was terribly upset. When I asked her what was wrong, she said some hysterical girl had threatened him and he was taking it out on her."

"Taking it out on her? What did she mean by that?"

"I don't know. I'm not a gossip and I don't pry."

If there's anything I'm sure of, it's that, Brendon thought grimly. "Mrs. Webster, what did she mean?"

"Karen had been staying at the New York apartment more and more these last months, ever since she met Edwin Rand. I have the feeling that Allan Grant let her know he was mighty sick of the situation. On the way to the airport, she said something like, I should be straightening this out with Allan, not running a driving service.

"I reminded her that the client was one of our most valuable, and that she had a real aversion to hired cars."

"Then the plane was late."

"Yes. That really upset Karen. But we went to the VIP lounge and had a drink. Then *Spartacus* came on. It's my—"

"Your favorite movie of all time. Also a very long one. And you do tend to fall asleep. Can you be sure that Karen Grant sat and watched the entire movie?"

"Well, I do know she was checking on the plane and went to make some phone calls."

"Mrs. Webster, her home in Clinton is forty-two miles from the airport. Was there any span of time when you did not see her for somewhere between two to two-and-a-half hours? I mean was it possible that she might have left you and driven to her home?"

"I really didn't think I slept but . . ." She paused.

"Mrs. Webster, what is it?"

"It's just that when we picked up our client and left the airport, Karen's car was parked in a different spot. It was so crowded when we arrived that we had quite a walk to the terminal, but when we left it was right across from the main door."

Moody sighed. "I wish you had told me this before, Mrs. Webster."

She looked at him, bewildered. "You didn't ask me."

101

IT WAS just like it had been in those months before Lee was locked up in the clinic, Opal thought. In rented cars, she and Bic began to follow her again. Some days they'd be parked across the street and watch Lee hurry from the garage to the clinic entrance, then wait however long it took until she came out again. Bic would spend the time staring at the door, so afraid of missing even one glimpse of her. Beads of perspiration would form on his forehead, his hands would grip the wheel when she reemerged.

"Wonder what she's been talking about today?" he'd ask, fear and anger in his voice. "She's alone in the room with that doctor, Opal. Maybe he's being tempted by her."

Weekdays Lee went to the clinic in the morning. Many afternoons she and Sarah would golf together, usually going to one of the local public courses. Afraid that Sarah would notice the car following them, Bic began to phone around to the starters to inquire about a reservation in the name of Kenyon. If there was one, he and Opal would occasionally drive to that course and try to run into Sarah and Lee in the coffee shop.

He never lingered at the table, just greeted them casually and kept going, but he missed nothing about Lee. Afterwards, he'd emotionally comment about her appearance. "That golf shirt just clings to her tender body . . . It was all I could do not to reach over and release the clip that was holding back that golden hair."

Because of the "Church of the Airways" program, they had to be in New York the better part of the weekend. Opal was secretly grateful for that. If they did get a glimpse of Lee and Sarah on Saturday or Sunday, the doctor and the same young man, Gregg Bennett, were always with them. That infuriated Bic.

One mid-August day he called to Opal to join him in Lee's room. The shades were drawn, and he was sitting in the rocker. "I have been praying for guidance and have received my answer," he told her. "Lee always goes to and returns from New York alone. She has a phone in her car. I have been able to get the number of that phone."

Opal cringed as Bic's face contorted and his eyes flashed with that strange compelling light. "Opal," he thundered, "do not think I have not been aware of your jealousy. I forbid you to trouble me with it again. Lee's earthly time is almost over. In the days that are left, you must allow me to fill myself with the sight and sound and scent of that pretty child."

102

THOMASINA PERKINS was thrilled to receive a note from Sarah Kenyon asking her to write a letter on Laurie's behalf to the judge who was going to sentence her.

You remember so clearly how terrified and frightened Laurie was, Sarah wrote, *and you're the only person who ever actually saw her with her abductors. We need to make the judge understand the trauma Laurie suffered when she was a small child. Be sure to include the name you thought you heard the woman call the man as they rushed Laurie from the diner.* Sarah concluded by writing that a known child abuser by that name had been in the Harrisburg area then and, while of course they couldn't prove it, she intended to suggest the possibility that he was the kidnapper.

266

Thomasina had told the story of seeing Laurie and calling the police so often that it could practically write itself. Until she got to the sticking point.

That day the woman had *not* called the man Jim. Thomasina knew that now with absolute certainty. She couldn't give that name to the judge. It would be like lying under oath. It troubled her to know that Sarah had wasted time and money tracking down the wrong person.

Thomasina was losing faith in Reverend Hawkins. She'd written to him a couple of times thanking him for the privilege of being on his show and explaining that, while she would never suggest that God had made a mistake, maybe they should have waited and kept listening to Him. It was just that God had given her the name of the counter boy first. Could they try again?

Reverend Hawkins hadn't bothered to answer her. Oh, she was on his mailing list, that was for sure. For every two dollars she donated, she got a letter asking for more.

Her niece had taped Thomasina's appearance on the "Church of the Airways" program, and Thomasina loved to watch it. But as her resentment of Reverend Hawkins grew she noticed more and more things about the taped segment. The way his mouth was so close to her ear when she heard the name. The way he didn't even get Laurie's name straight. He had referred to her at one point as Lee.

Thomasina's conscience was clear when she mailed a passionate letter to the judge, describing Laurie's panic and hysteria in lurid terms but without mentioning the name *Jim*. She sent a copy of the letter and an explanation to Sarah, pointing out the mistake the Reverend Hawkins himself had made by referring to Laurie as Lee.

103

"*I*T'S GETTING CLOSER," Laurie told Dr. Donnelly matter-of-factly as she kicked off her shoes and settled back on the couch.

"What is, Laurie?"

He expected her to talk about prison, but instead she said, "The knife."

He waited.

It was Kate who spoke to him now. "Doctor, I guess we've both done our best."

"Hey, Kate," he said, "that doesn't sound like you." Was Laurie becoming suicidal? he wondered.

A wry laugh. "Kate sees the handwriting on the wall, Doctor. Got a cigarette?"

"Sure. How's it going, Leona?"

"It's pretty nearly gone. Your golf is getting better."

"Thank you."

"You really like Sarah, don't you?"

"Very much."

"Don't let her be too unhappy, will you?"

"About what?"

Laurie stretched. "I have such a headache," she murmured. "It's as though it isn't just at night anymore. Even yesterday when Sarah and I were on the golf course I could suddenly see the hand that's holding the knife."

"Laurie, the memories are coming closer and closer to the surface. Can't you let them out?"

"I can't let go of the guilt." Was it Laurie or Leona or Kate speaking? For the first time Justin couldn't be sure. "I did such

268

bad things," she said, "disgusting things. Some secret part of me is remembering them."

Justin made a sudden decision. "Come on. We're going to take a walk in the park. Let's sit in the playground for a while and watch the kids."

The swings and slides, the jungle gym and seesaws were filled with young children. They sat on a park bench near the watchful mothers and nannies. The children were laughing, calling to each other, arguing about whose turn it was to be on the swing. Justin spotted a little girl who looked to be about four. She was happily bouncing a ball. Several times the nanny called to the child, "Don't go so far away, Christy." The child, totally absorbed in keeping the ball bouncing, did not seem to hear. Finally the nanny got up, hurried over and firmly caught the ball. "I said, stay in the playground," she scolded. "If you chased that ball in the road, one of those cars would hit you."

"I forgot." The small face looked forlorn and repentant, then, turning and seeing Laurie and Justin watching her, immediately brightened. She ran to them. "Do you like my beautiful sweater?" she asked.

The nanny came up. "Christy, you mustn't bother people." She smiled apologetically. "Christy thinks everything she puts on is beautiful."

"Well, it is," Laurie said. "It's a perfectly beautiful new sweater."

A few minutes later they started back for the clinic. "Suppose," Justin said, "that little girl, very absorbed in what she was doing, wandered too close to the road and someone grabbed her, put her in a car, disappeared with her and abused her. Do you think that years later she should blame herself?"

Laurie's eyes were welling with tears. "Point taken, Doctor."

"Then forgive yourself as readily as you would forgive

269

that child if something she couldn't help had happened to her today."

They went back into Justin's private office. Laurie stretched out on the couch. "If that little girl had been picked up today and put in a car . . ." she hesitated.

"Maybe you can imagine what might happen to her," Justin suggested.

"She wanted to go back home. Mommy would be angry that she went down to the road. There was a new neighbor whose son was seventeen years old and a fast driver. Mommy said the little girl must not run out in front anymore. She might get hurt by the car. They loved the little girl so much. They called her their miracle."

"But the people wouldn't take her home?"

"No. They drove and drove. She was crying, and the woman slapped her and said shut up. The man with the fuzzy arms picked her up and put her on his lap." Laurie's hands clenched and unclenched.

Justin watched as she clutched her shoulders. "Why are you doing that?"

"They told the little girl to get out of the car. It's so cold. She has to go to the bathroom, but he wants to take her picture so he makes her stand by the tree."

"The picture you tore up the day you first came to stay at the clinic made you remember that, didn't it."

"Yes. Yes."

"And the rest of the time the little girl stayed with him . . . the rest of the time *you* stayed with him . . ."

"He raped me," Laurie screamed. "I never knew when it would happen, but always after we sang the songs in the rocking chair he took me upstairs. Always then. Always then. He hurt me so much."

Justin rushed to comfort the sobbing girl. "It's okay," he said. "Just tell me this. Was it your fault?"

"He was so big. I tried to fight him. I couldn't make him stop," she shrieked. *"I couldn't make him stop."*

It was the moment to ask. "Was Opal there?"

"She's his wife."

Laurie gasped and bit her lip. Her eyes narrowed.

"Doctor, I told you that was a forbidden word." The nine-year-old boy would not allow any more memories to escape that day.

104

On AUGUST 17, while Gregg took Laurie to dinner and a play, Sarah and Brendon went to Newark Airport. They arrived at 8:55. "This is approximately the time Karen Grant and Anne Webster got here the night Allan Grant died," Moody told Sarah as they drove into the parking area. "The plane their client was on was more than three hours late, as were a lot of other planes that night. That means that the parking lot would be pretty full. Anne Webster said they had to walk quite a distance to the terminal."

Deliberately he parked his car almost at the end of the facility. "It's a pretty good hike to the United terminal," he observed. "Let's clock it at a normal pace. It should take five minutes at least."

Sarah nodded. She had told herself not to grasp at straws, not to be like so many family members of defendants she had prosecuted. Denial. Their husband or daughter or sister or brother was incapable of committing a crime, they'd argue. Even in the face of overwhelming evidence they'd be convinced there'd been some kind of horrible mistake.

But when she'd talked to Justin, he had been cautiously encouraging about Moody's theory that Karen Grant had both the opportunity and the motive to kill her husband. He said that he was beginning to accept the possibility that Laurie had no more than the four alter personalities they had met, all of whom consistently told him that Laurie was innocent.

As Sarah walked with Moody into the air-conditioned terminal, she welcomed the coolness and the relief from the muggy mid-August evening. The check-in lines reminded her of the wonderful trip to Italy she and Laurie had taken with their parents a little more than a year ago. Now it seemed as if that had been several lifetimes ago, she thought sadly.

"Remember, it was only after Karen Grant and Mrs. Webster got here that they learned the computer system had gone down and the plane was rescheduled for twelve-thirty arrival." Moody paused as he looked up at the listings of arrivals and departures. "What's your reaction if you're Karen Grant and edgy about your relationship with your husband? Maybe more than edgy if when you phoned him he'd told you he wanted a divorce?"

An image of Karen Grant came to Sarah's mind. In all these months she'd thought of Karen Grant as a grieving widow. In court at Laurie's plea bargain she'd been wearing black. It was odd, Sarah thought now as she remembered the scene. Maybe she was carrying it a bit far—not many people in their early thirties wear black as a sign of mourning anymore.

Sarah remarked on this fact to Brendon as they walked toward the VIP lounge. He nodded. "The widow Grant is always playing a part, and it shows. We know she and Anne Webster went up to the lounge and had a drink. The movie *Spartacus* started at nine o'clock that night on The Movie Channel. The receptionist who was here that night is on duty now," he told Sarah. "We'll talk to her."

The receptionist did not remember the night of January 28, but she did know and like Anne Webster. "I've been on the job ten years," she explained, "and I've never known a better travel agent. Only problem with Anne Webster is that whenever she kills time here, she takes over the television. She always puts on one of the movie stations and gets mighty stubborn if someone else wants to watch the news or something."

"Real problem," Brendon said sympathetically.

The receptionist laughed. "Oh, not really. I always tell the people who want to watch something different to just wait five minutes. Anne Webster can conk out faster than anyone I know. And once she's asleep, we change the channel."

They drove from the airport to Clinton. On the way, Moody theorized. "Let's say Karen was hanging around the airport that night, getting more and more worried that she can't talk her husband out of wanting a divorce. Webster is either engrossed in a movie or asleep and won't miss her. The plane won't be in until twelve-thirty."

"So she got in her car and went home," Sarah said.

"Exactly. Assume she let herself into the house with her key and went to the bedroom. Allan was asleep. Karen saw Laurie's tote bag and the knife and realized that if he were found stabbed to death, Laurie would be blamed for it."

On the way they discussed the fact that the subpoena to the bank in Chicago had not, so far, helped them.

The account had been opened in the name of Jane Graves, using an address in the Bahamas that turned out to be another mail drop. The deposit had been a draft from a numbered bank account in Switzerland.

"Almost impossible to get any information about Swiss depositors," Brendon said. "I'm inclined to think now that it was Karen Grant who hired Danny. She may have been stashing some of

273

Allen Grant's trust fund away, and as a travel agent, she knows her way around."

When they reached Clinton, the realtor's sign was still on the lawn of Allan Grant's home.

They sat in the car for several minutes, looking at the house. "It could happen. It makes sense," Sarah said. "But how do we prove it?"

"I talked to the secretary, Connie Santini, again today," Moody said. "She confirms everything we know. Karen Grant was living her own life exactly as she wanted to live it, using Allan Grant's income as a personal allowance. Putting on a show as the grieving widow, but it *is* a show. Her spirits have never been better, according to the secretary. I want you with me on August twenty-sixth when Anne Webster gets back from Australia. We're going to talk to that lady together."

"August twenty-sixth," Sarah said. "Five days before Laurie goes to prison."

105

"*IT'S THE LAST WEEK,*" Laurie told Justin Donnelly on August 24.

He watched as she leaned back on the couch, her hands clasped behind her head.

"Yesterday was fun wasn't it, Justin? I'm sorry. I'd rather call you Doctor in here."

"It was fun. You really are a terrific golfer, Laurie. You beat us all hands down."

"Even Gregg. Well, I'll be out of practice soon enough. Last night I was awake for a long time. I was thinking about that day when I was kidnapped. I could see myself in my pink bathing suit, going down the driveway to watch the people in the funeral procession. I thought it was a parade.

"When the man picked me up, I was still holding my music box. That song keeps going through my head . . . 'Eastside, westside, all around the town . . . Boys and girls together . . .'" She stopped.

Justin waited quietly.

"When the man with the hairy arms put me in the car, I asked him where we were going. The music box was still playing."

"Did anything special bring on those thoughts?"

"Maybe. Last night after you and Gregg left, Sarah and I sat up for a long time talking about that day. I told her that when we drove past the corner house, the one that was that ugly pink color, old Mrs. Whelan was on the porch. Isn't it funny to remember something like that?"

"Not really. All the memories are there. Once they're all out, the fear that they cause will go away."

" 'Boys and girls together . . .'" Laurie sang softly. "That's why the others came to be with me. We were boys and girls together."

"Boys? Laurie, is there another boy?"

Laurie swung her feet off the couch. One hand began smacking the other. "No, Doctor. There's only me." The young voice dropped to a whisper. "She didn't need anyone else. I always sent her away when Bic hurt her."

Justin had not caught the whispered name.

"Who hurt her?"

"Oh, gee," the boy alter said. "I didn't mean to tell. I'm glad you didn't hear me."

After the session, Justin Donnelly reminded himself that even

275

though he had not been able to hear the name the boy alter had unintentionally said aloud, it was very near the surface. It would come out again.

But next week at this time Laurie would be in prison. She'd be lucky if she saw a counselor every few months.

Justin knew that many of his colleagues did not believe in multiple personality disorder.

106

ANNE WEBSTER and her husband returned from their trip early on August 26. Moody managed to reach Webster at noon and persuaded her to see him and Sarah immediately. When they arrived in Bronxville, Webster was unexpectedly direct. "I've been thinking a lot about the night Allan died," she said. "You know nobody likes to feel like a fool. I let Karen get away with claiming that she hadn't moved the car. But you know something? I have proof that she did."

Moody's head tilted up. Sarah's lips went dry. "What kind of proof, Mrs. Webster?" she asked.

"I told you that Karen was upset on the drive to the airport. Something I didn't remember to tell you was that she snapped at me when I pointed out that she was very low on gas. Well she didn't get any on the way to the airport and she didn't get any on the way back from the airport and she didn't get any the next morning when I drove down to Clinton with her."

"Do you know if Karen Grant charges her gas, or pays cash?" Moody asked.

Webster smiled grimly. "You can bet if she bought gas that night it went on the company credit card."

"Where would last January's statements be?"

"In the office. Karen will never let me march in and go through the files, but Connie will do it if I ask. I'll give her a call."

She talked at length to her former secretary. When she hung up she said, "You're in luck. Karen's at an outing American Airlines is sponsoring today. Connie will be glad to look up the statements. She's mad clean through. She asked for a raise, and Karen turned her down."

On the way to New York, Moody warned Sarah, "You know of course that even if we could prove Karen Grant had been in the Clinton area that night there isn't a shred of proof that links her with her husband's death."

"I know," Sarah told him. "But Brendon, there must be something tangible we can put our hands on."

Connie Santini had a triumphant smile for them. "January statement from an Exxon station just off Route 78 and four miles from Clinton," she said, "and a copy of the receipt with Karen's signature. Boy, I'm going to quit this job. She's so darn cheap. I didn't take a raise all last year because business wasn't good. Now it's really picking up and she still won't part with an extra cent. I'll tell you this: She spends more money on jewelry than I make in a year."

Santini pointed across the lobby to L. Crown Jeweler. "She shops over there the way some people go to the cosmetics counter. But she's cheap with them too. The very day her husband died she'd bought a bracelet, then lost it. She had me on my hands and

277

knees searching for it. When the call came about Allan she was in Crown's raising hell that the bracelet had a lousy clasp. She'd lost it again. This time for good. Listen, there was nothing wrong with the clasp. She just didn't take the time to fasten it right, but you can be sure she made them replace it."

A bracelet, Sarah thought, *a bracelet!* In Allan Grant's bedroom the day of the plea bargain, Laurie, or rather, the boy alter, had acted out picking up something and shoving it in his pocket. It never occurred to me that the bracelet found with Laurie's blood-stained jeans might not be one of her own, she thought. I never asked to see it.

"Miss Santini, you've been a great help," Moody told her. "Will you be here for a little while?"

"Until five. I don't give her one extra minute."

"That's fine."

A young clerk was behind the counter of L. Crown Jewelers. Impressed by Moody's insinuation that he was from an insurance company and wanted to inquire about a certain lost bracelet, the clerk willingly looked up the records.

"Oh yes, sir. Mrs. Grant purchased a bracelet on January twenty-eighth. It was a new design from our showroom, twisted gold with silver going through it, giving the effect of diamonds. Quite lovely. It cost fifteen hundred dollars. But I don't understand why she'd put in a claim for it. We replaced it for her. She came in the next morning, most upset. She was sure it had fallen off her wrist shortly after she bought it."

"Why was she so sure of that?"

"Because she told us it had slipped off once at her desk before she lost it for good. Frankly, sir, the problem was that it had a new kind of catch, very secure, but not if you don't take the time to fasten it properly."

"Do you have the sales record?" Moody asked.

"Of course, but we did decide to replace it, sir. Mrs. Grant is a good customer."

"By any chance do you have a picture of the bracelet or a similar one?"

"I have both a picture and a bracelet. We've made several dozen of them since January."

"All alike? Was there anything different about that particular one?"

"The catch, sir. After the incident with Mrs. Grant we changed it on the others. We didn't want any repeat problems." He reached under the counter for a notebook. "You see the original catch clasped like this . . . the one we now use snaps this way and has a safety bar."

The clerk was a good artist.

A copy of the January 28 sales slip, a color photo of the bracelet and the signed and labeled sketch in hand, Sarah and Moody went back to the Global Travel Agency. Santini was waiting, her eyes alive with curiosity. She willingly dialed Anne Webster's number, then handed the phone to Moody, who pressed the speaker button.

"Mrs. Webster," he asked, "was there something about a missing bracelet the night you were at Newark airport with Karen Grant?"

"Oh yes. As I told you, Karen was driving the client and me back to New York. Suddenly she said, 'Damn it, I've lost it again.' Then she turned to me and, very upset, demanded to know whether or not I had noticed her bracelet in the airport."

"And had you?"

Webster hesitated. "I told a teeny-weeny fib. Actually I know she was wearing it in the VIP lounge, but after the way she carried on when she thought she'd lost it in the office . . . Well, I didn't want her to explode in front of the client. I said very positively that she hadn't been wearing it at the airport and that it was probably around her desk somewhere. But I did phone the airport that night, just in case someone turned it in. It's really all right. The jeweler replaced it."

Dear God, dear God, Sarah thought.

"Would you recognize it, Mrs. Webster?" Moody asked.

"Certainly. She showed it to Connie and me and told us about it being a new design."

Santini nodded vigorously.

"Mrs. Webster, I'll be back to you shortly. You've been a big help." In spite of yourself, Moody thought as he hung up the phone.

One last detail to put in place. Please, please, Sarah prayed as she dialed the office of the Hunterdon County prosecutor. She was put through to the prosecutor and told him what she needed. "I'll hold on." As she waited she told Moody, "They're sending someone to the evidence room."

They waited in silence for ten minutes, then Moody watched Sarah's face light up like a sunburst and then a rainbow as tears welled from her eyes. "Twisted gold with silver," she said. "Thank you. I need to see you first thing in the morning. Will Judge Armon be in his chambers?"

107

KAREN GRANT was thoroughly annoyed on Thursday morning to find that Connie Santini was not at her desk. I'm going to fire her, Karen thought as she snapped on lights and listened for messages. Santini had left one. She had an urgent errand but would be in sometime later. What's urgent about anything in *her* life? Karen thought as she opened her desk and took out the first draft of the statement she was planning to deliver in court at Laurie Kenyon's sentencing. It began: "Allan Grant was a husband beyond compare."

Karen should only know where I am right now, Connie Santini thought as she sat with Anne Webster in the small waiting area outside the prosecutor's private office. Sarah Kenyon and Mr. Moody were in talking to the prosecutor. Connie was fascinated by the charged atmosphere of the place. Phones ringing. Young attorneys rushing by, arms loaded with files. One of them looked over her shoulder and called, "Take a message. Can't talk now. I'm due in court."

Sarah Kenyon opened the door and said, "Will you come in now, please. The prosecutor wants to talk to you."

A moment later as she acknowledged the introduction to Prosecutor Levine, Anne Webster glanced down at his desk and noticed the object in a tagged plastic bag. "Oh for heaven's sake, there's Karen's bracelet," she said. "Where did you find it?"

An hour later, Prosecutor Levine and Sarah were in Judge Armon's chambers. "Your Honor," Levine said, "I don't know where to begin, but I'm here with Sarah Kenyon to jointly request an adjournment of Laurie Kenyon's sentencing for two weeks."

The judge's eyebrows raised. "Why?"

"Judge, I've never had anything like this happen before, especially where the defendent pled guilty. We now have reason to seriously question whether Laurie Kenyon committed this homicide. As you know, Miss Kenyon indicated to you that she didn't remember committing the homicide but was satisfied from the state's investigation that she had done so.

"Now some new and quite astonishing evidence has come to light that casts serious doubt on her culpability."

Sarah listened quietly as the prosecutor told the judge about the bracelet, the jewelry salesman's statement, the purchase of gas at the Clinton service station and then gave him the written affidavits of Anne Webster and Connie Santini.

They sat in silence for the three minutes it took Judge Armon to read the affidavits and examine the receipts. When he had finished, he shook his head and said, "Well, I've been on the bench for twenty years and I've never seen anything like this happen. Of course, under the circumstances, I'll adjourn the sentencing."

He looked at Sarah sympathetically as she sat gripping the arms of the chair, the mixture of emotions obvious in her face.

Sarah tried to keep her voice steady as she said, "Judge, on one level I'm obviously ecstatic and on another I'm devastated that I allowed her to plead guilty."

"Don't be so hard on yourself, Sarah," Judge Armon said. "We all know you've turned yourself inside out to defend her."

The prosecutor stood up. "I was going to talk with Mrs. Grant before the sentencing about the statement she wanted to make in court. Instead I think I'm going to have a little talk with her about how her husband died."

"What do you mean the sentencing isn't going to take place on Monday?" Karen asked indignantly. "What kind of snag? Mr. Levine, I think you should realize that this is a terrible ordeal for me. I don't want to have to face that girl again. Just preparing the statement I'm going to make to the judge is upsetting."

"These technicalities come up," Levine said soothingly. "Why don't you come in tomorrow around ten. I want to go over it with you."

Connie Santini arrived in the office at two o'clock fully expecting to have Karen Grant's wrath descend on her. The prosecutor had

282

warned her to say nothing to Karen about her meeting with him. Karen was preoccupied, however, and asked the secretary no questions. "You handle the phones," she told Connie. "Say I'm out. I'm working on my statement. I want that judge to know all I've been through."

The next morning, Karen dressed carefully for her meeting. It might be a little much to wear black today to the courtroom. Instead she chose a dark blue linen and matching pumps. She kept her makeup subdued.

The prosecutor did not keep her waiting. "Come in, Karen. I'm glad to see you."

He was always so pleasant and really a very attractive man. Karen smiled up at him. "I've prepared my statement for the judge. I think it really gets across everything I feel."

"Before we get to that, a couple of things have come up that I want to go over with you. Want to step in here?"

She was surprised that they did not go into his private office. Instead he took her into a smaller room. Several men and a steno-typist were already there. She recognized two of the men as the detectives who had spoken to her in the house the morning Allan's body was found.

There was something different about Prosecutor Levine. His voice was businesslike and remote as he said, "Karen, I'm going to read you your constitutional rights."

"What?"

"You have the right to remain silent. Do you understand that?"

Karen Grant felt the blood drain from her face. "Yes."

"You have a right to an attorney . . . anything you say can be used against you in a court of law . . ."

"Yes, I understand, but what the hell is going on? I'm the widow of the victim."

He continued to read her her rights, to ask if she understood

283

them. Finally he requested, "Will you read and sign the waiver-of-rights form and speak to us?"

"Yes, I will, but I think you're all crazy." Karen Grant's hand shook as she signed the paper.

The questions began. She became oblivious to the video camera, barely aware of the faint clicking of the keys as the stenographer's fingers flew over the keyboard.

"No, of course I didn't leave the airport that night. No. I wasn't parked in a different spot. That old bag Webster is always half-asleep. I sat through that lousy movie with her snoring beside me."

They showed her the charge card receipt for the gas she had purchased at the service station.

"That's a mistake. The date's a mistake. Those people never know what they're doing."

The bracelet.

"They sell plenty of those bracelets. What do you think, I'm the only customer that store has? Anyhow I lost it in the office. Even Anne Webster said I didn't have it on at the airport."

Karen's head started to pound and the prosecutor pointed out that the catch on her bracelet was one of a kind, that Anne Webster's sworn statement was that she *had* seen the bracelet on Karen's wrist in the airport and had called to report it missing.

Time passed as she snapped answers to their questions.

Her relationship with Allan? "It was perfect. We were crazy about each other. Of course he didn't ask me for a divorce on the phone that night."

Edwin Rand? "He's just a friend."

The bracelet? "I don't want to talk about the bracelet anymore. No, I didn't lose it in the bedroom."

The veins in Karen Grant's neck were throbbing. Her eyes were watering. She was twisting a handkerchief in her hands.

The prosecutor and detectives could sense that she was beginning to realize she could not talk her way out of it. She was beginning to feel the net closing around her.

The older detective, Frank Reeves, took the sympathetic approach. "I can understand how it happened. You went home to make up with your husband. He was asleep. You saw Laurie Kenyon's bag on the floor beside the bed. Maybe you thought that Allan had been lying to you after all about being involved with her. You snapped. The knife was there. A second later you realized what you'd done. It must have been a shock when I told you that we'd found the knife in Laurie's room."

As Reeves spoke, Karen's head bowed, her whole body sagged. Her eyes welling with tears, she said bitterly, "When I saw Laurie's bag I thought he had been lying to me. He had told me on the phone that he wanted a divorce, that there was someone else. When you told me she had the knife, I couldn't believe it. I couldn't believe Allan was really dead either. I never meant to kill him."

She looked imploringly into the faces of the prosecutor and detectives. "I really loved him, you know," she said. "He was so generous."

108

"*IT'S BEEN QUITE* a weekend," Justin said to Laurie as she settled herself on the couch.

"I still can't get it through my head," Laurie said. "Do you realize that this is the very hour I expected to be standing in court being sentenced?"

"How do you feel about Karen Grant?"

"I honestly don't know. I guess I'm having trouble believing that I had nothing to do with her husband's death."

"Believe it, Laurie," Justin said gently. He studied her carefully. The euphoria of the swiftly moving events had vanished. The aftershock of all the strain was going to show for a while. "I think it's a great idea for you and Sarah to get away on vacation for a couple of weeks. Do you remember that not long ago you told me you'd give anything to play the golf course at St. Andrews in Scotland? Now you can do it."

"Can I?"

"Of course. Laurie, I'd like to thank the little boy who's taken such good care of you. He was the one who knew you were innocent. Can I talk to him?"

"If you like."

She closed her eyes, paused, sat up as she opened them again. Her lips tightened. Her features softened. Her posture altered. A polite boyish voice said, "All right, Doctor. I'm here now."

"I just wanted to let you know that you've been great," Justin said.

"Not that great. If I hadn't taken that bracelet, Laurie wouldn't have been blamed for everything."

"That's not your fault. You did your best, and you're only nine years old. Laurie is twenty-two and she's really getting strong. I think that soon you and Kate and Leona and Debbie ought to start thinking about joining her completely. I've hardly seen Debbie in weeks. I haven't seen that much of Kate or Leona either. Don't you think it's time to release all the secrets to Laurie and help her to get well?"

Laurie sighed. "Gosh I have a headache today," she said in her normal voice as she settled back on the couch. "Something's different today, Doctor. The others seem to want me to do the talking."

Justin knew it was an important moment, one that must not be wasted. "That's because they want to become part of you, Laurie," he said carefully. "They always have been part of you, you know. Kate is your natural desire to take care of yourself. She's self-preservation. Leona is the woman in you. You've frozen your normal womanly responses so long they had to come out another way."

"In a sex kitten," Laurie suggested with a half smile.

"She is, or was, pretty sexy," Justin agreed. "Debbie is the little girl lost, the child who wanted to go home. You're home now, Laurie. You're safe."

"Am I?"

"You will be if you'll only let that nine-year-old boy put the rest of the puzzle together. He's admitted that one of the names you're forbidden to say is Opal. Let go a little more. Have him surrender his memories to you. Do you know the boy's name?"

"Now I do."

"Tell it to me, Laurie. Nothing will happen, I promise."

She sighed. "I hope not. His name is Lee."

109

THE PHONE would not stop ringing. Congratulations were pouring in. Sarah found herself saying the same thing over and over. "I know. It's a miracle. I don't think it's really sunk in yet."

Bouquets and baskets of flowers were arriving. The most elaborate basket came with the prayers and congratulations of the Reverend Bobby and Carla Hawkins.

"It's big enough to be from the chief mourner at a funeral," Sophie sniffed.

The words sent a clammy shock through Sarah. "Sophie, when you leave, take it with you, please. I don't care what you do with it."

"You're sure you don't need me anymore today?"

"Hey, give yourself a break." Sarah walked over to Sophie, hugged her. "We wouldn't have made it through all this without you. Gregg is coming over. His classes start next week, so he's leaving for Stanford tomorrow. He and Laurie are taking off for the day."

"And you?"

"I'm staying home. I need to collapse."

"No Dr. Donnelly?"

"Not tonight. He's got to drive to Connecticut for some meeting."

"I like him, Sarah."

"So do I."

Sophie was starting out the door when the phone rang. Sarah waved her off. "Don't worry, I'll get it."

It was Justin. There was something in his quick greeting that set off a warning signal to Sarah. "Is anything wrong?" she demanded.

"No, no," he said soothingly. "It's just that Laurie came up with a name today and I'm trying to remember in what context I heard it recently."

"What is it?"

"Lee."

Sarah frowned. "Let's see. Oh, I know. The letter Thomasina Perkins wrote me a couple of weeks ago. I told you about it. She's decided that she's stopped believing in Reverend Hawkins's miracles. In the letter she pointed out that while he was praying over her, he referred to Laurie as 'Lee.'"

"That's it," Justin said. "I noticed it myself the day I watched that program."

"How did Laurie use the name?" Sarah asked.

"It's what her nine-year-old boy alter calls himself. Of course it's probably just coincidence. Sarah, I've got to run. They need me upstairs. Laurie's on her way home. I'll call you later."

Sarah hung up slowly. A thought so frightening, so incredible and still so plausible burned in her mind. She dialed Betsy Lyons at the real estate agency. "Mrs. Lyons, please get out the file on our house. I'll be right over. I need to know the exact dates that the Hawkinses were in our house."

Laurie was on her way home. Gregg would be along any minute. As she ran from the apartment, Sarah remembered to hide the key under the mat for him.

110

*L*AURIE DROVE across Ninety-sixth Street, up the West Side Drive, over the George Washington Bridge, west on Route 4, north on Route 17. She knew why she had this terrible sense that her time was running out.

It was forbidden to tell the names. It was forbidden to tell what he had done to her. Her car phone rang. She pushed the ANSWER button.

It was the Reverend Hawkins. "Laurie, Sarah gave me your number. Are you on your way home?"

"Yes. Where is Sarah?"

"Right here. She's had a minor accident but she's all right, dear."

"Accident! What do you mean?"

"She came over to pick up some mail and has twisted her ankle. Can you come directly here?"

"Of course."

"Hurry, dear."

111

THE ISSUE of *People* magazine with the Reverend Bobby and Carla Hawkins on the cover arrived in mailboxes all over the country.

In Harrisburg, Thomasina Perkins oohed at the sight of that picture of the Hawkinses and almost forgave them their neglect of her. She opened to the cover story and gasped at the totally different picture of the Hawkinses taken twenty years ago. His gold earring; the powerful hairy arms; the beard. Her stringy, dark, straight hair. They were holding guitars. Memory flooded Thomasina as she read: "Bic and Opal, the would-be rock stars." *Bic.* The name that had haunted her for so many years.

Fifteen minutes after he spoke to Sarah, Justin Donnelly left his office to drive to Connecticut for the seminar he was attending. As he passed his secretary, he noticed the open magazine on her desk. He happened to glance at one of the pictures in the spread, and his blood ran cold. He grabbed the magazine. That heavy tree. The house was gone but the chicken coop in the rear . . . The caption read: "Site of the home from which Reverend Hawkins launched his ministry."

Justin raced back to his office and from Laurie's file grabbed the reconstructed picture and held it next to the one in the magazine. The tree, heavier in this new picture, but with that same gnarled, wide trunk; the edge of the chicken coop in the old picture, exactly the same as the side of the now-visible structure. The stone wall that ran beside the tree.

He raced from the clinic. His car was parked on the street. He'd call Sarah from the car phone. In his mind he could see the television program and the Reverend Bobby Hawkins praying over Thomasina Perkins, praying that she would be able to name the people who had abducted Lee.

In Teaneck, Betty Moody happily settled down to read the new issue of *People* magazine. An unusually relaxed Brendon was taking a couple of days off. His lip curled when he saw the picture of the Hawkinses on the cover. "Can't stand those two," he muttered as he looked over her shoulder. "What did they find to write about them?"

Betty flipped the pages to the cover story. "Sweet, Jesus," Moody muttered as he read: "Bic and *Opal,* the would-be rock stars . . ."

"What's the matter with me?" Brendon shouted. "It was plain as the nose on my face." He dashed for the foyer, stopping only long enough to grab his gun from the drawer.

112

SARAH SAT at Betsy Lyons's desk and analyzed the Kenyon-Hawkins file. "The first time Carla Hawkins came into this office was after our place went on the market," Sarah commented.

"But I didn't show it to her immediately."

"How did you happen to show it to her?"

"She was going through the book and noticed it."

"Did you ever leave her alone in our house?"

"Never," Lyons bristled.

"Mrs. Lyons, a knife disappeared from our kitchen around the end of January. I see Carla Hawkins was looking at the house several times just before that. It isn't easy to steal a carving knife from a wall bracket unless you have at least a little time alone. Do you remember if you left her in the kitchen by herself?"

Lyons bit her lip. "Yes," she said reluctantly. "She dropped her glove in Laurie's room, and I left her sitting in the kitchen while I retrieved it."

"All right. Something else. Isn't it pretty unusual for people not to bargain on the price of a house?"

"You were lucky, Sarah, to get that price in this market."

"I'm not sure about how much luck is involved. Isn't it highly unusual to offer to close, then allow the former owners to stay on until they decide to move and not even charge them rent?"

"It's extraordinary."

"I'm not surprised. One last observation. Look at these dates. Mrs. Hawkins often came out on Saturday around eleven."

"Yes."

"That was just the time Laurie was in therapy," Sarah said

quietly, "and they knew it." The chicken head that had so terrified Laurie. The knife. The picture in her journal. Those people in and out of the house with the boxes that hardly weighed a pound. Laurie's insistence on going back to the clinic the night she came home, right after the Hawkinses had stopped by. And . . . The *pink* house! Sarah thought. Carla Hawkins mentioned it that night I had dinner with them.

"Mrs. Lyons, did you ever tell Mrs. Hawkins that the corner house on our street used to be a garish pink?"

"I didn't know it had been pink."

She grabbed the phone. "I have to call home." Gregg Bennett answered.

"Gregg, I'm glad you're there. Make sure you stay with Laurie."

"She's not here," Gregg said. "I'd hoped she was with you. Sarah, Brendon Moody is here. Justin is on his way out. Sarah, the Hawkinses are the people who abducted Laurie. Justin and Moody are sure of it. Where is Laurie?"

With a certainty that went beyond reason, Sarah knew. "The house," she said. "I'm going to the house."

113

*L*AURIE DROVE down the familiar street, resisting the impulse to floor the accelerator. There were children playing on the lawn of one of the houses. Years ago Mama hadn't allowed her out front alone because of that boy who drove so fast.

Sarah. A twisted ankle isn't so bad, she tried to tell herself. But it wasn't that. There was something terribly wrong. She knew it. She'd sensed it all day.

She steered the car from the street into the driveway. Already the house seemed different. Mama's blue tieback draperies and scalloped shades had been so pretty. The Hawkinses had replaced them with blinds that, when closed, were totally black on the outside, giving the house a shuttered, unwelcoming look. Now it reminded her of another house, a dark, closed house where terrible things happened.

She hurried across the driveway, along the walk, up the porch steps to the door. An intercom had been installed. She must have been seen, because as she touched the bell she heard a woman say, "The door is unlocked. Come in."

She turned the handle, stepped into the foyer and closed the door behind her. The foyer, usually brightened by the light from the adjoining rooms, was now in semidarkness. Laurie blinked and looked around. There was no sound. "Sarah," she called. "Sarah."

"We're in your old room, waiting for you," a voice responded from a distance.

She began to climb the stairs, at first quickly, then with dragging footsteps.

Perspiration broke out on her forehead. The hand that clung to the railing became soaking wet, leaving a damp trail on the bannister. Her tongue felt thick and dry. Her breathing became quick, short gasps. She was at the top of the stairs, turning down the hallway. The door to her room was closed.

"Sarah!" she called.

"Come in, Lee!" This time the man's voice was impatient, as impatient as it used to be long ago when she didn't want to obey the command to go upstairs with him.

Despairingly she stood outside the bedroom door. She knew Sarah was not there. She had always known that someday they'd be waiting for her. Someday was now.

The door swung inward, opened by Opal. Her eyes were cold and hostile, just as they had been when Laurie first met her; a smile that was not a smile slashed her lips. Opal was wearing a short black skirt and a T-shirt that hugged her breasts. Her long, stringy dark hair, tousled and uncombed, hung limp on her shoulders. Laurie offered no resistance as Opal took her hand and led her across the room to where Bic was sitting in an old rocking chair, his feet bare, his shiny black chinos unbuttoned at the waist, his soiled T-shirt exposing his curly-haired arms. The dull gold earring in his ear swayed as he leaned forward, reaching out for her. He took her hands in his, made her stand before him, a truant child. A scrap of pink material was on his knee. Her bathing suit. The only light was from the night-light in the floor socket that Mama had always left on because Laurie was so afraid of the dark.

The loud thoughts were shrieking in her head.

An angry voice, scolding, *You little fool, you shouldn't have come.*

A child crying, *Don't make me do it.*

A boy's voice yelling, *Run. Run.*

A weary voice saying, *It's time to die for all the bad things we did.*

"Lee," Bic sighed. "You forgot your promise, didn't you? You talked about us to that doctor."

"Yes."

"You know what's going to happen to you?"

"Yes."

"What happened to the chicken?"

"You cut its head off."

"Would you rather punish yourself?"

"Yes."

"Good girl. Do you see the knife?"

He pointed to the corner. She nodded.

"Pick it up and come back to me."

The voices shouted at her as she walked across the room: *Don't!*

295

Run.

Get it. Do what he says. We're both tramps and we know it.

Closing her palm around the handle of the knife, she returned to him. She flinched at the vision of the chicken flopping at her feet. It was her turn.

He was so close to her. His breath was hot on her face. She had known that someday she would walk into a room and find him just like this, in the rocking chair.

His arms closed around her. She was on his lap, her legs dangling, his face brushing hers. He began to rock back and forth, back and forth. "You have been my temptation," he whispered. "When you die you will free me. Pray for forgiveness as we sing the beautiful song we always sang together. Then you will get up, kiss me goodbye, walk to the corner, put the knife against your heart and plunge it in. If you disobey, you know what I have to do to you."

His voice was deep but soft as he began, " 'Amazing Grace, how sweet the sound . . .' "

The rocking chair thudded back and forth on the bare floor. "Sing, Lee," he ordered sternly.

" 'That saved a wretch like me . . .' " His hands were caressing her shoulders, her arms, her neck. In a minute it will be all over, she promised herself. Her soprano voice rose clear and sweet. " 'I once was lost, but now am found . . . was blind but now I see.' " Her fingers pressed the blade of the knife against her heart.

We don't have to wait, Leona urged. *Do it now.*

296

114

JUSTIN DROVE FROM New York to New Jersey as fast as he dared, all the while trying to reassure himself that Laurie was safe. She was going directly home and meeting Gregg there. But there had been something about her this morning that troubled him. Resignation. That was the word. Why?

As soon as he'd reached the car he'd tried to phone Sarah to warn her about the Hawkinses, but there was no answer at the condo. Every ten minutes he pressed the redial button.

He had just started north on Route 17 when the phone was answered. Gregg was in the condo. Sarah was out, he told Justin. He expected Laurie any minute.

"Don't let Laurie out of your sight," Justin commanded. "The Hawkinses were her abductors. I'm certain of it."

"Hawkins! *That son of a bitch!*"

Gregg's outrage sharpened Justin's awareness of the enormous suffering Laurie had endured. All these months Hawkins had been circling around her, terrorizing her, trying to drive her into madness. He pressed his foot on the pedal. The car shot forward.

He was turning off Route 17 at the Ridgewood Avenue exit when the car phone rang.

It was Gregg. "I'm with Brendon Moody. Sarah thinks Laurie may be with Hawkins in the old house. We're on the way to it."

"I was only there twice. Give me directions."

As Gregg spat them out, Justin remembered the way. Around the railroad station, past the drugstore, straight on Godwin, left on Lincoln . . .

He didn't dare speed as he passed Graydon Pool. It was crowded, and families with young children were crossing the street, heading toward it.

297

An image came to Justin of a fragile Laurie confronting the monster who had kidnapped her when she was a four-year-old child in a pink bathing suit.

115

LAURIE'S BUICK was in the driveway. Sarah rushed from her car up the porch steps. She rang the bell repeatedly, then twisted the knob. The door was unlocked. As she pushed it open and ran into the foyer, she heard a door slam somewhere on the second floor.

"Laurie," she called.

Carla Hawkins, her blond hair disheveled, tying a robe as she came down the stairs, said frantically, "Sarah, Laurie came in a few minutes ago carrying a knife. She's threatening to kill herself. Bobby is talking her out of it. You mustn't startle her. Stay here with me."

Sarah pushed her aside and bounded up the stairs. At the top she looked around wildly. Down the hall the door to Laurie's room was closed. Her feet barely touched the floor as she rushed to it, then stopped. From inside she could hear the rise and fall of a man's voice. With painstaking care she opened the door.

Laurie was standing in the corner, staring blankly at Bobby Hawkins. She was holding the blade of a knife against her heart. The tip had already penetrated her flesh, and a trickle of blood was staining her blouse.

Hawkins was wrapped in a floor-length white terry-cloth robe, his hair loose and full. "You must do only what the Lord wants of you," he was saying. "Remember what is expected of you."

He's trying to make her kill herself, Sarah thought. Laurie, in a trancelike state, was unaware of her. Sarah was afraid to make a sudden move toward her. "Laurie," she said softly. "Laurie, look at me." Laurie's hand pushed the blade a fraction deeper.

"All sins must be punished," Hawkins said, his voice a hypnotic singsong. "You must not sin again."

Sarah saw the look of finality that came over Laurie's face. "Laurie, don't," she screamed. "Laurie, *don't!!*"

The voices were shrieking at her.

Lee was yelling, *Stop.*

Debbie was crying in terror.

Kate was shouting, *Wimp. Fool.*

Leona's voice was the loudest. *Get it over with!*

Someone else was crying. Sarah. Sarah, always so strong, always the caretaker, was coming toward her, her hands outstretched, tears streaking her face, begging, "Don't leave me. I love you."

The voices stilled. Laurie flung the knife across the room and stumbled forward to gather Sarah in her arms.

The knife was on the floor. His eyes glittering, his hair disheveled, the robe Opal had wrapped around him at the sound of the doorbell slipping from his shoulders, Bic bent down. His fingers grasped the handle of the knife.

Lee would never be his now. All the years of wanting her, fearing her memories were over. His ministry was over. She had been his temptation and his downfall. Her sister had kept him from her. Let them die together.

. . .

Laurie heard the hissing, swishing sound that had haunted her all these years, glimpsed the blade gleaming in the semidarkness, cutting the air in ever-widening circles, powered by the thick hairy arm.

"No," Laurie moaned. With a violent shove, she thrust Sarah away, out of the path of the knife.

Sarah, off balance, stumbled backwards and fell, her head smashing into the side of the rocker.

A terrible smile slashing his face, Bic advanced with measured step toward Laurie, the darting blade blocking her escape. Finally there was no place to go. Pressed against the wall, Laurie looked into the face of her executioner.

116

BRENDON MOODY floored the accelerator as he drove down Twin Oaks Road. "They're both here," he snapped as he saw the cars in the driveway. Gregg at his heels, he raced to the house. Why was the front door ajar?

There was an unnatural silence about the darkened rooms. "Check this floor," he ordered. "I'm going upstairs."

At the end of the hallway the door was open. Laurie's bedroom. He ran toward it. Some instinct made him draw his gun. He heard a moan as he reached the doorway and took in the nightmarish scene.

Sarah was lying on the floor, dazed, trying to struggle to her feet. Blood trickled from her forehead.

Carla Hawkins stood frozen a few feet from Sarah.

Laurie was backed into a corner of the room, her hands raised to her throat, staring at the wild-eyed figure approaching her, sweeping a knife in ever-widening arcs.

Bic Hawkins raised the knife high in the air, looked down into Laurie's face, inches from his own, and whispered, "Goodbye, Lee."

It was the instant Brendon Moody needed. His bullet found its target, the throat of Laurie's abductor.

Justin rushed into the house as Gregg was racing through the foyer to the staircase. "Upstairs," Gregg shouted. The shot sounded as they reached the landing.

She had always known it would happen this way. The knife entering her throat. Sticky warm blood splashing over her face and arms.

But now the knife was gone. The droplets of blood spattered over her were not her blood. It was Bic, not she, who had slumped and fallen. It was his eyes, not hers, staring up.

Laurie watched motionless as the gleaming, compelling eyes flickered and closed forever.

Justin and Gregg reached the doorway of the bedroom together. Carla Hawkins, kneeling beside the body, was pleading, "Come back, Bic. A miracle. You can perform miracles."

Brendon Moody, his hand at his side, still holding the gun, stood dispassionately observing them.

The three men watched as Sarah struggled to her feet. Laurie walked to her, her hands outstretched. They stood looking at each other for a long minute. Then in a firm voice Laurie said, "It's over, Sarah. It's really over."

117

TWO WEEKS LATER, Sarah and Justin stood at the security check in Newark Airport and watched Laurie walk down the corridor to the gate for United Airlines flight 19 to San Francisco.

"Being near Gregg, finishing college at UCSF is the best possible choice for her now," Justin assured Sarah as he noticed the worried expression that replaced her bright goodbye smile.

"I know it is. She can play a lot of golf, get her game back, get her degree. Be independent and still have Gregg there for her. They're so good together. She doesn't need me anymore, at least not in the same way."

At the bend in the corridor, Laurie turned, smiled and blew a kiss.

She's different, Sarah thought. Confident, sure of herself. I've never seen her look that way before.

She pressed her fingertips to her lips and returned it.

As Laurie's slender form disappeared around the corner, Sarah felt Justin's arm comfortingly around her shoulders.

"Save the rest of the kisses for me, luv."

I'LL BE SEEING YOU

FOR MY NEWEST GRANDCHILD
JEROME WARREN DERENZO
'SCOOCHIE'
WITH LOVE AND JOY

ACKNOWLEDGMENTS

The writing of this book required considerable research. It is with great gratitude I acknowledge those who have been so wonderfully helpful.

B. W. Webster, M.D., Associate Director, Reproductive Resource Center of Greater Kansas City; Robert Shaler, Ph.D., Director of Forensic Biology, New York City Medical Examiner's Office; Finian I. Lennon, Mruk & Partners, Management Consultants – Executive Search; Leigh Ann Winick, Producer Fox/5 TV News; Gina and Bob Scrobogna, Realty Executives, Scottsdale, Arizona; Jay S. Watnick, JD, ChFC, CLU, President of Namco Financial Associates, Inc.; George Taylor, Director – Special Investigation Unit, Reliance National Insurance Company; James F. Finn, Retired Partner, Howard Needles Tammen & Bergendoff, Consulting Engineers; Sergeant Ken Lowman (Ret.), Stamford, Conn., City Police.

Forever thanks to my longtime editor, Michael V. Korda, and his associate, senior editor Chuck Adams, for their terrific and vital guidance. Sine qua non.

As always, my agent Eugene H. Winick and my publicist Lisl Cade have been there every step of the way.

Special thanks to Judith Glassman for being my other eyes and my daughter Carol Higgins Clark for her ideas and for helping to put the final pieces of the puzzle together.

And to my dear family and friends, now that this is over, I'm happy to say I'll Be Seeing You!

His honour rooted in dishonour stood,
And faith unfaithful kept him falsely true.
– Alfred, Lord Tennyson

Part One

1

Meghan Collins stood somewhat aside from the cluster of other journalists in Emergency at Manhattan's Roosevelt Hospital. Minutes before, a retired United States senator had been mugged on Central Park West and rushed here. The media were milling around, awaiting word of his condition.

Meghan lowered her heavy tote bag to the floor. The wireless mike, cellular telephone and notebooks were causing the strap to dig into her shoulder blade. She leaned against the wall and closed her eyes for a moment's rest. All the reporters were tired. They'd been in court since early afternoon, awaiting the verdict in a fraud trial. At nine o'clock, just as they were leaving, the call came to cover the mugging. It was now nearly eleven. The crisp October day had turned into an overcast night that was an unwelcome promise of an early winter.

It was a busy night in the hospital. Young patients carrying a bleeding toddler were waved past the registration desk through the door to the examination area. Bruised and shaken passengers of a car accident consoled each other as they awaited medical treatment.

Outside, the persistent wail of arriving and departing ambulances added to the familiar cacophony of New York traffic.

A hand touched Meghan's arm. 'How's it going, Counselor?'

It was Jack Murphy from Channel 5. His wife had gone through NYU Law School with Meghan. Unlike

3

Meghan, however, Liz was practicing law. Meghan Collins, Juris Doctor, had worked for a Park Avenue law firm for six months, quit and got a job at WPCD radio as a news reporter. She'd been there three years now and for the past month had been borrowed regularly by PCD Channel 3, the television affiliate.

'It's going okay, I guess,' Meghan told him. Her beeper sounded.

'Have dinner with us soon,' Jack said. 'It's been too long.' He rejoined his cameraman as she reached to get her cellular phone out of the bag.

The call was from Ken Simon at the WPCD radio news desk. 'Meg, the EMS scanner just picked up an ambulance heading for Roosevelt. Stabbing victim found on Fifty-sixth Street and Tenth. Watch for her.'

The ominous ee-aww sound of an approaching ambulance coincided with the staccato tapping of hurrying feet. The trauma team was heading for the Emergency entrance. Meg broke the connection, dropped the phone in her bag and followed the empty stretcher as it was wheeled out to the semicircular driveway.

The ambulance screeched to a halt. Experienced hands rushed to assist in transferring the victim to the stretcher. An oxygen mask was clamped on her face. The sheet covering her slender body was bloodstained. Tangled chestnut hair accentuated the blue-tinged pallor of her neck.

Meg rushed to the driver's door. 'Any witnesses?' she asked quickly.

'None came forward.' The driver's face was lined and weary, his voice matter-of-fact. 'There's an alley between two of those old tenements near Tenth. Looks like somone came up from behind, shoved her in it and stabbed her. Probably happened in a split second.'

'How bad is she?'

'As bad as you can get.'

'Identification?'

4

'None. She'd been robbed. Probably hit by some druggie who needed a fix.'

The stretcher was being wheeled in. Meghan darted back into the emergency room behind it.

One of the reporters snapped, 'The senator's doctor is about to give a statement.'

The media surged across the room to crowd around the desk. Meghan did not know what instinct kept her near the stretcher. She watched as the doctor about to start an IV removed the oxygen mask and lifted the victim's eyelids.

'She's gone,' he said.

Meghan looked over a nurse's shoulder and stared down into the unseeing blue eyes of the dead young woman. She gasped as she took in those eyes, the broad forehead, arched brows, high cheekbones, straight nose, generous lips.

It was as though she was looking into a mirror.

She was looking at her own face.

2

Meghan took a cab to her apartment in Battery Park City, at the very tip of Manhattan. It was an expensive fare, but it was late and she was very tired. By the time she arrived home, the numb shock of seeing the dead woman was deepening rather than wearing off. The victim had been stabbed in the chest, possibly four to five hours before she was found. She'd been wearing jeans, a lined denim jacket, running shoes and socks. Robbery had probably been the motive. Her skin was tanned. Narrow bands of lighter skin on her wrist and several fingers suggested that rings and a watch were missing. Her pockets were empty and no handbag was found.

Meghan switched on the foyer light and looked across the room. From her windows she could see Ellis Island and the Statue of Liberty. She could watch the cruise ships being piloted to their berths on the Hudson River. She loved downtown New York, the narrowness of the streets, the sweeping majesty of the World Trade Center, the bustle of the financial district.

The apartment was a good-sized studio with a sleeping alcove and kitchen unit. Meghan had furnished it with her mother's castoffs, intending eventually to get a larger place and gradually redecorate. In the three years she'd worked for WPCD that had not happened.

She tossed her coat over a chair, went into the bathroom and changed into pajamas and a robe. The apartment was pleasantly warm, but she felt chilled to the point of illness. She realized she was avoiding looking into the vanity mirror. Finally she turned and studied herself as she reached for the cleansing cream.

Her face was chalk white, her eyes staring. Her hands trembled as she released her hair so that it spilled around her neck.

In frozen disbelief she tried to pick out differences between herself and the dead woman. She remembered that the victim's face had been a little fuller, the shape of her eyes round rather than oval, her chin smaller. But the skin tone and the color of the hair and the open, unseeing eyes were so very like her own.

She knew where the victim was now. In the medical examiner's morgue, being photographed and fingerprinted. Dental charts would be made.

And then the autopsy.

Meghan realized she was trembling. She hurried into the kitchenette, opened the refrigerator and removed the carton of milk. Hot chocolate. Maybe that would help.

She settled on the couch and hugged her knees, the

6

steaming cup in front of her. The phone rang. It was probably her mother, so she hoped her voice sounded steady when she answered it.

'Meg, hope you weren't asleep.'

'No, just got in. How's it going, Mom?'

'All right, I guess. I heard from the insurance people today. They're coming over tomorrow afternoon again. I hope to God they don't ask any more questions about that loan Dad took out on his policies. They can't seem to fathom that I have no idea what he did with the money.'

In late January, Meghan's father had been driving home to Connecticut from Newark Airport. It had been snowing and sleeting all day. At seven-twenty, Edwin Collins made a call from his car phone to a business associate, Victor Orsini, to set up a meeting the next morning. He told Orsini he was on the approach to the Tappan Zee Bridge.

In what may have been only a few seconds later, a fuel tanker spun out of control on the bridge and crashed into a tractor trailer, causing a series of explosions and a fireball that engulfed seven or eight automobiles. The tractor trailer smashed into the side of the bridge and tore open a gaping hole before plunging into the swirling, icy waters of the Hudson River. The fuel tanker followed, dragging with it the other disintegrating vehicles.

A badly injured eyewitness who'd managed to steer out of the direct path of the fuel tanker testified that a dark blue Cadillac sedan spun out in front of him and disappeared through the gaping steel. Edwin Collins had been driving a dark blue Cadillac.

It was the worst disaster in the history of the bridge. Eight lives were lost. Meg's sixty-year-old father never made it home that night. He was assumed to have died in the explosion. The New York Thruway authorities were still searching for scraps of wreckage and bodies,

7

but now, nearly nine months later, no trace had as yet been found of either him or his car.

A memorial mass had been offered a week after the accident, but because no death certificate had been issued, Edwin and Catherine Collins' joint assets were frozen and the large insurance policies on his life had not been paid.

Bad enough for Mom to be heartbroken without the hassle these people are giving her, Meg thought. 'I'll be up tomorrow afternoon, Mom. If they keep stalling, we may have to file suit.'

She debated, then decided that the last thing her mother needed was to hear that a woman with a striking resemblance to Meghan had been stabbed to death. Instead she talked about the trial she'd covered that day.

For a long time, Meghan lay in bed, dozing fitfully. Finally she fell into a deep sleep.

A high-pitched squeal pulled her awake. The fax began to whine. She looked at the clock: it was quarter-past four. What on earth? she thought.

She switched on the light, pulled herself up on one elbow and watched as paper slowly slid from the machine. She jumped out of bed, ran across the room and reached for the message.

It read: MISTAKE. ANNIE WAS A MISTAKE.

3

Tom Weicker, fifty-two-year-old news director of PCD Channel 3, had been borrowing Meghan Collins from the radio affiliate with increasing frequency. He was in the process of handpicking another reporter for the on-air news team and had been rotating the candidates, but now he had made his final decision: Meghan Collins.

He reasoned that she had good delivery, could ad lib at the drop of a hat and always gave a sense of immediacy and excitement to even a minor news item. Her legal training was a real plus at trials. She was damn good looking and had natural warmth. She liked people and could relate to them.

On Friday morning, Weicker sent for Meghan. When she knocked at the open door of his office, he waved her in. Meghan was wearing a fitted jacket in tones of pale blue and rust brown. A skirt in the same fine wool skimmed the top of her boots. Classy, Weicker thought, perfect for the job.

Meghan studied Weicker's expression, trying to read his thoughts. He had a thin, sharp-featured face and wore rimless glasses. That and his thinning hair made him look older than his age and more like a bank teller than a media power-house. It was an impression quickly dispelled, however, when he began to speak. Meghan liked Tom but knew that his nickname, 'Lethal Weicker', had been earned. When he began borrowing her from the radio station he'd made it clear that it was a tough, lousy break that her father had lost his life in

9

the bridge tragedy, but he needed her reassurance that it wouldn't affect her job performance.

It hadn't, and now Meghan heard herself being offered the job she wanted so badly.

The immediate, reflexive reaction that flooded through her was, I can't wait to tell Dad!

Thirty floors below, in the garage of the PCD building, Bernie Heffernan, the parking attendant, was in Tom Weicker's car, going through the glove compartment. By some genetic irony, Bernie's features had been formed to give him the countenance of a merry soul. His cheeks were plump, his chin and mouth small, his eyes wide and guileless, his hair thick and rumpled, his body sturdy, if somewhat rotund. At thirty-five the immediate impression he gave to observers was that he was a guy who, though wearing his best suit, would fix your flat tire.

He still lived with his mother in the shabby house in Jackson Heights, Queens, where he'd been born. The only times he'd been away from it were those dark, nightmarish periods when he was incarcerated. The day after his twelfth birthday he was sent to a juvenile detention center for the first of a dozen times. In his early twenties he'd spent three years in a psychiatric facility. Four years ago he was sentenced to ten months in Riker's Island. That was when the police caught him hiding in a college student's car. He'd been warned a dozen times to stay away from her. Funny, Bernie thought – he couldn't even remember what she looked like now. Not her and not any of them. And they had all been so important to him at the time.

Bernie never wanted to go to jail again. The other inmates frightened him. Twice they beat him up. He had sworn to Mama that he'd never hide in shrubs and look in windows again, or follow a woman and try to kiss her. He was getting very good at controlling his temper too. He'd hated the psychiatrist who kept warning Mama that one day that vicious temper would get Bernie into trouble no one could fix. Bernie knew that nobody had to worry about him anymore.

His father had taken off when he was a baby. His embittered mother no longer ventured outside, and at home Bernie had to endure her incessant reminders of all the inequities life had inflicted on her during her seventy-three years and how much he owed her.

Well, whatever he 'owed' her, Bernie managed to spend most of his money on electronic equipment. He had a radio that scanned police calls, another radio powerful enough to receive programs from all over the world, a voice-altering device.

At night he dutifully watched television with his mother. After she went to bed at ten o'clock, however, Bernie snapped off the television, rushed down to the basement, turned on the radios and began to call talk show hosts. He made up names and backgrounds to give them. He'd call a right-wing host and rant liberal values, a liberal host and sing the praises of the extreme right. In his call-in persona, he loved arguments, confrontations, trading insults.

Unknown to his mother he also had a forty-inch television and a VCR in the basement and often watched movies he had brought home from porn shops.

The police scanner inspired other ideas. He began to go through telephone books and circle numbers that were listed in women's names. He would dial one of those numbers in the middle of the night and say he was calling from a cellular phone outside her home and was about to break in. He'd whisper that maybe he'd just pay a visit, or maybe he'd kill her. Then Bernie would sit and chuckle as he listened to the police scanners sending a squad car rushing to the address. It was almost as good as peeking in windows or following women, and he never had to worry about the headlights of a police car suddenly shining on him, or a cop on a loudspeaker yelling, 'Freeze.'

The car belonging to Tom Weicker was a gold mine of information for Bernie. Weicker had an electronic address book in the glove compartment. In it he kept the names, addresses and numbers of the key staff of the station. The big shots, Bernie thought, as he copied numbers onto his own electronic pad. He'd even reached Weicker's wife at home one night. She had begun to shriek when he told her he was at the back door and on his way in.

Afterwards, recalling her terror, he'd giggled for hours.

What was getting hard for him now was that for the first time since he was released from Riker's Island, he had that scary feeling of not being able to get someone out of his mind. This one was a reporter. She was so pretty that when he opened the car door for her it was a struggle not to touch her.

Her name was Meghan Collins.

4

Somehow Meghan was able to accept Weicker's offer calmly. It was a joke among the staff that if you were too gee-whiz-thanks about a promotion, Tom Weicker would ponder whether or not he'd made a good choice. He wanted ambitious, driven people who felt any recognition given them was overdue.

Trying to seem matter-of-fact, she showed him the faxed message. As he read it he raised his eyebrows. 'What's this mean?' he asked. 'What's the "mistake"? Who is Annie?'

'I don't know. Tom, I was at Roosevelt Hospital when

the stabbing victim was brought in last night. Has she been identified?'

'Not yet. What about her?'

'I suppose you ought to know something,' Meghan said reluctantly. 'She looks like me.'

'She resembles you?'

'She could almost be my double.'

Tom's eyes narrowed. 'Are you suggesting that this fax is tied into that woman's death?'

'It's probably just coincidence, but I thought I should at least let you see it.'

'I'm glad you did. Let me keep it. I'll find out who's handling the investigation on that case and let him take a look at it.'

For Meghan, it was a distinct relief to pick up her assignments at the news desk.

It was a relatively tame day. A press conference at the mayor's office at which he named his choice for the new police commissioner, a suspicious fire that had gutted a tenement in Washington Heights. Late in the afternoon, Meghan spoke to the medical examiner's office. An artist's sketch of the dead girl and her physical description had been issued by the Missing Persons Bureau. Her fingerprints were on the way to Washington to be checked against government and criminal files. She had died of a single deep stab wound in the chest. Internal bleeding had been slow but massive. Both legs and arms had been broken some years ago. If not claimed in thirty days, her body would be buried in potter's field in a numbered grave. Another Jane Doe.

At six o'clock that evening, Meghan was just leaving work. As she'd been doing since her father's disappearance, she was going to spend the weekend in Connecticut with her mother. On Sunday afternoon, she was assigned to cover an event at the Manning Clinic, an assisted reproduction facility located forty minutes from their home in Newtown. The clinic was having its

13

annual reunion of children born as a result of in vitro fertilization carried out there.

The assignment editor collared her at the elevator. 'Steve will handle the camera on Sunday at Manning. I told him to meet you there at three.'

'Okay.'

During the week, Meghan used a company vehicle. This morning she'd driven her own car uptown. The elevator jolted to a stop at the garage level. She smiled as Bernie spotted her and immediately began trotting to the lower parking level. He brought up her white Mustang and held the door open for her. 'Any news about your dad?' he asked solicitously.

'No, but thanks for asking.'

He bent over, bringing his face close to hers. 'My mother and I are praying.'

What a nice guy! Meghan thought, as she steered the car up the ramp to the exit.

5

Catherine Collins' hair always looked as though she'd just run a hand through it. It was a short, curly mop, now tinted ash blond, that accentuated the pert prettiness of her heart-shaped face. She occasionally reminded Meghan that it was a good thing she'd inherited her own father's determined jaw. Otherwise, now that she was fifty-three, she'd look like a fading Kewpie doll, an impression enhanced by her diminutive size. Barely five feet tall, she referred to herself as the house midget.

Meghan's grandfather Patrick Kelly had come to the United States from Ireland at age nineteen, 'with the clothes on my back and one set of underwear rolled under my arm', as the story went. After working days as a dishwasher in the kitchen of a Fifth Avenue hotel and nights with the cleaning crew of a funeral home, he'd concluded that, while there were a lot of things people could do without, nobody could give up eating or dying. Since it was more cheerful to watch people eat than lie in a casket with carnations scattered over them, Patrick Kelly decided to put all his energies into the food business.

Twenty-five years later, he built the inn of his dreams in Newtown, Connecticut, and named it Drumdoe after the village of his birth. It had ten guest rooms and a fine restaurant that drew people from a radius of fifty miles. Pat completed the dream by renovating a charming farmhouse on the adjoining property as a home. He then chose a bride, fathered Catherine and ran his inn until his death at eighty-eight.

His daughter and granddaughter were virtually raised in that inn. Catherine now ran it with the same dedication to excellence that Patrick had instilled in her, and her work there had helped her cope with her husband's death.

Yet, in the nine months since the bridge tragedy, she had found it impossible not to believe that someday the door would open and Ed would cheerfully call, 'Where are my girls?' Sometimes she still found herself listening for the sound of her husband's voice.

Now, in addition to all the shock and grief, her finances had become an urgent problem. Two years earlier, Catherine had closed the inn for six months, mortgaged it and completed a massive renovation and redecoration project.

The timing could not have been worse. The reopening coincided with the downward trend of the economy. The payments on the new mortgage were not being met by present income, and quarterly taxes were coming

15

due. Her personal account had only a few thousand dollars left in it.

For weeks after the accident, Catherine had steeled herself for the call that would inform her that her husband's body had been retrieved from the river. Now she prayed for that call to come and end the uncertainty.

There was such a total sense of incompletion. Catherine would often think that people who ignored funeral rites didn't understand that they were necessary to the spirit. She wanted to be able to visit Ed's grave. Pat, her father, used to talk about 'a decent Christian burial'. She and Meg would joke about that. When Pat spotted the name of a friend from the past in the obituary column, she or Meg would tease, 'Oh, by God, I hope he had a decent Christian burial.'

They didn't joke about that anymore.

On Friday afternoon, Catherine was in the house, getting ready to go to the inn for the dinner hour. Talk about TGIF, she thought. Friday meant Meg would soon be home for the weekend.

The insurance people were due momentarily. If they'll even give me a partial payout until the Thruway divers found wreckage of the car, Catherine thought as she fastened a pin on the lapel of her houndstooth jacket. I need the money. They're just trying to wiggle out of double indemnity, but I'm willing to waive that until they have the proof they keep talking about.

But when the two somber executives arrived it was not to begin the process of payment. 'Mrs Collins,' the older of the two said, 'I hope you will understand our position. We sympathize with you and understand the predicament you are in. The problem is that we cannot authorize payment on your husband's policies without a death certificate, and that is not going to be issued.'

Catherine stared at him. 'You mean it's not going to be issued until they have absolute proof of his death?

16

But suppose his body was carried downriver clear into the Atlantic?'

Both men looked uneasy. The younger one answered her. 'Mrs Collins, the New York Thruway Authority, as owner and operator of the Tappan Zee Bridge, has conducted exhaustive operations to retrieve both victims and wreckage from the river. Granted, the explosions meant that the vehicles were shattered. Nevertheless, heavy parts like transmissions and engines don't disintegrate. Besides the tractor trailer and fuel tanker, six vehicles went over the side, or seven if we were to include your husband's car. Parts from all the others have been retrieved. All the other bodies have been recovered as well. There isn't so much as a wheel or tire or door or engine part of a Cadillac in the riverbed below the accident site.'

'Then you're saying . . .' Catherine was finding it hard to form the words.

'We're saying that the exhaustive report on the accident about to be released by the Thruway Authority categorically states that Edwin Collins could not have perished in the bridge tragedy that night. The experts feel that even though he may have been in the vicinity of the bridge, no one believes Edwin Collins was a victim. We believe he escaped being caught with the cars that were involved in the accident and took advantage of that propitious happening to make the disappearance he was planning. We think he reasoned he could take care of you and your daughter through the insurance and go on to whatever new life he had already planned to begin.'

17

6

Mac, as Dr Jeremy MacIntyre was known, lived with his seven-year-old son, Kyle, around the bend from the Collins family. The summers of his college years at Yale, Mac had worked as a waiter at the Drumdoe Inn. In those summers he'd formed a lasting attachment for the area and decided that someday he'd live there.

Growing up, Mac had observed that he was the guy in the crowd the girls didn't notice. Average height, average weight, average looks. It was a reasonably accurate description, but actually Mac did not do himself justice. After they took a second look, women *did* find a challenge in the quizzical expression in his hazel eyes, an endearing boyishness in the sandy hair that always seemed wind tousled, a comforting steadiness in the authority with which he would lead them on the dance floor or tuck a hand under their elbow on an icy evening.

Mac had always known he would be a doctor someday. By the time he began his studies at NYU medical school he had begun to believe that the future of medicine was in genetics. Now thirty-six, he worked at LifeCode, a genetic research laboratory in Westport, some fifty minutes southeast of Newtown.

It was the job he wanted, and it fit into his life as a divorced, custodial father. At twenty-seven Mac had married. The marriage lasted a year and a half and produced Kyle. Then one day Mac came home from the lab to find a babysitter and a note. It read: 'Mac, this isn't for me. I'm a lousy wife and a lousy mother.

We both know it can't work. I've got to have a crack at a career. Take good care of Kyle. Goodbye, Ginger.'

Ginger had done pretty well for herself since then. She sang in cabarets in Vegas and on cruise ships. She'd cut a few records, and the last one had hit the charts. She sent Kyle expensive presents for his birthday and Christmas. The gifts were invariably too sophisticated or too babyish. She'd seen Kyle only three times in the seven years since she'd taken off.

Despite the fact that it had almost come as a relief, Mac still harbored residual bitterness over Ginger's desertion. Somehow, divorce had never been a part of his imagined future, and he still felt uncomfortable with it. He knew that his son missed having a mother, so he took special care and special pride in being a good, attentive father.

On Friday evenings, Mac and Kyle often had dinner at the Drumdoe Inn. They ate in the small, informal grill, where the special Friday menu included individual pizzas and fish and chips.

Catherine was always at the inn for the dinner hour. Growing up, Meg had been a fixture there too. When she was ten and Mac a nineteen-year-old busboy, she had wistfully told him that it was fun to eat at home. 'Daddy and I do sometimes, when he's here.'

Since her father's disappearance, Meg spent just about every weekend at home and joined her mother at the inn for dinner. But this Friday night there was no sign of either Catherine or Meg.

Mac acknowledged that he was disappointed, but Kyle, who always looked forward especially to seeing Meg, dismissed her absence. 'So she's not here. Fine.'

'Fine' was Kyle's new all-purpose word. He used it when he was enthusiastic, disgusted or being cool. Tonight, Mac wasn't quite sure what emotion he was hearing. But hey, he told himself, give the kid space. If something's really bothering him it'll come out sooner

19

or later, and it certainly can't have anything to do with Meghan.

Kyle finished the last of the pizza in silence. He was mad at Meghan. She always acted like she really was interested in the stuff that he did, but Wednesday afternoon, when he was outside and had just taught his dog, Jake, to stand up on his hind legs and beg, Meghan had driven past and ignored him. She'd been going real slow, too, and he'd yelled to her to stop. He knew she'd seen him, because she'd looked right at him. But then she'd speeded up the car, driven off, and hadn't even taken time to see Jake's trick. Fine.

He wouldn't tell his dad about it. Dad would say that Meghan was just upset because Mr Collins hadn't come home for a long time and might have been one of the people whose car went into the river off the bridge. He'd say that sometimes when people were thinking about something else, they could go right past people and not even see them. But Meg *had* seen Kyle Wednesday and hadn't even bothered to wave to him.

Fine, he thought. Just fine.

7

When Meghan arrived home she found her mother sitting in the darkened living room, her hands folded in her lap. 'Mom, are you okay?' she asked anxiously. 'It's nearly seven-thirty. Aren't you going to Drumdoe?' She switched on the light and took in Catherine's blotched, tear-stained face. She sank to her knees and grabbed her mother's hands. 'Oh God, did they find him? Is that it?'

'No, Meggie, that's not it.' Haltingly Catherine Collins related the visit from the insurers.

Not Dad, Meghan thought. He couldn't, wouldn't do this to Mother. Not to her. There had to be a mistake. 'That's the craziest thing I ever heard,' she said firmly.

'That's what I told them. But Meg, why would Dad have borrowed so much on the insurance? That haunts me. And even if he did invest it, I don't know where. Without a death certificate, my hands are tied. I can't keep up with expenses. Phillip has been sending Dad's monthly draw from the company, but that's not fair to him. Most of the money due him in commissions has been in for some time. I know I'm conservative by nature, but I certainly wasn't when I renovated the inn. I really overdid it. Now I may have to sell Drumdoe.'

The inn. It was Friday night. Her mother should be there now, in her element, greeting guests, keeping a watchful eye on the waiters and busboys, the table settings, sampling the dishes in the kitchen. Every detail automatically checked and rechecked.

'Dad didn't do this to you,' Meg said flatly. 'I just know that.'

Catherine Collins broke into harsh, dry sobs. 'Maybe Dad used the bridge accident as a chance to get away from me. But why, Meg? I loved him so much.'

Meghan put her arms around her mother. 'Listen,' she said firmly, 'you were right the first time. Dad would never do this to you, and one way or the other, we're going to prove it.'

21

8

The Collins and Carter Executive Search office was located in Danbury, Connecticut. Edwin Collins had started the firm when he was twenty-eight, after having worked five years for a Fortune 500 company based in New York. By then he realized that working within the corporate structure was not for him.

Following his marriage to Catherine Kelly, he'd relocated his office to Danbury. They wanted to live in Connecticut, and the location of Edwin's office was not important since he spent much of his time traveling throughout the country, visiting clients.

Some twelve years before his disappearance, Collins had brought Phillip Carter into the business.

Carter, a Wharton graduate with the added attraction of a law degree, had previously been a client of Edwin's, having been placed by him in jobs several times. The last one before they joined forces was with a multinational firm in Maryland.

When Collins was visiting that client, he and Carter would have lunch or a drink together. Over the years they had developed a business-oriented friendship. In the early eighties, after a difficult midlife divorce, Phillip Carter finally left his job in Maryland to become Collins' partner and associate.

They were opposites in many ways. Collins was tall, classically handsome, an impeccable dresser and quietly witty, while Carter was bluff and hearty, with attractively irregular features and a thick head of graying hair. His clothes were expensive, but never looked quite put

22

together. His tie was often pulled loose from the knot. He was a man's man, whose stories over a drink brought forth bursts of laughter, a man with an eye for the ladies, too.

The partnership had worked. For a long time Phillip Carter lived in Manhattan and did reverse commuting to Danbury, when he was not traveling for the company. His name often appeared in the columns of the New York newspapers as having attended dinner parties and benefits with various women. Eventually he bought a small house in Brookfield, ten minutes from the office, and stayed there with increasing frequency.

Now fifty-three years old, Phillip Carter was a familiar figure in the Danbury area.

He regularly worked at his desk for several hours after everyone else had left for the day because, since a number of clients and candidates were located in the Midwest and on the West Coast, early evening in the East was a good time to contact them. Since the night of the bridge tragedy, Phillip rarely left the office before eight o'clock.

When Meghan called at five to eight this evening, he was reaching for his coat. 'I was afraid it was coming to this,' he said after she'd told him about the visit from the insurers. 'Can you come in tomorrow around noon?'

After he hung up he sat for a long time at his desk. Then he picked up the phone and called his accountant. 'I think we'd better audit the books right now,' he said quietly.

9

When Meghan arrived at the Collins and Carter Executive Search offices at two o'clock on Saturday, she found three men working with calculators at the long table that usually held magazines and plants. She did not need Phillip Carter's explanation to confirm that they were auditors. At his suggestion, they went into her father's private office.

She had spent a sleepless night, her mind a battleground of questions, doubts and denial. Phillip closed the door and indicated one of the two chairs in front of the desk. He took the other one, a subtlety she appreciated. It would have hurt to see him behind her father's desk.

She knew Phillip would be honest with her. She asked, 'Phillip, do you think it's remotely possible that my father is still alive and chose to disappear?'

The momentary pause before he spoke was answer enough. 'You *do* think that?' she prodded.

'Meg, I've lived long enough to know that anything is possible. Frankly, the Thruway investigators and the insurers have been around here for quite a while asking some pretty direct questions. A couple of times I've wanted to toss them out bodily. Like everyone else, I expected Ed's car, or wreckage from it, would be recovered. It's possible that a lot of it would have been carried downstream by the tide or become lodged in the riverbed, but it doesn't help that not a trace of the car has been found. So to answer you, yes, it's possible. And

24

no, I can't believe your father capable of a stunt like that.'

It was what she expected to hear, but that didn't make it easier. Once when she was very little, Meghan had tried to take a burning piece of bread out of the toaster with a fork. She felt as though she was experiencing again the vivid pain of electrical current shooting through her body.

'And of course it doesn't help that Dad took the cash value out of his policies a few weeks before he disappeared.'

'No, it doesn't. I want you to know that I'm doing the audit for your mother's sake. When this becomes public knowledge, and be sure it will, I want to be able to have a certified statement that our books are in perfect order. This sort of thing starts rumors flying, as you can understand.'

Meghan looked down. She had dressed in jeans and a matching jacket. It occurred to her that this was the kind of outfit the dead woman was wearing when she was brought into Roosevelt Hospital. She pushed the thought away. 'Was my father a gambler? Would that explain his need for a cash loan?'

Carter shook his head. 'Your father wasn't a gambler, and I've seen enough of them, Meg.' He grimaced. 'Meg, I wish I could find an answer, but I can't. Nothing in Ed's business or personal life suggested to me that he would choose to disappear. On the other hand, the lack of physical evidence from the crash is necessarily suspicious, at least to outsiders.'

Meghan looked at the desk, the executive swivel chair behind it. She could picture her father sitting there, leaning back, his eyes twinkling, his hands clasped, fingers pointing up in what her mother called 'Ed's saint-and-martyr pose'.

She could see herself running into this office as a child. Her father always had candy for her, gooey chocolate bars, marshmallows, peanut brittle. Her mother

25

had tried to keep that kind of candy from her. 'Ed,' she'd protest, 'don't give her that junk. You'll ruin her teeth.'

'Sweets to the sweet, Catherine.'

Daddy's girl. Always. He was the fun parent. Mother was the one who made Meghan practice the piano and make her bed. Mother was the one who'd protested when she quit the law firm. 'For heaven's sake, Meg,' she had pleaded, 'give it more than six months; don't waste your education.'

Daddy had understood. 'Leave her alone, love,' he'd said firmly. 'Meg has a good head on her shoulders.'

Once when she was little Meghan had asked her father why he traveled so much.

'Ah, Meg,' he'd sighed. 'How I wish it wasn't necessary. Maybe I was born to be a wandering minstrel.'

Because he was away so much, when he came home he always tried to make it up. He'd suggest that instead of going to the inn he'd whip up dinner for the two of them at home. 'Meghan Anne,' he'd tell her, 'you're my date.'

This office has his aura, Meg thought. The handsome cherrywood desk he'd found in a Salvation Army store and stripped and refinished himself. The table behind it with pictures of her and her mother. The lion's-head bookends holding leather-bound books.

For nine months she had been mourning him as dead. She wondered if at this moment she was mourning him more. If the insurers were right, he had become a stranger. Meghan looked into Phillip Carter's eyes. 'They're not right,' she said aloud. 'I believe my father is dead. I believe that some wreckage of his car will still be found.' She looked around. 'But in fairness to you, we have no right to tie up this office. I'll come in next week and pack his personal effects.'

'We'll take care of that, Meg.'

'No. Please. I can sort things out better here. Mother's

26

in rough enough shape without watching me do it at home.'

Phillip Carter nodded. 'You're right, Meg. I'm worried about Catherine too.'

'That's why I don't dare tell her about what happened the other night.' She saw the deepening concern on his face as she told him about the stabbing victim who resembled her and the fax that came in the middle of the night.

'Meg, that's bizarre,' he said. 'I hope your boss follows it up with the police. We can't let anything happen to you.'

As Victor Orsini turned his key in the door of the Collins and Carter offices, he was surprised to realize it was unlocked. Saturday afternoon usually meant he had the place to himself. He had returned from a series of meetings in Colorado and wanted to go over mail and messages.

Thirty-one years old with a permanent tan, muscular arms and shoulders and a lean disciplined body, he had the look of an outdoorsman. His jet black hair and strong features were indicative of his Italian heritage. His intensely blue eyes were a throwback to his British grandmother.

Orsini had been working for Collins and Carter for nearly seven years. He hadn't expected to stay so long, in fact he'd always planned to use this job as a stepping-stone to a bigger firm.

His eyebrows raised when he pushed open the door and saw the auditors. In a deliberately impersonal tone, the head man told Orsini that Phillip Carter and Meghan Collins were in Edwin Collins' private office. He then hesitantly acquainted Victor with the insurers' theory that Collins had chosen to disappear.

'That's crazy.' Victor strode across the reception area and knocked on the closed door.

27

Carter opened it. 'Oh, Victor, good to see you. We didn't expect you today.'

Meghan turned to greet him. Orsini realized she was fighting back tears. He groped for something reassuring to say but could come up with nothing. He had been questioned by the investigators about the call Ed Collins made to him just before the accident. 'Yes,' he'd said at the time, 'Edwin said he was getting on the bridge. Yes, I'm sure he didn't say he was getting off it. Do you think I can't hear? Yes, he wanted to see me the next morning. There wasn't anything unusual about that. Ed used his car phone all the time.'

Victor suddenly wondered how long it would be before anyone questioned that it was his word alone that placed Ed Collins on the ramp to the Tappan Zee that night. It was not difficult for him to mirror the concern on Meghan's face when he shook the hand she extended to him.

10

At three o'clock on Sunday afternoon, Meg met Steve Boyle, the PCD cameraman, in the parking lot of the Manning Clinic.

The clinic was on a hillside two miles from Route 7 in rural Kent, a forty-minute drive north from her home. It had been built in 1890 as the residence of a shrewd businessman whose wife had had the good sense to restrain her ambitious husband from creating an ostentatious display on his meteoric rise to the status of merchant prince. She convinced him that, instead of the

28

pseudopalazzo he had planned, an English manor house was better suited to the beauty of the countryside.

'Prepared for children's hour?' Meghan asked the cameraman as they trudged up the walk.

'The Giants are on and we're stuck with the Munchkins,' Steve groused.

Inside the mansion, the spacious foyer functioned as a reception area. Oak-paneled walls held framed pictures of the children who owed their existence to the genius of modern science. Beyond, the great hall had the ambiance of a comfortable family room, with groupings of furniture that invited intimate conversations or could be angled for informal lectures.

Booklets with testimonials from grateful parents were scattered on tables. 'We wanted a child so badly. Our lives were incomplete. And then we made an appointment at the Manning Clinic . . .' 'I'd go to a friend's baby shower and try not to cry. Someone suggested I look into in vitro fertilization, and Jamie was born fifteen months later . . .' 'My fortieth birthday was coming, and I knew it would soon be too late . . .'

Every year, on the third Sunday in October, the children who had been born as a result of IVF at the Manning Clinic were invited to return with their parents for the annual reunion. Meghan learned that this year three hundred invitations were sent and over two hundred small alumni accepted. It was a large, noisy and festive party.

In one of the smaller sitting rooms, Meghan interviewed Dr George Manning, the silver-haired, seventy-year-old director of the clinic, and asked him to explain in vitro fertilization.

'In the simplest possible terms,' he explained, 'IVF is a method by which a woman who has great difficulty conceiving is sometimes able to have the baby or babies she wants so desperately. After her menstrual cycle has been monitored, she begins treatment. Fertility drugs are administered so that her ovaries are stimulated to release an abundance of follicles, which are then retrieved.

'The woman's partner is asked to provide a semen sample to inseminate the eggs contained in the follicles in the laboratory. The next day an embryologist checks to see which, if any, eggs have been fertilized. If success was achieved, a physician will transfer one or more of the fertilized eggs, which are now referred to as embryos, to the woman's uterus. If requested, the rest of the embryos will be cryopreserved for later implanation.

'After fifteen days, blood is drawn for the first pregnancy test.' The doctor pointed to the great hall. 'And as you can see from the crowd we have here today, many of those tests prove positive.'

'I certainly can,' Meg agreed. 'Doctor, what is the ratio of success to failure?'

'Still not as high as we'd prefer, but improving constantly,' he said solemnly.

'Thank you, Doctor.'

Trailed by Steve, Meghan interviewed several of the mothers, asking them to share their personal experiences with in vitro fertilization.

One of them, posing with her three handsome offspring, explained, 'They fertilized fourteen eggs and implanted three. One of them resulted in a pregnancy, and here he is.' She smiled down at her elder son. 'Chris is seven now. The other embryos were cryopreserved, or, in simpler terms, frozen. I came back five years ago, and Todd is the result. Then I tried again last year, and Jill is three months old. Some of the embryos didn't survive thawing, but I still have two cryopreserved embryos in the lab. In case I ever find time on my hands for another kid,' she said laughing as the four-year-old darted away.

'Have we got enough, Meghan?' Steve asked. 'I'd like to catch the last quarter of the Giants game.'

'Let me talk to one more staff member. I've been

30

watching that woman. She seems to know everybody's name.'

Meg went over to the woman and glanced at her name tag. 'May I have a word with you, Dr Petrovic?'

'Of course.' Petrovic's voice was well modulated, with a hint of an accent. She was of average height, with hazel eyes and refined features. She seemed courteous rather than friendly. Still, Meg noticed that she had a cluster of children around her.

'How long have you been at the clinic, Doctor?'

'It will be seven years in March. I'm the embryologist in charge of the laboratory.'

'Would you care to comment on what you feel about these children?'

'I feel that each one of them is a miracle.'

'Thank you, Doctor.'

'We've got enough footage inside,' Meg told Steve when they left Petrovic. 'I do want a shot of the group picture, though. They'll be gathering for it in a minute.'

The annual photo was taken on the front lawn outside the mansion. There was the usual confusion that attended lining up children from toddler age to nine-year-olds, with mothers holding infants standing in the last row and flanked by staff members.

The Indian summer day was bright, and as Steve focused the camera on the group, Meghan had the fleeting thought that every one of the children looked well dressed and happy. Why not? she thought. They were all desperately wanted.

A three-year-old ran from the front row to his pregnant mother, who was standing near Meghan. Blue eyed and golden haired, with a sweet, shy smile, he threw his arms around his mother's knees.

'Get a shot of that,' Meghan told Steve. 'He's adorable.' Steve held the camera on the little boy as his mother cajoled him to rejoin the other children.

'I'm right here, Jonathan,' she assured him as she placed him back in line. 'You can see me. I promise I'm

31

not going away.' She returned to where she had been standing.

Meghan walked over to the woman. 'Would you mind answering a few questions?' she asked, holding out the mike.

'I'd be glad to.'

'Will you give us your name and tell us how old your little boy is?'

'I'm Dina Anderson, and Jonathan is almost three.'

'Is your expected baby also the result of in vitro fertilization?'

'Yes, as a matter of fact, he's Jonathan's identical twin.'

'Identical twin!' Meghan knew she sounded astonished.

'I know it sounds impossible,' Dina Anderson said happily, 'but that's the way it is. It's extremely rare, but an embryo can split in the laboratory just the way it would in the womb. When we were told that one of the fertilized eggs had divided, my husband and I decided that I would try to give birth to each twin separately. We felt that individually they might each have a better chance for survival in my womb, and actually it's practical. I've got a responsible job, and I'd hate to have left two infants with a nanny.'

The photographer for the clinic had been snapping pictures. A moment later he yelled, 'Okay kids, thanks.' The children scattered, and Jonathan ran to his mother. Dina Anderson scooped up her son in her arms. 'I can't imagine life without him,' she said. 'And in about ten days we'll have Ryan.'

What a human interest segment that would make, Meghan thought. 'Mrs Anderson,' she said persuasively, 'if you're willing, I'd like to talk to my boss about doing a feature story on your twins.'

11

On the way back to Newtown, Meghan used the car phone to call her mother. Her alarm at getting the answering machine turned to relief when she dialed the inn and was told Mrs Collins was in the dining room. 'Tell her I'm on my way,' she instructed the receptionist, 'and that I'll meet her there.'

For the next fifteen minutes Meghan drove as though on automatic pilot. She was excited about the possibility of the feature story she would pitch to Weicker. And she could get some guidance on it from Mac. He was a specialist in genetics. He'd be able to give her expert advice and reading material she could study to know more about the whole spectrum of assisted reproduction, including the statistics on success and failure rates. When the traffic slowed to a halt, she picked up her car phone and dialed his number.

Kyle answered. Meghan raised her eyebrow at the way his tone changed when he realized she was the caller. What's eating him? she wondered, as he pointedly ignored her greeting and passed the phone to his father.

'Hi, Meghan. What can I do for you?' As always the sound of Mac's voice gave Meghan a stab of familiar pain. She'd called him her best friend when she was ten, had a crush on him when she was twelve, and had fallen in love with him by the time she was sixteen. Three years later he married Ginger. She'd been at the wedding, and it was one of the hardest days of her life. Mac had been crazy about Ginger, and Meg suspected that even after seven years, if Ginger had walked in the door and drop-

33

ped her suitcase, he'd *still* want her. Meg would never let herself admit that no matter how hard she tried, she'd never been able to stop loving Mac.

'I could use some professional help, Mac.' As the car passed the blocked lane and picked up speed, she explained the visit to the clinic and the story she was putting together. 'And I sort of need the information in a hurry so I can pitch the whole thing to my boss.'

'I can give it to you right away. Kyle and I are just heading for the inn. I'll bring it along. Want to join us for dinner?'

'That works out fine. See you.' She broke the connection.

It was nearly seven when she reached the outskirts of town. The temperature was dropping, and the afternoon breeze had turned to gusts of wind. The headlights caught the trees, still heavy with leaves that were now restlessly moving, sending shadows over the road. At this moment, they made her think of the dark, choppy water of the Hudson.

Concentrate on how you'll pitch the idea of doing a special on the Manning Clinic to Weicker, she told herself fiercely.

Phillip Carter was in Drumdoe, at a window table set for three. He waved Meghan over. 'Catherine's in the kitchen giving the chef a hard time,' he told her. 'The people over there' – he nodded to a nearby table – 'wanted the beef rare. Your mother said what they got could have passed for a hockey puck. In fact, it was medium rare.'

Meghan sank into a chair and smiled. 'The best thing that could happen to her would be if the chef quit. Then she'd have to get back in the kitchen. It would keep her mind off things.' She reached across the table and touched Carter's hand. 'Thanks for coming over.'

'I hope you haven't eaten. I've managed to make Catherine promise to join me.'

34

'That's great, but how about if I have coffee with you? Mac and Kyle should be here any minute, and I said I'd join them. The truth is, I need to pick Mac's brain.'

At dinner, Kyle continued to be aloof to Meghan. Finally she raised her eyebrows in a questioning look at Mac, who shrugged and murmured, 'Don't ask me.' Mac cautioned her about the feature story she was planning. 'You're right. There are a lot of failures, and it's a very expensive procedure.'

Meg looked across the table at Mac and his son. They were so alike. She remembered the way her father had pressed her hand at Mac's wedding. He'd understood. He'd always understood her.

When they were ready to leave, she said, 'I'll sit with Mother and Phillip for a few minutes.' She put an arm round Kyle. 'See you, buddy.'

He pulled away.

'Hey, come on,' Meghan said. 'What's all this about?'

To her surprise she saw tears well in his eyes. 'I thought you were my friend.' He turned swiftly and ran to the door.

'I'll get it out of him,' Mac promised as he rushed to catch up with his son.

At seven o'clock, in nearby Bridgewater, Dina Anderson was holding Jonathan on her lap and sipping the last of her coffee as she told her husband about the party at the Manning Clinic. 'We may be famous,' she said. 'Meghan Collins, that reporter from Channel 3, wants to get the go-ahead from her boss to be in the hospital when the baby is born and get early pictures of Jonathan with his brand-new brother. If her boss agrees, she might want to do updates from time to time on how they interact.'

Donald Anderson looked doubtful. 'Honey, I'm not sure we need that kind of publicity.'

'Oh, come on. It could be fun. And I agree with

35

Meghan that if more people who want babies understood the different kinds of assisted birth, they'd realize IVF really is a viable option. This guy was certainly worth all the expense and effort.'

'This guy's head is going in your coffee.' Anderson got up, walked around the table and took his son from his wife's arms. 'Bedtime for Bonzo,' he announced, then added, 'If you want to do it, it's okay with me. I guess it would be fun to have some professional tapes of the kids.'

Dina watched affectionately as her blue-eyed, blond husband carried her equally fair child to the staircase. She had all Jonathan's baby pictures in readiness. It would be such fun to compare them with Ryan's pictures. She still had one cryopreserved embryo at the clinic. In two years we'll try for another baby, and maybe that one will look like me, she thought, glancing across the room to the mirror over the serving table. She studied her reflection, her olive skin, hazel eyes, coal black hair. 'That wouldn't be too bad a deal either,' she murmured to herself.

At the inn, lingering over a second cup of coffee with her mother and Phillip, Meghan listened as he soberly discussed her father's disappearance.

'Edwin's borrowing so heavily on his insurance without telling you plays right into the insurers' hands. As they told you, they're taking it as a signal that for his own reasons he was accumulating cash. Just as they won't pay his personal insurance, I've been notified they won't settle the partnership insurance either, which would be paid to you as satisfaction for his senior partnership in Executive Search.'

'Which means,' Catherine Collins said quietly, 'that because I cannot prove my husband is dead I stand to lose everything. Phillip, is Edwin owed any more money for past work?'

His answer was simple. 'No.'

36

'How is the headhunter business this year?'

'Not good.'

'You've advanced us $45,000 while we've been waiting for Edwin's body to be found.'

He suddenly looked stern. 'Catherine, I'm glad to do it. I only wish I could increase it. When we have proof of Ed's death, you can repay me out of the business insurance.'

She put a hand over his. 'I can't let you do that, Phillip. Old Pat would spin in his grave if he thought I was living on borrowed money. The fact is, unless we can find some proof that Edwin did die in that accident, I will lose the place my father spent his life creating, and I'll have to sell my home.' She looked at Meghan. 'Thank God I have you, Meggie.' That was when Meghan decided not to drive back to New York City as she had planned, but to stay the night.

When she and her mother got back to the house, by unspoken consent they did not talk any more about the man who had been husband and father. Instead they watched the ten o'clock news, then prepared for bed. Meghan knocked on the door of her mother's bedroom to say good night. She realized that she no longer thought of it as her parents' room. When she opened the door, she saw with a thrust of pain that her mother had moved her pillows to the center of the bed.

Meghan knew that was a clear message that if Edwin Collins was alive, there was no room for him anymore in this house.

37

12

Bernie Heffernan spent Sunday evening with his mother, watching television in the shabby sitting room of their bungalow-type home in Jackson Heights. He vastly preferred watching from the communications center he had created in the crudely finished basement room, but always stayed upstairs until his mother went to bed at ten. Since her fall ten years earlier, she never went near the rickety basement stairs.

Meghan's segment about the Manning Clinic was aired on the six o'clock news. Bernie stared at the screen, perspiration beading his brow. If he were downstairs now, he could be taping Meghan on his VCR.

'Bernard!' Mama's sharp voice broke into his reverie.

He plastered on a smile. 'Sorry, Mama.'

Her eyes were enlarged behind the rimless bifocals. 'I asked you if they ever found that woman's father.'

He'd mentioned Meghan's father to Mama once and always regretted it. He patted his mother's hand. 'I told her that we're praying for her, Mama.'

He didn't like the way Mama looked at him. 'You're not thinking on that woman, are you, Bernard?'

'No, Mama. Of course not, Mama.'

After his mother went to bed, Bernie went down to the basement. He felt tired and dispirited. There was only one way to get some relief.

He began his calls immediately. First the religious station in Atlanta. Using the voice-altering device, he shouted insults at the preacher until he was cut off.

Then he dialed a talk show in Massachusetts and told the host he'd overheard a murder plot against him.

At eleven he began calling women whose names he had checked off in the phone book. One by one he warned them that he was about to break in. From the sound of their voices he could picture how they looked. Young and pretty. Old. Plain. Slim. Heavy. Mentally he'd create the face, filling in the details of their features with each additional word they said.

Except tonight. Tonight they all had the same face.

Tonight they all looked like Meghan Collins.

13

When Meghan went downstairs Monday morning at six-thirty she found her mother already in the kitchen. The aroma of coffee filled the room, juice had been poured and bread was in the toaster. Meghan's protest that her mother should not have gotten up so early died on her lips. From the deep shadows around Catherine Collins' eyes, it was clear that she had slept little if at all.

Like me, Meghan thought, as she reached for the coffeepot. 'Mother, I've done a lot of thinking,' she said. Carefully choosing her words, she continued, 'I can't understand a single reason why Dad would choose to disappear. Let's say there was another woman. That certainly could happen, but if it did, Dad could have asked you for a divorce. You'd have been devastated, of course, and I'd have been angry for you, but in the end we're both realists, and Dad knew that. The insurance companies are hanging everything on the fact

39

that they haven't found either his body or the car, and that he borrowed against his own policies. But they were *his* policies, and as you said, he may have wanted to make some kind of investment he knew you wouldn't approve of. It *is* possible.'

'Anything's possible,' Catherine Collins said quietly, 'including the fact that I don't know what to do.'

'I do. We're going to file suit demanding payment of those policies, including double indemnity for accidental death. We're not going to sit back and let those people tell us that Dad pulled this on you.'

At seven o'clock Mac and Kyle sat across from each other at their kitchen table. Kyle had gone to bed still refusing to discuss his coolness toward Meg, but this morning his mood had changed. 'I was thinking,' he began.

Mac smiled. 'That's a good start.'

'I mean it. Remember last night Meg was talking about the case she was covering in court all day Wednesday?'

'Yes.'

'Then she couldn't have been up here Wednesday afternoon.'

'No, she wasn't.'

'Then I didn't see her drive by the house.'

Mac looked into his son's serious eyes. 'No, you wouldn't have seen her Wednesday afternoon. I'm sure of that.'

'I guess it was just somebody who looked a lot like her.' Kyle's relieved smile revealed two missing teeth. He glanced down at Jake, who was stretched out under the table. 'Now, by the time Meg gets a chance to see Jake when she comes home next weekend, he'll be *perfect* at begging.'

At the sound of his name, Jake jumped up and lifted his front paws.

'I'd say he's perfect at begging now,' Mac said dryly.

*

Meghan drove directly to the West Fifty-sixth Street garage entrance of the PCD building. Bernie had the driver's door open at the exact moment she shifted into Park. 'Hi, Miss Collins.' His beaming smile and warm voice brought a responsive smile to her lips. 'My mother and I saw you at that clinic, I mean we saw the news last night with you on. Must have been fun to be with all those kids.' His hand came out to assist her from the car.

'They were awfully cute, Bernie,' Meghan agreed.

'My mother said it seems kind of weird – you know what I mean – having babies the way those people do. I'm not much for all these crazy scientific fads.'

Breakthroughs, not fads, Meghan thought. 'I know what you mean,' she said. 'It does seem a little like something out of *Brave New World*.'

Bernie stared blankly at her.

'See you.' She headed for the elevator, her leather folder tucked under her arm.

Bernie watched her go, then got in her car and drove it down to the lower level of the garage. Deliberately he put it in a dark corner at the far wall. During lunch break all the guys chose a car to relax in, where they'd eat and read the paper or doze. The only management rule was to make sure you didn't smear ketchup on the upholstery. Ever since some dope burned the leather armrest of a Mercedes, no one was allowed to smoke, even in cars where the ashtray was filled with butts. The point was, nobody saw anything funny about always taking a break in the same car or the same couple of cars. Bernie felt happy sitting in Meghan's Mustang. It had a hint of the perfume she always wore.

Meghan's desk was in the Bull Pen on the thirtieth floor. Swiftly she read the assignment sheet. At eleven o'clock she was to be at the arraignment of an indicted inside stock trader.

41

Her phone rang. It was Tom Weicker. 'Meg, can you come in right away?'

There were two men in Weicker's private office. Meghan recognized one of them, Jamal Nader, a soft-spoken black detective whom she'd run into a number of times in court. They greeted each other warmly. Weicker introduced the other man as Lt Story.

'Lt Story is in charge of the homicide you covered the other night. I gave him the fax you received.'

Nader shook his head. 'That dead girl really is a lookalike for you, Meghan.'

'Has she been identified?' Meghan asked.

'No.' Nader hesitated. 'But she seems to have known you.'

'Known me?' Meghan stared at him. 'How do you figure that?'

'When they brought her into the morgue Thursday night they went through her clothing and found nothing. They sent everything to the district attorney's office to be stored as evidence. One of our guys went over it again. The lining of the jacket pocket had a deep fold. He found a sheet of paper torn from a Drumdoe Inn notepad. It had your name and direct phone number at WPCD written on it.'

'My name!'

Lt Story reached into his pocket. The piece of paper was encased in plastic. He held it up. 'Your first name and the number.'

Meghan and the two detectives were standing at Tom Weicker's desk. Meghan gripped the desktop as she stared at the bold letters, the slanted printing of the numbers. She felt her lips go dry.

'Miss Collins, do you recognize that handwriting?' Story asked sharply.

She nodded. 'Yes.'

'Who . . . ?'

She turned her head, not wanting to see that familiar writing anymore. 'My father wrote that,' she whispered.

14

On Monday morning, Phillip Carter reached the office at eight o'clock. As usual he was the first to arrive. The staff was small, consisting of Jackie, his fifty-year-old secretary, the mother of teenagers; Milly, the grandmotherly part-time bookkeeper, and Victor Orsini.

Carter had his own computer adjacent to his desk. In it he kept files that only he could access, files that listed his personal data. His friends joked about his love for going to land auctions, but they would have been astonished at the amount of rural property he had quietly amassed over the years. Unfortunately for him, much of the land he had acquired cheaply had been lost in his divorce settlement. The property he bought at sky-high prices he acquired after the divorce.

As he inserted the key in the computer he reflected that when Jackie and Milly learned that Edwin Collins' presumed death was being challenged, they would not lack for noon-hour gossip.

His essential sense of privacy recoiled at the notion that he would ever be the subject of one of the avid discussions Jackie and Milly shared as they lunched on salads that seemed to him to consist mostly of alfalfa sprouts.

The subject of Ed Collins' office worried him. It had seemed the decent thing to leave it as it was until the official pronouncement of his death, but now it was just as well Meghan had said she wanted to pack up her father's personal effects. One way or the other, Edwin Collins would never use it again.

43

Carter frowned. Victor Orsini. He just couldn't like the man. Orsini had always been closer to Ed, but he did a damn good job, and his expertise in the field of medical technology was absolutely necessary today, and particularly valuable now that Ed was gone. He had handled most of that area of the business.

Carter knew there was no way to avoid giving Orsini Ed's office when Meghan had finished clearing it out. Victor's present office was cramped and had only one small window.

Yes, for the present, he needed the man, like him or not.

Nevertheless, Phillip's intuition warned him that there was an elusive factor about Victor Orsini's makeup that should never be ignored.

Lt Story allowed a copy of the plastic-enclosed scrap of paper to be made for Meghan. 'How long ago were you assigned that phone number at the radio station?' he asked her.

'In mid-January.'

'When was the last time you saw your father?'

'On January 14th. He was leaving for California on a business trip.'

'What kind of business?'

Meghan's tongue felt thick, her fingers were chilled as she held the photocopy with her name looking incongruously bold against the white background. She told him about Collins and Carter Executive Search. It was obvious that Detective Jamal Nader had already told Story that her father was missing.

'Did your father have this number in his possession when he left?'

'He must have. I never spoke to him or saw him again after the fourteenth. He was due home on the twenty-eighth.'

'And he died in the Tappan Zee Bridge accident that night.'

44

'He called his associate Victor Orsini as he was starting onto the bridge. The accident happened less than a minute after their phone conversation. Someone reported seeing a dark Cadillac spin into the fuel tanker and go over the side.' It was useless to conceal what this man could learn by one phone call. 'I must tell you that the insurance companies have now refused to pay his policies on the basis that at least parts of all the other vehicles have been found, but there's been no trace of my father's car. The Thruway divers claim that if the car went into the river at that point, they should have located it.' Meghan's chin went up. 'My mother is filing suit to have the insurance paid.'

She could see the skepticism in the eyes of all three men. To her own ears – and with this paper in her hand – she sounded like one of those unfortunate witnesses she had seen in court trials, people who stick doggedly to their testimony even in the face of irrefutable proof that they are either mistaken or lying.

Story cleared his throat. 'Miss Collins, the young woman who was murdered Thursday night bears a striking resemblance to you and was carrying a slip of paper with your name and phone number written on it in your father's handwriting. Have you any explanation?'

Meghan stiffened her back. 'I have no idea why that young woman was carrying that piece of paper. I have no idea how she got it. She did look a lot like me. For all I know my father might have met her and commented on the similarity and said, "If you're ever in New York, I'd like you to meet my daughter." People do resemble each other. We all know that. My father was in the kind of business where he met many people; knowing him, that would be the kind of comment he'd make. There is one thing I am sure of, if my father were alive, he would not have deliberately disappeared and left my mother financially paralyzed.'

45

She turned to Tom. 'I'm assigned to cover the Baxter arraignment. I'd better get moving.'

'You okay?' Tom asked. There was no hint of pity in his manner.

'I'm absolutely fine,' Meghan said quietly. She did not look at Story or Nader.

It was Nader who spoke. 'Meghan, we're in touch with the FBI. If there's been any report of a missing woman who fits the description of Thursday night's stabbing victim, we'll have it soon. Maybe a lot of answers are tied up together.'

15

Helene Petrovic loved her job as embryologist in charge of the laboratory of the Manning Clinic. Widowed at twenty-seven, she had emigrated to the United States from Rumania, gratefully accepted the largess of a family friend, worked for her as a cosmetician and begun to go to school at night.

Now forty-eight, she was a slender, handsome woman whose eyes never smiled. During the week, Helene lived in New Milford, Connecticut, five miles from the clinic, in the furnished condo she rented. Weekends were spent in Lawrenceville, New Jersey, in the pleasant colonial-style house she owned. The study off her bedroom there was filled with pictures of the children she had helped bring into life.

Helene thought of herself as the chief pediatrician of a nursery for newborns on the maternity ward of a fine hospital. The difference was that the embryos in her

46

care were more vulnerable than the frailest preemie. She took her responsibility with fierce seriousness.

Helene would look at the tiny vials in the laboratory, and, knowing the parents and sometimes the siblings, in her mind's eye she saw the children who might someday be born. She loved them all, but there was one child she loved the best, the beautiful towhead whose sweet smile reminded her of the husband she had lost as a young woman.

The arraignment of the stockbroker Baxter on inside trader charges took place in the courthouse on Centre Street. Flanked by his two attorneys, the impeccably dressed defendant pleaded not guilty, his firm voice suggesting the authority of the boardroom. Steve was Meg's cameraman again. 'What a con artist. I'd almost rather be back in Connecticut with the Munchkins.'

'I wrote up a memo and left it for Tom – about doing a feature on that clinic. This afternoon I'm going to pitch it to him,' Meghan said.

Steve winked. 'If I ever have kids, I hope to have them the old-fashioned way, if you know what I mean.'

She smiled briefly. 'I know what you mean.'

At four o'clock, Meghan was again in Tom's office. 'Meghan, let me get this straight. You mean this woman is about to give birth to the identical twin of her three-year-old?'

'That's exactly what I mean. That kind of divided birth has been done in England, but it's news here. Plus the mother in this case is quite interesting. Dina Anderson is a bank vice president, very attractive and well spoken, and obviously a terrific mother. And the three-year-old is a doll.

'Another point is that so many studies have shown that identical twins, even when separated at birth, grow up with identical tastes. It can be eerie. They may marry people with the same name, call their children by the

47

same names, decorate their houses in the same colors, wear the same hairstyle, choose the same clothes. It would be interesting to know how the relationship would change if one twin is significantly older than the other.

'Think about it,' she concluded. 'It's only fifteen years since the miracle of the first test tube baby, and now there are thousands of them. There are more new breakthroughs in assisted reproduction methods every day. I think ongoing segments on the new methods – and updates on the Anderson twins – could be terrific.'

She spoke eagerly, warming to her argument. Tom Weicker was not an easy sell.

'How sure is Mrs Anderson that she's having the identical twin?'

'Absolutely positive. The cryopreserved embryos are in individual tubes, marked with the mother's name, Social Security number and date of her birth. And each tube is given its own number. After Jonathan's embryo was transferred, the Andersons had two embryos, his identical twin and one other. The tube with his identical twin was specially labeled.'

Tom got up from his desk and stretched. He'd taken off his coat, loosened his tie and opened his collar button. The effect was to soften his usual flinty exterior.

He walked over to the window, stared down at the snarled traffic on West Fifty-sixth Street, then turned abruptly. 'I liked what you did with the Manning reunion yesterday. We've gotten good response. Go ahead with it.'

He was letting her do it! Meghan nodded, reminding herself that enthusiasm was out of order.

Tom went back to his desk. 'Meghan, take a look at this. It's an artist's sketch of the woman who was stabbed Thursday night.' He handed it to her.

Even though she had seen the victim, Meghan's mouth went dry when she looked at the sketch. She read the statistics, 'Caucasian, dark brown hair, blue-

48

green eyes, 5'6", slender build, 120 pounds, 24–28 years old.' Add an inch to the height and they'd describe her.

'If that "mistake" fax was on the level and meant you were the intended victim, it's pretty clear why this girl is dead,' Weicker commented. 'She was right in this neighborhood, and the resemblance to you is uncanny.'

'I simply don't understand it. Nor do I understand how she got that slip of paper with my father's writing.'

'I spoke to Lt Story again. We both agreed that until the killer is found it would be better to pull you off the news beat, just in case there is some kind of nut gunning for you.'

'But, Tom – ' she protested. He cut her off.

'Meghan, concentrate on that feature. It could make a darned good human interest story. If it works, we'll do future segments on those kids. But as of now, you are off the news beat. Keep me posted,' he snapped as he sat down and pulled out a desk drawer, clearly dismissing her.

16

By Monday afternoon, the Manning Clinic had settled down from the excitement of the weekend reunion. All traces of the festive party were gone, and the reception area was restored to its usual quiet elegance.

A couple in their late thirties was leafing through magazines as they waited for their first appointment. The receptionist, Marge Walters, looked at them sympathetically. She had had no problem having three children in the first three years of her marriage. Across the room an obviously nervous woman in her twenties

49

was holding her husband's hand. Marge knew the young woman had an appointment to have embryos implanted in her womb. Twelve of her eggs had become fertilized in the lab. Three would be implanted in the hope that one might result in a pregnancy. Sometimes more than one embryo developed, leading to a multiple birth.

'That would be a blessing, not a problem,' the young woman had assured Marge when she signed in. The other nine embryos would be cryopreserved. If a pregnancy did not result this time, the young woman would come back and be implanted with some of those embryos.

Dr Manning had called an unexpected lunchtime staff meeting. Unconsciously, Marge riffled her fingers through short blond hair. Dr Manning had told them that PCD Channel 3 was going to do a television special on the clinic and tie it in with the impending birth of Jonathan Anderson's identical twin. He asked that all cooperation be given to Meghan Collins, respecting of course the privacy of the clients. Only those clients who agreed in writing would be interviewed.

Marge hoped that she'd get to appear in the special. Her boys would get such a kick out of it.

To the right of her desk were the offices for senior staff. The door leading to those offices opened and one of the new secretaries came out, her step brisk. She paused at Marge's desk long enough to whisper, 'Something's up. Dr Petrovic just came out of Manning's office. She's very upset, and when I went in, he looked as though he was about to have a heart attack.'

'What do you think is going on?' Marge asked.

'I don't know, but she's cleaning out her desk. I wonder if she quit – or was fired?'

'I can't imagine her choosing to leave this place,' Marge said in disbelief. 'That lab is her whole life.'

On Monday evening, when Meghan picked up her car, Bernie had said, 'See you tomorrow, Meghan.'

She had told him that she wouldn't be around the office for a while, that she would be on special assignment in Connecticut. Saying that to Bernie had been easy, but as she drove home, she wrestled with the problem of how to explain to her mother that she'd been switched from the news team after just getting the job.

She'd simply have to say that the station wanted the feature to be completed quickly because of the impending birth of the Anderson baby. Mom's upset enough without having to worry that I might have been an intended murder victim, Meghan thought, and she'd be a wreck if she knew about the slip of paper with Dad's writing.

She exited Interstate 84 onto Route 7. Some trees still had leaves, although the vivid colors of mid-October had faded. Fall had always been her favorite season, she reflected. But not this year.

A part of her brain, the legal part, the portion that separated emotion from evidence, insisted that she begin to consider all the reasons why that paper with her name and phone number could have been in the dead woman's pocket. It's not disloyal to examine all the possibilities, she reminded herself fiercely. A good defense lawyer must always see the case through the prosecutor's eyes as well.

Her mother had gone through all the papers that were in the wall safe at home. But she knew her mother had not examined the contents of the desk in her father's study. It was time to do that.

She hoped she had taken care of everything at the newsroom. Before she left, Meg made a list of her ongoing assignments for Bill Evans, her counterpart from the Chicago affiliate, who would sub for her on the news team while the murder investigation was going on.

Her appointment with Dr Manning was set for tomorrow at eleven o'clock. She'd asked him if she

51

could go through an initial information and counseling session as though she were a new client. During a sleepless night, something else had occurred to her. It would be a nice touch to get some tape on Jonathan Anderson helping his mother prepare for the baby. She wondered if the Andersons had any home videos of Jonathan as a newborn.

When she reached home, the house was empty. That had to mean her mother was at the inn. Good, Meghan thought. It's the best place for her. She lugged in the fax machine they'd lent her at the office. She'd hook it up to the second line in her father's study. At least I won't be awakened by crazy, middle-of-the-night messages, she thought as she closed and locked the door and began switching on lights against the rapidly approaching darkness.

Meghan sighed unconsciously as she walked around the house. She'd always loved this place. The rooms weren't large. Her mother's favorite complaint was that old farmhouses always looked bigger on the outside than they actually were. 'This place is an optical illusion,' she would lament. But in Meghan's eyes there was great charm in the intimacy of the rooms. She liked the feel of the slightly uneven floor with its wide boards, the look of the fireplaces and the French doors and the built-in corner cupboards of the dining room. In her eyes they were the perfect setting for the antique maple furniture with its lovely warm patina, the deep comfortable upholstery, the colorful hand-hooked rugs.

Dad was away so much, she thought as she opened the door of his study, a room that she and her mother had avoided since the night of the bridge accident. But you always knew he was coming back, and he was so much fun.

She snapped on the desk lamp and sat in the swivel chair. This room was the smallest on the first floor. The fireplace was flanked by bookshelves. Her father's favorite chair, maroon leather with a matching ottoman,

52

had a standing lamp on one side and a piecrust table on the other.

The table as well as the mantel held clusters of family pictures: her mother and father's wedding portrait; Meghan as a baby; the three of them as she grew up; old Pat, bursting with pride in front of the Drumdoe Inn. The record of a happy family, Meghan thought, looking from one to another of a group of framed snapshots.

She picked up the picture of her father's mother, Aurelia. Taken in the early thirties when she was twenty-four, it showed clearly that she had been a beautiful woman. Thick wavy hair, large expressive eyes, oval face, slender neck, sable skins over her suit. Her expression was the dreamy posed look that photographers of that day preferred. 'I had the prettiest mother in Pennsylvania,' her father would say, then add, 'and now I have the prettiest daughter in Connecticut. You look like her.' His mother had died when he was a baby.

Meghan did not remember ever having seen a picture of Richard Collins. 'We never got along,' her father had told her tersely. 'The less I saw of him, the better.'

The phone rang. It was Virginia Murphy, her mother's right-hand at the inn. 'Catherine wanted me to see if you were home and if you wanted to come over for dinner.'

'How is she, Virginia?' Meghan asked.

'She's always good when she's here, and we have a lot of reservations tonight. Mr Carter is coming at seven. He wants your mother to join him.'

Hmm, Meghan thought. She'd always suspected that Phillip Carter was developing a warm spot in his heart for Catherine Collins. 'Will you tell Mom that I have an interview in Kent tomorrow and need to do a lot of research for it? I'll fix something here.'

When she hung up, she resolutely got out her briefcase and pulled from it all the newspaper and magazine human interest stories on in vitro fertilization a

53

researcher at the station had assembled for her. She frowned when she found several cases where a clinic was sued because tests showed the woman's husband was not the biological father of the child. 'That is a pretty serious mistake to make,' she said aloud, and decided that it was an angle that should be touched on in one segment of the feature.

At eight o'clock she made a sandwich and a pot of tea and carried them back to the study. She ate while she tried to absorb the technical material Mac had given her. It was, she decided, a crash course in assisted reproductive procedures.

The click of the lock a little after ten meant that her mother was home. She called, 'Hi, I'm in here.'

Catherine Collins hurried into the room. 'Meggie, you're all right?'

'Of course. Why?'

'Just now when I was coming up the driveway I got the queerest feeling about you, that something was wrong – almost like a premonition.'

Meghan forced a chuckle, got up swiftly and hugged her mother. 'There *was* something wrong,' she said. 'I've been trying to absorb the mysteries of DNA, and believe me, it's tough. I now know why Sister Elizabeth told me I had no head for science.'

She was relieved to see the tension ease from her mother's face.

Helene Petrovic swallowed nervously as she packed the last of her suitcases at midnight. She left out only her toiletries and the clothes she would wear in the morning. She was frantic to be finished with it all. She had become so jumpy lately. The strain had become too much, she decided. It was time to put an end to it.

She lifted the suitcase from the bed and placed it next to the others. From the foyer, the faint click of a turning lock reached her ears. She jammed her hand against her

54

mouth to muffle a scream. He wasn't supposed to come tonight. She turned around to face him.

'Helene?' His voice was polite. 'Weren't you planning to say goodbye?'

'I . . . I was going to write you.'

'That won't be necessary now.'

With his right hand, he reached into his pocket. She saw the glint of metal. Then he picked up one of the bed pillows and held it in front of him. Helene did not have time to try to escape. Searing pain exploded through her head. The future that she had planned so carefully disappeared with her into the blackness.

At four a.m. the ringing of the phone tore Meghan from sleep. She fumbled for the receiver.

A barely discernible, hoarse voice whispered, 'Meg.'

'Who is this?' She heard a click and knew her mother was picking up the extension.

'It's Daddy, Meg. I'm in trouble. I did something terrible.'

A strangled moan made Meg fling down the receiver and rush into her mother's room. Catherine Collins was slumped on the pillow, her face ashen, her eyes closed. Meg grasped her arms. 'Mom, it's some sick, crazy fool,' she said urgently. 'Mom!'

Her mother was unconscious.

17

At seven-thirty Tuesday morning, Mac watched his lively son leap onto the school bus. Then he got in his car for the drive to Westport. There was a nippy

55

bite in the air, and his glasses were fogging over. He took them off, gave them a quick rub and automatically wished that he were one of the happy contact lens wearers whose smiling faces reproached him from poster-sized ads whenever he went to have his glasses adjusted or replaced.

As he drove around the bend in the road he was astonished to see Meg's white Mustang about to turn into her driveway. He tapped the horn and she braked.

He pulled up beside her. In unison they lowered their windows. His cheerful, 'What are you up to?' died on his lips as he got a good look at Meghan. Her face was strained and pale, her hair disheveled, a striped pajama top visible between the lapels of her raincoat. 'Meg, what's wrong?' he demanded.

'My mother's in the hospital,' she said tonelessly.

A car was coming up behind her. 'Go ahead,' he said. 'I'll follow you.'

In the driveway, he hurried to open the car door for Meg. She seemed dazed. How bad is Catherine? he thought, worried. On the porch, he took Meg's house key from her hand. 'Here, let me do that.'

In the foyer, he put his hands on her shoulders. 'Tell me.'

'They thought at first she'd had a heart attack. Fortunately they were wrong, but there is a chance that she's building up to one. She's on medication to head it off. She'll be in the hospital for at least a week. They asked – get this – had she been under any stress?' An uncertain laugh became a stifled sob. She swallowed and pulled back. 'I'm okay, Mac. The tests showed no heart damage as of now. She's exhausted, heartsick, worried. Rest and some sedatives are what she needs.'

'I agree. Wouldn't hurt you either. Come on. You could use a cup of coffee.'

She followed him into the kitchen. 'I'll make it.'

'Sit down. Don't you want to take your coat off?'

56

'I'm still cold.' She attempted a smile. 'How can you go out on a day like this without a coat?'

Mac glanced down at his gray tweed jacket. 'My topcoat has a loose button. I can't find my sewing kit.'

When the coffee was ready, he poured them each a cup and sat opposite her at the table. 'I suppose with Catherine in the hospital you'll come here to sleep for a while.'

'I was going to anyhow.' Quietly she told him all that had been happening: about the victim who resembled her, the note that had been found in the victim's pocket, the middle-of-the-night fax. 'And so,' she explained, 'the station wants me off the firing line for the time being, and my boss gave me the Manning Clinic assignment. And then early this morning the phone rang and . . .' She told him about the call and her mother's collapse.

Mac hoped the shock he was feeling did not show in his face. Granted, Kyle had been with them Sunday night at dinner. She might not have wanted to say anything in front of him. Even so, Meg had not even hinted that less than three days earlier she had seen a murdered woman who might have died in her place. Likewise, she had not chosen to confide in Mac about the decision of the insurers.

From the time she was ten years old and he was a college sophomore working summers at the inn, he'd been the willing confidante of her secrets, everything from how much she missed her father when he was away, to how much she hated practicing the piano.

The year and a half of Mac's marriage was the only time he hadn't seen the Collinses regularly. He'd been living here since the divorce, nearly seven years now, and believed that he and Meg were back on their big brother-little sister basis. Guess again, he thought.

Meghan was silent now, absorbed in her own thoughts, clearly neither looking for nor expecting help or advice from him. He remembered Kyle's remark: *I thought you were my friend*. The woman Kyle had seen

57

driving past the house on Wednesday, the one he'd thought was Meghan. Was it possible that she was the woman who died a day later?

Mac decided instantly not to discuss this with Meghan until he had questioned Kyle tonight and had a chance to think. But he did have to ask her something else. 'Meg, forgive me, but is there any chance however remote that it was your father calling this morning?'

'No. No. I'd know his voice. So would my mother. The one we heard was surreal, not as bad as a computer voice, but not right.'

'He said he was in trouble.'

'Yes.'

'And the note in the stabbing victim's pocket was in his writing.'

'Yes.'

'Did your father ever mention anyone named Annie?'

Meghan stared at Mac.

Annie! She could hear her father teasing as he called, *Meg . . . Meggie . . . Meghan Anne . . . Annie . . .*

She thought in horror, *Annie* was always his pet name for me.

18

On Tuesday morning, from the front windows of her home in Scottsdale, Arizona, Frances Grolier could see the first glimmer of light begin to define the McDowell Mountains, light that she knew would become strong and brilliant, constantly changing the hues and tones and colors reflected on those masses of rock.

She turned and walked across the long room to the

back windows. The house bordered on the vast Pima Indian reservation and offered a view of the primordial desert, stark and open, edged by Camelback Mountain; desert and mountain now mysteriously lighted in the shadowy pink glow that preceded the sunrise.

At fifty-six, Frances had somehow managed to retain a fey quality that suited her thin face, thick mass of graying brown hair and wide, compelling eyes. She never bothered to soften the deep lines around her eyes and mouth with makeup. Tall and reedy , she was most comfortable in slacks and a loose smock. She shunned personal publicity, but her work as a sculptor was known in art circles, particularly for her consummate skill in molding faces. The sensitivity with which she captured below-the-surface expressions was the hallmark of her talent.

Long ago she had made a decision and stuck by it without regret. Her lifestyle suited her well. But now . . .

She shouldn't have expected Annie to understand. She should have kept her word and told her nothing. Annie had listened to the painful explanation, her eyes wide and shocked. Then she'd walked across the room and deliberately knocked over the stand holding the bronze bust.

At Frances' horrified cry, Annie had rushed from the house, jumped in her car and driven away. That evening Frances tried to phone her daughter at her apartment in San Diego. The answering machine was on. She'd phoned every day for the last week and always got the machine. It would be just like Annie to disappear indefinitely. Last year, after she'd broken her engagement to Greg, she'd flown to Australia and backpacked for six months.

With fingers that seemed to be unable to obey the signals from her brain, Frances resumed her careful repair of the bust she had sculpted of Annie's father.

From the moment she entered his office at two o'clock

on Tuesday afternoon, Meghan could sense the difference in Dr George Manning's attitude. On Sunday, when she'd covered the reunion, he had been expansive, co-operative, proud to display the children and the clinic. On the phone yesterday, when she'd made the appointment, he'd been quietly enthusiastic. Today the doctor looked every day of his seventy years. The healthy pink complexion she had noted earlier had been replaced by a gray pallor. The hand that he extended to her had a slight tremor.

This morning, before he left for Westport, Mac had insisted that she phone the hospital and check on her mother. She was told that Mrs Collins was sleeping and that her blood pressure had improved satisfactorily and was now in the high-normal range.

Mac. What had she seen in his eyes as he said goodbye? He'd brushed her cheek with his usual light kiss, but his eyes held another message. Pity? She didn't want it.

She'd laid down for a couple of hours, not sleeping but at least dozing, sloughing off some of the heavy-eyed numbness. Then she'd showered, a long, hot shower that took some of the achiness from her shoulders. She'd dressed in a dark green suit with a fitted jacket and calf-length skirt. She wanted to look her best. She had noticed that the adults at the Manning Clinic reunion were well dressed, then reasoned that people who could afford to spend somewhere between ten and twenty thousand dollars in the attempt to have a baby certainly had discretionary income.

At the Park Avenue firm where she'd set out to practice law, it was a rule that no casual dress was permitted. As a radio and now television reporter, Meghan had observed that people being interviewed seemed to be naturally more expansive if they felt a sense of identity with the interviewer.

She wanted Dr Manning to subconsciously think of her and talk to her as he would to a prospective client.

Now, standing in front of him, studying him, she realized that he was looking at her the way a convicted felon looked at the sentencing judge. Fear was the emotion emanating from him. But why should Dr Manning be afraid of her?

'I'm looking forward to doing this special more than I can tell you,' she said as she took the seat across the desk from him. 'I – '

He interrupted. 'Miss Collins, I'm afraid that we can't cooperate on any television feature. The staff and I had a meeting, and the feeling was that many of our clients would be most uncomfortable if they saw television cameras around here.'

'But you were happy to have us on Sunday.'

'The people who were here on Sunday have children. The women who are newcomers, or those who have not succeeded in achieving a successful pregnancy, are often anxious and depressed. Assisted reproduction is a very private matter.' His voice was firm, but his eyes betrayed his nervousness. About what, she wondered?

'When we spoke on the phone,' she said, 'we agreed that no one would be interviewed or caught on-camera who wasn't perfectly willing to discuss being a client here.'

'Miss Collins, the answer is no, and now I'm afraid I'm due at a meeting.' He rose.

Meghan had no choice but to stand up with him. 'What happened, Doctor?' she asked quietly. 'You must know I'm aware that there's got to be a lot more to this sudden change than belated concern for your clients.'

He did not reply. Meghan left the office and walked down the corridor to the reception area. She smiled warmly at the receptionist and glanced at the nameplate on the desk. 'Mrs Walters, I have a friend who'd be very interested in any literature I can give her about the clinic.'

Marge Walters looked puzzled. 'I guess Dr Manning

61

forgot to give you all the stuff he had his secretary put together for you. Let me call her. She'll bring it out.'

'If you would,' Meghan said. 'The doctor *was* willing to cooperate with the story I've been planning.'

'Of course. The staff love the idea. It's good publicity for the clinic. Let me call Jane.'

Meghan crossed her fingers, hoping Dr Manning had not told his secretary of his decision to refuse to be involved in the planned special. Then, as she watched, Walters' expression changed from a smile to a puzzled frown. When she replaced the receiver, her open and friendly manner was gone. 'Miss Collins, I guess you know that I shouldn't have asked Dr Manning's secretary for the file.'

'I'm only asking for whatever information a new client might request,' Meghan said.

'You'd better take that up with Dr Manning.' She hesitated. 'I don't mean to be rude, Miss Collins, but I work here. I take orders.'

It was clear that there would be no help from her. Meghan turned to go, then paused. 'Can you tell me this? Was there very much concern on the part of the staff about doing the feature? I mean, was it everybody or just a few who objected at the meeting?'

She could see the struggle in the other woman. Marge Walters was bursting with curiosity. The curiosity won. 'Miss Collins,' she whispered, 'yesterday at noon we had a staff meeting and everyone applauded the news that you were doing a special. We were joking about who'd get to be on-camera. I can't imagine what changed Dr Manning's mind.'

19

Mac found his work in the LifeCode Research Laboratory, where he was a specialist in genetic therapy, to be rewarding, satisfying and all-absorbing.

After he left Meghan, he drove to the lab and got right to work. As the day progressed, however, he admitted to himself that he was having trouble concentrating. A dull sense of apprehension seemed to be paralyzing his brain and permeating his entire body so that his fingers, which could as second nature handle the most delicate equipment, felt heavy and clumsy. He had lunch at his desk and, as he ate, tried to analyze the tangible fear that was overwhelming him.

He called the hospital and was told that Mrs Collins had been removed from the intensive care unit to the cardiac section. She was sleeping, and no calls were being put through.

All of which is good news, Mac thought. The cardiac section was probably only a precaution. He felt sure Catherine would be all right and the enforced rest would do her good.

It was his worry about Meghan that caused this blinding unease. Who was threatening her? Even if the incredible were true and Ed Collins was still alive, surely the danger was not coming from him?

No, his concern all came back to the victim who looked like Meghan. By the time he'd tossed out the untasted half of his sandwich and downed the last of his cold coffee, Mac knew that he would not rest until

63

he had gone to the morgue in New York to see that woman's body.

Stopping at the hospital on his way home that evening, Mac saw Catherine, who was clearly sedated. Her speech was markedly slower than her usual spirited delivery. 'Isn't this nonsense, Mac?' she asked.

He pulled up a chair. 'Even stalwart daughters of Erin are allowed time out every now and then, Catherine.'

Her smile was acknowledgment. 'I guess I've been traveling on nerve for a while. You know everything, I suppose.'

'Yes.'

'Meggie just left. She's going over to the inn. Mac, that new chef I hired! I swear he must have trained at a takeout joint. I'll have to get rid of him.' Her face clouded. 'That is, if I can figure a way to hang on to Drumdoe.'

'I think you'd better put aside that kind of worry for at least a little while.'

She sighed. 'I know. It's just that I can *do* something about a bad chef. I can't *do* anything about insurers who won't pay and nuts who call in the middle of the night. Meg said that kind of sick call is just a sign of the times, but it's so rotten, so upsetting. She's shrugging it off, but you can understand why I'm worried.'

'Trust Meg.' Mac felt like a hypocrite as he tried to sound reassuring.

A few minutes later he stood up to go. He kissed Catherine's forehead. Her smile had a touch of resiliency. 'I have a great idea. When I fire the chef, I'll send him over to this place. Compared to what they served me for dinner, he comes through like Escoffier.'

Marie Dileo, the daily housekeeper, was setting the table when Mac got home, and Kyle was sprawled on the floor doing his homework. Mac pulled Kyle up on the couch beside him. 'Hey, fellow, tell me something.

64

The other day, how much of a look did you get at the woman you thought was Meg?'

'A pretty good look,' Kyle replied. 'Meg came over this afternoon.'

'She did?'

'Yes. She wanted to see why I was mad at her.'

'And you told her?'

'Uh-huh.'

'What'd she say?'

'Oh, just that Wednesday afternoon she was in court and that sometimes when people are on television other people like to see where they live. That stuff. Just like you, she asked how good a look I got at that lady. And I told her that the lady was driving very, very slow. That's why when I saw her, I ran down the driveway and I called to her. And she stopped the car and looked at me and rolled down the window and then she just took off.'

'You didn't tell me all that.'

'I said that she saw me and then drove away fast.'

'You didn't say she stopped and rolled down the window, pal.'

'Uh-huh. I *thought* she was Meg. But her hair was longer. I told Meg that too. You know, it was around her shoulders. Like that picture of Mommy.'

Ginger had sent Kyle one of her recent publicity pictures, a head shot with her blond hair swirling around her shoulders, her lips parted, revealing perfect teeth, her eyes wide and sensuous. In the corner she'd written, 'To my darling little Kyle, Love and kisses, Mommy.'

A publicity picture, Mac had thought in disgust. If he'd been home when it arrived, Kyle would never have seen it.

After stopping to see Kyle, visiting her mother and checking on the inn, Meghan arrived home at seven-thirty. Virginia had insisted on sending dinner home with her, a chicken potpie, salad and the warm salty

65

rolls Meghan loved. 'You're as bad as your mother,' Virginia had fussed. 'You'll forget to eat.'

I probably would have, Meghan thought as she changed quickly into old pajamas and a robe. It was an outfit that dated back to college days and was still her favorite for an early, quiet evening of reading or watching television.

In the kitchen, she sipped a glass of wine and nibbled on a salt roll as the microwave oven zapped the temperature of the potpie to steaming hot.

When it was ready, she carried it on a tray into the study and settled down in her father's swivel chair. Tomorrow she would begin digging into the history of the Manning Clinic. Researchers at the television station could quickly come up with all the background available on it. And on Dr Manning, she thought. I'd like to know if there are any skeletons in *his* closet, she told herself.

Tonight she had a different project in mind, however. She absolutely had to find any shred of evidence that might link her father to the dead woman who resembled her, the woman whose name might be Annie.

A suspicion had insinuated itself into her mind, a suspicion so incredible that she could not bring herself to consider it yet. She only knew that it was absolutely essential to go through all her father's personal papers immediately.

Not surprisingly the desk drawers were neat. Edwin Collins had been innately tidy. Writing paper, envelopes and stamps were precisely placed in the slotted side drawer. His day-at-a-glance calendar was filled out for January and early February. After that, only standing dates were entered. Her mother's birthday. Her birthday. The spring golf club outing. A cruise her parents had planned to take to celebrate their thirtieth wedding anniversary in June.

Why would anyone who was planning to disappear

mark his calendar for important dates months in advance? she wondered. That didn't make sense.

The days he had been away in January or had planned to be away in February simply carried the name of a city. She knew the details of those trips would have been listed in the business appointment book he carried with him.

The deep bottom drawer on the right was locked. Meghan searched in vain for a key, then hesitated. Tomorrow she might be able to get a locksmith, but she did not want to wait. She went into the kitchen, found the toolbox and brought back a steel file. As she hoped, the lock was old and easily forced open.

In this drawer stacks of envelopes were held together by rubber bands. Meghan picked up the top packet and glanced through it. All except the first envelope were written in the same hand.

That one contained only a newspaper clipping from the *Philadelphia Bulletin*. Below the picture of a handsome woman, the obituary notice read:

Aurelia Crowley Collins, 75, a lifelong resident of Philadelphia, died in St Paul's Hospital on 9 December of heart failure.

Aurelia Crowley Collins! Meghan gasped as she studied the picture. The wide-set eyes, the wavy hair that framed the oval face. It was the same woman, now aged, whose portrait was prominently placed on the table a few feet away. *Her grandmother*

The date on the clipping was two years old. Her grandmother had been alive until two years ago! Meghan leafed through the other envelopes in the packet she was holding. They all came from Philadelphia. The last one was postmarked two and a half years ago.

She read one, then another, and another. Unbelieving, she went through the other stacks of envelopes. At random, she kept reading. The earliest note went back thirty years. All contained the same plea.

Dear Edwin,
I had hoped that perhaps this Christmas I might have word from you. I pray that you and your family are well. How I would love to see my granddaughter. Perhaps someday you will allow that to happen.
With love,
Mother

Dear Edwin,
We are always supposed to look ahead. But as one grows older, it is much easier to look back and bitterly regret the mistakes of the past. Isn't it possible for us to talk, even on the telephone? It would give me so much happiness.
Love,
Mother

After a while Meg could not bear to read any more, but it was clear from their worn appearance that her father must have pored over them many times.

Dad, you were so kind, she thought. Why did you tell everyone your mother was dead? What did she do to you that was so unforgivable? Why did you keep these letters if you were never going to make peace with her?

She picked up the envelope that had contained the obituary notice. There was no name, but the address printed on the flap was a street in Chestnut Hill. She knew that Chestnut Hill was one of Philadelphia's most exclusive residential areas.

Who was the sender? More important, what kind of man had her father really been?

20

In Helene Petrovic's charming colonial home in Lawrenceville, New Jersey, her niece, Stephanie, was cross and worried. The baby was due in a few weeks, and her back hurt. She was always tired. As a surprise, she had gone to the trouble of preparing a hot lunch for Helene, who had said she planned to get home by noon.

At one-thirty, Stephanie had tried to phone her aunt, but there was no answer at the Connecticut apartment. Now, at six o'clock, Helene had still not arrived. Was anything wrong? Perhaps some last-minute errands came up and Helene had lived alone so long she was not used to keeping someone else informed of her movements.

Stephanie had been shocked when on the phone yesterday Helene told her that she had quit her job, effective immediately. 'I need a rest and I'm worried about you being alone so much,' Helene had told her.

The fact was that Stephanie loved being alone. She had never known the luxury of being able to lie in bed until she decided to make coffee and get the paper that had been delivered in the predawn hours. On really lazy days, still resting in bed, she would eventually watch the morning television programs.

She was twenty but looked older. Growing up, it had been her dream to be like her father's younger sister, Helene, who had left for the United States twenty years ago, after her husband died.

Now that same Helene was her anchor, her future, in a world that no longer existed as she knew it. The

69

bloody, brief revolution in Rumania had cost her parents their lives and destroyed their home. Stephanie had moved in with neighbors whose tiny house had no room for another occupant.

Over the years, Helene had occasionally sent a little money and a gift package at Christmas. In desperation, Stephanie had written to her imploring help.

A few weeks later she was on the plane to the United States.

Helene was so kind. It was just that Stephanie fiercely wanted to live in Manhattan, get a job in a beauty salon and go to cosmetician school at night. Already her English was excellent, though she'd arrived here last year knowing only a few English words.

Her time had almost come. She and Helene had looked at studio apartments in New York. They found one in Greenwich Village that would be available in January, and Helene had promised they would go shopping to decorate it.

This house was on the market. Helene had always said she was not going to give up her job and the place in Connecticut until it sold. What had made her change her mind so abruptly now, Stephanie wondered?

She brushed back the light brown hair from her broad forehead. She was hungry again and might as well eat. She could always warm up dinner for Helene when she arrived.

At eight o'clock, as she was smiling at a rerun of *The Golden Girls*, the front door bell pealed.

Her sigh was both relieved and vexed. Helene probably had an armful of packages and didn't want to search for her key. She gave a last look at the set. The program was about to end. After being so late, couldn't Helene have waited one more minute? she wondered as she hoisted herself up from the couch.

Her welcoming smile faded and vanished at the sight of a tall policeman with a boyish face. In disbelief she

70

heard that Helene Petrovic had been shot to death in Connecticut.

Before grief and shock encompassed her, Stephanie's one clear thought was to frantically ask herself, *what will become of me?* Only last week Helene had talked about her intention of changing her will, which left everything she had to the Manning Clinic Research Foundation. Now it was too late.

21

By eight o'clock on Tuesday evening, traffic in the garage had slowed down to a trickle. Bernie, who frequently worked overtime, had put in a twelve hour day and it was time to go home.

He didn't mind the overtime. The pay was good and so were the tips. All these years the extra money had paid for his electronic equipment.

This evening when he went to the office to check out he was worried. He hadn't realized the big boss was on the premises when at lunchtime that day he'd sat in Tom Weicker's car and flipped through the glove compartment again for possible items of interest. Then he'd looked up to see the boss staring through the car window. The boss had just walked away, not saying a word. That was even worse. If he'd snarled at him it would have cleared the air.

Bernie punched the time clock. The evening manager was sitting in the office and called him over. His face wasn't friendly. 'Bernie, clean out your locker.' He had an envelope in his hand. 'This covers salary, vacation and sick days and two weeks severance.'

71

'But . . .' The protest died on Bernie's lips as the manager raised a hand.

'Listen, Bernie, you know as well as I do that we've had complaints of money and personal items disappearing from cars that were parked in this garage.'

'I never took a thing.'

'You had no damn business going through Weicker's glove compartment, Bernie. You're through.'

When he got home, still angry and upset, Bernie found that his mother had a frozen macaroni and cheese dinner ready to be put in the microwave. 'It's been a terrible day,' she complained as she took the wrapper off the package. 'The kids from down the block were yelling in front of the house. I told them to shut up and they called me an old bat. You know what I did?' She did not wait for an answer. 'I called the cops and complained. Then one of them came over, and he was rude to me.'

Bernie grasped her arm. 'You brought the cops in here, Mama? Did they go downstairs?'

'Why would they go downstairs?'

'Mama, I don't want the cops in here, ever.'

'Bernie, I haven't been downstairs in years. You're keeping it clean down there, aren't you? I don't want dust filtering up. My sinuses are terrible.'

'It's clean, Mama.'

'I hope so. You're not a neat person. Like your father.' She slammed the door of the microwave. 'You hurt my arm. You grabbed it hard. Don't do that again.'

'I won't, Mama. I'm sorry, Mama.'

The next morning, Bernie left for work at the usual time. He didn't want his mother to know he got fired. Today, however, he headed for a car wash a few blocks from the house. He paid to have the full treatment on his eight-year-old Chevy. Vacuum, clean out trunk, polish the dashboard, wash, wax. When the car came

72

out, it was still shabby but respectable, the basic dark green color recognizable.

He never cleaned his car except for the few times a year his mother announced she was planning to go to church on the following Sunday. Of course it would be different if he were taking Meghan for a ride. He'd really have it shining for her.

Bernie knew what he was going to do. He had thought about it all night. Maybe there was a reason he'd lost his job at the garage. Maybe it was all part of a greater plan. For weeks it hadn't been enough to see Meghan only in the few minutes when she dropped off or picked up her Mustang or a Channel 3 car.

He wanted to be around her, to take pictures of her that he could play during the night on his VCR.

Today he'd buy a video camera on Forty-seventh Street.

But he had to make money. No one was a better driver, so he could earn it by using his car as a gypsy cab. That would give him a lot of freedom too. Freedom to drive to Connecticut where Meghan Collins lived when she wasn't in New York.

He had to be careful not to be noticed.

'It's called "obsession", Bernie,' the shrink at Riker's Island had explained when Bernie begged to know what was wrong with him. 'I think we've helped you, but if that feeling comes over you again, I want you to talk to me. It will mean that you might need some medication.'

Bernie knew he didn't need any help. He just needed to be around Meghan Collins.

73

22

The body of Helene Petrovic lay all Tuesday in the bedroom where she had died. Never friendly with her neighbors, she'd already said goodbye to the few with whom she exchanged greetings, and her car was hidden from sight in the garage of her rented condo.

It was only when the owner of the condo stopped by late that afternoon that she found the dead woman at the foot of the bed.

The death of a quiet embryologist in New Milford, Connecticut, was briefly mentioned on New York television news programs. It wasn't much of a story. There was no evidence of a break-in, no apparent sexual attack. The victim's purse with two hundred dollars in it was in the room, so robbery was ruled out.

A neighbor across the street volunteered that Helene Petrovic had one visitor she'd observed, a man who always came late at night. She'd never really gotten a good look at him but knew he was tall. She figured he was a boyfriend, because he always pulled his car into the other side of Petrovic's garage. She knew he had to have left during the night, because she'd never seen him in the morning. How often had she seen him? Maybe a half-dozen times. The car? A late model dark sedan.

After the discovery of her grandmother's obituary notice, Meghan had phoned the hospital and was told that her mother was sleeping and that her condition was satisfactory. Tired to the bone, she'd rummaged through the medicine cabinet for a sleeping pill, then

74

gone to bed and slept straight through until her alarm woke her at six-thirty a.m.

An immediate call to the hospital reassured her that her mother had had a restful night and her vital signs were normal.

Meghan read the *Times* over coffee, and in the Connecticut section was shocked to read of the death of Dr Helene Petrovic. There was a picture of the woman. In it, the expression in her eyes was both sad and enigmatic. I talked with her at Manning, Meghan thought. She was in charge of the lab with the cryopreserved embryos. Who had murdered that quiet, intelligent woman? Meghan wondered. Another thought struck her. According to the paper, Dr Petrovic had quit her job and had planned on moving from Connecticut the next morning. Did her decision have anything to do with Dr Manning's refusal to cooperate on the television special?

It was too early to call Tom Weicker, but it probably wasn't too late to catch Mac before he left for work. Meghan knew there was something else she had to face, and now was as good a time as any.

Mac's hello was hurried.

'Mac, I'm sorry. I know this is a bad time to call but I have to talk to you,' Meghan said.

'Hi, Meg. Sure. Just hang on a minute.'

He must have put his hand over the phone. She heard his muffled but exasperated call, 'Kyle, you left your homework on the dining room table.'

When he got back on he explained, 'We go through this every morning. I tell him to put his homework in his schoolbag at night. He doesn't. In the morning he's yelling that he lost it.'

'Why don't *you* put it in his schoolbag at night?'

'That doesn't build character.' His voice changed. 'Meg, how's your mother?'

'Good. I really think she's okay. She's a strong lady.'

'Like you.'

75

'I'm not that strong.'

'Too strong for my taste, not telling me about that stabbing victim. But that's a conversation we'll have another time.'

'Mac, could you stop by for three minutes on your way out?'

'Sure. As soon as His Nibs gets on the bus.'

Meghan knew that she had no more than twenty minutes to shower and dress before Mac arrived. She was brushing her hair when the bell rang. 'Have a quick cup of coffee,' she said. 'What I'm about to ask isn't easy.'

Was it only twenty-four hours ago they had sat across from each other at this table? she wondered. It seemed so much longer. But yesterday she'd been in near-shock. Today, knowing her mother was almost certainly all right, she was able to face and accept whatever stark truth came to light.

'Mac,' she began, 'you're a DNA specialist.'

'Yes.'

'The woman who was stabbed Thursday night, the one who resembles me so much?'

'Yes.'

'If her DNA was compared to mine, could kinship be established?'

Mac raised his eyebrows and studied the cup in his hand. 'Meg, this is the way it works. With DNA testing we can positively know if any two people had the same mother. It's complicated, and I can show you in the lab how we do it. Within the ninety-ninth percentile we can establish if two people had the same father. It's not as absolute as the mother-child scenario, but we can get a very strong indication of whether or not we're dealing with half siblings.'

'Can that test be done on me and the dead woman?'

'Yes.'

76

'You don't seem surprised that I'm asking about it, Mac.'

He put down the coffee cup and looked at her squarely. 'Meg, I already had decided to go to the morgue and see that woman's body this afternoon. They have a DNA lab in the medical examiner's office. I was planning to make sure they were preserving a sample of her blood before she's removed to potter's field.'

Meg bit her lip. 'Then you're thinking in the same direction I am.' She blinked her eyes to blot out the vivid memory of the dead woman's face. 'I have to see Phillip this morning and stop in at the hospital,' she continued. 'I'll meet you at the medical examiner's. What time is good for you?'

They agreed to meet around two o'clock. As Mac drove away he reflected that there was no good time to look down at the dead face of a woman who resembled Meghan Collins.

23

Phillip Carter heard the news report detailing Dr Helene Petrovic's death on his way to the office. He made a mental note to have Victor Orsini follow up immediately on the vacancy her death had left at Manning Clinic. She had, after all, been hired at Manning through Collins and Carter. Those jobs paid well, and there would be another good fee if Collins and Carter was commissioned to find a replacement.

He arrived at the office at a quarter of nine and spotted Meghan's car parked in one of the stalls near the entrance of the building. She had obviously been

77

waiting for him, because she got out of her car as he parked.

'Meg, what a nice surprise.' He put an arm around her. 'But for goodness sake, you have a key. Why didn't you go inside?'

Meg smiled briefly. 'I've just been here a minute.' Besides, she thought, I'd feel like an intruder walking in.

'Catherine's all right, isn't she?' he asked.

'Doing really well.'

'Thank God for that,' he said heartily.

The small reception room was pleasant with its brightly slipcovered couch and chair, circular coffee table and paneled walls. Meghan once again had a reaction of intense sadness as she hurried through it. This time they went into Phillip's office. He seemed to sense that she did not want to go into her father's office again.

He helped her off with her coat. 'Coffee?'

'No thanks. I've had three cups already.'

He settled behind his desk. 'And I'm trying to cut down, so I'll wait. Meg, you look pretty troubled.'

'I am.' Meghan moistened her lips. 'Phillip, I'm beginning to think I didn't know my father at all.'

'In what way?'

She told him about the letters and the obituary notice she had found in the locked drawer, then watched as Phillip's expression changed from concern to disbelief.

'Meg, I don't know what to tell you,' he said when she finished. 'I've known your father for years. Ever since I can remember, I've understood that his mother died when he was a kid, his father remarried and he had a lousy childhood, living with the father and stepmother. When my father was dying, your dad said something I never forgot. He said, "I envy you being able to mourn a parent."'

'Then you never knew either?'

'No, of course not.'

'The point is, why did he have to lie about it?' Meg

78

asked, her voice rising. She clasped her hands together and bit her lip. 'I mean, why not tell my mother the truth? What did he have to gain by deceiving her?'

'Think about it, Meg. He met your mother, told her his family background as he'd told it to everyone else. When they started getting interested in each other it would have been pretty difficult to admit he'd lied to her. And can you imagine your grandfather's reaction if he'd learned that your father was ignoring his own mother for whatever reason?'

'Yes, I can see that. But Pop's been dead for so many years. Why couldn't he . . . ?' Her voice trailed off.

'Meg, when you start living a lie, it gets harder with every passing day to straighten it out.'

Meghan heard the sound of voices in the outside office. She stood up. 'Can we keep this between us?'

'Of course.'

He got up with her. 'What are you going to do?'

'As soon as I'm sure Mother is okay I'm going to the address in Chestnut Hill that was on the envelope with the obituary notice. Maybe I'll get some answers there.'

'How's the feature story on the Manning Clinic going?'

'It's not. They're stonewalling me. I've got to find a different in vitro facility to use. Wait a minute. You or Dad placed someone at Manning, didn't you?'

'Your dad handled it. As a matter of fact, it's that poor woman who was shot yesterday.'

'Dr Petrovic? I met her last week.'

The intercom buzzed. Phillip Carter picked up the phone. 'Who? All right, I'll take it.'

'A reporter from the *New York Post*,' he explained to Meghan. 'God knows what they want of me.'

Meghan watched as Phillip Carter's face darkened. 'That's absolutely impossible.' His voice was husky with outrage. 'I . . . I will not comment until I have personally spoken with Dr Iovino at New York Hospital.'

He replaced the receiver and turned to Meghan. 'Meg,

79

that reporter has been checking on Helene Petrovic. They never heard of her at New York Hospital. Her credentials were fraudulent, and we're responsible for her getting the job in the laboratory at Manning.'

'But didn't you check her references before you submitted her to the clinic?'

Even as she asked the question, Meghan knew the answer, she could see it in Phillip's face. Her father had handled Helene Petrovic's file. It would have been up to him to validate the information on her curriculum vitae.

24

Despite the best efforts of the entire staff of the Manning Clinic there was no hiding the tension that permeated the atmosphere. Several new clients watched uneasily as a van with a CBS television logo on the sides pulled into the parking area and a reporter and cameraman hurried up the walkway.

Marge Walters was at her receptionist best, firm with the reporter. 'Dr Manning declines to be interviewed until he has investigated the allegations,' she said. She was unable to stop the cameraman, who began to video-tape the room and its occupants.

Several clients stood up. Marge rushed over to them. 'This is all a misunderstanding,' she pleaded, suddenly realizing she was being recorded.

One woman, her hands shielding her face, exploded in anger. 'This is an outrage. It's tough enough to have to resort to this kind of procedure to have a baby

80

without being on the eleven o'clock news.' She ran from the room.

Another said, 'Mrs Walters, I'm leaving too. You'd better cancel my appointment.'

'I understand.' Marge forced a sympathetic smile. 'When would you like to reschedule?'

'I'll have to check my appointment book. I'll call.'

Marge watched the retreating women. No you won't, she thought. Alarmed, she noticed Mrs Kaplan, a client on her second visit to the clinic, approach the reporter.

'What's this all about?' she demanded.

'What it's all about is that the person in charge of the Manning Clinic lab for the last six years apparently was not a doctor. In fact her only training seems to have been as a cosmetologist.'

'My God. My sister had in vitro fertilization here two years ago. Is there any chance she didn't receive her own embryo?' Mrs Kaplan clenched her hands together.

God help us, Marge thought. That's the end of this place. She'd been shocked and saddened when she heard on the morning news of Dr Helene Petrovic's death. It was only when she arrived at work an hour ago that she'd heard the rumor of something being wrong with Petrovic's credentials. But hearing the reporter's stark statement and watching Mrs Kaplan's response made her realize the enormity of the possible consequences.

Helene Petrovic had been in charge of the cryopreserved embryos. Dozens upon dozens of test tubes, no bigger than half an index finger, each one containing a potentially viable human being. Mislabel even one of them and the wrong embryo might be implanted in a woman's womb, making her a host mother, but not the biological mother of a child.

Marge watched the Kaplan woman rush from the room followed by the reporter. She looked out the window. More news vans were pulling in. More reporters were attempting to question the women who had just left the reception area.

81

She saw the reporter from PCD Channel 3 getting out of a car. Meghan Collins. That was her name. She was the one who'd been planning to do the television special that Dr Manning called off so abruptly . . .

Meghan was not sure if she really should be here, especially since her father's name was certain to come up in the course of the investigation into Helene Petrovic's credentials. As she left Phillip Carter's office she'd been beeped by the news desk and told that Steve, her cameraman, would meet her at the Manning Clinic. 'Weicker okayed it,' she was assured.

She'd tried to reach Weicker earlier, but he was not yet in. She felt she had to speak to him about the possible conflict of interest. It was easier for the moment, however, to simply accept the assignment. The odds were that the lawyers for the clinic would not permit any interviews with Dr Manning anyway.

She did not attempt to join the rest of the media in flinging questions to the departing clients. Instead she spotted Steve and motioned for him to follow her inside. She opened the door quietly. As she had hoped, Marge Walters was at her desk, speaking urgently into the phone. 'We've got to cancel all of today's appointments,' she was insisting. 'You'd better tell them in there that they've got to make some kind of statement. Otherwise the only thing the public is going to see is women bolting out of here.'

As the door closed behind Steve, Walters looked up. 'I can't talk any more,' she said hurriedly and clicked down the receiver.

Meghan did not speak until she was settled in the chair across from Walters' desk. The situation required tact and careful handling. She had learned not to fire questions at a defensive interviewee. 'This is a pretty rough morning for you, Mrs Walters,' she said soothingly.

82

She watched as the receptionist brushed a hand over her forehead. 'You bet it is.'

The woman's tone was guarded, but Meghan sensed in her the same conflict she had noticed yesterday. She realized the need for discretion, but she was dying to talk to someone about all that had been going on. Marge Walters was a born gossip.

'I met Dr Petrovic at the reunion,' Meghan said. 'She seemed like a lovely person.'

'She was,' Walters agreed. 'It's hard to believe she wasn't qualified for the job she was doing. But her early medical training was probably in Rumania. With all the changes in government over there, I'll bet anything they find out she had all the degrees she needed. I don't understand about New York Hospital saying she didn't train there. I bet that's a mistake too. But finding that out may come too late. This bad publicity will ruin this place.'

'It could,' Meghan agreed. 'Do you think that her quitting had something to do with Dr Manning's decision to cancel our session yesterday?'

Walters looked at the camera Steve was holding.

Quickly Meghan added, 'If you can tell me anything that will balance all this negative news I'd like to include it.'

Marge Walters made up her mind. She trusted Meghan Collins. 'Then let me tell you that Helene Petrovic was one of the most wonderful, hardest working people I've ever met. No one was happier than she when an embryo was brought to term in its mother's womb. She loved every single embryo in that lab and used to insist on having the emergency generator tested regularly to be sure that in case of power failure the temperature would stay constant.'

Walters' eyes misted. 'I remember Dr Manning telling us at a staff meeting last year how he'd rushed to the clinic during that terrible snowstorm in December, when all the electricity went down, to make sure the emer-

83

gency generator was working. Guess who arrived a minute behind him? Helene Petrovic. And she hated driving in snow or ice. It was a special fear of hers, yet she drove here in that storm. She was that dedicated.'

'You're telling me exactly what I felt when I interviewed her,' Meghan commented. 'She seemed to be a very caring person. I could see it in the way she was interacting with the children during the picture session on Sunday.'

'I missed that. I had to go to a family wedding that day. Can you turn off the camera now?'

'Of course.' Meghan nodded to Steve.

Walters shook her head. 'I wanted to be here. But my cousin Dodie finally married her boyfriend. They've only been living together for eight years. You should have heard my aunt. You'd think a nineteen-year-old out of convent school was the bride. I swear to God the night before the wedding I bet she told Dodie how babies come to be born.'

Walters grimaced as the incongruity of her remark in this clinic occurred to her. 'How most of them come to be born, I mean.'

'Is there any chance I can see Dr Manning?' Meghan knew if there was a chance it was through this woman.

Walters shook her head. 'Just between us, an assistant state attorney and some investigators are with him now.'

That wasn't surprising. Certainly they were looking into Helen Petrovic's abrupt departure from the clinic and asking questions about her personal life. 'Did Helene have any particularly close friends here?'

'No. Not really. She was very nice but a little formal – you know what I mean. I thought maybe it was because she was from Rumania. Although when you think about it, the Gabor women came from there, and they've had more than their share of close friends, especially Zsa Zsa.'

'I'm quite sure the Gabors are Hungarian, not Rumanian. So Helene Petrovic didn't have any particular friends or an intimate relationship you're aware of?'

'The nearest to it was Dr Williams. He used to be Dr Manning's assistant, and I wondered if there wasn't a little something going on between him and Helene. I saw them at dinner one night when my husband and I went to a little out-of-the-way place. They didn't look happy when I stopped by their table to say hello. But that was just one time six years ago, right after she started working here. I have to say I kept my eye on them after that and they never acted at all special to each other.'

'Is Dr Williams still here?'

'No. He was offered a job to open and run a new facility and he took it. It's the Franklin Center in Philadelphia. It has a wonderful reputation. Between us, Dr Williams was a top-drawer manager. He put together the whole medical team here, and believe me, he did a terrific job.'

'Then he was the one who hired Petrovic?'

'Technically, but they always hire the top staff through one of those headhunter outfits that recruits and screens them for us. Even so, Dr Williams worked here for about six months after Helene came on staff, and believe me, he'd have noticed if she seemed incompetent.'

'I'd like to talk with him, Mrs Walters.'

'Please call me Marge. I wish you *would* talk to him. He'd tell you how wonderful Helene was in that lab.'

Meghan heard the front door opening. Walters looked up. 'More cameras! Meghan, I'd better not say any more.'

Meghan stood up. 'You've been a great help.'

Driving home, Meghan reflected that she would not give Dr Williams the chance to put her off over the phone. She'd go to the Franklin Center in Philadelphia and try to see him. With luck she could persuade him to tape an interview for the in vitro feature.

85

What would he have to say about Helene Petrovic? Would he defend her, like Marge Walters? Or woud be be outraged that Petrovic had managed to deceive him, as she had deceived all her other colleagues?

And, Meghan wondered, what would she learn at her other stop in the Philadelphia area? The house in Chestnut Hill, from which someone had notified her father of his mother's death.

25

Victor Orsini and Phillip Carter never socialized for lunch. Orsini knew that Carter considered him to be Edwin Collins' protégé. When the job at Collins and Carter had come up nearly seven years ago it had been between Orsini and another candidate. Orsini had been Ed Collins' choice. From the beginning his relationship with Carter was cordial, but never warm.

Today, however, after they had both ordered the baked sole and house salad, Orsini was in full sympathy with Carter's obvious distress. There had been reporters in the office and a dozen phone calls from the media asking how it was possible that Collins and Carter had not detected the lies in Helene Petrovic's curriculum vitae.

'I told them the simple truth,' Phillip Carter said as he drummed his fingers nervously on the tablecloth. 'Ed always researched prospective candidates meticulously, and it was his case. It only adds fuel to the fire that Ed is missing and the police are openly saying they don't believe he died in the bridge accident.'

86

'Does Jackie remember anything about the Petrovic case?' Orsini asked.

'She'd just started working for us then. Her initials are on the letter, but she has no memory of it. Why should she? It was a usual glowing recommendation attached to the curriculum vitae. After he received it Dr Manning had a meeting with Petrovic and hired her.'

Orsini said, 'Of all the fields in which to have been caught verifying fraudulent references, medical research is about the worst.'

'Yes, it is,' Phillip agreed. 'If any mistakes were made by Helene Petrovic and the Manning Clinic is sued, there's a damn good chance the clinic will sue us.'

'And win.'

Carter nodded glumly. 'And win.' He paused. 'Victor, you worked more directly with Ed than you did with me. When he called you from the car phone that night, he talked about wanting to meet with you in the morning. Was that all he said?'

'Yes, that's all. Why?'

'Damn it, Victor,' Phillip Carter snapped, 'let's stop playing games! If Ed did manage to get over the bridge safely, do you have any inkling from that conversation whether he might have been in the state of mind to use the accident as his opportunity to disappear?'

'Look, Phillip, he said he wanted to make sure I was in the office in the morning,' Orsini replied, his voice taking on an edge. 'It was a lousy connection. That's all I can tell you.'

'I'm sorry. I keep looking for anything that might start to make sense.' Carter sighed. 'Victor, I've been meaning to speak to you. Meghan is clearing out Ed's personal things from his office on Saturday. I want you to take that office as of Monday. We haven't had a great year but we can certainly refurbish it within reason.'

'Don't worry about that right now.'

They had little else to say to each other.

Orsini noticed that Phillip Carter did not hint that

87

after the matter of Ed Collins' legal situation was somehow straightened out, he would offer Orsini a partnership. He knew that offer would never be made. For his part it was only a matter of weeks before the position he'd almost gotten on the Coast last year became available again. The guy they'd hired for the job didn't work out. This time Orsini was being offered a bigger salary, a vice presidency and stock options.

He wished that he could leave today. Pack up and fly out there right now. But under the circumstances that was impossible. There was something he wanted to find, something he wanted to check out at the office, and now that he could move into Ed's old office, the search might be easier.

26

Bernie stopped at a diner on Route 7 just outside Danbury. He settled on a stool at the counter and ordered the deluxe hamburger, French fries and coffee. Increasingly content as he munched and swallowed, he reviewed with satisfaction the busy hours he'd spent since he left home this morning.

After the car was cleaned up, he'd purchased a chauffeur's hat and dark jacket at a secondhand store in lower Manhattan. He'd reasoned that outfit would give him a leg up on all the other gypsy cabs in New York. Then he'd headed for La Guardia Airport and stood near the baggage area, with the other chauffeurs waiting to make pickups.

He lucked out right away. Some guy about thirty or so came down the escalator and searched the name cards drivers were holding. There was no one waiting for him. Bernie could read the guy's mind. He'd probably hired a driver from one of the dirt-cheap services and was kicking himself. Most of the drivers from those places were guys who had just arrived in New York and spent their first six months on the job getting lost.

Bernie had approached the man, offered to take him into the city, warned that he didn't have a fancy limo but a nice clean car and bragged he was the best driver anyone could hire. He quoted a price of twenty bucks to drive the fellow to West Forty-eighth Street. He got him there in thirty-five minutes and received a ten-dollar tip. 'You are a hell of a driver,' the man said as he paid.

Bernie remembered the compliment with pleasure as he reached for a French fry and smiled to himself. If he kept making money this way, adding it to his severance and vacation pay, he could last a long time before Mama knew he wasn't at the old job. She never called him there. She didn't like talking on the phone. She said it gave her one of her headaches.

And here he was, free as a bird, not accountable to anyone and out to see where Meghan Collins lived. He had bought a street map of the Newtown area and studied it. The Collins house was on Bayberry Road, and he knew how to get there.

At exactly two o'clock he was driving slowly past the white-shingled house with the black shutters. His eyes narrowed as he drank in every detail. The large porch. Nice. Kind of elegant. He thought of the people next door to his house in Jackson Heights who had poured concrete over most of their minuscule backyard and now grandly referred to the lumpy surface as their patio.

Bernie studied the grounds. There was a huge rhododendron at the left corner of the macadam driveway, a weeping willow off center in the middle of the lawn. Evergreens made a vivid hedge separating the Collins place from the next property.

Well satisfied, Bernie leaned his foot on the acceler-

89

ator. In case he was being watched, he certainly wouldn't be dope enough to do a U-turn here. He drove around the bend, then jammed on his brakes. He'd almost hit a stupid dog.

A kid came flying across the lawn. Through the window, Bernie could hear him frantically calling the dog. 'Jake! Jake!'

The dog ran to the kid, and Bernie was able to start up the car again. The street was quiet enough that through the closed window, he could hear the kid yell, 'Thanks, mister. Thanks a lot.'

Mac arrived at the medical examiner's office on East Thirty-first Street at one-thirty. Meghan was not due until two o'clock, but he had phoned and made an appointment with Dr Kenneth Lyons, the director of the lab. He was escorted to the fifth floor, where in Dr Lyons' small office, he explained his suspicions.

Lyons was a lean man in his late forties with a ready smile and keen, intelligent eyes. 'That woman has been a puzzle. She certainly didn't have the look of someone who would simply disappear and not be missed. We were planning to take a DNA sample from her before the body is taken to potter's field anyway. It will be very simple to take a sample from Miss Collins as well and see if there's the possibility of kinship.'

'That's what Meghan wants to do.'

The doctor's secretary was seated at a desk near the window. The phone rang and she picked it up. 'Miss Collins is downstairs.'

It wasn't just the normal apprehension of viewing a dead body in the morgue that Mac saw in Meghan's face as he stepped from the elevator. Something else had added to the pain in her eyes, the drawn, tired lines around her mouth. It seemed to him that there was a sadness in her that was removed from the grief she had lived with since her father's disappearance.

But she smiled when she saw him, a quick, relieved

smile. She's so pretty, he thought. Her chestnut hair was tousled around her head, a testament to the sharp afternoon wind. She was wearing a black-and-white tweed suit and black boots. The zippered jacket reached her hips, the narrow skirt was calf length. A black turtleneck sweater accentuated the paleness of her face.

Mac introduced her to Dr Lyons. 'You'll be able to study the victim more closely downstairs than in the viewing room,' Lyons said.

The morgue was antiseptically clean. Rows of lockers lined the walls. The murmur of voices could be heard from behind the closed door of a room with an eight-foot window on the corridor. The curtains were drawn over the window. Mac was sure an autopsy was being performed.

An attendant led them down the corridor almost to the end. Dr Lyons nodded to him and he reached for the handle of a drawer.

Noiselessly, the drawer slid out. Mac stared down at the nude, refrigerated body of the young woman. There was a single deep stab wound in her chest. Slender arms lay at her sides; her fingers were open. He took in the narrow waist, slim hips, long legs, high-arched feet. Finally he studied the face.

The chestnut hair was matted on her shoulders, but he could imagine it with the same wind-tossed life as Meghan's hair. The mouth, generous and with the promise of warmth, the thick eyelashes that arched over the closed eyes, the dark brows that accentuated the high forehead.

Mac felt as though a violent punch had caught him in the stomach. He felt dazed, nauseated, light-headed. This could be Meg, he thought, *this was meant to happen to Meg.*

91

27

Catherine Collins touched the button at her hand, and the hospital bed tilted noiselessly up until she stopped it at a semireclining position. For the last hour, since the lunch tray was taken out, she had tried to sleep, but it was useless. She was irritated at herself for her desire to escape into sleep. It's time to face up to life, my girl, she told herself sternly.

She wished she had a calculator and the account books of the inn. She needed to figure out for herself how long she could hold on before she was forced to sell Drumdoe. The mortgage, she thought – that damn mortgage! Pop would never have put so much money in the place. Do without and make do, that had been his slogan when he was a greenhorn. How often had she heard that?

But once he got his inn and his house he'd been the most generous husband and father. Provided you weren't ridiculously extravagant, of course.

And I was ridiculous giving that decorator so much leeway, Catherine thought. But that's water under the bridge.

The analogy made her shiver. It brought to mind the horrible photographs of wrecked cars being hauled to the surface from under the Tappan Zee Bridge. She and Meghan had studied the photos with magnifying glasses, dreading to find what they were expecting to see: some part of a dark blue Cadillac.

Catherine threw back the covers, got out of bed and reached for her robe. She walked across the room to the tiny bathroom and splashed water on her face, then looked in the mirror and grimaced. Put on a little war paint, dear, she told herself.

Ten minutes later she was back in bed and feeling somewhat better. Her short blond hair was brushed; blusher on her cheeks and lipstick had camouflaged the gaunt pallor she had seen in the mirror; a blue silk bed jacket made her feel presentable to possible visitors. She knew Meghan was in New York for the afternoon, but there was always the chance someone else might drop by.

Someone did. Phillip Carter tapped on the partially open door. 'Catherine, may I come in?'

'You bet.'

He bent down and kissed her cheek. 'You look much better.'

'I feel much better. In fact I'm trying to get out of here, but they want me to stay a couple of days more.'

'Good idea.' He pulled the one comfortable chair close to the bed and sat down.

He was wearing a casual tan jacket, dark brown slacks and a brown-and-beige print tie, Catherine noticed. His strong male presence made her ache for her husband.

Edwin had been strikingly handsome. She had met him thirty-one years ago, at a party after a Harvard-Yale football game. She was dating one of the Yale players. She had noticed Ed on the dance floor. The dark hair, the deep blue eyes, the tall thin body.

The next dance, Edwin had cut in on her, and the next day he was ringing the bell at the farmhouse, a dozen roses in his hand. 'I'm courting you, Catherine,' he announced.

Now Catherine tried to blink back sudden tears.

'Catherine?' Phillip's hand was holding hers.

'I'm fine,' she said, withdrawing her hand.

'I don't think you'll feel that way in a few minutes. I wish I could have spoken to Meg before I came.'

93

'She had to go into the city. What is it, Phillip?'

'Catherine, you may have read about the woman who was murdered in New Milford.'

'That doctor. Yes. How awful.'

'Then you haven't heard that she wasn't a doctor, that her credentials were falsified and that she was placed at the Manning Clinic by our company?'

Catherine bolted up. 'What?'

A nurse hurried in. 'Mrs Collins, there are two investigators from the New Milford police in the lobby who need to speak with you. The doctor is on his way. He wants to be here but said I should warn you they'll be up in a few minutes.'

Catherine waited until she heard retreating footsteps in the corridor before she asked, 'Phillip, you know why those people are here?'

'Yes, I do. They were in the office an hour ago.'

'Why? Forget about waiting for the doctor. I have no intention of collapsing again. Please, I do need to know what I'm facing.'

'Catherine, the woman who was murdered last night in New Milford was Ed's client. Ed had to have known her credentials were falsified.' Phillip Carter turned away as though to avoid seeing the pain he knew he was going to inflict. 'You know that the police don't think Ed was drowned in the bridge accident. A neighbor who lives across the street from Helene Petrovic's apartment said Petrovic was visited regularly late at night by a tall man who drove a dark sedan.' He paused, his expression grim. 'She saw him there two weeks ago. Catherine, when Meg called the ambulance the other night a squad car came as well. When you came to, you told the policeman you'd had a call from your husband.'

Catherine tried to swallow but could not. Her mouth and lips were parched. She had the incongruous thought that this is what it must be like to experience severe thirst. 'I was out of it. I meant to say Meg had a call from someone saying he was her father.'

94

There was a tap on the door. The doctor spoke as he came in. 'Catherine, I'm terribly sorry about this. The assistant state attorney insists that the investigators of a murder in New Milford ask you a few questions, and I could not in conscience say you weren't well enough to see them.'

'I'm well enough to see them,' Catherine said quietly. She looked at Phillip. 'Will you stay?'

'I certainly will.' He got up as the investigators followed a nurse into the room.

Catherine's first impression was surprise that one of them was a woman, a young woman around Meghan's age. The other was a man she judged to be in his late thirties. It was he who spoke first, apologizing for the intrusion, promising to take only a few moments of her time, introducing himself and his partner. 'This is Special Investigator Arlene Weiss. I'm Bob Marron.' He got straight to the point. 'Mrs Collins, you were brought here in shock because your daughter received a phone call in the middle of the night from someone who claimed to be your husband?'

'It wasn't my husband. I'd know his voice anywhere, under any circumstances.'

'Mrs Collins, I'm sorry to ask you this, but do you still believe your husband died last January?'

'I absolutely believe he is dead,' she said firmly.

'Beautiful roses for you, Mrs Collins,' a voice chirped as the door was pushed open. It was one of the volunteers in pink jackets who delivered flowers to the rooms, brought around the book cart and helped feed the elderly patients.

'Not now,' Catherine's doctor snapped.

'No, it's all right. Just put them on the nightstand.' Catherine realized she welcomed the intrusion. She needed a moment to get hold of herself. Again stalling for time, she reached for the card the volunteer was detaching from the ribbon on the vase.

She glanced at it, then froze, her eyes filled with

horror. As everyone stared at her, she held up the card with trembling fingers, fighting to retain her composure. 'I didn't know dead people could send flowers,' she whispered.

She read it aloud. ' "My dearest. Have faith in me. I promise this will all work out." ' Catherine bit her lip. 'It's signed, "Your loving husband, Edwin." '

Part Two

28

On Wednesday afternoon, investigators from Connecticut drove to Lawrenceville, New Jersey, to question Stephanie Petrovic about her murdered aunt.

Trying to ignore the restless stirring in her womb, Stephanie clasped her hands together to keep them from trembling. Having grown up in Rumania under the Ceauşescu regime, she had been trained to fear the police, and even though the men who were sitting in her aunt's living room seemed very kind and were not wearing uniforms, she knew enough not to trust them. People who trusted the police often ended up in prison, or worse.

Her aunt's lawyer, Charles Potters, was there as well, a man who reminded her of an official of the village where she had been born. He too was being kind, but she sensed that his kindness was of the impersonal variety. He would do his duty and he had already informed her that his duty was to carry out the terms of Helene's will, which left her entire estate to the Manning Clinic.

'She intended to change it,' Stephanie had told him. 'She planned to take care of me, to help me while I went to cosmetology school, to get me an apartment. She promised she would leave money to me. She said I was like a daughter to her.'

'I understand. But since she did not change her will, the only thing I can say is that until this house is sold you may live in it. As trustee, I can probably arrange

99

to hire you as a caretaker until a sale is completed. After that, I'm afraid, legally you're on your own.'

On her own! Stephanie knew that unless she could get a green card and a job there was no way she could stay in this country.

One of the policemen asked if there were any man who had been her aunt's particular friend.

'No. Not really,' she asnwered. 'Sometimes in the evening we go to parties given by other Rumanians. Sometimes Helene would go to concerts. Often on Saturday or Sunday, she would go out for three or four hours. She never told me where.' But Stephanie knew of no man at all in her aunt's life. She told again how surprised she had been when Helene abruptly quit her job. 'She was planning to give up work as soon as she sold her house. She wanted to move to France for a while.' Stephanie knew she was stumbling over the English words. She was so afraid.

'According to Dr Manning, he had no inkling that she was contemplating leaving the clinic,' the investigator named Hugo said in Rumanian.

Stephanie flashed a look of gratitude at him and switched to her native language as well. 'She told me that Dr Manning would be very upset and she dreaded breaking the news to him.'

'Did she have another job in mind? It would have meant her credentials being checked again.'

'She said she wanted to take some time off to rest.'

Hugo turned to the lawyer. 'What was Helene Petrovic's financial situation?'

Charles Potters answered, 'I can assure you it was quite good. Doctor, or rather Ms Petrovic lived very carefully and made good investments. This house was paid off, and she had eight hundred thousand dollars in stocks, bonds and cash.'

So much money, Stephanie thought, and now she would not have a penny of it. She rubbed her hand across her forehead. Her back hurt. Her feet were swol-

100

len. She was so tired. Mr Potters was helping her arrange the funeral mass. It would be held at St Dominic's on Friday.

She looked around. This room was so pretty, with its blue brocaded upholstery, polished tables, fringed lamps and pale blue carpet. This whole house was so pretty. She'd liked being in a place like this. Helene had promised that she could take some things from here for her apartment in New York. What would she do now? What was the policeman asking?

'When do you expect your baby, Stephanie?'

Tears gushed down her cheeks as she answered. 'In two weeks.' She burst out, 'He told me it was my problem and he's moved to California. He won't help me. I don't know where to find him. I don't know what to do.'

29

The shock that Meghan had felt at once again seeing the dead woman who resembled her had dulled by the time a vial of blood was drawn from her arm.

She did not know quite what reaction she expected from Mac when he viewed the body. The only one she had detected was a tightening of his lips. The only comment he made was that he found the resemblance so startling he felt the DNA comparison was absolutely necessary. Dr Lyons voiced the same opinion.

Neither she nor Mac had eaten lunch. They left the medical examiner's office in separate cars and drove to one of Meg's favorite spots, Neary's on Fifty-seventh Street. Seated side by side on a banquette in the cozy restaurant, over a club sandwich and coffee, Meghan told Mac about Helene Petrovic's falsified credentials and her father's possible involvement.

Jimmy Neary came over to inquire about Meghan's mother. When he learned Catherine was in the hospital, he brought his portable phone to the table for Meghan to call her.

Phillip answered.

'Hi, Phillip,' Meghan said. 'Just thought I'd phone and see how Mom is doing. Would you put her on, please?'

'Meg, she's had a pretty nasty shock.'

'What kind of shock?' Meghan demanded.

'Somebody sent her a dozen roses. You'll understand when I read the card to you.'

Mac had been looking across the room at the framed pictures of the Irish countryside. At Meghan's gasp, he turned to her, then watched as her eyes widened in shock. Something's happened to Catherine, he thought. 'Meg, what is it?' He took the phone from her shaking fingers. 'Hello . . .'

'Mac, I'm glad you're there.'

It was Phillip Carter's voice, even now, sounding confident and in charge.

Mac put his arm around Meghan as Carter tersely related the events of the past hour. 'I'm staying with Catherine for a while,' he concluded. 'She was pretty upset at first, but she's calmer now. She says she wants to speak to Meg.'

'Meg, it's your mother,' Mac said, holding the receiver out to her. For a moment he wasn't sure Meghan had heard him, but then she reached for the phone. He could see the effort she was making to sound matter-of-fact.

'Mom, you're sure you're okay? . . . What do I think? I think it's some kind of cruel joke too. You're right, Dad would never do anything like that. . . . I know . . . I know how tough it is. . . . Come on, you certainly do have the strength to handle this. You're old Pat's daughter, aren't you?

'I have an appointment with Mr Weicker at the station in an hour. Then I'll come directly to the hospital. . . . Love you too. Let me talk to Phillip for a minute.

'Phillip, stay with her, won't you? She shouldn't be alone now. . . . Thanks.'

When Meg replaced the receiver, she cried, 'It's a miracle my mother didn't have a full-blown heart attack, what with investigators asking about Dad and those roses being delivered.' Her mouth quivered and she bit her lip.

Oh, Meg, Mac thought. He ached to put his arms around her, to hold her to him, to kiss the pain from her eyes and lips. Instead he tried to reassure her about the primary fear that he knew was paralyzing her.

'Catherine isn't going to have a heart attack,' he said firmly. 'At least put that worry out of your mind. I mean it, Meg. Now, did I get it right from Phillip that the police are trying to tie your dad to that Petrovic woman's death?'

'Apparently. They kept coming back to the neighbor who said a tall man with a dark late-model sedan visited Petrovic regularly. Dad was tall. He drove a dark sedan.'

'So do thousands of other tall men, Meg. That's ridiculous.'

'I know it is. Mom knows it too. But the police categorically don't believe Dad was in the bridge accident, which means to them that he's probably still alive. They want to know why he vouched for Petrovic's falsified credentials. They asked Mom if she thought he might have had some kind of personal relationship with Petrovic.'

'Do you believe that he's alive, Meg?'

'No, I don't. But if he put Helene Petrovic in that job knowing she was a fraud, something was wrong. Unless she somehow fooled him too.'

'Meg, I've known your father since I was a college freshman. If there's one point on which I can reassure you, it's that Edwin Collins is or was a very gentle man. What you told Catherine is absolutely true. That middle-of-the-night phone call and sending those flowers your mother received just aren't things your father would have done. They're the kind of games cruel people play.'

'Or demented people.' Meghan straightened up as though just aware of Mac's arm around her. Quietly, Mac removed it.

He said, 'Meg, flowers have to be paid for, with cash, with a credit card, with a charge account. How was the payment for the roses handled?'

'I gather the investigators are hot onto that scenario.' Jimmy Neary offered an Irish coffee.

Meghan shook her head. 'I sure could use one, Jimmy, but we'd better take a rain check. I have to get to the office.'

Mac was going back to work. Before they got into their cars, he put his hands on her shoulders. 'Meg, one thing. Promise me you'll let me help.'

'Oh, Mac,' she sighed, 'I think you've had your share of the Collins family's problems for a while. How long did Dr Lyons say it would take to get the results of the DNA comparison?'

'Four to six weeks,' Mac said. 'I'll call you tonight, Meg.'

Half an hour later, Meghan was sitting in Tom Weicker's office. 'That was a hell of a good interview with the receptionist at the Manning Clinic,' he told her. 'No one else has anything like it. But in view of your father's connection to Petrovic, I don't want you to go near that place again.'

It was what she expected to hear. She looked squarely at him. 'The Franklin Center in Philadelphia has a terrific reputation. I'd like to substitute that in vitro facility for Manning in the feature.' She waited, dreading to hear that he was pulling her off that too.

She was relieved when he said, 'I want the feature completed as soon as possible. Everybody's buzzing about in vitro fertilization because of Petrovic. The timing is great. When can you go to Philadelphia?'

'Tomorrow.'

She felt dishonest not telling Tom that Dr Henry Williams, who headed the Franklin Center, had worked with Helene Petrovic at Manning. But, she reasoned, if she had any chance of getting in to talk to Williams it would be as a PC reporter, not as the daughter of the man who had submitted Petrovic's bogus résumé and glowingly recommended her.

Bernie drove to Manhattan from Connecticut. Seeing Meghan's house brought back memories of all the other times he'd followed a girl home, then hidden in her car or garage or even in the shrubbery around her house, just so he could watch her. It was like being in a different world where it was just the two of them alive, even though the girl didn't know he was there.

He knew he had to be near Meghan, but he'd have to be careful. Newtown was a ritzy little community, and cops in places like that were always on the lookout for strange cars driving around a neighborhood.

Suppose I'd hit that dog, Bernie thought as he drove through the Bronx toward the Willis Avenue bridge. The kid who owned it probably would have started yelling his head off. People would have rushed out to see what happened. One of them might have started asking questions, like what's a guy in a gypsy cab doing in this neighborhood, on a dead end street? If somebody'd called the cops, they might have checked my record, Bernie thought. He knew what that would mean.

There was only one thing for him to do. When he got to midtown Manhattan, he drove to the discount shop on Forty-seventh Street where he acquired most of his electronic gadgets. For a long time he'd had his eye on a real state-of-the-art video camera there. Today he bought that and a police scanner radio for the car.

He then went to an art supply store and bought sheets of pink paper. This year pink was the color of the press passes the police issued to the media. He had one at home. A reporter had dropped it in the garage. On his computer, he could copy it and make up a press pass that looked official, and he'd also make himself a press parking permit to stick in his windshield.

There were bunches of local cable stations around that no one paid any attention to. He'd say he was from one of them. He'd be Bernie Heffernan, news reporter.

Just like Meghan.

The only problem was, he was going through his vacation and severance pay too fast. He had to keep money coming in. Fortunately he managed to pick up a fare to Kennedy Airport and one back into the city before it was time to go home.

At dinner his mother was sneezing. 'Are you getting a cold, Mama?' he asked solicitously.

'I don't get colds. I just have allergies,' she snapped. 'I think there's dust in this house.'

'Mama, you know there's no dust here. You're a good housekeeper.'

'Bernard, are you keeping the basement clean? I'm trusting you. I don't dare attempt those stairs after what happened.'

'Mama, it's fine.'

They watched the six o'clock news together and saw Meghan Collins interviewing the receptionist at the Manning Clinic.

Bernie leaned forward, drinking in Meghan's profile as she asked questions. His hands and forehead grew damp.

Then the remote selector was yanked from his hand.

As the television clicked off, he felt a stinging slap on his face. 'You're starting again, Bernard,' his mother screamed. 'You're watching that girl. I can tell. I can just tell! Don't you ever learn?'

When Meghan got to the hospital, she found her mother fully dressed. 'Virginia brought me some clothes. I've got to get out of here,' Catherine Collins said firmly. 'I can't just lie in this bed and think. It's too unsettling. At least at the inn I'll be busy.'

'What did the doctor say?'

'At first he objected, of course, but now he agrees, or at least he's willing to sign me out.' Her voice faltered. 'Meggie, don't try to change my mind. It really is better if I'm home.'

Meghan hugged her fiercely. 'Are you packed yet?'

'Down to the toothbrush. Meg, one more thing. Those investigators want to talk to you. When we get home, you have to call and set up an appointment with them.'

The phone was ringing when Meghan pushed open the front door of the house. She ran to get it. It was Dina Anderson. 'Meghan. If you're still interested in being around when the baby is born, start making plans. The doctor is going to put me into Danbury Medical Center on Monday morning and induce labor.'

'I'll be there. Is it all right if I come up Sunday afternoon with a cameraman and take some pictures of you and Jonathan getting ready for the baby?'

'That will be fine.'

Catherine Collins went from room to room, turning on the lights. 'It's so good to be home,' she murmured.

'Do you want to lie down?'

'That's the last thing in the world I want to do. I'm going to soak in a tub and get properly dressed and then we're going to have dinner at the inn.'

'Are you sure?' Meghan watched as her mother's chin went up and her mouth settled in a firm line.

'I'm very sure. Things are going to get a lot worse before they get better, Meg. You'll see that when you talk to those investigators. But no one is going to think that we're hiding out.'

'I think Pop's exact words were, "Don't let the bastards get you." I'd better call those people from the state attorney's office.'

John Dwyer was the assistant state attorney assigned to the Danbury courthouse. His jurisdiction included the town of New Milford.

At forty, Dwyer had been in the state attorney's office for fifteen years. During those years, he'd sent some upstanding citizens, pillars of the community, to prison for crimes ranging from fraud to murder. He'd also prosecuted three people who'd faked their deaths in an attempt to collect insurance.

Edwin Collins' supposed death in the Tappan Zee Bridge tragedy had generated much sympathetic coverage in the local media. The family was well known in the area, and the Drumdoe Inn was an institution.

The fact that Collins' car almost certainly had not gone over the side of the bridge and his role in the verification of Helene Petrovic's bogus credentials had changed a shocking suburban murder to a statewide scandal. Dwyer knew that the State Department of Health was sending medical investigators to the Manning Clinic to determine how much damage Petrovic might have done in the lab there.

Late Wednesday afternoon, Dwyer had a meeting in his office with the investigators from the New Milford police, Arlene Weiss and Bob Marron. They had managed to get Petrovic's file from the State Department in Washington.

Weiss reviewed the specifics of it for him. 'Petrovic came to the United States twenty years ago, when she was twenty-seven. Her sponsor ran a beauty salon on Broadway. Her visa application lists her education as high school graduate with some training at a cosmetology school in Bucharest.'

'No medical training?' Dwyer asked.

'None that she listed,' Weiss confirmed.

Bob Marron looked at his notes. 'She went to work at her friend's salon, stayed there eleven years and in the last couple took secretarial courses at night.'

Dwyer nodded.

'Then she was offered a job as a secretary at the Dowling Assisted Reproduction Center in Trenton, New Jersey. That's when she bought the Lawrenceville house.

'Three years later, Collins placed her at the Manning Clinic as an embryologist.'

'What about Edwin Collins? Does his background check out?' Dwyer asked.

'Yes. He's a Harvard Business graduate. Never been in trouble. Senior partner in the firm. Got a gun permit about ten years ago after he was held up at a red light in Bridgeport.'

The intercom buzzed. 'Miss Collins returning Mr Marron's call.'

'That's Collins' daughter?' Dwyer asked.

'Yes.'

'Get her in here tomorrow.'

Marron took the phone and spoke to Meghan, then looked at the assistant state attorney. 'Eight o'clock tomorrow morning all right? She's driving to Philadelphia on assignment and needs to come in early.'

Dwyer nodded.

After Marron confirmed the appointment with Meghan and replaced the receiver, Dwyer leaned back in his swivel chair. 'Let's see what we have. Edwin Collins disappeared and is presumed dead. But now his wife receives flowers from him, which you tell me were charged to his credit card.'

'The order was phoned in to the florist. The credit

109

card has never been canceled. On the other hand, until this afternoon, it hasn't been used since January,' Weiss said.

'Wasn't it tagged after his disappearance to see if there was activity on the account?'

'Until the other day, Collins was presumed to have drowned. There was no reason to put an alert on his cards.'

Arlene Weiss was looking over her notes. 'I want to ask Meghan Collins about something her mother said. That phone call that landed Mrs Collins in the hospital, the one that she swears didn't sound like her husband . . .'

'What about it?'

'She thought she heard the caller say something like, "I'm in terrible trouble." What did that mean?'

'We'll ask the daughter what she thinks when we talk to her tomorrow,' Dwyer said. 'I know what I think. Is Edwin Collins still listed as missing-presumed-dead?'

Marron and Weiss nodded together. Assistant State Attorney Dwyer got up. 'We probably should change that. Here's the way I see it. One, we've established Collins' connection to Petrovic. Two, he almost certainly did not die in the bridge accident. Three, he took all the cash value from his insurance policies a few weeks before he disappeared. Four, no trace of his car has been found, but a tall man in a dark sedan regularly visited the Petrovic woman. Five, the phone call, the use of the credit card, the flowers. I say it's enough. Put out an APB on Edwin Collins. Make it, "Wanted for questioning in the murder of Helene Petrovic." '

30

Just before five o'clock, Victor Orsini received the call he was afraid might come. Larry Downes, president of Downes and Rosen, phoned to tell him that it would be better all around if he held off giving notice at Collins and Carter.

'For how long, Larry?' Victor asked quietly.

'I don't know,' Downes said evasively. 'This fuss about the Petrovic woman will all die down eventually, but you have too much negative feedback attached to you for you to come here now. And if it turns out that Petrovic mixed up any of those embryos at the clinic, there'll be hell to pay, and you know it. You guys placed her there, and you'll be held responsible.'

Victor protested. 'I'd just started when Helene Petrovic's application was submitted to the Manning Clinic. Larry, you let me down last winter.'

'I'm sorry, Victor. But the fact is, you were there six weeks before Petrovic began working at Manning. That means you were there when the investigation into her credentials should have been taking place. Collins and Carter is a small operation. Who's going to believe you weren't aware of what was going on?'

Orsini swallowed. When he spoke to the reporters he'd said that he'd never heard of Petrovic, that he'd barely been hired when she was okayed for Manning. They hadn't picked up that he'd obviously been in the office when her application was processed. He tried one more argument. 'Larry, I've helped you people a lot this year.'

'Have you, Victor?'

'You placed candidates with three of our best accounts.'

'Perhaps our candidates for the jobs were stronger.'

'Who told you those corporations were looking to fill positions?'

'I'm sorry, Victor.'

Orsini stared at the receiver as the line went dead. Don't call us. We'll call you, he thought. He knew the job with Downes and Rosen probably would never be given to him now.

Milly poked her head into his office. 'I'm on my way. Hasn't it been a terrible day, Mr Orsini? All those reporters coming in and all those calls.' Her eyes were snapping with excitement.

Victor could just see her at her dinner table tonight, repeating with relish every detail of the day. 'Is Mr Carter back?'

'No. He phoned that he was going to stay with Mrs Collins at the hospital and then go directly home. You know, I think he's getting sweet on her.'

Orsini did not answer.

'Well, good night, Mr Orsini.'

'Good night, Milly.'

While her mother was dressing, Meghan slipped into the study and took the letters and obituary notice from the drawer in her father's desk. She hid them in her briefcase and prayed her mother would not notice the faint scratches on the desk where the file had slipped when she was breaking into the drawer. Meghan would have to tell her about the letters and the death notice evenually, but not yet. Maybe after she'd been to Philadelphia she might have some sort of explanation.

She went upstairs to her own bathroom to wash her face and hands and freshen her makeup. After hesitating a moment, she decided to call Mac. He had said he'd call her, and she didn't want him to think anything was wrong. More wrong than it already is, she corrected herself.

Kyle answered. 'Meg!' It was the Kyle she knew, delighted to hear her voice.

'Hi, pal. How's it going?'

'Great. But today was really bad.'

'Why?'

'Jake nearly got killed. I was throwing a ball to him. He's getting real good at catching it, but I threw too hard and it went in the street and he ran out and some guy almost hit him. I mean you should have seen the guy stop his car. Like just *stop*. That car *shook*.'

'I'm glad Jake's okay, Kyle. Next time toss the ball to him in the backyard. You've got more room.'

'That's what Dad said. He's grabbing the phone, Meg. See you.'

Mac came on. 'I was not grabbing it. I reached for it. Hi, Meg. You've gotten all the news from this end. How's it going?'

She told him that her mother was home. 'I'm driving to Philadelphia tomorrow for the feature I'm trying to put together.'

'Will you also check out that address in Chestnut Hill?'

'Yes. Mother doesn't know about that or those letters.'

'She won't hear it from me. When will you get back?'

'Probably not before eight o'clock. It's nearly a four-hour drive to Philadelphia.'

'Meg.' Mac's voice became hesitant. 'I know that you don't want me interfering, but I wish you'd let me help. I sense sometimes that you're avoiding me.'

'Don't be silly. We've always been good buddies.'

'I'm not sure we are anymore. Maybe I've missed something. What happened?'

What happened, Meghan thought, is that I can't think of that letter I wrote you nine years ago, begging you not to marry Ginger, without writhing in humiliation.

What happened is that I'll never be anything more than your little buddy and I've managed to separate myself from you. I can't risk going through Jeremy MacIntyre withdrawal again.

'Nothing happened, Mac,' she said lightly. 'You're still my buddy. I can't help it if I don't talk about piano lessons anymore. I gave them up years ago.'

That night when she went to her mother's room to turn down the bed she switched the ringer on the phone to the off position. If there were any more nocturnal calls, they would be heard only by her.

31

Dr Henry Williams, the sixty-five-year-old head of the Franklin Assisted Reproduction Center in the renovated old town section of Philadelphia, was a man who looked vaguely like everyone's favorite uncle. He had a head of thick graying hair, a gentle face that reassured even the most nervous patient. Very tall, he had a slight stoop that suggested he was in the habit of bending down to listen.

Meghan had phoned him after her meeting with Tom Weicker, and he had readily agreed to an appointment. Now Meghan sat in front of his desk in the cheerful office with its framed pictures of babies and young children covering the walls.

'Are these all children born through in vitro fertilization?' Meghan asked.

'Born through assisted reproduction,' Williams corrected. 'Not all are in vitro births.'

'I understand, or at least I believe I do. In vitro is when the eggs are removed from the ovaries and fertilized with semen in the laboratory.'

'Correct. You realize that the woman has been given fertility drugs so that her ovaries will release a number of eggs at the same time?'

'Yes. I understand that.'

'There are other procedures we practice, all variations of in vitro fertilization. I suggest I give you some literature that explains them. Basically it amounts to a lot of heavy-duty terms that all boil down to assisting a woman to have the successful pregnancy she craves.'

'Would you be willing to be interviewed on-camera, to let us do some footage on the facilities and speak to some of your clients?'

'Yes. Frankly we're proud of our operation, and favorable publicity is welcome. I would have one stipulation. I'll contact several of our clients and ask if they'd be willing to speak to you. I don't want you approaching them. Some people do not choose to let their families know that they have used assisted birth procedures.'

'Why would they object? I should think they'd just be happy to have the baby.'

'They are. But one woman whose mother-in-law learned about the assisted birth openly said that, because of her son's very low sperm count, she doubted if it was her son's child. Our client actually had DNA testing done on her, the husband and the baby to prove it was the biological offspring of both parents.'

'Some people do use donor embryos, of course.'

'Yes, those who simply cannot conceive on their own. It's actually a form of adoption.'

'I guess it is. Doctor, I know this is a terrible rush, but could I come back late this afternoon with a cameraman? A woman in Connecticut is giving birth very soon to the identical twin of her son who was born three years ago through in vitro fertilization. We'll be doing follow-up stories on the progress of the children.'

Williams' expression changed, becoming troubled. 'Sometimes I wonder if we don't go too far. The psychological aspects of identical twins being born at separate times concerns me greatly. Incidentally, when the embryo splits in two and one is cryopreserved, we call it the clone, not the identical twin. But to answer your question, yes, I'd be available later today.'

'I can't tell you how grateful I am. We'll do some establishing shots outside and in the reception area. I'll lead in with when the Franklin Center started. That's about six years ago, I understand.'

'Six years ago this past September.'

'Then I'll stick to specific questions about in vitro fertilization and the freezing, I mean cryopreservation, of the clone, as in Mrs Anderson's case.'

Meghan got up to go. 'I've got some fast arrangements to make. Would four o'clock be all right for you?'

'It should be fine.'

Meghan hesitated. She had been afraid to ask Dr Williams about Helen Petrovic before she established some rapport with him, but she could not wait any longer. 'Dr Williams, I don't know if the papers here have carried the story, but Helene Petrovic, a woman who worked in the Manning Clinic, was found murdered, and it's come out that her credentials were falsified. You knew her and actually worked with her, didn't you?'

'Yes, I did.' Henry Williams shook his head. 'I was Dr Manning's assistant, and I knew everything that went on in that clinic and who was doing the job. Helene Petrovic certainly fooled me. She kept that lab the way labs should be kept. It's terrible that she falsified credentials, but she absolutely seemed to know what she was doing.'

Meghan decided to take a chance that this kindly man would understand why she needed to ask probing questions. 'Doctor, my father's firm and specifically my father have been accused of verifying Helene Petrovic's lies. Forgive me, but I must try to find out more about her. The receptionist at Manning Clinic saw you and Helene Petrovic at dinner. How well did you get to know her?'

Henry Williams looked amused. 'You mean Marge Walters. Did she also tell you that as a courtesy I always took a new staff member at Manning to dinner? An informal welcome . . .'

'No, she didn't. Did you know Helene Petrovic before she went to Manning?'

'No.'

'Have you had any contact with her since you left?'

'None at all.'

The intercom buzzed. He picked up the receiver and listened. 'Hold it for a moment, please,' he said, turning to Meghan.

She took her cue. 'Doctor, I won't take any more of your time. Thank you so much.' Meghan picked up her shoulder bag and left.

When the door closed behind her, Dr Henry Williams again put the receiver to his ear. 'Put the call through now, please.'

He murmured a greeting, listened, then said nervously, 'Yes, of course I'm alone. She just left. She'll be back at four with a camerman. Don't tell me to be careful. What kind of fool do you take me for?'

He replaced the receiver, suddenly infinitely weary. After a moment, he picked it up again and dialed. 'Everything under control over there?' he asked.

Her Scottish ancestors called it second sight, the gift had turned up in a woman in different generations of Clan Campbell. This time it was Fiona Campbell Black who was granted it. A psychic who was regularly called upon by police departments throughout the country to help solve crimes and by families frantic to find missing loved ones, Fiona treated her extraordinary abilities with profound respect.

Married twenty years, she lived in Litchfield, Connecticut, a lovely old town that was settled in the early seventeenth century.

On Thursday afternoon Fiona's husband, Andrew Black, a lawyer with offices in town, came home for lunch. He found her sitting in the breakfast room, the morning paper spread in front of her, her eyes reflective, her head tilted as though she were expecting to hear a voice or sound she did not want to miss.

Andrew Black knew what that meant. He took off his coat, tossed it on a chair and said, 'I'll fix us something.'

Ten minutes later when he came back with a plate of sandwiches and a pot of tea, Fiona raised her eyebrows. 'It happened when I saw this.' She held up the local newspaper with Edwin Collins' picture on the front page. 'They want this man for questioning in the Petrovic woman's death.'

Black poured the tea. 'I read that.'

'Andrew, I don't want to get involved, but I think I have to. I'm getting a message about him.'

'How clear is it?'

'It isn't. I have to handle something that belongs to him. Should I call the New Milford police or go directly to his family?'

'I think it's better to go through the police.'

'I suppose so.' Slowly, Fiona ran her fingertips over the grainy reproduction of Edwin Collins' face. 'So much evil,' she murmured, 'so much death and evil surrounding him.'

32

Bernie's first fare on Thursday morning was from Kennedy Airport. He parked the Chevy and wandered over to where the suburban buses picked up and deposited passengers. Bernie glanced at the schedule. A bus for Westport was due in, and a group of people were waiting for it. One couple in their thirties had two small kids and a lot of luggage. Bernie decided that they'd be good prospects.

'Connecticut?' he asked them, his smile genial.

'We're not taking a cab,' the woman snapped impatiently as she grabbed the two-year-old's hand. 'Billy, stay with me,' she scolded. 'You can't run around here.'

'Forty bucks plus tolls,' Bernie said. 'I've got a pickup around Westport, so any fare I get is found money.'

The husband was trying to hang on to a squirming three-year-old. 'You got a deal.' He did not bother to look to his wife for approval.

Bernie had run his car through the car wash and vacuumed the interior again. He saw the disdain that initially flashed on the woman's face turn to approval at the Chevy's clean interior. He drove carefully, never above the speed limit, no quick changes from lane to lane. The man sat in front with him. The woman was in the back, the kids strapped in beside her. Bernie made a mental note to buy some car seats and keep them in the trunk.

The man directed Bernie to Exit 17 off the Connecticut Turnpike. 'It's just a mile and a half from here.'

When they reached the pleasant brick home on Tuxedo Road, Bernie was rewarded with a ten dollar tip.

He drove back to the Connecticut Turnpike, south to Exit 15 and once again got on Route 7. It was as though he couldn't stop the car from going to where Meghan lived. Be careful, he tried to tell himself. Even with the camera and the press pass it might look suspicious for him to be on her street.

He decided to have a cup of coffee and think about it. He pulled in at the next diner. There was a newspaper vending machine in the vestibule between the outer and inner doors. Through the glass, Bernie saw the headline, all about the Manning Clinic. That was where Meghan had done the interview yesterday, the one he and Mama had watched. He fished in his pocket for change and bought a paper.

Over coffee he read the article. The Manning Clinic was about forty minutes away from Meghan's town. There'd probably be media hanging around there because they were checking out the laboratory where that woman had worked.

Maybe Meghan would be there too. She'd been there yesterday.

Forty minutes later Bernie was on the narrow, winding road that led from the quaint center of Kent to the Manning Clinic. After he left the diner he'd sat in the car and studied the map of this area so carefully that it was easy to figure out the most direct way to get there.

Just as he'd hoped, there were a number of media vans in the parking lot of the clinic. He parked at a distance from them and stuck his parking permit in the windshield. Then he studied the press pass he'd created. It would have taken an expert to spot that it wasn't genuine. It listed him as Bernard Heffernan, Channel 86, Elmira, New York. It was a local community station, he reminded himself. If anyone asked why that community would be interested in this story, he'd say they were thinking of building a facility like the Manning Clinic there.

Satisfied that he had his story straight, Bernie got out of the car and pulled on his windbreaker. Most reporters and cameramen didn't dress up. He decided to wear dark glasses, then got his new video camera from the trunk. State of the art, he told himself proudly. It had cost a bundle. He'd put it on his credit card. He'd rubbed some dust on it from the basement so it didn't look too new, and he'd painted the Channel 86 call letters on the side.

There were a dozen or so reporters and cameramen in the clinic's lobby. They were interviewing a man who Bernie could see was stonewalling them. He was saying, 'I repeat, the Manning Clinic is proud of its success in assisting women to have the children they so ardently desire. It is our belief that, despite the information on her visa application, Helene Petrovic may have trained as an embryologist in Rumania. None of the professionals who worked with her detected the slightest word or action on her part that suggested she did not thoroughly know her job.'

'But if she made mistakes?' one reporter asked. 'Suppose she mixed up those frozen embryos and women have given birth to other people's children?'

'We will perform DNA analysis for any parents who wish the clinical test for themselves and their child. The results take four to six weeks to achieve, but they are irrefutable. If parents wish to have that testing done at a different facility, we will pay the expense. Neither Dr Manning nor any of the senior staff expect a problem in that area.'

Bernie looked around. Meghan wasn't here. Should he ask people if they'd seen her? No, that would be a mistake. Just be part of the crowd, he cautioned himself.

But as he'd hoped, no one was paying any attention

121

to him. He pointed his camera at the guy answering questions and turned it on.

When the interview was over, Bernie left with the group, taking care not to get too close to any of the others. He had spotted a PCD cameraman but did not recognize the burly man who was holding the mike. At the foot of the porch steps, a woman stopped her car and got out. She was pregnant and obviously upset. A reporter asked, 'Ma'am, are you a client here?'

Stephanie Petrovic tried to shield her face from the cameras as she cried. 'No. No. I just came to beg them to share my aunt's money with me. She left everything to the clinic. I am thinking that perhaps somebody from here killed her because they were afraid that after she quit she would change her will. If I could prove that, wouldn't her money be mine?'

For long minutes, Meghan sat in her car in front of the handsome limestone house in Chestnut Hill, twenty miles from downtown Philadelphia. The graceful lines of the three-story residence were accentuated by the mullioned windows, antique oak door and the slate roof that gleamed in shades of deep green in the early afternoon sun.

The walkway that threaded through the broad expanse of lawn was bordered by rows of azaleas that Meghan was sure would bloom with vivid beauty in the spring. A dozen slender white birches were scattered like sentinels throughout the property.

The name on the mailbox was C.J. Graham. Had she ever heard that name from her father? Meghan didn't think so.

She got out of the car and went slowly up the walk. She hesitated a moment, then rang the bell and heard the faint peal of chimes sound inside the house. A moment later the door was opened by a maid in uniform.

'Yes?' Her inquiry was polite but guarded.

Meghan realized she did not know who she should ask to see. 'I would like a word with whoever lives in this house who might have been a friend of Aurelia Collins.'

'Who is it, Jessie?' a man's voice called.

Behind the maid, Meghan saw a tall man with snow white hair, approaching the door.

'Invite the young woman in, Jessie,' he directed. 'It's cold out there.'

Meghan stepped inside. As the door closed, the man's eyes narrowed. He waved her closer. 'Come in, please. Under the light.' A smile broke over his face. 'It's Annie, isn't it? My dear, I'm glad to see you again.'

233

Catherine Collins had an early breakfast with Meghan before Meg left to meet with the investigators at the Danbury courthouse and then to drive to Philadelphia. Catherine carried a second cup of coffee upstairs and turned on the television in her room. On the local news she heard that her husband's official listing with the law was no longer missing-presumed-dead, but had been changed to wanted-for-questioning in the Petrovic death.

When Meg called to say she was finished with the investigators and about to leave for Philadelphia, Catherine asked, 'Meg, what did they ask you?'

'The same kind of questions they asked you. You know they're convinced Dad is alive. So far they have him guilty of fraud and murder. God knows what else they'll come up with. You're the one who warned me yesterday that it was going to get worse before it got better. You sure were right.'

Something in Meg's voice chilled Catherine. 'Meg, there's something you're not telling me.'

'Mom, I have to go. We'll talk tonight, I promise.'

'I don't want anything held back.'

'I swear to God I won't hold anything back.'

The doctor had cautioned Catherine to stay at home and rest for at least a few days. Rest and give myself a real heart attack worrying, she thought as she dressed. She was going to the inn.

She'd been away only a few days, but she could see a difference. Virginia was good but missed small details. The flower arrangement on the registration desk was drooping. 'When did this come?' Catherine asked.

'Just this morning.'

'Call the florist and ask him to replace it.' The roses she had received in the hospital were dewy fresh, Catherine rememebered.

The tables in the dining room were set for lunch. Catherine walked from one to the other, examining them, a busboy behind her. 'We're short a napkin here, and on the table by the window. A knife is missing there and that saltcellar looks grimy.'

'Yes, ma'am.'

She went into the kitchen. The old chef had retired in July after twenty years. His replacement, Clive D'Arcette, had come with impressive experience, despite being only twenty-six years old. After four months, Catherine was coming to the conclusion that he was a good second banana, but couldn't yet do the job on his own.

He was preparing the luncheon specials when Catherine entered the kitchen. She frowned as she noticed the grease spatters on the stove. Clearly they came from the dinner preparation the night before. The garbage

124

bin had not been emptied. She tasted the hollandaise sauce. 'Why is it salty?' she asked.

'I wouldn't call it salty, Mrs Collins,' D'Arcette said, his tone just missing politeness.

'But I would, and I suspect anyone who orders it would.'

'Mrs Collins, you hired me to be the chef here. Unless I can be the chef and prepare food my way, this situation won't work.'

'You've made it very easy for me,' Catherine said. 'You're fired.'

She was tying an apron around her waist when Virginia Murphy hurried in. 'Catherine, where's Clive going? He just stormed past me.'

'Back to cooking school, I hope.'

'You're supposed to be resting.'

Catherine turned to her. 'Virginia, my salvation is going to be at this stove for as long as I can hang onto this place. Now what specials did Escoffier line up for today?'

They served forty-three lunches as well as sandwiches in the bar. It was a good seating. As the new orders slowed down, Catherine was able to go into the dining room. In her long white apron, she went from table to table, stopping for a moment at each. She could see the questioning eyes behind the warm smiles of greeting.

I don't blame people for being curious, with all they're hearing, she thought. I would be too. But these are my friends. This is my inn, and no matter what truth comes out, Meg and I have our place in this town.

Catherine spent the late afternoon in the office going over the books. If the bank will let me refinance and I hock or sell my jewelry, she decided, I might be able to hang on for six months longer at least. By then maybe we'll know something about the insurance. She closed her eyes. If only she hadn't been fool enough to put the house in both her and Edwin's names after Pop died . . .

Why did I do it? she wondered. I know why. I didn't want Edwin to think of himself as living in my house. Even when Pop was alive, Edwin had always insisted on paying for the utilities and repairs. 'I have to feel as though I belong here,' he'd said. Oh, Edwin! What had he called himself? Oh yes, 'a wandering minstrel'. She'd always thought of that as a joke. Had he meant it as a joke? Now she wasn't so certain.

She tried to remember verses of the old Gilbert and Sullivan song he used to sing. Only the opening line and one other came back to her. The first line was, 'A wandering minstrel, I, a thing of shreds and patches.' The other line: 'And to your humors changing, I tune my subtle song.'

Plaintive words when you analyzed them. Why had Edwin felt they applied to him?

Resolutely, Catherine went back to studying the accounts. The phone rang as she closed the last book. It was Bob Marron, one of the investigators who had come to see her in the hospital. 'Mrs Collins, when you weren't home I took a chance on calling you at the inn. Something has come up. We felt we needed to pass on this information to you, though we certainly don't necessarily recommend that you act on it.'

'I don't know what you're talking about,' Catherine said flatly.

She listened as Marron told her that Fiona Black, a psychic who had worked with them on cases of missing persons, had called. 'She says she is getting very strong vibrations about your husband and would like to be able to handle something of his,' Marron concluded.

'You're trying to send me some quack?'

'I know how you feel, but do you remember the Talmadge child who was missing three years ago?'

'Yes.'

'It was Mrs Black who told us to concentrate the search in the construction area near the town hall. She saved that kid's life.'

126

'I see.' Catherine moistened her lips with her tongue. Anything is better than not knowing, she told herself. She tightened her grasp on the receiver. 'What does Mrs Black want of Edwin's? Clothing? A ring?'

'She's here now. She'd like to come to your house and select something if that's possible. I'd bring her over in half an hour.'

Catherine wondered if she should wait for Meg before she met this woman. Then she heard herself say, 'Half an hour will be fine. I'm on my way home now.'

Meghan felt frozen in time as she stood in the foyer with the courtly man who obviously believed they had met before. Through lips almost too numb to utter the words, she managed to say, 'My name isn't Annie. It's Meghan. Meghan Collins.'

Graham looked closely at her. 'You're Edwin's daughter, aren't you?'

'Yes, I am.'

'Come with me, please.' He took her arm and guided her through the door to the study, on the right of the foyer. 'I spend most of my time in here,' he told her as he led her to the couch and settled himself in a high-backed wing chair. 'Since my wife passed away, this house seems awfully big to me.'

Meghan realized that Graham had seen her shock and distress and was trying to defuse it. But she was beyond phrasing her questions diplomatically. She opened her purse and took out the envelope with the obituary notice. 'Did you send this to my father?' she asked.

'Yes, I did. He didn't acknowledge it, but then I never expected that he would. I was so sorry when I read about the accident last January.'

'How do you know my father?' Meghan asked.

'I'm sorry,' he apologized. 'I don't think I've introduced myself. I'm Cyrus Graham. Your father's stepbrother.'

127

His stepbrother! I never knew this man existed, Meghan thought.

'You called me "Annie" just now,' she said. 'Why?'

He answered her with a question. 'Do you have a sister, Meghan?'

'No.'

'And you don't remember meeting me with your father and mother about ten years ago in Arizona?'

'I've never been there.'

'Then I'm totally confused,' Graham told her.

'Exactly when and where in Arizona did you think we met?' Meghan asked urgently.

'Let's see. It was in April, close to eleven years ago. I was in Scottsdale. My wife had spent a week in the Elizabeth Arden Spa, and I was picking her up the next morning. The evening before, I stayed at the Safari Hotel in Scottsdale. I was just leaving the dining room when I spotted Edwin. He was sitting with a woman who might have been in her early forties and a young girl who looked very much like you.' Graham looked at Meghan. 'Actually, both you and she resemble Edwin's mother.'

'My grandmother.'

'Yes.' Now he looked concerned. 'Meghan, I'm afraid this is distressing you.'

'It's very important that I know everything I can about the people who were with my father that night.'

'Very well. You realize it was a brief meeting, but since it was the first time I'd seen Edwin in years it made an impression on me.'

'When had you seen him before that?'

'Not since he graduated from prep school. But even though thirty years had passed, I recognized him instantly. I went over to the table and got a mighty chilly reception. He introduced me to his wife and daughter as someone he'd known growing up in Philadelphia. I took the hint and left immediately. I knew through Aurelia

128

that he and his family lived in Connecticut and simply assumed that they were vacationing in Arizona.'

'Did he introduce the woman he was with as his wife?'

'I think so. I can't be sure about that. He may have said something like "Frances and Annie, this is Cyrus Graham." '

'You're positive the girl's name was *Annie?*'

'Yes, I am. And I know the woman's name was Frances.'

'How old was Annie then?'

'About sixteen, I should think.'

Meghan thought, that would make her about twenty-six now. She shivered. And she's lying in the morgue in my place.

She realized Graham was studying her.

'I think we could use a cup of tea,' he said. 'Have you had lunch?'

'Please don't bother.'

'I'd like you to join me. I'll ask Jessie to put something together for us.'

When he left the room, Meghan clasped her hands on her knees. Her legs felt weak and wobbly, as though if she stood up they would not support her. *Annie,* she thought. A vivid memory sprang into her mind of discussing names with her father. 'How did you pick Meghan Anne for me?'

'My two favorite names in the world are Meghan and Annie. And that's how you became Meghan Anne.'

You got to use your two favorite names, after all, Dad, Meghan thought bitterly. When Cyrus Graham returned, followed by the maid carrying a luncheon tray, Meghan accepted a cup of tea and a finger sandwich.

'I can't tell you how shocked I am,' she said, and was glad she was able to at least sound calm. 'Now tell me about *him*. Suddenly my father has become a total stranger to me.'

It was not a pretty story. Richard Collins, her grandfather, had married seventeen-year-old Aurelia Crowley when she became pregnant. 'He felt it was the honorable thing,' Graham said. 'He was much older and divorced her almost immediately, but he did support her and the baby with reasonable generosity. A year later, when I was fourteen, Richard and my mother married. My own father was dead. This was the Graham family home. Richard Collins moved in, and it was a good marriage. He and my mother were both rather rigid, joyless people, and as the old saying goes, God made them and matched them.'

'And my father was raised by his mother?'

'Until he was three years old, at which point Aurelia fell madly in love with someone from California who did not want to be saddled with a child. One morning she arrived here and deposited Edwin with his suitcases and toys. My mother was furious. Richard was even more furious, and little Edwin was devastated. He worshiped his mother.'

'She abandoned him to a family where he wasn't wanted?' Meghan asked incredulously.

'Yes. Mother and Richard took him in out of duty, but certainly not out of desire. I'm afraid he was a difficult little boy. I can remember him standing every day with his nose pressed to the window, so positive was he that his mother would come back.'

'And did she?'

'Yes. A year later. The great love affair went sour, and she came back and collected Edwin. He was over-joyed and so were my parents.'

'And then . . .'

'When he was eight, Aurelia met someone else and the scenario was repeated.'

'Dear God!' Meghan said.

'This time Edwin was really impossible. He appar-ently thought that if he behaved very badly they'd find a way to send him back to his mother. It was an interesting morning around here when he put the garden hose in the gas tank of Mother's new sedan.'

'Did they send him home?'

'Aurelia had left Philadelphia again. He was sent to boarding school and then to camp during the summer. I was away at college and then in law school and only saw him occasionally. I did visit him at school once and was astonished to see that he was very popular with his schoolmates. Even then he was telling people that his mother was dead.'

'Did he ever see her again?'

'She came back to Philadelphia when he was sixteen. This time she stayed. She had finally matured and taken a job in a law office. I understand she tried to see Edwin, but it was too late. He wanted nothing to do with her. The pain was too deep. From time to time over the years she contacted me to ask if I ever heard from Edwin. A friend had sent me a clipping reporting his marriage to your mother. It gave the name and address of his firm. I gave the clipping to Aurelia. From what she told me, she wrote to him around his birthday and at Christmas every year but never heard back. In one of our conversations I told her about the meeting in Scottsdale. Perhaps I had no business sending the obituary notice to him.'

'He was a wonderful father to me and a wonderful husband to my mother,' Meghan said. She tried to blink back the tears that she felt welling in her eyes. 'He traveled a great deal in his job. I can't believe he could have had another life, another woman he may have called his wife, perhaps another daughter he must have loved too. But I'm beginning to think it must be true. How else do you explain Annie and Frances? How can anybody expect my mother and me to forgive that deception?'

It was a question she was asking of herself, not of Cyrus Graham, but he answered it. 'Meghan, turn around.' He pointed to the prim row of windows behind

131

the couch. 'That center window is the one where a little boy stood watch every afternoon, looking for his mother. That kind of abandonment does something to the soul and the psyche.'

34

At four o'clock, Mac phoned Catherine at home to see how she was feeling. When he did not get an answer he tried her at the inn. Just as the operator was about to put him through to Catherine's office, the intercom on his desk began to buzz. 'No, that's all right,' he said hurriedly. 'I'll try her later.'

The next hour was busy, and he did not get to phone again. He was just at the outskirts of Newtown when he dialed her at the house from the car phone. 'I thought if you were home I'd stop by for few minutes, Catherine,' he said.

'I'd be glad for the moral support, Mac.' Catherine quickly told him about the psychic and that she and the investigator were on their way.

'I'll be there in five minutes.' Mac replaced the receiver and frowned. He didn't believe in psychics. God knows what Meg is hearing about Edwin in Chestnut Hill today, he thought. Catherine's just about at the end of her rope, and they don't need some charlatan creating any more trouble for them.

He pulled into the Collins' driveway as a man and a woman were getting out of a car in front of the house. The investigator and the psychic, Mac thought.

He caught up with them on the porch. Bob Marron introduced first himself and then Mrs Fiona Black, saying only that she was someone who hoped to assist in locating Edwin Collins.

Mac was prepared to see a real display of hocus-pocus and calculated fakery. Instead he found himself in grudging admiration of the contained and poised woman who greeted Catherine with compassion. 'You've had a very bad time,' she said. 'I don't know if I can help you, but I know I have to try.'

Catherine's face was drawn, but Mac saw the flicker of hope that came into it. 'I believe in my heart that my husband is dead,' she told Fiona Black. 'I know the police don't believe that. It would be so much easier if there were some way of being certain, some way of proving it, of finding out once and for all.'

'Perhaps there is.' Fiona Black pressed Catherine's hands in hers. She walked slowly into the living room, her manner observant. Catherine stood next to Mac and Investigator Marron, watching her.

She turned to Catherine. 'Mrs Collins, do you still have your husband's clothes and personal items here?'

'Yes. Come upstairs,' she said, leading the way.

Mac felt his heart beating faster as they followed her. There was something about Fiona Black. She was not a fraud.

Catherine brought them to the master bedroom. On the dresser there was a twin frame. One picture was of Meghan. The other of Catherine and Edwin in formal dress. Last New Year's Eve at the inn, Mac thought. It had been a festive night.

Fiona Black studied the picture, then said, 'Where is his clothing?'

Catherine opened the door to a walk-in closet. Mac remembered that years ago she and Edwin had broken through the wall to the small adjoining bedroom and made two walk-in closets for themselves. This one was Edwin's. Rows of jackets and slacks and suits. Floor-to-ceiling shelves with sport shirts and sweaters. A shoe rack.

133

Catherine was looking at the contents of the closet. 'Edwin had wonderful taste in clothes. I always had to pick out my father's ties,' she said. It was as though she was reminiscing to herself.

Fiona Black walked into the closet, her fingers lightly touching the lapel of one coat, the shoulder of another. 'Do you have favorite cuff links or a ring of his?'

Catherine opened a dresser drawer. 'This was the wedding ring I gave him. He mislaid it one day. We thought it was lost. He was so upset I replaced it, then found this one where it had slipped behind the dresser. It had gotten a bit tight, so he kept wearing the new one.'

Fiona Black took the thin band of gold. 'May I take this for a few days? I promise not to lose it.'

Catherine hesitated, then said, 'If you think it will be useful to you.'

The cameraman from the PCD Philadelphia Affiliate met Meghan at quarter of four outside the Franklin Center, 'Sorry this is such a rush job,' she apologized.

The lanky cameraman, who introduced himself as Len, shrugged. 'We're used to it.'

Meghan was glad that it was necessary to concentrate on this interview. The hour she had spent with Cyrus Graham, her father's stepbrother, was so painful that she had to put thoughts of it aside until, bit by bit, she could accept it. She had promised her mother she would hold nothing back from her. It would be difficult, but she would keep that promise. Tonight they would talk it out.

She said, 'Len, at the opening, I'd like to get a wide shot of the block. These cobbled streets aren't the way people think about Philadelphia.'

'You should have seen this area before the renovation,' Len said as he began to roll tape.

Inside the Center they were greeted by the receptionist. Three women sat in the waiting room. All looked

134

well groomed and were carefully made up. Meghan was sure these were the clients whom Dr Williams had contacted to be interviewed.

She was right. The receptionist introduced her to them. One was pregnant. On-camera she explained that this would be her third child to be born by in vitro fertilization. The other two each had one child and were planning to attempt another pregnancy with their cryopreserved embryos.

'I have eight frozen embryos,' one of them said happily as she smiled into the lens. 'They'll transfer three of them, hoping one will take. If not, I'll wait a few months, then I'll have others thawed and try again.'

'If you succeed immediately in achieving a pregnancy, will you be back next year?' Meghan asked.

'Oh no. My husband and I only want two children.'

'But you'll still have cryopreserved embryos stored in the lab here, won't you?'

The woman agreed. 'Yes, I will,' she said. 'We'll pay to have them stored. Who knows? I'm only twenty-eight. I might change my mind. In a few years I may be back, and it's nice to know I have other embryos already available to me.'

'Provided any of them survive the thawing process?' Meghan asked.

'Of course.'

Next they went into Dr Williams' office. Meg took a seat opposite him for the interview. 'Doctor, again thank you for having us,' she said. 'What I wish you would do at the outset is explain in vitro fertilization as simply as you did to me earlier. Then, if you'll allow us to have some footage of the lab, and show us how cryopreserved embryos are kept, we won't take up any more of your time.'

Dr Williams was an excellent interview. Admirably succinct, he quickly explained the reasons why women might have trouble conceiving and the procedure of in vitro fertilization. 'The patient is given fertility drugs to

135

stimulate the production of eggs; the eggs are retrieved from her ovaries; in the lab they are fertilized, and the desired result is that we achieve viable embryos. Early embryos are transferred to the mother's womb, usually two or three at a time, in hopes that at least one will result in a successful pregnancy. The others are cryopreserved, or in layman's language, frozen, for eventual later use.'

'Doctor, in a few days, as soon as it is born, we are going to see a baby whose identical twin was born three years ago,' Meghan said. 'Will you explain to our viewers how it is possible for identical twins to be born three years apart?'

'It is possible, but very rare, that the embryo divides into two identical parts in the Petri dish just as it could in the womb. In this case, apparently the mother chose to have one embryo transferred immediately, the other cryopreserved for transfer later. Fortunately, despite great odds, both procedures were successful.'

Before they left Dr Williams' office, Len panned the camera across the wall with the pictures of children born through assisted reproduction at the Center. Next they shot footage of the lab, paying particular attention to the long-term storage containers where cryopreserved embryos, submerged in liquid nitrogen, were kept.

It was nearly five-thirty when Meghan said, 'Okay, it's a wrap. Thanks everyone. Doctor, I'm so grateful.'

'I am too,' he assured her. 'I can guarantee you that this kind of publicity will generate many inquiries from childless couples.'

Outside, Len put his camera in the van and walked with Meghan to her car. 'Kind of gets you, doesn't it?' he asked. 'I mean, I have three kids and I'd hate to think they started life in a freezer like those embryos.'

'On the other hand, those embryos represent lives that wouldn't have come into existence at all without this process,' Meghan said.

As she began the long drive back to Connecticut she

realized that the smooth, pleasant interview with Dr Williams had been a respite.

Now her thoughts were back to the moment Cyrus Graham had greeted her as Annie. Every word he said in their time together replayed in her mind.

That same evening, at eight-fifteen, Fiona Black phoned Bob Marron. 'Edwin Collins is dead,' she said quietly. 'He has been dead for many months. His body is submerged in water.'

35

It was nine-thirty when Meghan arrived home on Thursday night, relieved to find that Mac was waiting with her mother. Seeing the question in his eyes, she nodded. It was a gesture not lost on her mother.

'Meg, what is it?'

Meg could catch the lingering aroma of onion soup. 'Any of that left?' She waved her hand in the direction of the kitchen.

'You didn't have any dinner? Mac, pour her a glass of wine while I heat something up.'

'Just soup, Mom, please.'

When Catherine left, Mac came over to her. 'How bad was it,' he asked, his voice low.

She turned away, not wanting him to see the weary tears that threatened to spill over. 'Pretty bad.'

'Meg, if you want to talk to your mother alone, I'll get out of here. I just thought she needed company, and Mrs Dileo was willing to stay with Kyle.'

'That was nice of you, Mac, but you shouldn't have

137

left Kyle. He looks forward to you coming home so much. Little kids shouldn't be disappointed. Don't ever let him down.'

She felt that she was babbling. Mac's hands were holding her face, turning it to him.

'Meggie, what's the matter?'

Meg pressed her knuckles to her lips. She must not break down. 'It's just . . .'

She could not go on. She felt Mac's arms around her. Oh God, to just let go, to be held by him. The letter. Nine years ago he had come to her with the letter she had written, the letter that begged him not to marry Ginger . . .

'I think you'd rather I didn't save this,' he'd said then. He'd put his arm around her then as well, she remembered. 'Meg, someday you'll fall in love. What you feel for me is something else. Everyone feels that way when a best friend gets married. There's always the fear that everything will be different. It won't be that way between us. We'll always be buddies.'

The memory was as sharp as a dash of cold water. Meg straightened up and stepped back. 'I'm all right, I'm just tired and hungry.' She heard her mother's footsteps and waited until she was back in the room. 'I have some pretty disturbing news for you, Mom.'

'I think I should leave you two to talk it out,' Mac said.

It was Catherine who stopped him. 'Mac, you're family. I wish you'd stay.'

They sat at the kitchen table. It seemed to Meghan that she could feel her father's presence. He was the one who would fix the late-evening supper if the restaurant had been crowded and her mother too busy to eat. He was a perfect mimic, taking on the mannerisms of one of the captains dealing with a cranky guest. 'This table is not satisfactory? The banquette? Of course. A draft? But there is no window open. The inn is sealed shut.

138

Perhaps it is the air flowing between your ears, madame.'

Sipping a glass of wine, the steaming soup so appetizing, but untouched until she could tell them about the meeting in Chestnut Hill, Meghan talked about her father. She deliberately told about his childhood first, about Cyrus Graham's belief that the reason he turned his back on his mother was that he could not endure the chance of her abandoning him again.

Meghan watched her mother's face and found the reaction she had hoped for, pity for the little boy who had not been wanted, for the man who could not risk being hurt a third time.

But then it was necessary to tell her about the meeting in Scottsdale between Cyrus Graham and Edwin Collins.

'He introduced another woman as his wife?' There was no expression in her mother's voice.

'Mom, I don't know. Graham knew that Dad was married and had a daughter. He assumed that Dad was with his wife and daughter. Dad said something to him like, "Frances and Annie, this is Cyrus Graham." Mom, did Dad have any other relatives you know about? Is it a possibility that we have cousins in Arizona?'

'For God's sake, Meg, if I didn't know that your grandmother was alive all those years, how would I know about cousins?' Catherine Collins bit her lip. 'I'm sorry.' Her expression changed. 'You say your father's stepbrother thought you were Annie. You looked that much like her?'

'Yes.' Meg looked imploringly at Mac.

He understood what she was asking. 'Meg,' he said, 'I don't think there's any point in not telling your mother why we went to New York yesterday.'

'No, there isn't. Mom, there's something else you have to know . . .' She looked steadily at her mother as she told her what she had hoped to conceal.

When she finished, her mother sat staring past her as though trying to understand what she had been hearing.

Finally, in a steady voice that was almost a monotone, she said, 'A girl was stabbed who looked like you, Meg? She was carrying a piece of paper from Drumdoe Inn with your name and work number in Dad's handwriting? Within hours after she died, you got a fax that said, "Mistake. Annie was a mistake"?'

Catherine's eyes became bleak and frightened.

'You went to have your DNA checked against hers because you thought you might be related to that girl.'

'I did it because I'm trying to find answers.'

'I'm glad I saw that Fiona woman tonight,' Catherine burst out. 'Meg, I don't suppose you'll approve, but Bob Marron of the New Milford police phoned this afternoon . . .'

Meg listened as her mother spoke of Fiona Black's visit. It's bizarre, she thought, but no more bizarre than anything else that's happened these last months.

At ten-thirty, Mac got up to leave. 'If I may give advice, I'd suggest that both of you go to bed,' he said.

Mrs Dileo, Mac's housekeeper, was watching television when he arrived home. 'Kyle was so disappointed when you didn't get home before he fell asleep,' she said. 'Well, I'll be on my way.'

Mac waited until her car pulled out, then turned off the outside lights and locked the door. He went in to look at Kyle. His small son was hunched in the fetal position, the pillow bunched under his head.

Mac tucked the covers around him, bent down and kissed the top of his head. Kyle seemed to be just fine, a pretty normal kid, but now Mac asked himself if he was ignoring any signals that Kyle might be sending out. Most other seven-year-olds grew up with mothers. Mac wasn't sure if the overwhelming surge of tenderness he felt now was for his son, or for the little boy Edwin Collins had been fifty years ago in Philadelphia.

140

Or for Catherine and Meghan, who surely were the victims of the unhappy childhood of their husband and father.

Meghan and Catherine saw Stephanie Petrovic's impassioned interview at the Manning Clinic on the eleven o'clock news. Meg listened as the anchorman reported that Stephanie Petrovic had lived with her aunt in their New Jersey home. 'The body is being shipped to Rumania; the memorial mass will be held at noon in St Dominic's Rumanian Church in Trenton,' he finished.

'I'm going to that mass,' Meghan told her mother. 'I want to talk to that girl.'

At eight o'clock Friday morning, Bob Marron received a call at home. An illegally parked car, a dark blue Cadillac sedan, had been ticketed in Battery Park City, Manhattan, outside Meghan Collins' apartment house. The car was registered to Edwin Collins, and appeared to be the car he was driving the evening he disappeared.

As Marron dialed State Attorney John Dwyer he said to his wife, 'The psychic sure dropped the ball on this one.'

Fifteen minutes later, Marron was telling Meghan about the discovery of her father's car. He asked if she and Mrs Collins could come to John Dwyer's office. He would like to see them together as soon as possible.

36

Early Friday morning, Bernie watched again the replay of the interview he had taped at the Manning Clinic. He didn't hold the camera steady enough, he decided. The picture wobbled. He'd be more careful next time.

'Bernard!' His mother was yelling for him at the top of the stairs. Reluctantly he turned off the equipment.

'I'll be right there, Mama.'

'Your breakfast is getting cold.' His mother was wrapped in her flannel robe. It had been washed so often that the neck and the sleeves and the seat were threadbare. Bernie had told her that she washed it too much, but Mama said she was a clean person, that in her house you could eat off the floors.

This morning Mama was in a bad mood. 'I was sneezing a lot last night,' she told him as she dished out oatmeal from the pot on the stove. 'I think I smelled dust coming from the basement just now. You do mop the floor down there, don't you?'

'Yes, I do, Mama.'

'I wish you'd fix those cellar stairs so I can get down there and see for myself.'

Bernie knew that his mother would never take a chance on those stairs. One of the steps was broken, and the bannister was wobbly.

'Mama, those stairs are dangerous. Remember what happened to your hip – and now, what with your arthritis, your knees are really bad.'

'Don't think I'm taking a chance like that again,' she

snapped. 'But see that you keep it mopped. I don't know why you spend so much time down there anyhow.'

'Yes, you do, Mama. I don't need much sleep, and if I have the television on in the living room, it keeps you awake.' Mama had no idea about all the electronic equipment he had and she never would.

'I didn't sleep much last night. My allergies were at me.'

'I'm sorry, Mama.' Bernie finished the lukewarm oatmeal. 'I'll be late.' He grabbed his jacket.

She followed him to the door. When he was going down the walk, she called after him, 'I'm glad to see you're keeping the car decent for a change.

After the phone call from Bob Marron, Meghan hurriedly showered, dressed and went down to the kitchen. Her mother was already there, preparing breakfast.

Catherine's attempt at a cheery 'Good morning, Meg' froze on her lips as she saw Meg's face. 'What is it?' she asked. 'I did hear the phone ring when I was in the shower, didn't I?'

Meg took both her mother's hands in hers. 'Mom, look at me. I'm going to be absolutely honest with you. I thought for months that Daddy was lost on the bridge that night. With all that's happened this past week I need to make myself think as a lawyer and reporter. Look at all the possibilities, weigh each one carefully. I tried to make myself consider whether he might be alive and in serious trouble. But I know ... I am sure ... that what has gone on these last few days was something Dad would never do to us. That call, the flowers ... and now ...' She stopped.

'And now, what, Meg?'

'Dad's car was found in the city, illegally parked outside my apartment building.'

'Mother of God!' Catherine's face went ashen.

'Mom, someone else put it there. I don't know why, but there's a reason behind all of this. The assistant

143

state attorney wants to see us. He and his investigators are going to try to persuade us that Dad is alive. They didn't know him. We did. Whatever else may have been wrong in his life, he wouldn't send those flowers or leave his car where he'd be sure it would be found. He'd know how frantic we'd be. When we have this meeting, we're going to stick to our guns and defend him.'

Neither one of them cared about food. They brought steaming cups of coffee out to the car. As Meghan backed out of the garage, trying to sound matter-of-fact, she said, 'It may be illegal to drive one-handed, but coffee does help.'

'That's because we're both so cold, inside and out. Look, Meg. The first dusting of snow is on the lawn. It's going to be a long winter. I've always loved winter. Your father hated it. That was one of the reasons he didn't mind traveling so much. Arizona is warm all year, isn't it?'

When they passed the Drumdoe Inn, Meghan said, 'Mom, look over there. When we get back I'm going to drop you at the inn. You're going to work, and I'm going to start looking for answers. Promise me you won't say anything about what Cyrus Graham told me yesterday. Remember, he only assumed the woman and girl Dad was with ten years ago were you and me. Dad never introduced them except by their names, Frances and Annie. But until we can do some checking on our own, let's not give the state attorney any more reason to destroy Dad's reputation.'

Meghan and Catherine were escorted immediately to John Dwyer's office. He was waiting there with investigators Bob Marron and Arlene Weiss. Meghan took the chair next to her mother, her hand protectively covering hers.

It was quickly apparent what was wanted. All three, the attorney and the officers, were convinced that Edwin

144

Collins was alive and about to directly contact his wife and daughter. 'The phone call, the flowers, now his car,' Dwyer pointed out. 'Mrs Collins, you knew your husband had a gun permit?'

'Yes, I did. He got it about ten years ago.'

'Where did he keep the gun?'

'Locked up in his office or at home.'

'When did you last see it?'

'I don't remember having seen it in years.'

Meghan broke in, 'Why are you asking about my father's gun? Was it found in the car?'

'Yes, it was,' John Dwyer said quietly.

'That wouldn't be unusual,' Catherine said quickly. 'He wanted it for the car. He had a terrible experience in Bridgeport ten years ago when he was stopped at a traffic light.'

Dwyer turned to Meghan. 'You were away all day in Philadelphia, Miss Collins. It's possible your father is aware of your movements and knew you had left Connecticut. He might have assumed that you could be found in your apartment. What I must emphatically request is that if Mr Collins does contact either one of you, you must insist that he come here and talk with us. It will be much better for him in the long run.'

'My husband won't be contacting us,' Catherine said firmly. 'Mr Dwyer, didn't some people try to abandon their cars that night on the bridge?'

'Yes. I believe so.'

'Wasn't a woman who left her car hit by one of the other vehicles, and didn't she barely escape being dragged over the side of the bridge?'

'Yes.'

'Then consider this. My husband might have abandoned his car and gotten caught in that carnage. Someone else might have driven it away.'

Meghan saw exasperation mingled with pity in the assistant state attorney's face.

Catherine Collins saw it too. She got up to go. 'How

145

long does it usually take Mrs Black to reach a premise about a missing person?' she asked.

Dwyer exchanged glances with his investigators. 'She already has,' he said reluctantly. 'She believes your husband has been dead a long time, that he is lying in water.'

Catherine closed her eyes and swayed. Involuntarily, Meghan grasped her mother's arms, afraid she was about to faint.

Catherine's entire body was trembling. But when she opened her eyes, her voice was firm as she said, 'I never thought I would find comfort in a message like that, but in this place, and listening to you, I *do* find comfort in it.'

The consensus of the media about Stephanie Petrovic's impassioned interview was that she was a disappointed potential heir. Her accusation of a possible plot by the Manning Clinic to kill her aunt was dismissed as frivolous. The clinic was owned by a private group of investors and run by Dr Manning, whose credentials were impeccable. He still refused to speak to the press, but it was clear that in no way did he stand to personally gain by Helene Petrovic's bequest to embryo research at the clinic. After her outburst Stephanie had been taken to the office of a Manning Clinic senior staff member who would not comment on the conversation.

Helene's lawyer, Charles Potters, was appalled when he read about the episode. On Friday morning before the memorial mass, he came to the house and with ill-concealed outrage imparted his feelings to Stephanie. 'No matter what her background turns out to be, your aunt was devoted to her work at the clinic. For you to create a scene like that would have been horrifying to her.'

When he saw the misery in the young woman's face, he relented. 'I know you've been through a great deal,' he told her. 'After the mass you'll have a chance to rest. I thought some of Helene's friends from St Dominic's were planning to stay with you?'

'I sent them home,' Stephanie said. 'I hardly know them, and I'm better off by myself.'

After the lawyer left, she propped pillows on the couch and lay down. Her unwieldy body made it difficult to get comfortable. Her back hurt all the time now. She felt so alone. But she didn't want those old women around, eyeing her, talking about her.

She was grateful that Helene had left specific instructions that upon her death there was to be no wake, that her body was to be sent to Rumania and buried in her husband's grave.

She dozed off and was awakened by the peal of the telephone. Who now, she wondered wearily. It was a pleasant woman's voice. 'Miss Petrovic?'

'Yes.'

'I'm Meghan Collins from PCD Channel 3. I wasn't at the Manning Clinic when you were there yesterday, but I saw your statement on the eleven o'clock news.'

'I don't want to talk about that. My aunt's lawyer is very upset with me.'

'I wish you would talk with me. I might be able to help you.'

'How can you help me? How can anyone help me?'

'There are ways. I'm calling from my car phone. I'm on my way to the mass. May I take you out to lunch afterwards?'

She sounds so friendly, Stephanie thought, and I need a friend. 'I don't want to be on television again.'

'I'm not asking you to be on television. I'm asking you to talk to me.'

Stephanie hesitated. When the service is over, she thought, I don't want to be with Mr Potters and I don't want to be with those old women from the Rumanian Society. They're all gossiping about me. 'I'll go to lunch with you,' she said.

147

Meghan dropped her mother at the inn, then drove to Trenton as fast as she dared.

On the way she made a second phone call to Tom Weicker's office to tell him that her father's car had been located.

'Does anyone else know about the car being found?' he asked quickly.

'Not yet. They're trying to keep it quiet. But we both know it's going to leak out.' She tried to sound offhand. 'At least Channel 3 can have the inside track.'

'It's turning into a big story, Meg.'

'I know it is.'

'We'll run it immediately.'

'That's why I'm giving it to you.'

'Meg, I'm sorry.'

'Don't be. There's a rational answer to all this.'

'When is Mrs Anderson's baby due?'

'They're putting her in the hospital on Monday. She's willing to have me go to her home Sunday afternoon and tape her and Jonathan getting the room ready for the baby. She has infant pictures of Jonathan that we can use. When the baby is born, we'll compare the newborn shots.'

'Stay with it, at least for the present.'

'Thanks, Tom,' she said, 'and thanks for the support.'

Phillip Carter spent much of Friday afternoon being questioned about Edwin Collins. With less and less patience, Carter answered questions that grew more and more pointed. 'No, we have never had another instance in which there was a question of fraudulent credentials. Our reputation has been impeccable.'

Arlene Weiss asked about the car. 'When it was found in New York it had twenty-seven thousand miles on the odometer, Mr Carter. According to the service record booklet, it had been serviced the preceding October, just a little over a year ago. At that time it had twenty-one

148

thousand miles on it. How many miles did Mr Collins put on the car in an average month?'

'I would say that depended entirely on his schedule. We have company cars and turn them in every three years. It's up to us to have them serviced. I'm fairly meticulous. Edwin tended to be a bit lax.'

'Let me put it this way,' Bob Marron said, 'Mr Collins vanished in January. Between October last year and January, was it likely that he put six thousand miles on the car?'

'I don't know. I can give you his appointments for those months and try to figure out through expense accounts to which of those he would have driven.'

'We need to try to estimate how much the car has been used since January,' Marron said. 'We'd also like to see the car phone bill for January.'

'I assume you want to check on the time he made the call to Victor Orsini. The insurance company has already looked into that. The call was made less than a minute before the accident on the Tappan Zee Bridge.'

They asked about Collins and Carter's financial status. 'Our books are in order. They have been thoroughly audited. The last few years, like many businesses, we experienced the cutbacks of the recession. The kind of companies we deal with were letting people go, not hiring them. However, I know of no reason why Edwin would have had to borrow several hundred thousand dollars on his life insurance.'

'Your firm would have received a commission from the Manning Clinic for placing Petrovic?'

'Of course.'

'Did Collins pocket that commission?'

'No, the auditors found it.'

'No one questioned Helene Petrovic's name on the $6,000 payment when it came in?'

'The copy of the Manning client statement in our files had been doctored. It reads "Second installment due for placing Dr Henry Williams." There was no second installment due.'

'Then clearly Collins didn't place her so he could swindle the firm out of $6,000.'

'I would say that's obvious.'

When they finally left, Phillip Carter tried without success to concentrate on the work on his desk. He could hear the phone in the outer office ringing. Jackie buzzed him on the intercom. A reporter from a supermarket tabloid was on the phone. Phillip curtly refused the call, realizing that the only calls that day had come from the media. Collins and Carter had not heard from a single client.

37

Meghan slipped into St Dominic's church at twelve-thirty, at the midpoint on the sparsely attended mass for Helene Petrovic. In keeping with the wishes of the deceased, it was a simple ceremony without flowers or music.

There was a scattering of neighbors from Lawrence-ville in attendance as well as a few older women from the Rumanian Society. Stephanie was seated with her lawyer, and as they left the church, Meghan introduced herself. The young woman seemed glad to see her.

'Let me say goodbye to these people,' she said, 'and then I'll join you.'

Meghan watched as the polite murmurs of sympathy were expressed. She saw no great manifestation of grief from anyone. She walked over to two women who had

150

just come out of church. 'Did you know Helene Petrovic well?' she asked.

'As well as anyone,' one of them replied pleasantly. 'Some of us go to concerts together. Helene joined us occasionally. She was a member of the Rumanian Society and was notified of any of our activities. Sometimes she would show up.'

'But not too often.'

'No.'

'Did she have any very close friends?'

The other woman shook her head. 'Helene kept to herself.'

'How about men? I met Mrs Petrovic. She was a very attractive woman.'

They both shook their heads. 'If she had any special men friends, she never breathed a word about it.'

Meghan noted that Stephanie was saying goodbye to the last of the people from church. As she walked over to join her, she heard the lawyer caution, 'I wish you would not speak to that reporter. I'd be glad to drive you home or take you to lunch.'

'I'll be fine.'

Meghan took the young woman's arm as they walked down the rest of the steps. 'These are pretty steep.'

'And I'm so clumsy now. I keep getting in my own way.'

'This is your territory,' Meghan said when they were in the car. 'Where would you like to eat?'

'Would you mind if we went back to the house? People have left so much food there, and I'm feeling so tired.'

'Of course.'

When they reached the Petrovic home, Meghan insisted that Stephanie rest while she prepared lunch. 'Kick your shoes off and put your feet up on the couch,' she said firmly. 'We have a family inn, and I was raised in the kitchen there. I'm used to preparing meals.'

As she heated soup and laid out a plate of cold

151

chicken and salad, Meghan studied the surroundings. The kitchen had a French country house decor. The tiled walls and terracotta floor were clearly custom made. The appliances were top of the line. The round oak table and chairs were antiques. Obviously a lot of care – and money – had gone into the place.

They ate in the dining room. Here too the upholstered armchairs around the trestle table were obviously expensive. The table shone with the patina of fine old furniture. Where did the money come from? Meghan wondered. Helene had worked as a cosmetician until she got a job as a secretary in the clinic in Trenton, and from there she went to Manning.

Meghan did not have to ask questions. Stephanie was more than willing to discuss her problems. 'They are going to sell this house. All the money from the sale and eight hundred thousand dollars is going to the clinic. But it's so unfair. My aunt promised to change her will. I'm her only relative. That's why she sent for me.'

'What about the baby's father?' Meghan asked. 'He can be made to help you.'

'He's moved away.'

'He can be traced. In this country there are laws to protect children. What is his name?'

Stephanie hesitated. 'I don't want to have anything to do with him.'

'You have a right to be taken care of.'

'I'm going to give up the baby for adoption. It's the only way.'

'It may not be the only way. What is his name and where did you meet him?'

'I . . . I met him at one of the Rumanian affairs in New York. His name is Jan. Helene had a headache that night and left early. He offered to drive me home.' She looked down. 'I don't like to talk about being so foolish.'

'Did you go out with him often?'

'A few times.'

'You told him about the baby?'

'He called to say he was going to California. That was when I told him. He said it was my problem.'

'When was that?'

'Last March.'

'What kind of work does he do?'

'He's a . . . mechanic. Please, Miss Collins, I don't want anything to do with him. Don't lots of people want babies?'

'Yes, they do. But that was what I meant when I said I could help you. If we find Jan, he'll have to support the baby and help you at least until you can get a job.'

'Please leave him alone. I'm afraid of him. He was so angry.'

'Angry because you told him he was the father of your baby?'

'Don't keep asking me about him!' Stephanie pushed her chair away from the table. 'You said you'd help. Then find me people who will take the baby and give me some money.'

Meghan said contritely, 'I'm sorry, Stephanie. The last thing I came here to do was to upset you. Let's have a cup of tea. I'll clean up later.'

In the living room she propped an extra pillow behind Stephanie's back and pulled an ottoman over for her feet.

Stephanie smiled apologetically. 'You're very kind. I was rude. It is just that so much has happened so fast.'

'Stephanie, what you're going to need is to have someone sponsor you for a green card until you can get a job. Surely your aunt had one good friend who might help you out.'

'You mean if one of her friends sponsored me, I might be able to stay.'

'Yes. Isn't there someone, maybe someone who owes your aunt a favor?'

153

Stephanie's expression brightened. 'Oh, yes, there may indeed be someone. Thank you, Meghan.'

'Who is the friend?' Meghan asked swiftly.

'I may be wrong,' Stephanie said, suddenly nervous. 'I must think about it.'

She would not say anything more.

It was two o'clock. Bernie had gotten a couple of trips out of La Guardia Airport in the morning, then took a fare from Kennedy Airport to Bronxville.

He had had no intention of going to Connecticut that afternoon. But when he left the Cross County he found himself turning north. He had to go back to Newtown.

There was no car in the driveway of Meghan's house. He cruised along the curving road to the cul-de-sac, then turned around. The kid and his dog were nowhere in sight. That was good. He didn't want to be noticed.

He drove past Meghan's house again. He couldn't hang around here.

He drove past the Drumdoe Inn. Wait a minute, he thought. This is the place her mother owns. He'd read that in the paper yesterday. In an instant he'd made a U-turn and driven into the parking lot. There's got to be a bar, he thought. Maybe I can have a beer and even order a sandwich.

Suppose Meghan was there. He'd tell her the same story he told the others, that he was working for a local cable station in Elmira. There was no reason she shouldn't believe him.

The inn's lobby was medium size and had paneled walls and blue-and-red checked carpeting. There was no one behind the desk. To the right, he could see a few people in the dining room and busboys clearing tables. Well, lunch hour was pretty well over, he thought. The bar was to the left. He could see that it was empty, except for the bartender. He went to the bar, sat on one of the stools, ordered a beer and asked for the menu.

154

After he decided on a hamburger he started talking to the bartender. 'This is a nice place.'

'Sure is,' the bartender agreed.

The guy had a name tag that read 'Joe'; he looked to be about fifty. The local newspaper was on the back bar. Bernie pointed to it.

'I read yesterday's paper. Looks like the family that owns this place has a lot of problems.'

'They sure do,' Joe agreed. 'Damn shame. Mrs Collins is the nicest woman you'd ever want to know and her daughter, Meg, is a doll.'

Two men came in and sat at the end of the bar. Joe filled their orders, then stayed talking with them. Bernie looked around as he finished his hamburger and beer. The back windows looked out over the parking lot. Beyond that was a wooded area that extended behind the Collins house.

Bernie had an interesting thought. If he drove here at night he could park in the lot with the cars from the dinner crowd and slip into the woods. Maybe from there he could take pictures of Meghan in her house. He had a zoom lens. It should be easy.

Before he left he asked Joe if they had valet parking.

'Just on Friday and Saturday nights,' Joe told him.

Bernie nodded. He decided that he'd be back Sunday night.

Meghan left Stephanie Petrovic at two o'clock. At the door she said, 'I'll keep in touch with you and I want to know when you're going to the hospital. It's tough to have your first baby without anyone close to you around.'

'I'm getting scared about it,' Stephanie admitted. 'My mother had a hard time when I was born. I just want it over with.'

The image of the troubled young face stayed with Meghan. Why was Stephanie so adamant about not trying to get child support from the father? Of course

155

if she was determined to give the baby up for adoption, it was probably a moot point.

There was another stop Meghan wanted to make before she started home. Trenton was not far from Lawrenceville, and Helene Petrovic had worked there as a secretary in the Dowling Center, an assisted reproduction facility. Maybe somebody there would remember the woman, although she'd left the place for the Manning Clinic six years ago. Meghan was determined to find out more about her.

The Dowling Assisted Reproduction Center was in a small building connected to Valley Memorial Hospital. The reception room held only a desk and one chair. Clearly this place was not on the scale of the Manning Clinic.

Meghan did not show her PCD identification. She was not here as a reporter. When she told the receptionist she wanted to speak to someone about Helene Petrovic, the woman's face changed. 'We have nothing more to say on the matter. Mrs Petrovic worked here as a secretary for three years. She never was involved in any medical procedures.'

'I believe that,' Meghan said. 'But my father is being held responsible for placing her at the Manning Clinic. I need to speak to someone who knew her well. I need to know if my father's firm ever requested a reference for her.'

The woman looked hesitant.

'Please,' Meghan said quietly.

'I'll see if the director is available.'

The director was a handsome gray-haired woman of about fifty. When Meghan was escorted into her office, she introduced herself as Dr Keating. 'I'm a Ph.D., not a physician,' she said briskly. 'I'm concerned with the business end of the center.'

She had Helene Petrovic's file in her drawer. 'The

156

state attorney's office in Connecticut requested a copy of this two days ago,' she commented.

'Do you mind if I take notes?' Meghan asked.

'Not at all.'

The file contained information that had been reported in the papers. On her application form to Dowling, Helene Petrovic had been truthful. She had applied for a secretarial position, giving her work background as a cosmetician and citing her recently acquired certificate from the Woods Secretarial School in New York.

'Her references checked out,' Dr Keating said. 'She made a nice appearance and had a pleasant manner. I hired her and was very satisfied with her the three years she was here.'

'When she left, did she tell you she was going to the Manning Clinic?'

'No. She said that she planned to take a job as a cosmetician in New York again. She said a friend was opening a salon. That's why we didn't find it surprising that we were never contacted for a reference.'

'Then you had no dealings with Collins and Carter Executive Search?'

'None at all.'

'Dr Keating, Mrs Petrovic managed to pull the wool over the eyes of the medical staff in the Manning Clinic. Where do you think she got the knowledge to handle cryopreserved embryos?'

Keating frowned. 'As I told the Connecticut investigators, Helene was fascinated with medicine and particularly the kind that is done here, the process of assisted reproduction. She used to read the medical books when work was slow and often would visit the laboratory and observe what was going on there. I might add that she would never have been allowed to step into the laboratory alone. As a matter of fact, we never allow fewer than two qualified staff people to be present. It's a sort of fail-safe system. I think it should be a law in every facility of this kind.'

'Then you think she picked up her medical knowledge through observation and reading?'

'It's hard to believe that someone who had no opportunity to do hands-on work under supervision would be able to fool experts, but it's the only explanation I have.'

'Dr Keating, all I hear is that Helene Petrovic was very nice, well respected but a loner. Was that true here?'

'I would say so. To the best of my knowledge she never socialized with the other secretaries or anyone on this staff.'

'No male friends?'

'I don't know for sure, but I always suspected that she was seeing someone from the hospital. Several times when she was away from her desk one of the other girls picked up her phone. They began to tease her about who was her Dr Kildare. Apparently the message was to call an extension in the hospital.'

'You wouldn't know which extension?'

'It was over six years ago.'

'Of course.' Meghan got up. 'Dr Keating, you've been so kind. May I give you my phone number just in case you remember anything that you think might be of assistance?'

Keating reached out her hand. 'I know the circumstances, Miss Collins. I wish I could help.'

When she was getting into her car, Meghan studied the impressive structure that was Valley Memorial Hospital. Ten stories high, half the length of a city block, hundreds of windows from which lights were beginning to gleam in the late afternoon.

Was it possible that behind one of those windows there was a doctor who had helped Helene Petrovic to perfect her dangerous deception?

Meghan was exiting onto route 7 when the five o'clock news came on. She listened to the WPCD radio station

158

bulletin: 'Assistant State Attorney John Dwyer has confirmed that the car Edwin Collins was driving the night of the Tappan Zee Bridge disaster last January has been located outside the Manhattan apartment of his daughter. Ballistic tests show that Collins' gun, found in the car, was the murder weapon that killed Helene Petrovic, the laboratory worker whose fraudulent credentials he allegedly presented to the Manning Clinic. A warrant has just been issued for Edwin Collins' arrest on suspicion of homicide.'

38

Dr George Manning left the clinic at five o'clock on Friday afternoon. Three new patients had canceled their appointments, so far only a half dozen or so worried parents had called to inquire about DNA tests to assure themselves that their children were their biological offspring. Dr Manning knew that it would take only one verified case of a mixup to cause alarm in every woman who had borne a child through treatment at the clinic. For good and sufficient reasons he dreaded the next few days.

Wearily he drove the eight miles to his home in South Kent. It was such a shame, such a damn shame, he thought. Ten years of hard work and a national reputation ruined, virtually overnight. Less than a week ago he had been celebrating the annual reunion and looking forward to retirement. On his seventieth birthday last January he had announced that he would stay at his post just one more year.

The most galling memory was that Edwin Collins

had called when he read an account of the birthday celebration and retirement plans and asked if Collins and Carter could once again serve the Manning Clinic!

On Friday evening, when Dina Anderson put her three-year-old son to bed, she hugged him fiercely. 'Jonathan, I think your twin isn't going to wait till Monday to be born,' she told him.

'How's it going, honey?' her husband asked when she went downstairs.

'Five minutes apart.'

'I'd better alert the doctor.'

'So much for Jonathan and me being on-camera, getting the room ready for Ryan.' She winced. 'You'd better tell my mother to get right over, and let the doctor know I'm on my way to the hospital.'

Half an hour later, in Danbury Medical Center, Dina Anderson was being examined. 'Would you believe the contractions stopped?' she asked in disgust.

'We're going to keep you,' the obstetrician told her. 'If nothing happens during the night, we'll start an IV to induce labor in the morning. You might as well go home, Don.'

Dina pulled her husband's face down for a kiss. 'Don't look so worried, Daddy. Oh, and will you phone Meghan Collins and alert her that Ryan will probably be around by tomorrow. She wants to be there to tape him as soon as he's in the nursery. Be sure to bring the pictures of Jonathan as a newborn. She's going to show them with the baby so everyone can see that they're exactly alike. And let Dr Manning know. He was so sweet. He called today to ask how I was doing.'

The next morning, Meghan and her cameraman, Steve, were in the lobby of the hospital, awaiting word of the delivery of Ryan. Donald Anderson had given them Jonathan's newborn infant pictures. When the baby was in the nursery, they would be allowed to videotape him. Jonathan would be brought to the hospital by Dina's mother, and they'd be able to take a brief shot of the family together.

With a reporter's eye, Meghan observed the activity in the lobby. A young mother, her infant in her arms, was being wheeled to the door by a nurse. Her husband followed, struggling with suitcases and flower arrangements. From one of the bouquets floated a pink balloon inscribed, 'It's a Girl'.

An exhausted-looking couple came out of the elevator holding the hands of a four-year-old with a cast on his arm and a bandage on his head. An expectant mother crossed the lobby and entered the door marked ADMITTANCE.

Seeing these families, Meghan was reminded of Kyle. What kind of mother would walk out on a six-month-old baby?

The cameraman was studying Jonathan's pictures. 'I'll get the same angle,' he said. 'Kind of weird when you think you know exactly what the kid's gonna look like.'

'Look,' Meghan said. 'That's Dr Manning coming in. I wonder if he's here because of the Andersons.'

Upstairs in the delivery room, a loud wail brought a smile to the faces of the doctors, the nurses and the Andersons. Pale and exhausted, Dina looked up at her husband and saw the shock on his face. Frantically she pulled herself up on one elbow. 'Is he okay?' she cried. 'Let me see him.'

'He's fine, Dina,' the doctor said, holding up the squalling infant with the shock of bright red hair.

'That's not Jonathan's twin!' Dina screamed. 'Whose baby have I been carrying?'

39

'It always rains on Saturday,' Kyle grumbled as he flipped from channel to channel on the television set. He was sitting cross-legged on the carpet, Jake beside him.

Mac was deep in the morning paper. 'Not always,' he said absently. He glanced at his watch. It was almost noon. 'Turn to Channel 3. I want to catch the news.'

'Okay.' Kyle clicked the remote. 'Look, there's Meg!'

Mac dropped the paper. 'Turn up the volume.'

'You're always telling me to turn it down.'

'Kyle!'

'Okay. Okay.'

Meg was standing in the lobby of a hospital. 'There is a frightening new development in the Manning Clinic case. Following the murder of Helene Petrovic, and the discovery of her faudulent credentials, there has been concern that the late Ms Petrovic may have made serious mistakes in handling the cryopreserved embryos. An hour ago a baby, expected to be the clone of his three-year-old brother, was born here in Danbury Medical Center.'

Mac and Kyle watched as the camera angle widened.

'With me is Dr Allan Neitzer, the obstetrician who just delivered Dina Anderson of a son. Doctor, will you tell us about the baby?'

'The baby is a healthy, beautiful eight-pound boy.'

'But it is not the identical twin of the Andersons' three-year-old son?'

'No, it is not.'

'Is it Dina Anderson's biological child?'

'Only DNA tests can establish that.'

'How long will they take?'

'Four to six weeks.'

'How are the Andersons reacting?'

'Very upset. Very worried.'

'Dr Manning was here. He went upstairs before we could speak to him. Has he seen the Andersons?'

'I can't coment on that.'

'Thank you, Doctor.' Meghan turned to face the camera directly. 'We'll be here with this unfolding story. Back to you in the newsroom, Mike.'

'Turn it off, Kyle.'

Kyle pressed the remote button, and the screen went blank. 'What did that mean?'

It means big problems, Mac thought. How many more mistakes had Helene Petrovic made at Manning? Whatever they were, no doubt Edwin Collins would be held equally responsible for them. 'It's pretty complicated, Kyle.'

'Is anything wrong for Meg?'

Mac looked into his son's face. The sandy hair so like his own that never stayed in place was falling on his forehead. The brown eyes that he'd inherited from Ginger had lost their usual meery twinkle. Except for the color of the eyes, Kyle was a MacIntyre through and through. What would it be like, Mac wondered, to look in your son's face and realize he might not belong to you.

He put an arm around Kyle. 'Things have been rough for Meg lately. That's why she looks worried.'

'Next to you and Jake, she's my best friend,' Kyle said soberly.

At the mention of his name, Jake thumped his tail.

Mac smiled wryly. 'I'm sure Meg will be flattered to hear it.' Not for the first time in these last few days, he wondered if his blind stupidity in not realizing his feelings for Meg had forever relegated him in her eyes to the status of friend and buddy.

163

Meghan and the cameraman sat in the lobby of Danbury Medical Center. Steve seemed to know that she did not want to talk. Neither Donald Anderson nor Dr Manning had come downstairs.

'Look, Meg,' Steve said suddenly, 'isn't that the other Anderson kid?'

'Yes, it is. That must be the grandmother with him.'

They both jumped up, followed them across the lobby and caught them at the elevator. Meg turned on the mike. Steve began to roll tape.

'I wonder if you would speak to us for a moment,' Meghan asked the woman. 'Aren't you Dina Anderson's mother and Jonathan's grandmother?'

'Yes, I am.' The well-bred voice was distressed. Silver hair framed a troubled face.

By her expression, Meghan knew the woman was aware of the problem.

'Have you spoken to your daughter or son-in-law since the baby was born?'

'My son-in-law phoned me. Please. We want to get upstairs. My daughter needs me.' She stepped into the elevator, the little boy's hand grasped tightly in her own.

Meghan did not try to detain her.

Jonathan was wearing a blue jacket that matched the blue of his eyes. His cheeks were rosy accents to his fair complexion. His hood was down, and raindrops had beaded the white-gold hair that was shaped in Buster Brown style. He smiled and waved. 'Bye-bye,' he called as the elevator doors began to close.

'That's some good-looking kid,' Steve observed.

'He's beautiful,' Meghan agreed.

They returned to their seats. 'Do you think Manning will give a statement?' Steve asked.

'If I were Dr Manning, I'd be talking to my lawyers.' And Collins and Carter Executive Search will need their lawyers too, she thought.

Meghan's beeper sounded. She pulled out her cellular phone, called the news desk and was told that Tom

Weicker wanted to talk to her. 'If Tom's in on Saturday, something's up,' she murmured.

Something was up. Weicker got right to the point. 'Meg, Dennis Cimini is on his way to relieve you. He took a helicopter, so he should be there soon.'

She was not surprised. The special about identical twins being born three years apart had become a much bigger story. It was now tied into the Manning Clinic scandal and the murder of Helene Petrovic.

'All right, Tom.' She sensed there was more.

'Meg, you told the Connecticut authorities about the dead woman who resembles you and the fact that she had a note in her pocket in your father's handwriting.'

'I felt I had to tell them. I was sure the New York detectives would contact them at some point about it.'

'There's been a leak somewhere. They also learned that you went to the morgue for a DNA test. We've got to carry the story right away. The other stations have it.'

'I understand, Tom.'

'Meg, as of now you're on leave. Paid leave of course.'

'All right.'

'I'm sorry, Meg.'

'I know you are. Thanks.' She broke the connection. Dennis Cimini was coming through the revolving door to the lobby. 'I guess that does it. See you around, Steve,' she said. She hoped her bitter disappointment wasn't obvious to him.

40

There was an auction coming up on property near the Rhode Island border. Phillip Carter had planned to take a look at it.

He needed a day away from the office and the myriad problems of the past week. The media had been omnipresent. The investigators had been in and out. A talk show host had actually asked him to be on a program about missing persons.

Victor Orsini had not been off the mark when he said that every word uttered or printed about Helene Petrovic's fraudulent credentials was a nail in the coffin of Collins and Carter.

On Saturday just before noon, Carter was at his front door when the phone rang. He debated about answering, then picked up the receiver. It was Orsini.

'Phillip, I had the television on. The fat's in the fire. Helene Petrovic's first known mistake at the Manning Clinic was just born.'

'What's that supposed to mean?'

Orsini explained. As Phillip listened, his blood chilled.

'This is just the beginning,' Orsini said. 'How much insurance does the company have to cover this?'

'There isn't enough insurance in the world to cover it,' Carter said quietly as he hung up.

You believe you have everything under control, he thought, but you never do. Panic was not a familiar emotion, but suddenly events were closing in on him.

In the next moment he was thinking of Catherine and Meghan. There was no further consideration of a leisurely drive to the country. He would call Meg and Catherine later. Maybe he could join them for dinner this evening. He wanted to know what they were doing, what they were thinking.

When Meg got home at one-thirty, Catherine had lunch ready. She'd seen the news brief broadcast from the hospital.

'It was probably my last one for Channel 3,' Meg said quietly.

For a little while, both too overwhelmed to speak, the two women ate in silence. Then Meg said, 'Mom, as bad as it is for us, can you imagine how the women feel who underwent in vitro fertilization at the Manning Clinic? With the Anderson mix-up there isn't one of them who isn't going to wonder if she received her own embryo. What will happen when errors can be traced and a biological and host mother both claim the same child?'

'I can imagine what it would be like.' Catherine Collins reached across the table and grasped Meg's hand. 'Meggie, I've lived for nearly nine months on such an emotional seesaw that I'm punch drunk.'

'Mom, I know how it's been for you.'

'Hear me out. I have no idea how all this will end, but I do know one thing. *I can't lose you.* If somebody killed that poor girl thinking it was you, I can only pity her with all my heart and thank God on my knees that you're the one who's alive.'

They both jumped as the door bell rang.

'I'll get it,' Meg said.

It was an insured package for Catherine. She ripped it open. Inside was a note and a small box. She read the note aloud: 'Dear Mrs Collins, I am returning your husband's wedding ring. I have rarely felt such certainty as I did when I told investigator Bob Marron that Edwin Collins died many months ago.

167

'My thoughts and prayers are with you, Fiona Campbell Black.'

Meghan realized that she was glad to see tears wash away some of the pain that was etched on her mother's face.

Catherine took the slender gold ring from the box and closed her hand over it.

41

Late Saturday in Danbury Medical Center, a sedated Dina Anderson was dozing in bed, Jonathan asleep beside her. Her husband and mother were sitting silently by the bedside. The obstetrician, Dr Neitzer, came to the door and beckoned to Don.

He stepped outside. 'Any word?'

The doctor nodded. 'Good, I hope. On checking your blood type, your wife's, Jonathan's and the baby's, we find that the baby certainly could be your biological child. You are A positive, your wife is O negative, the baby is O positive.'

'Jonathan is A positive.'

'Which is the other blood type consistent with the child of A positive and O negative parents.'

'I don't know what to think,' Don said. 'Dina's mother swears the baby looks like her own brother when he was born. There's red hair on that side of the family.'

'The DNA test will establish absolutely whether or not the baby is biologically yours, but that will take four weeks minimum.'

'And what do we do in the meantime?' Don asked,

168

angrily. 'Bond to it, love it and maybe find out we have to give it to someone else from the Manning Clinic? Or do we let it lie in a nursery until we know whether or not it's ours?'

'It isn't good for any baby in the early weeks of life to be left in a nursery,' Doctor Neitzer replied. 'Even our very sick babies are handled as much as possible by the mothers and fathers. And Dr Manning says—'

'Nothing Dr Manning says interests me,' Don interrupted. 'All I've ever heard since the embryo split nearly four years ago was how the embryo of Jonathan's twin was in a specially marked tube.'

'Don, where are you?' a weak voice called.

Anderson and Dr Neitzer went back into the room. Dina and Jonathan were both awake. She said, 'Jonathan wants to see his new brother.'

'Honey, I don't know . . .'

Dina's mother stood up and looked hopefully at her daughter.

'I do. I agree with Jonathan. I carried that baby for nine months. For the first three I was spotting and terrified I'd lose it. The first moment I felt life I was so happy I cried. I love coffee and couldn't have one sip of it because that kid doesn't like coffee. He's been kicking me so hard I haven't had a decent sleep in three months. Whether or not he's my biological child, by God I've earned him and I want him.'

'Honey, Dr Neitzer says the blood tests show it may be our child.'

'That's good. Now, will you please have someone bring my baby to me.'

At two-thirty Dr Manning, accompanied by his lawyer and a hospital official, entered the hospital's auditorium.

The hospital official made a firm announcement. 'Dr Manning will read a prepared statement. He will not take questions. After that I request that all of you leave

169

the premises. The Andersons will not make any statements, nor will they permit any pictures.'

Dr Manning's silver hair was rumpled, and his kindly face was strained as he put on his glasses and in a hoarse voice began to read:

'I can only apologize for the distress the Anderson family is experiencing. I firmly believe Mrs Anderson gave birth to her own biological child today. She had two cryopreserved embryos in the laboratory at our clinic. One was her son Jonathan's identical twin; the other his sibling.

'Last Monday, Helene Petrovic admitted to me that she had had an accident in the laboratory at the time she was handling the Petri dishes containing those two embryos. She slipped and fell. Her hand hit and overturned one of the lab dishes before the embryos were transferred to the test tubes. She believed the remaining dish contained the identical twin and put it in the specially marked tube. The other embryo was lost.'

Dr Manning took off his glasses and looked up.

'If Helene Petrovic was telling the truth, and I have no reason to doubt it, I repeat, Dina Anderson today gave birth to her biological son.'

Questions were shouted at him. 'Why didn't Petrovic tell you at that time?'

'Why didn't you warn the Andersons immediately?'

'How many more mistakes do you think she made?'

Dr Manning ignored them all and walked unsteadily from the room.

Victor Orsini called Phillip Carter after the Saturday evening news broadcast. 'You'd better think of getting lawyers in to represent the firm,' he told Carter.

Carter was just ready to leave for dinner at the Drumdoe Inn. 'I agree. This is too big for Leiber to handle, but he can probably recommend someone.'

Leiber was the lawyer the company kept on retainer.

'Phillip, if you don't have plans for the evening, how

about dinner? There's an old saying, misery loves company.'

'Then I've got the right plans. I'm meeting Catherine and Meg Collins.'

'Give them my best. See you Monday.'

Orsini hung up and walked over to the window. Candlewood Lake was tranquil tonight. The lights from the houses that bordered it were brighter than usual. Dinner parties, Orsini thought. He was sure his name would come up at all of them. Everyone around here knew he worked for Collins and Carter.

His call to Phillip Carter had elicited the information he wanted: Carter was safely tied up for the evening. Victor could go to the office now. He'd be absolutely alone and could spend a couple of hours going through the personal files in Edwin Collins' office. Something had begun to nag at him, and it was vital that he give those files a final check before Meghan moved them out.

Meghan, Mac and Phillip met for dinner at the Drumdoe Inn at seven-thirty. Catherine was in the kitchen where she'd been since four o'clock.

'Your mother has guts,' Mac said.

'You bet she does,' Meg agreed. 'Did you catch the evening news? I watched PCD, and the lead story was the combination of the Anderson baby mix-up, the Petrovic murder, my resemblance to the woman in the morgue and the warrant for Dad's arrest. I gather all the stations led with it.'

'I know,' Mac said quietly.

Phillip raised his hand in a gesture of helplessness. 'Meg, I'd do anything to help you and your mother, anything to try to find some explanation for Edwin sending Petrovic to Manning.'

'There is an explanation,' Meg said. 'I believe that and so does Mother, which is what gave her the courage to come down here and put on an apron.'

171

'She's not planning to handle the kitchen herself indefinitely?' Philip protested.

'No. Tony, the head chef who retired last summer, phoned today and offered to come back and help out for a while. I told him that was wonderful but warned him not to take over. The busier Mother is, the better for her. But he's in there now. She'll be able to join us soon.'

Meghan felt Mac's eyes on her and looked down to avoid the compassion she saw in them. She had known that tonight everyone in the dining room would be studying her and her mother to see how they were holding up. She had deliberately chosen to wear red: a calf-length skirt and cowl-neck cashmere sweater with gold jewelry.

She'd made herself up carefully with blusher and lipstick and eyeshadow. I guess I don't look like an unemployed reporter, she decided, glimpsing herself in the mirror as she left the house.

The disconcerting part was that she was sure that Mac could see behind her façade. He'd guess that in addition to everything else, she was worried sick about her job.

Mac had ordered wine. When it was poured, he raised his glass to her. 'I have a message from Kyle. When he knew we were having dinner together he said to tell you he's coming to scare you tomorrow night.'

Meg smiled. 'Of course; tomorrow's Halloween. What's Kyle wearing?'

'Very original. He's a ghost, a really scary ghost, or so he claims. I'm taking him and some other kids trick-or-treating tomorrow afternoon, but he wants to save you for tomorrow night. So if there's a thump on the window after dark, be prepared.'

'I'll make sure I'm home. Look, here's Mother.'

Catherine kept a smile on her lips as she walked across the dining room. She was constantly stopped by people jumping up from their tables to embrace her.

172

When she joined them, she said, 'I'm so glad we came here. It's a heck of a lot better than sitting at home thinking.'

'You look *wonderful*,' Phillip said. 'You're a real trouper.'

The admiration in his eyes was not lost on Meg. She glanced at Mac. He had seen it too.

Be careful, Phillip. Don't crowd Mother, Meghan thought.

She studied her mother's rings. The diamonds and emeralds she was wearing shone brilliantly under the small table lamp. Earlier that evening her mother had told her that on Monday she intended to hock or sell her jewelry. A big tax payment was due on the inn the following week. Catherine had said, 'My only regret about giving up the jewelry is that I so wanted it for you.'

I don't care about myself, Meg thought now, but . . .

'Meg? Are you ready to order?'

'Oh, sorry.' Meghan smiled apologetically and glanced down at the menu in her hand.

'Try the Beef Wellington,' Catherine said. 'It's terrific. I should know. I made it.'

During dinner, Meg was grateful that Mac and Phillip steered the conversation onto safe subjects, everything from the proposed paving of local roads to Kyle's championship soccer team.

Over cappuccino, Phillip asked Meg what her plans were. 'I'm so sorry about the job,' he said.

Meg shrugged. 'I'm certainly not happy about it, but maybe it will turn out all right. You see, I keep thinking that nobody really knows anything about Helene Petrovic. She's the key to all this. I'm determined to turn up something about her that may give us some answers.'

'I wish you would,' Phillip said. 'God knows *I'd* like some answers.'

'Something else,' Meg added, 'I never got to clear out Dad's office. Would you mind if I go in tomorrow?'

173

'Go in whenever you want, Meg. Can I help you?'

'No thanks. I'll be fine.'

'Meg, call me when you're finished,' Mac said. 'I'll come over and carry things to the car.'

'Tomorrow's your day to trick or treat with Kyle,' Meg reminded him. 'I can handle it.' She smiled at the two men. 'Many thanks, guys, for being with us tonight. It's good to have friends at a time like this.'

In Scottsdale, Arizona, at nine o'clock on Saturday night, Frances Grolier sighed as she put down her pearwood-handled knife. She had a commission to do a fifteen-inch bronze of a young Navaho boy and girl as a presentation to the guest of honor at a fund-raising dinner. The deadline was fast approaching and Frances was totally unsatisfied with the clay model she had been working on.

She had not managed to capture the questioning expression she had seen in the sensitive faces of the children. The pictures she had taken of them had caught it, but her hands were simply unable to execute her clear vision of what the sculpture should be.

The trouble was that she simply could not concentrate on her work.

Annie. She had not heard from her daughter for nearly two weeks now. All the messages she'd left on her answering machine had been ignored. In the last few days she'd called Annie's closest friends. No one had seen her.

She could be anywhere, Frances thought. She could have accepted an assignment to do a travel article on some remote, godforsaken place. As a freelance travel writer, Annie came and went on no set schedule.

I raised her to be independent, Frances told herself. I raised her to be free, to take chances, to take from life what she wanted.

Did I teach her that to justify my own life? she wondered.

174

It was a thought that had come to her repeatedly in the last few days.

There was no use trying to work any more tonight. She went to the fireplace and added logs from the basket. The day had been warm and bright, but now the desert night was sharply cool.

The house was so quiet. There might never again be the heart-pounding anticipation of knowing that he was coming soon. As a little girl, Annie often asked why Daddy traveled so much.

'He has a very important job with the government,' Frances would tell her.

As Annie grew up she became more curious. 'What kind of job is it, Dad?'

'Oh, a sort of watchdog, honey.'

'Are you in the CIA?'

'If I were, I'd never tell you.'

'You are, aren't you?'

'Annie, I work for the government and get a lot of frequent-flyer miles in the process.'

Remembering, Frances went into the kitchen, put ice in a glass and poured a generous amount of Scotch over it. Not the best way to solve problems, she told herself.

She put the drink down, went into the bath off the bedroom and showered, scrubbing away the bits of dried clay that were clinging to the crevices in her palms. Putting on gray silk pajamas and a robe, she retrieved the Scotch and settled on the couch in front of the fireplace. Then she picked up the Associated Press item she had torn from page ten of the morning newspaper, a summary of the report issued by the New York State Thruway Authority on the Tappan Zee Bridge disaster.

In part it read: 'The number of victims who perished in the accident has been reduced from eight to seven. Exhaustive search has revealed no trace of the body of Edwin R. Collins, nor wreckage from his car.'

Now Frances was haunted by the question, is it possible that Edwin is still alive?

He'd been so upset about business the morning he left.

He'd had a growing fear that his double life would be exposed and that both his daughters would despise him.

He'd had chest pains recently, which were diagnosed as being caused by anxiety.

He'd given her a bearer bond for two hundred thousand dollars in December. 'In case anything happens to me,' he had said. Had he been planning to find a way to drop out of both his lives when he said that?

And where was Annie? Frances agonized, with a growing sense of foreboding.

Edwin had an answering machine in his private office. Over the years, if Frances ever had to reach him, the arrangement was that she would call between midnight and five a.m. Eastern time. He always beeped in for messages by six o'clock and then erased them.

Of course that number was disconnected. Or was it?

It was a few minutes past ten in Arizona, past midnight on the East Coast.

She picked up the receiver and dialed. After two rings, Ed's recorded announcement began. 'You have reached 203–555–2867. At the beep please leave a brief message.'

Frances was so startled at hearing his voice that she almost forgot why she was calling. Could this possibly mean that he is alive? she wondered. And if Ed is alive somewhere, does he ever check this machine?

She had nothing to lose. Hurriedly Frances left the message they'd agreed upon. 'Mr Collins, please call Palomino Leather Goods. If you're still interested in that briefcase, we have it in stock.'

Victor Orsini was in Edwin Collins' office, still going through the files, when the private phone rang. He jumped. Who in hell would call an office at this hour?

The answering machine clicked on. Sitting in Collins'

176

chair, Orsini listened to the modulated voice as it left the brief message.

When the call was completed, Orsini sat staring at the machine for long minutes. No business calls about a briefcase are made at this hour, he thought. That's some kind of code. Someone expects Ed Collins to get that message. It was one more confirmation that some mysterious person believed Ed was alive and out there somewhere.

A few minutes later, Victor left. He had not found the object of his search.

42

On Sunday morning, Catherine Collins attended the ten o'clock mass at St Paul's, but she found it difficult to keep her mind on the sermon. She had been christened in this church, married in it, buried her parents from it. She had always found comfort here. For so long she had prayed at mass that Edwin's body would be found, prayed for resignation to his loss, for the strength to go on without him.

What was she asking of God now? Only that He keep Meg safe. She glanced at Meg, sitting beside her, completely still, seemingly attentive to the homily, but Catherine suspected that her daughter's thoughts were far away as well.

A fragment from the *Dies Irae* came unbidden into Catherine's mind. 'Day of wrath and day of mourning. Lo, the world in ashes burning.'

I'm angry and I'm hurt and my world is in ashes,

177

Catherine thought. She blinked back sudden tears and felt Meg's hand close over hers.

When they left church they stopped for coffee and sticky buns at the local bakery, which had a half-dozen tables in the rear of the shop. 'Feel better?' Meg asked.

'Yes,' Catherine said briskly. 'These sticky buns will do it every time. I'm going with you to Dad's office.'

'I thought we'd agreed I should clear it out. That's why we're in two cars.'

'It's no easier for you than it is for me. It will go faster if we're together, and some of that stuff will be heavy to carry.'

Her mother's voice held the note of finality that Meghan knew ended further debate.

Meghan's car was filled with boxes for packing. She and her mother lugged them to the building. When they opened the door into the Collins and Carter office suite, they were surprised to find that it was warm and the lights were on.

'Ten to one Phillip came in early to get the place ready,' Catherine observed. She looked around the reception room. 'It's surprising how seldom I came here,' she said. 'Your dad traveled so much, and even when he wasn't on the road he was usually out on appointments. And of course I was always tied to the inn.'

'I probably was here more than you,' Meg agreed. 'I used to come here after school sometimes and catch a ride home with him.'

She pushed open the door to her father's private office. 'It's just as he left it,' she told her mother. 'Phillip has been awfully generous to keep it undisturbed this long. I know Victor really should have been using it.'

For a long moment they both studied the room: his desk, the long table behind it with their pictures, the wall unit with bookcases and file cabinets in the same

178

cherrywood finish as the desk. The effect was uncluttered and tasteful.

'Edwin bought and refinished that desk,' Catherine said. 'I'm sure Phillip wouldn't mind if we had it picked up.'

'I'm sure he wouldn't.'

They began by collecting the pictures and stacking them in a box. Meghan knew they both sensed that the faster the office took on an impersonal look, the easier it would be. Then she suggested, 'Mom, why don't you start with the books. I'll go through the desk and files.'

It was only when she was seated at the desk that she saw the blinking light on the answering machine, which sat on a low table next to the swivel chair.

'Look at this.'

Her mother came over to the desk. 'Is anyone still leaving messages on Dad's machine?' she asked incredulously, then leaned down to look at the call display. 'There's just one. Let's hear it.'

Bewildered, they listened to the message and then the computer voice of the machine saying, 'Sunday, October thirty-first, twelve-oh-nine a.m. End of final message.'

'That message came in only hours ago!' Catherine exclaimed. 'Who leaves a business message in the middle of the night? And when would Dad have ordered a briefcase?'

'It could be a mistake,' Meghan said. 'Whoever called didn't leave a return number or a name.'

'Wouldn't most salespeople leave a phone number if they wanted to confirm an order, especially if the order was placed months ago? Meg, that message doesn't make sense. And that woman doesn't sound like an order clerk to me.'

Meg slipped the tape out of the machine and put it in her shoulder bag. 'It doesn't make sense,' she agreed. 'We're only wasting time trying to figure it out here. Let's get on with this packing and listen to it again at home.'

179

She looked quickly through the desk drawers and found the usual assortment of stationery, notepads, paper clips, pens and highlighters. She remembered that when he went over a candidate's curriculum vitae, her father had marked the most favorable aspects of the résumé in yellow, the least favorable in pink. Quickly she transferred the contents of the desk to boxes.

Next she tackled the files. The first one seemed to have copies of her father's expense account reports. Apparently the bookkeeper kept the original and returned a photocopy with Paid stamped across the top.

'I'm going to take these files home,' she said. 'They're Dad's personal copies of originals already in the company records.'

'Is there any point in taking them?'

'Yes, there just might be some reference to Palomino Leather Goods.'

They were finishing the last box when they heard the outside door open. 'It's me,' Phillip called.

He came in, wearing a shirt open at the neck, sleeveless sweater, corduroy jacket and slacks. 'Hope it was comfortable when you got here,' he said. 'I stopped by this morning for a minute. This place gets mighty chilly over a weekend if the thermostat is down.'

He surveyed the boxes. 'I knew you'd need a hand. Catherine, will you please put down that box of books.'

'Dad called her "Mighty Mouse," ' Meg said. 'This is nice of you, Phillip.'

He saw the top of an expense file sticking out of one of the boxes. 'Are you sure you want all that stuff? It's nuts and bolts, and you and I went all through it, Meg, looking for any insurance policies that might not have been in the safe.'

'We might as well take it,' Meg said. 'You'd only have to dispose of it anyhow.'

'Phillip, the answering machine was blinking when we came in here.' Meghan took out the tape, snapped it into the machine and played it.

She saw the look of astonishment on his face. 'Obviously you don't get it either.'

'No. I don't.'

It was fortunate that both she and her mother had brought their cars. The trunks and backseats were crammed by the time the last box had been carried down.

They refused Phillip's offer to follow them and help unload. 'I'll have a couple of the busboys from the inn take care of it,' Catherine said.

As Meghan drove home she knew that every hour she was not tracking down information on Helene Petrovic she would be going through every line of every page of her father's records.

If there was someone else in Dad's life, she thought, and if that woman in the morgue is the Annie that Cyrus Graham met ten years ago, there might be some link in his files that I can trace back to them.

Some instinct told her that Palomino Leather Goods might prove to be that link.

In Kyle's eyes, the trick-or-treating had been absolutely great. On Sunday evening he spread his collection of assorted candies, cookies, apples and pennies on the den floor while Mac prepared dinner.

'Don't eat any of that junk now,' Mac warned.

'I know, Dad. You told me twice.'

'Then maybe it'll start sinking in.' Mac tested the hamburgers on the grill.

'Why do we always have hamburgers on Sunday when we're home?' Kyle asked. 'They're better at McDonald's.'

'Many thanks.' Mac flipped them onto toasted buns. 'We have hamburgers on Sunday because I cook hamburgers better than anything else. I take you out most Fridays. I make pasta when we're home on Saturdays, and Mrs Dileo cooks good food the rest of the week. Now eat up if you want to put your costume on again and scare Meg.'

Kyle took a couple of bites of his hamburger. 'Do you like Meg, Dad?'

'Yes, I do. Very much. Why?'

'I wish she'd come here more. She's fun.'

I wish she'd come here more too, Mac thought, but it doesn't look as though that's going to happen. Last night when he'd offered to help her with the packing up of her father's office she'd cut him off so fast his head had been spinning.

Stay away. Don't get too close. We're just friends. She might as well put up a sign.

She'd certainly grown up a lot from the nineteen-year-old kid who had a crush on him and wrote a letter telling him she loved him and please don't marry Ginger.

He wished he had the letter now. He also wished she'd feel that way again. He certainly regretted he hadn't taken her advice about Ginger.

Then Mac looked at his son. No I don't, he thought. I couldn't and wouldn't undo having this kid.

'Dad, what's the matter?' Kyle asked. 'You look worried.'

'That's what you said about Meg when you saw her on television yesterday.'

'Well, she did and so do you.'

'I'm just worried that I might have to learn how to cook something else. Finish up and get your costume on.'

It was seven-thirty when they left the house. Kyle deemed it satisfactorily dark outside for ghosts. 'I bet there really are ghosts out,' he said. 'On Halloween all the dead people get out of their graves and walk around.'

'Who told you that?'

'Danny.'

'Tell Danny that's a tall tale everyone tells on Halloween.'

They walked around the curve in the road and

182

reached the Collins property. 'Now, Dad, you wait here near the hedge where Meg can't see you. I'll go around in back and bang on the window and howl. Okay?'

'Okay. Don't scare her too much.'

Swinging his skull-shaped lantern, Kyle raced around the back of the Collins house. The dining room shades were up, and he could see Meg sitting at the table with a bunch of papers in front of her. He had a good idea. He'd go right to the edge of the woods and run from there to the house, yelling 'Whoo, whoo,' and then he'd bang on the window. That should really scare Meg.

He stepped between two trees, spread his arms and began to wave them about. As his right hand went back, he felt flesh, smooth flesh, then an ear. He heard breathing. Whirling his head around, he saw the form of a man, crouching behind him, the light reflecting off a camera lens. A hand grabbed his neck. Kyle wiggled loose and began to scream. Then he was shoved forward with a violent push. As he fell, he dropped his lantern and began clawing the ground, his hand closing over something. Still screaming, he scrambled to his feet and ran toward the house.

That's some realistic yell, Mac thought, when he first heard Kyle's scream. Then, as the terrified shriek continued, he began to run toward the woods. Something had happened to Kyle. With a burst of speed he raced across the lawn and behind the house.

From inside the dining room, Meg heard the screaming and ran to the back door. She yanked it open and grabbed Kyle as he stumbled through the door and fell into her arms, sobbing in terror.

That was the way Mac found them, their arms around each other, Meg rocking his son back and forth, soothing him. 'Kyle, it's okay. It's okay,' she kept repeating.

It took minutes before he could tell them what had happened. 'Kyle, it's all those stories about the dead walking that makes you think you're seeing things,' Mac said. 'There was nothing there.'

183

Calmer now, drinking the hot cocoa Meg had made for him, Kyle was adamant. 'There was so a man there, and he had a camera. I know. I fell when he pushed me, but I picked up something. Then I dropped it when I saw Meg. Go see what it is, Dad.'

'I'll get a flashlight, Mac,' Meg said.

Mac went outside and began moving the beam back and forth over the ground. He did not have to go far. Only a few feet from the back porch he found a gray plastic box, the kind used to carry videotapes.

He picked it up and walked back to the woods, still shining the light before him. He knew it was useless. No intruder stands around waiting to be discovered. The ground was too hard to see footprints, but he found Kyle's lantern directly in line with the dining room windows. From where he was standing he could see Meg and Kyle clearly.

Someone with a camera had been here watching Meg, maybe taping her. Why?

Mac thought of the dead girl in the morgue, then hurried back across the lawn to the house.

That stupid kid! Bernie thought as he ran through the woods to his car. He'd parked it near the end of the Drumdoe Inn parking lot but not so far away that it stood out. There were about forty cars scattered through the lot now, so his Chevy certainly wouldn't have been particularly noticed. He hurriedly tossed his camera in the trunk and drove through town toward Route 7. He was careful to go not more than five miles above the speed limit. But he knew that driving too slow was a red flag to the cops too.

Had that kid gotten a good look at him? He didn't think so. It was dark, and the kid was scared. A few seconds more and he could have moved backwards and the kid wouldn't have known he was there.

Bernie was furious. He'd been enjoying watching

184

Meghan through the camera, and he'd had such a clear view of her. He was sure he had great tapes.

On the other hand he'd never seen anyone so frightened as that kid had been. He felt tingly and alive and almost energized just thinking about it. To have such power. To be able to record someone's expressions and movements and secret little gestures, like the way Meghan kept tucking her hair behind her ear when she was concentrating. To scare someone so much that he screamed and cried and ran like that little kid just now.

To watch Meghan, her hands, her hair . . .

43

Stephanie Petrovic had a fitful night, finally falling into a heavy sleep. When she awakened at ten-thirty on Sunday morning, she opened her eyes lazily and smiled. At last things were working out.

She had been warned never to breathe his name, to forget she'd ever met him, but that was before Helene was murdered and before Helene lost the chance to change her will.

On the telephone he was so kind to her. He promised he would take care of her. He would make arrangements to have the baby adopted by people who would pay one hundred thousand dollars for it.

'So much?' she had asked, delighted.

He reassured her that there would be no problem.

He would also arrange to get her a green card. 'It will be fake, but no one will ever be able to tell the difference,' he had said. 'However, I suggest that you move someplace where no one knows you. I wouldn't

185

want anyone to recognize you. Even in a big place like New York City people bump into each other, and in your case they'd start asking questions. You might try California.'

Stephanie knew she would love California. Maybe she could get a job in a spa there, she thought. With one hundred thousand dollars she'd be able to get the training she'd need. Or maybe she could just get a job right away. She was like Helene. Being a beautician came to her naturally. She loved that kind of work.

He was sending a car for her at seven o'clock tonight. 'I don't want the neighbors to see you moving out,' he'd told her.

Stephanie wanted to luxuriate in bed, but she was hungry. Only ten days more and the baby will be born and then I can go on a diet, she promised herself.

She showered, then dressed in the maternity clothes she had come to hate. Then she began to pack. Helene had tapestry luggage in the closet. Why shouldn't I have it? Stephanie thought. Who deserves it more?

Because of the pregnancy, she had so few clothes, but once she was back to her normal size she'd fit in Helene's things again. Helene had been a conservative dresser, but all her clothes were expensive and in good taste. Stephanie went through the closet and dresser drawers, rejecting only what she absolutely did not like.

Helene had a small safe on the floor of her closet. Stephanie knew where she kept the combination, so she opened it. It didn't contain much jewelry, but there were a few very good pieces, which she slipped into a cosmetic bag.

It was a shame she couldn't move the furniture out there. On the other hand, she knew from pictures she'd seen that in California they didn't use old-fashioned upholstered furniture and dark woods like mahogany.

She did go through the house and chose some Dresden figurines to take with her. Then she remembered the table silver. The big chest was too heavy to carry, so

186

she put the silver in plastic bags and fastened rubber bands around them to keep it from rattling in the suitcase.

The lawyer, Mr Potters, called at five o'clock to see how she was feeling. 'Perhaps you'd like to join my wife and me for dinner, Stephanie.'

'Oh, thank you,' she said, 'but someone from the Rumanian Society is going to drop in.'

'Fine. We just didn't want you to be lonesome. Remember, be sure to call me if you need anything.'

'You're so kind, Mr Potters.'

'Well, I only wish I could do more for you. Unfortunately, where the will is concerned, my hands are tied.'

I don't need your help, Stephanie thought as she hung up the phone.

Now it was time to write the letter. She composed three versions before she was satisfied. She knew that some of her spelling was bad, and she had to look up some words, but at last it seemed to be all right. It was to Mr Potters:

Dear Mr Potters,

I am happy to say that Jan, the father of my baby, is the one who came to see me. We are going to get married and he will take care of us. He must get back to his job right away so I am leaving with him. He now works in Dallas.

I love Jan very much and I know you will be pleassed for me.

Thank you.

Stephanie Petrovic

The car came for her promptly at seven. The driver carried her bags out. Stephanie left the note and house key on the dining room table, turned off the lights, closed the door behind her and hurried through the darkness, down the flagstone walk to the waiting vehicle.

187

*

On Monday morning, Meghan tried to phone Stephanie Petrovic. There was no answer. She settled down at the dining room table, where she had begun to go through her father's business files.

She immediately noticed something. He'd been registered and billed for five days at the Four Seasons Hotel in Beverly Hills, from 23 January to 28 January, the day he flew to Newark and disappeared. After the first two days there were no extra charges on that bill. Even if he ate most of his meals out, Meghan thought, people send for breakfast or make a phone call or open the room bar and have a drink – something.

On the other hand, if he'd been on the concierge floor, it would be very like her father just to go to the courtesy buffet and help himself to juice, coffee and a roll. He was a light-breakfast eater.

The first two days, however, did have extra charges on the bill, like the valet, a bottle of wine, an evening snack, phone calls. She made a note of the dates of the three days when there were no extra expenses.

There might be a pattern, she thought.

At noon she tried Stephanie again, and again the phone was not answered. At two o'clock she began to be alarmed and phoned the lawyer, Charles Potters. He assured her that Stephanie was fine. He'd spoken to her the evening before and she'd said someone from the Rumanian Society was dropping by.

'I'm glad,' Meghan said. 'She's a very frightened girl.'

'Yes, she is,' Potters agreed. 'Something that isn't generally known is that when someone leaves an entire estate to a charity or a medical facility such as the Manning Clinic, if a close relative is needy and inclined to try to break the will, the charity or facility may quietly offer a settlement. However, after Stephanie went on television literally accusing the clinic of being responsible for her aunt's murder, any such settlement was out of the question. It would seem like hush money.'

'I understand,' Meghan said. 'I'll keep trying Stephanie, but will you ask her to call me if you hear from her? I still think someone should go after the man who got her pregnant. If she gives away her baby, she may someday regret it.'

Meghan's mother had gone to the inn for the breakfast and lunch service, and she returned to the house just as Meg was finishing the conversation with Potters. 'Let me get busy with you,' she said, taking a seat next to her at the dining room table.

'Actually you can take over,' Meghan told her. 'I really have to drive to my apartment and get clothes and pick up my mail. It's the first of November, and all the little window envelopes will be in.'

The evening before, when her mother had returned from the inn, she had told her about the man with the camera who had frightened Kyle. 'I asked someone at the station to check it out for me; I haven't heard yet, but I'm sure one of those sleazy programs is putting together a story on us and Dad and the Andersons,' she said. 'Sending someone to spy on us is the way they work.' She had not allowed Mac to call the police.

She showed her mother what she was doing with the files. 'Mom, watch the hotel receipts for times when there were no extra expenses for three or four days in a row. I'd like to see if it only happened when Dad was in California.' She did not say that Los Angeles was half an hour by plane from Scottsdale.

'And as for Palomino Leather Goods,' Catherine said, 'I don't know why, but that name has been churning around in my mind. I feel as though I've heard it before, but a long time ago.'

Meghan still had not decided if she would stop at PCD on her way to the apartment. She was wearing comfortable old slacks and a favorite sweater. It'll do, she thought. That was one of the aspects she had loved about the job, the behind-the-scenes informality.

She brushed her hair quickly and realized that it was

growing too long. She liked it to be collar length. Now it was touching her shoulders. The dead girl's hair had been on her shoulders. Her hands suddenly cold, Meghan reached back, twisted her hair into a French knot and pinned it up.

When she was leaving, her mother said, 'Meg, why don't you go out to dinner with some of your friends? It will do you good to get away from all this.'

'I'm not much in the mood for social dinners,' Meg said, 'but I'll call and let you know. You'll be at the inn?'

'Yes.'

'Well, when you're here after dark be sure to keep the draperies drawn.' She raised her hand, palm upright and outward, fingers spread. 'As Kyle would say, "Give me a high five."'

Her mother raised her hand and touched her daughter's palm in response. 'You've got it.'

They looked at each other for a long minute, then Catherine said briskly, 'Drive carefully.'

It was the standard warning ever since Meg had gotten her driving permit at age sixteen.

Her answer was always in the same vein. Today she said, 'Actually I thought I'd tailgate a tractor trailer.' Then she wanted to bite her tongue. The accident on the Tappan Zee Bridge had been caused by a fuel truck tailgating a tractor trailer.

She knew her mother was thinking the same thing when she said, 'Dear God, Meg, it's like walking through a mine field, isn't it? Even the kind of joking remark that has been part of the fabric of our lives has been tainted and twisted. Will it ever end?'

That same Monday morning, Dr George Manning was again questioned in Assistant State Attorney John Dwyer's office. The questions had become sharper with an edge of sarcasm in them. The two investigators sat quietly as their boss handled the interrogation.

190

'Doctor,' Dwyer asked, 'can you explain why you didn't tell us immediately that Helene Petrovic was afraid that she had mixed up the Anderson embryos?'

'Because she wasn't sure.' George Manning's shoulders slumped. His complexion, usually a healthy pink, was ashen. Even the admirable head of silver hair seemed a faded, graying white. Since the Anderson baby's birth he had aged visibly.

'Dr Manning, you've said repeatedly that founding and running the assisted reproduction clinic has been the great achievement of your lifetime. Were you aware that Helene Petrovic was planning to leave her rather considerable estate to research at your clinic?'

'We had talked about it. You see, the level of success in our field is still not anything like what we would wish. It's very expensive for a woman to have in vitro fertilization, anywhere from ten to twenty thousand dollars. If a pregnancy is not achieved, the process starts all over. While some clinics claim a one out of five success ratio, the honest figure is closer to one out of ten.'

'Doctor, you are very anxious to see the ratio of successful pregnancies at your clinic improved?'

'Yes, of course.'

'Wasn't it quite a blow to you last Monday when Helene Petrovic not only quit but admitted she might have made a very serious mistake?'

'It was devastating.'

'Yet, even when she was found murdered, you withheld the very important reason for quitting that she had given you.' Dwyer leaned across his desk. 'What else did Ms Petrovic tell you at that meeting last Monday, Doctor?'

Manning folded his hands together. 'She said that she was planning to sell her house in Lawrenceville and move away, that she might go to France to live.'

'And what did you think of that plan?'

191

'I was stunned,' he whispered. 'I was sure she was running away.'

'Running away from what, Doctor?'

George Manning knew it was all over. He could not protect the clinic any longer. 'I had the feeling that she was afraid that if the Anderson baby was not Jonathan's twin, it would start an investigation that might reveal many mistakes in the lab.'

'The will, Doctor. Did you also think that Helene Petrovic would change her will?'

'She told me she was sorry, but it was necessary. She planned to take a long time off from work and now she had family to consider.'

John Dwyer had found the answer he had guessed was there. 'Dr Manning, when was the last time you spoke to Edwin Collins?'

'He called me the day before he disappeared.' Dr George Manning did not like what he saw in Dwyer's eyes. 'It was the first contact I had had with him either by phone or letter since he placed Helene Petrovic in my clinic,' he said, looking away, unable to cope with the disbelief and mistrust he was reading in the demeanor of the assistant state attorney.

44

Meghan decided to skip going to the office and reached her apartment building at four o'clock. Her mailbox was overflowing. She fished out all the envelopes and ads and throwaways, then took the elevator up to her fourteenth-floor apartment.

She immediately opened the windows to blow away

the smell of stale heat, then stood for a moment looking out over the water to the Statue of Liberty. Today the lady seemed remote and formidable in the shadows cast by the late afternoon sun.

Often when she looked at it she thought of her grandfather, Pat Kelly, who had come to this country as a teenager with nothing and worked so hard to make his fortune.

What would her grandfather think if he knew that his daughter Catherine might lose everything he had worked for because her husband had cheated on her for years?

Scottsdale, Arizona. Meg looked over the waters of New York Harbor and realized what had been bothering her. Arizona was in the Southwest. Palomino had the sound of the Southwest.

She went over to the phone, dialed the operator and asked for the area code for Scottsdale, Arizona.

Next she dialed Arizona information.

When she reached that operator, she asked, 'Do you have a listing for an Edwin Collins or an E. R. Collins?'

There was none.

Meg asked another question. 'Do you have a listing for Palomino Leather Goods?'

There was a pause, then the operator said, 'Please hold for the number.'

Part Three

45

On Monday evening when Mac got home from work, Kyle was his usual cheerful self. He informed his father that he had told all the kids at school about the guy in the woods.

'They all said how scared they'd be,' he explained with satisfaction. 'I told them how I really ran fast and got away from him. Did you tell your friends about it?'

'No, I didn't.'

'It's okay if you want to,' Kyle said magnanimously.

As Kyle turned away, Mac held his arm. 'Kyle, wait a minute.'

'What's the matter?'

'Let me take a look at something.'

Kyle was wearing an open-necked flannel shirt. Mac pushed it back, revealing yellowish and purple bruises at the base of his son's neck. 'Did you get these last night?'

'I told you that guy grabbed me.'

'You said he pushed you.'

'First he grabbed me, but I got away.'

Mac swore under his breath. He had not thought to examine Kyle the night before. He'd been wearing the ghost costume, and under that, a white turtleneck shirt. Mac had thought that Kyle had only been pushed by the intruder with the camera. Instead he had been grabbed around the neck. Strong fingers had caused those bruises.

Mac kept an arm around his son as he dialed the

197

police. Last night he had reluctantly gone along with Meghan when she pleaded with him not to call them.

'Mac, it's bad enough now without giving the media a fresh angle on all this,' she had said. 'Mark my words, somebody will write that Dad is hanging around the house. The assistant state attorney is sure he's going to contact us.'

I've let Meg keep me out of this long enough, Mac thought grimly. She's not going to any longer. That wasn't just some cameraman hanging around out there.

The phone was answered on the first ring. 'State Trooper Thorne speaking.'

Fifteen minutes later a squad car was at the house. It was clear the two policemen were not pleased that they had not been called earlier. 'Dr MacIntyre, last night was Halloween. We're always worried that some nut might be hanging around, hoping to pick up a kid. That guy might have gone somewhere else in town.'

'I agree I should have called,' Mac said, 'but I don't think that man was looking for children. He was directly in line with the dining room windows of the Collins' home, and Meghan Collins was in full view.'

He saw the looks the cops exchanged. 'I think the state attorney's office should know about this,' one of them said.

All the way home from her apartment, the bitter truth had been sinking in. Meghan knew she now had virtual confirmation that her father had a second family in Arizona.

When she'd phoned the Palomino Leather Goods Shop she'd spoken to the owner. The woman was astonished when asked about the message on the answering machine. 'That call didn't come from here,' she said flatly.

She did confirm that she had a customer named Mrs

E. R. Collins who had a daughter in her twenties. After that she refused to give information over the phone.

It was seven-thirty when Meg reached Newtown. She turned into the driveway and was surprised to see Mac's red Chrysler and an unfamiliar sedan parked in front of the house. Now what? she thought, alarmed. She pulled up behind them, parked and hurried up the porch steps, realizing that any unexpected occurrence was enough to start her heart pounding with dread.

Special Investigator Arlene Weiss was in the living room with Catherine, Mac and Kyle. There was no apology in Mac's voice when he told Meg why he'd called the local police and then the assistant state attorney's office about the intruder. In fact, Meg was sure from the clipped way he spoke to her that he was angry. Kyle had been manhandled and terrified; he might have been strangled by some lunatic, and I wouldn't let Mac notify the police, she thought. She didn't blame him for being furious.

Kyle was sitting between Catherine and Mac on the couch. He slid down and came across the room to her. 'Meg, don't look so sad. I'm okay.' He put his hands on her cheeks. 'Really, I'm okay.'

She looked into his serious eyes, then hugged him fiercely. 'You bet you are, pal.'

Weiss did not stay long. 'Miss Collins, believe it or not, we want to help you,' she said as Meghan accompanied her to the door. 'When you don't report, or allow other people to report, incidents like last night's, you are hindering this investigation. We could have had a police vehicle here in a few minutes if you'd called. According to Kyle, that man was carrying a large camera that would have slowed him down. Please, is there anything else we should know?'

'Nothing,' Meg said.

'Mrs Collins tells me that you were at your apartment. Did you find any more faxed messages?'

'No.' She bit her lip, thinking of her call to Palomino Leather Goods.

Weiss stared at her. 'I see. Well, if you remember anything that you think will interest us, you know where to reach us.'

When Weiss left, Mac said to Kyle, 'Go into the den. You can watch television for fifteen minutes. Then we have to go.'

'That's okay, Dad. There's nothing good on. I'll stay here.'

'It wasn't a suggestion.'

Kyle jumped up. 'Fine. You don't have to get sore about it.'

'Right, Dad,' Meghan agreed. 'You don't have to get sore about it.'

Kyle gave her a high five as he passed her chair.

Mac waited until he heard the click of the den door. 'What did you find out while you were at your apartment, Meghan?'

Meg looked at her mother. 'The location of the Palomino Leather Goods Shop and that they have a customer named Mrs E. R. Collins.'

Ignoring her mother's gasp, she told them about her call to Scottsdale.

'I'm flying out there tomorrow,' she said. 'We have to know if their Mrs Collins is the woman Cyrus Graham saw with Dad. We can't be sure until I meet her.'

Catherine Collins hoped the hurt she saw in her daughter's face was not mirrored in her own expression when she said quietly, 'Meggie, if you look so much like that dead young woman, and the woman in Scottsdale is that girl's mother, it could be terrible for her to see you.'

'Nothing is going to make it easy for whoever turns out to be the mother of that girl.'

She was grateful that they did not try to dissuade her. Instead Mac said, 'Meg, don't tell anyone, and I mean

200

anyone, where you're going. How long do you expect to stay?'

'Overnight at the most.'

'Then for all anyone will know, you're at your apartment. Leave it at that.'

When he collected Kyle, he said, 'Catherine, if Kyle and I come to the inn tomorrow night, do you think you'd have time to join us for dinner?'

Catherine managed a smile. 'I'd love to. What should I have on the menu, Kyle?'

'Chicken McNuggets?' he asked hopefully.

'Are you trying to run me out of business? Come on inside. I brought home some cookies. Take a couple with you.' She led him into the kitchen.

'Catherine is very tactful,' Mac said. 'I think she knew I wanted a minute with you. Meg, I don't like you going out there alone, but I think I understand. Now I want the truth. Is there anything you're holding back?'

'No.'

'Meg, I won't let you shut me out anymore. Get used to that idea. How can I help?'

'Call Stephanie Petrovic in the morning, and if she's not there, call her lawyer. I have a funny feeling about Stephanie. I've tried to reach her three or four times, and she's been out all day. I even called her from the car half an hour ago. Her baby is due in ten days and she feels lousy. The other day she was exhausted after her aunt's funeral and couldn't wait to lie down. I can't imagine her being gone so long. Let me give you the numbers.'

When Mac and Kyle left a few minutes later, Mac's kiss was not the usual friendly peck on the cheek. Instead, as his son had done earlier, he held Meg's face in his hands.

'Take care of yourself,' he ordered, as his lips closed firmly over hers.

201

46

Monday had been a bad day for Bernie. He got up at dawn, settled in the cracked Naugahyde recliner in the basement, and began to watch over and over the video he'd taken of Meghan from his hiding place in the woods. He'd wanted to see it when he got home last night, but his mother had demanded he keep her company.

'I'm alone too much, Bernard,' she'd complained. 'You never used to go out so much on weekends. You haven't got a girl have you?'

'Of course not, Mama,' he'd said.

'You know all the trouble you've gotten into because of girls.'

'None of that was my fault, Mama.'

'I didn't say it was your fault. I said that girls are poison for you. Stay away from them.'

'Yes, Mama.'

When Mama got in one of those moods, the best thing Bernie could do was to listen to her. He was still afraid of her. He still shivered thinking of the times when he was growing up and she'd suddenly appear with the strap in her hands. 'I saw you looking at that smut on television, Bernard. I can read those filthy thoughts in your head.'

Mama would never understand that what he felt for Meghan was pure and beautiful. It was just that he wanted to be around Meghan, wanted to see her, wanted to feel like he could always get her to look up and smile at him. Like last night. If he had tapped at the window and she'd recognized him, she wouldn't have been scared. She'd have run to the door to let him in. She'd have said, 'Bernie, what are you doing here?' Maybe she'd have made a cup of tea for him.

Bernie leaned forward. He was getting to the good part again, where Meghan looked so intent on what she was doing as she sat at the head of the dining room table with all those papers in front of her. With the zoom lens he'd managed to get close-ups of her face. There was something about the way she was beginning to moisten her lips that thrilled him. Her blouse was open at the neck. He wasn't sure if he could see the beat of her pulse there or if he only imagined that.

'Bernard! Bernard!'

His mother was at the head of the stairs, shouting down to him. How long had she been calling?

'Yes, Mama. I'm coming.'

'It took you long enough,' she snapped when he reached the kitchen. 'You'll be late for work. What were you doing?'

'Straightening up a little. I know you want me to leave it neat.'

Fifteen minutes later he was in the car. He drove down the block, unsure of where to go. He knew he should try to pick up some fares at the airport. With all the equipment he was buying, he needed to make some money. He had to force himself to turn the wheel and head in the direction of La Guardia.

He spent the day driving back and forth to the airport. It went well enough until late afternoon when some guy kept complaining to him about the traffic. 'For Pete's sake, get in the left lane. Can't you see this one is blocked?'

Bernie had begun thinking about Meghan again, about whether it would be safe to drive past her house once it got dark.

A minute later the passenger snapped, 'Listen, I knew

203

I should have taken a cab. Where'd you learn to drive? Keep up with the traffic, for God's sake.'

Bernie was at the last exit on the Grand Central Parkway before the Triborough Bridge. He took a sharp right onto the street parallel to the parkway and pulled the car to the curb.

'What the hell do you think you're doing?' the passenger demanded.

The guy's big suitcase was next to Bernie in the front seat. He leaned over, opened the door and pushed it out. 'Get lost,' he ordered. 'Get yourself a taxi.'

He spun his head to look into the passenger's face. Their eyes locked.

The passenger's expression changed to one of panic. 'All right, take it easy. Sorry if I got you upset.'

He jumped out of the car and yanked his suitcase away just as Bernie floored the accelerator. Bernie cut through side streets. He'd better go home. Otherwise he'd go back and smash that big mouth.

He began to take deliberate deep breaths. That's what the prison psychiatrist told him to do when he felt himself getting mad. 'You've got to handle that anger, Bernie,' he'd warned him. 'Unless you want to spend the rest of your life in here.'

Bernie knew he could never go back to prison again. He'd do anything to keep that from happening.

On Tuesday morning, Meghan's alarm went off at four a.m. She had a reservation on America West Flight 9, leaving from Kennedy Airport at seven-twenty-five. She had no trouble getting up. Her sleep had been uneasy. She showered, running the water as hot as she could stand it, glad to feel some of the taut muscles in her neck and back loosen.

As she pulled on underwear and stockings she listened to the weather report on the radio. It was below freezing in New York. Arizona, of course, was another matter.

204

Cool in the evenings at this time of year, but she understood it could be fairly warm during the day.

A tan, lightweight wool jacket and slacks with a print blouse seemed to be a good choice. Over it she'd wear her Burberry without the lining. She quickly packed the few things she'd need for an overnight stay.

The smell of coffee greeted her as she started down the stairs. Her mother was in the kitchen. 'You shouldn't have gotten up,' Meg protested.

'I wasn't sleeping.' Catherine Collins toyed with the belt of her terry-cloth robe. 'I didn't offer to go with you, Meg, but now I'm having second thoughts. Maybe I shouldn't let you do this alone. It's just that if there is another Mrs Edwin Collins in Scottsdale, I don't know what I could say to her. Was she as ignorant as I about what was going on? Or did she knowingly live a lie?'

'I hope by the end of the day I'll have some answers,' Meg said, 'and I absolutely know that it's better I do this alone.' She took a few sips of grapefruit juice and swallowed a little coffee. 'I've got to get going. It's a long ride to Kennedy Airport. I don't want to get caught in rush-hour traffic.'

Her mother walked her to the door. Meg hugged her briefly. 'I get into Phoenix at eleven o'clock, mountain time. I'll call you late this afternoon.'

She could feel her mother's eyes on her as she walked to the car.

The flight was uneventful. She had a window seat and for long periods of time gazed down at the puffy cushion of white clouds. She thought of her fifth birthday when her mother and father took her to DisneyWorld. It was her first flight. She'd sat at the window, her father beside her, her mother across the aisle.

Over the years her father had teased her about the question she'd asked that day. 'Daddy, if we got out of the plane, could we walk on the clouds?'

He'd told her that he was sorry to say the clouds wouldn't hold her up. 'But I'll always hold you up, Meggie Anne,' he'd promised.

And he had. She thought of the awful day when she'd tripped just before the finish line of a race and had cost her high school track team the state championship. Her father had been waiting when she'd slunk out of the gym, not wanting to hear the consoling words of her teammates or see the disappointment on their faces.

He had offered understanding, not consolation. 'There are some events in our lives, Meghan,' he'd told her, 'that no matter how old we get, the memory still hurts. I'm afraid you've just chalked up one of those events.'

A wave of tenderness swept over Meghan and then was gone as she remembered the times when her father's claim of pressing business had kept him away. Sometimes even on holidays like Thanksgiving and Christmas. Was he celebrating them in Scottsdale? With his other family? Holidays were always so busy at the inn. When he wasn't home, she and her mother would have dinner there with friends, but her mother would be up and down greeting guests and checking the kitchen.

She remembered being fourteen and taking jazz dance lessons. When her father came home from one of his trips, she'd shown him the newest steps she'd mastered.

'Meggie,' he'd sighed, 'jazz is good music and a fine dance form, but the waltz is the dance of the angels.' He'd taught her the Viennese waltz.

It was a relief when the pilot announced that they were beginning the descent into Sky Harbor International Airport, where the outside temperature was seventy degrees.

Meghan took her things from the overhead compartment and waited restlessly for the cabin door to open. She wanted to get through this day as quickly as possible.

The car rental agency was in the Barry Goldwater

206

terminal. Meghan stopped to look up the address of the Palomino Leather Goods Shop and when she signed for a car asked the clerk for directions.

'That's in the Bogota section of Scottsdale,' the clerk said. 'It's a wonderful shopping area that will make you think you're in a medieval town.'

On a map she outlined the route for Meghan. 'You'll be there in twenty-five minutes,' she said.

As she drove, Meghan absorbed the beauty of the mountains in the distance and the cloudless, intensely blue sky. When she had cleared the commercial sections, palms and orange trees and saguaro cactuses began to dot the landscape.

She passed the adobe-style Safari Hotel. With its bright oleanders and tall palms, it looked serene and inviting. This was where Cyrus Graham said he had seen his stepbrother, her father, nearly eleven years ago.

The Palomino Leather Goods Shop was a mile farther down on Scottsdale Road. Here the buildings had castle-like towers and crenellated parapet walls. Cobblestone streets contributed to an old-world effect. The boutiques that lined the streets were small, and all of them looked expensive. Meghan turned left into the parking area past Palomino Leather Goods and got out of the car. She found it disconcerting to realize that her knees were trembling.

The pungent scent of fine leather greeted her when she entered the shop. Purses ranging in size from clutches to tote bags were tastefully grouped on shelves and tables. A display case held wallets, key rings and jewelry. Brief-cases and luggage were visible in the larger area a few steps down and to the rear of the entry level.

There was only one other person in the shop, a young woman with striking Indian features and thick, dark hair that cascaded down her back. She looked up from her position behind the cash register and smiled. 'May I help you?' There was no hint of recognition in her voice or manner.

Meghan thought quickly. 'I hope so. I'm only in town for a few hours and I wanted to look up some relatives. I don't have their address and they're not listed in the phone book. I know they shop here and I hoped I might be able to get the address or phone number from you.'

The clerk hesitated. 'I'm new. Maybe you could come back in about an hour. The owner will be in then.'

'Please,' Meghan said. 'I have so little time.'

'What's the name? I can see if they have an account.'

'E. R. Collins.'

'Oh,' the clerk said, 'you must have called yesterday.'

'That's right.'

'I was here. After she spoke to you, the owner, Mrs Stoges, told me about Mr Collins' death. Was he a relative?'

Meghan's mouth went dry. 'Yes. That's why I'm anxious to stop in on the family.'

The clerk turned on the computer. 'Here's the address and phone number. I'm afraid I have to phone Mrs Collins and ask permission to give it to you.'

There was nothing to do but nod. Meghan watched the buttons on the phone being rapidly pressed.

A moment later the clerk said into the receiver. 'Mrs Collins? This is the Palomino Leather Goods Shop. There's a young lady here who would like to see you, a relative. Is it all right if I give her your address?'

She listened then looked at Meghan. 'May I ask your name?'

'Meghan. Meghan Collins.'

The clerk repeated it, listened, then said goodbye and hung up. She smiled at Meg. 'Mrs Collins would like you to come right over. She lives only ten minutes from here.'

47

Frances stood, looking out the window at the back of the house. A low stucco wall crowned by a wrought-iron rail enclosed the pool and patio. The property ended at the border of the vast expanse of desert that was the Pima Indian Reservation. In the distance, Camelback Mountain glistened under the midday sun. An incongruously beautiful day for all secrets to be laid open, she thought.

Annie had gone to Connecticut after all, had looked up Meghan and sent her here. Why should Annie have honored her father's wishes, Frances asked herself fiercely. What loyalty does she owe to him or to me?

In the two-and-a-half days since she'd left the message on Edwin's answering machine, she'd waited in an agony of hope and dread. The call she'd just received from Palomino was not the one she'd hoped to get. But at least Meghan Collins might be able to tell her when she had seen Annie, perhaps where Frances could reach her.

The chimes rang through the house, soft, melodious, but chilling. Frances turned and walked to the front door.

When Meghan stopped in front of 1006 Doubletree Ranch Road she found a one-storey, cream-colored stucco house with a red tile roof, on the edge of the desert. Vivid red hibiscus and cactuses framed the front of the dwelling, complementing the stark beauty of the mountain range in the distance.

On her way to the door she passed the window and caught a glimpse of the woman inside. She couldn't see her face but could tell that the woman was tall and very thin, with hair loosely pinned in a chignon. She seemed to be wearing some sort of smock.

Meghan rang the bell, then the door opened.

The woman gave a startled gasp. Her face went ashen. 'Dear God,' she whispered. 'I knew you looked like Annie, but I had no idea. . . . ' Her hand flew up to her mouth, pressing against her lips in a visible effort to silence the flow of words.

This is Annie's mother and she doesn't know that Annie is dead. Horrified, Meghan thought, It's going to be worse for her that I'm here. What would it be like for Mom if Annie had been the one to go to Connecticut and tell her I was dead?

'Come in, Meghan.' The woman stood aside, still clutching the handle of the door, as though supporting herself on it. 'I'm Frances Grolier.'

Meghan did not know what kind of person she had expected to find, but not this woman with her fresh-scrubbed looks, graying hair, sturdy hands and thin, lined face. The eyes she was looking into were shocked and distressed.

'Didn't the clerk at Palomino call you Mrs Collins when she phoned?' Meghan asked.

'The tradespeople know me as Mrs Collins.'

She was wearing a gold wedding band. Meghan looked at it pointedly.

'Yes,' France Grolier said. 'For appearance sake, your father gave that to me.'

Meghan thought of the way her mother had convulsively gripped the wedding band the psychic had returned to her. She looked away from Frances Grolier, suddenly filled with an overwhelming sense of loss. Impressions of the room filtered through the misery of this moment.

210

The house was divided into living and studio areas extending from the front to the back.

The front section was the living room. A couch in front of the fireplace. Earth-tone tiles on the floor.

The maroon leather chair and matching ottoman to the side of the fireplace were exact replicas of the ones in her father's study, Meghan realized with a start. Bookshelves within easy reach of the chair. Dad certainly liked to feel at home wherever he was, Meghan thought bitterly.

Framed photographs prominently displayed on the mantel drew her like a magnet. They were family groups of her father with this woman and a young girl who might easily be her sister, and who was – or rather had been – her half sister.

One picture especially riveted her. It was a Christmas scene. Her father holding a five- or six-year-old on his lap, surrounded by presents. A young Frances Grolier kneeling behind him, arms around his neck. All wearing pyjamas and robes. A joyous family.

Was that one of the Christmas Days I spent praying for a miracle, that suddenly Daddy would come through the door? Meghan wondered.

Sickening pain encompassed her. She turned away and saw against the far wall the bust on a pedestal. With feet that now seemed too leaden to move she made her way to it.

A rare talent had shaped this bronze image of her father. Love and understanding had caught the hint of melancholy behind the twinkle in the eyes, the sensitive mouth, the long, expressive fingers folded under the chin, the fine head of hair with the lock that always strayed forward onto his forehead.

She could see that cracks along the neck and forehead had been skillfully repaired.

'Meghan?'

She turned, dreading what she must now tell this woman.

211

Frances Grolier crossed the room to her. Her voice pleading, she said, 'I'm prepared for anything you feel about me, but *please* . . . I must know about Annie. Do you know where she is? And what about your father? Has he been in touch with you?'

Keeping his promise to Meghan, Mac tried unsuccessfully to phone Stephanie Petrovic at nine o'clock on Tuesday morning. Hourly phone calls continued to bring no response.

At twelve-fifteen he called Charles Potters, the lawyer for the estate of Helene Petrovic. When Potters got on the phone, Mac identified himself and stated his reason for phoning and was immediately told that Potters too was concerned.

'I tried Stephanie last night,' Potters explained. 'I could tell that Miss Collins was disturbed by her absence. I'm going over to the house now. I have a key.'

He promised to call back.

An hour and a half later, his voice trembling with indignation, Potters told Mac about Stephanie's note. 'That deceitful girl,' he cried. 'She helped herself to whatever she could carry! The silver. Some lovely Dresden. Practically all of Helene's wardrobe. Her jewelry. Those pieces were insured for over fifty thousand dollars. I'm notifying the police. This is a case of common theft.'

'You say she left with the father of her baby?' Mac asked. 'From what Meghan told me, I find that very hard to believe. She had the sense that Stephanie was frightened at the suggestion that she go after him for child support.'

'Which may have been an act,' Potters said. 'Stephanie Petrovic is a very cold young woman. I can assure you that the main source of her grief over her aunt's death was the fact that Helene had not changed her will as Stephanie claimed she planned to do.'

'Mr Potters, do you believe Helene Petrovic planned to change her will?'

'I have no way of knowing that. I do know that in the weeks before her death, Helene had put her house on the market and converted her securities to bearer bonds. Fortunately those were not in her safe.'

When Mac put down the phone, he leaned back in his chair.

How long could any amateur, no matter how gifted, pull the wool over the eyes of trained experts in the field of reproductive endocrinology and in vitro fertilization? he mused. Yet Helene Petrovic had managed it for years. I couldn't have done it, Mac thought, remembering his intense medical training.

According to Meghan, while Petrovic was working at the Dowling Assisted Reproduction Center she spent a lot of time hanging around the laboratory. She might also have been seeing a doctor from Valley Memorial, the hospital with which the center was affiliated.

Mac made up his mind. He would take tomorrow off. There were some things best handled in person. Tomorrow he was going to drive to Valley Memorial in Trenton and see the director of the facility. He needed to try to get some records.

Mac had met and liked Dr George Manning but was shocked and concerned that Manning had not immediately warned the Andersons about the potential embryo mix-up. There was no question he'd been hoping for a cover-up.

Now Mac wondered if there was any possibility that Helene Petrovic's abrupt decision to quit the clinic, change her will, sell her house and move to France might have more sinister reasons than her fear of an error in the laboratory. Particularly, he reasoned, since it might still be proven that the Anderson's baby was their biological child, if not the identical twin they'd expected.

Mac wanted to learn if there was any possibility that

Dr George Manning had been connected to Valley Memorial at any point in the several years that Helene Petrovic worked in the adjacent facility.

Manning would not be the first man to throw aside his professional life for a woman, nor would he be the last. Technically, Petrovic had been hired through Collins and Carter Executive Search. Yet only yesterday Manning had admitted that he had spoken to Edwin Collins the day before Collins disappeared. Had they been in collusion over those credentials? Or had someone else on the Manning staff helped her out? The Manning Clinic was only about ten years old. Their annual reports would list the names of the senior staff. He'd get his secretary to copy them for him.

Mac pulled out a pad, and in his neat penmanship, which his colleagues joked was so uncharacteristic of the medical profession, wrote:

1. Edwin Collins believed dead in bridge accident, 28 January; no proof.
2. Woman who resembles Meg (Annie?) fatally stabbed, 21 October.
3. 'Annie' may have been seen by Kyle the day before her death.
4. Helene Petrovic fatally shot hours after she quit her job at Manning, 25 October.
   (Edwin Collins placed Helene Petrovic at Manning Clinic, vouching for the accuracy of her false credentials.)
5. Stephanie Petrovic claimed conspiracy by Manning Clinic to prevent her aunt from changing her will.
6. Stephanie Petrovic vanished sometime between late afternoon of 31 October and 2 November, leaving a note claiming she was rejoining the father of her child, a man she apparently feared.

None of it made sense. But there was one thing he

214

was convinced was true. Everything that had happened was connected in a logical way. Like genes, he thought. The minute you understand the structure everything falls into place.

He put aside the pad. He had work to do if he was planning to take tomorrow off for the trip to Dowling. It was four o'clock. That meant it was two o'clock in Arizona. He wondered how Meg was doing, how the day, which must be incredibly difficult for her, was progressing.

Meg stared at Frances Grolier. 'What do you mean have I heard from my father?'

'Meghan, the last time he was here, I could see that the world was closing in on him. He was so frightened, so depressed. He said he wished he could just disappear.

'Meghan, you must tell me. *Have you seen Annie?*'

Only a few hours ago, Meg had remembered her father's warning that some events cause unforgettable pain. Compassion engulfed her as she saw the dawning horror in the eyes of Annie's mother.

Frances grasped her arms. 'Meghan, is Annie sick?'

Meghan could not speak. She answered the note of hope in the frantic question with a barely perceptible shake of her head.

'Is she . . . is Annie dead?'

'I'm so sorry.'

'No. That can't be.' Frances Grolier's eyes searched Meghan's face, pleading. 'When I opened the door . . . even though I knew you were coming . . . for that split second, I thought it was Annie. I knew how alike you were. Ed showed me pictures.' Grolier's knees buckled.

Meghan grasped her arms, helped her to sit down on the couch. 'Isn't there someone I can tell, somebody you'd like to have with you now?'

'No one,' Grolier whispered. 'No one.' Her pallor turning a sickly gray, she stared into the fireplace as though suddenly unaware of Meghan's presence.

Meghan watched helplessly as Frances Grolier's pupils became dilated, her expression vacant. She's going into shock, Meghan thought.

Then, in a voice devoid of emotion, Grolier asked, 'What happened to my daughter?'

'She was stabbed. I happened to be in the emergency room when she was brought in.'

'Who . . . ?'

Grolier did not complete the question.

'Annie may have been a mugging victim,' Meghan said quietly. 'She had no identification except a slip of paper with my name and phone number on it.'

'The Drumdoe Inn notepaper?'

'Yes.'

'Where is my daughter now?'

'The . . .the medical examiner's building in Manhattan.'

'You mean the morgue.'

'Yes.'

'How did you find me, Meghan?'

'Through the message you left the other night to call the Palomino Leather Goods Shop.'

A ghastly smile tugged at Frances Grolier's lips. 'I left that message hoping to reach your father. Annie's father. He always put you first, you know. So afraid that you and your mother would find out about us. Always so afraid.'

Meghan could see that shock was being replaced by anger and grief. 'I am so sorry.' It was all she could think to say. From where she was sitting, she could see the Christmas picture. I'm so sorry for all of us, she thought.

'Meghan, I have to talk to you, but not now. I need to be alone. Where are you staying?'

'I'll try to get a room at the Safari Hotel.'

'I'll call you there later. Please go.'

As Meghan closed the door, she heard the steady sobbing, low rhythmic sounds that tore at her heart.

She drove to the hotel, praying that it would not be full, that no one would see her and think she was Annie. But the check-in was fast, and ten minutes later she closed the door of the room and sank down on the bed, her emotions a combination of enormous pity, shared pain and icy fear.

Frances Grolier clearly believed it possible that her lover, Edwin Collins, was alive.

48

On Tuesday morning, Victor Orsini moved into Edwin Collins' private office. The day before, the cleaning service had washed the walls and windows and cleaned the carpet. Now the room was antiseptically clean. Orsini had no interest in even thinking about redecorating it. Not with the way things were going.

He knew that on Sunday Meghan and her mother had cleared the office of Collins' personal effects. He assumed they had heard the message on the answering machine and taken the tape. He could only imagine what they thought of it.

He had hoped they wouldn't bother with Collins' business records, but they'd taken all of them. Sentiment? He doubted it. Meghan was smart. She was looking for something. Was it the same thing he was so anxious to find? Was it somewhere in those papers? Would she find it?

Orsini paused in the unpacking of his books. He'd spread the morning paper on the desk, the desk that belonged to Edwin Collins and soon would be moved to the Drumdoe Inn. A front-page update on the Manning

Clinic scandal announced that state medical investigators had been in the clinic on Monday and already rumors were rampant that Helene Petrovic may have made many serious mistakes. Empty vials had been found among the ones containing cryopreserved embryos, suggesting that Petrovic's lack of medical skill may have resulted in embryos being improperly labeled or even destroyed.

An independent source who refused to be identified pointed out that, at the very least, clients who were paying handsomely for maintenance of their embryos were being overcharged. In the worst possible scenario, women who might not be able to again produce eggs for possible fertilization might have lost their chance for biological motherhood.

Featured next to the story was a reproduction of Edwin Collins' letter strongly recommending 'Dr' Helene Petrovic to Dr George Manning.

The letter had been written March 21st, nearly seven years ago, and was stamped received on March 22nd.

Orsini frowned, hearing again the accusing, angry voice of Collins, calling him from the car phone that last night. He stared at the newspaper and Edwin's bold signature on the letter of recommendation. Perspiration broke out on his forehead. Somewhere in this office or in the files Meghan Collins had taken home is the incriminating evidence that will bring down this house of cards, he thought. But will anyone find it?

For hours, Bernie was unable to calm the rage the sneering passenger had triggered in him. As soon as his mother went to bed Monday night, he'd rushed downstairs to play his videotapes of Meghan. The news tapes had her voice, but the one he'd taken from the woods behind her house was his favorite. It made him wildly restless to be near her again.

He played the tapes through the night, only going to bed as a hint of dawn flickered through the slit in the cardboard he had placed over the narrow basement window. Mama would notice if his bed had not been slept in.

He got into bed fully dressed and pulled up the covers just in time. The creaking of the mattress in the next room warned that his mother was waking up. A few minutes later the door of his room opened. He knew she was looking in at him. He kept his eyes shut. She wouldn't expect him to wake up for another fifteen minutes.

After the door closed again, he hunched up in bed, planning his day.

Meghan had to be in Connecticut. But where? At her house? At the inn? Maybe she gave her mother a hand in running the inn. What about the New York apartment? Maybe she was there.

He got up promptly at seven, took off his sweater and shirt, put on his pajama top in case Mama saw him and went out to the bathroom. There he splashed water on his face and hands, shaved, brushed his teeth and combed his hair. He smiled at his reflection in the mirror on the medicine cabinet. Everyone had always told him he had a warm smile. Trouble was the silver was peeling behind the glass, and the mirror gave back a distorted image like the ones in amusement parks. He didn't look warm and friendly now.

Then, as Mama had taught him to do, he reached down for the can of cleanser, shook a liberal amount of the gritty powder into the sink, rubbed it in vigorously with a sponge, rinsed it away and dried the sink with the rag Mama always left folded over the side of the tub.

Back in the bedroom he made his bed, folded his pajama top, put on a clean shirt and carried the soiled one to the hamper.

Today Mama had bran flakes in his cereal bowl. 'You look tired, Bernard,' she said sharply. 'Are you getting enough rest?'

219

'Yes, Mama.'

'What time did you go to bed?'

'I guess about eleven o'clock.'

'I woke up to go to the bathroom at eleven-thirty. You weren't in bed then.'

'Maybe it was a little later, Mama.'

'I thought I heard your voice. Were you talking to someone?'

'No, Mama. Who would I be talking to?'

'I thought I heard a woman's voice.'

'Mama, it was the television.' He gulped the cereal and tea. 'I have to be at work early.'

She watched him from the door. 'Be home on time for dinner. I don't want to be fussing in the kitchen all night.'

He wanted to tell her that he expected to work overtime but didn't dare. Maybe he'd call her later.

Three blocks away he stopped at a public telephone. It was cold, but the shiver he felt as he dialed Meghan's apartment had more to do with anticipation than chill. The phone rang four times. When the answering machine clicked on, he hung up.

He then dialed the house in Connecticut. A woman answered. It must be Meghan's mother, Bernie thought. He deepened his voice, quickened its pace. He wanted to sound like Tom Weicker.

'Good morning, Mrs Collins. Is Meghan there?'

'Who is this?'

'Tom Weicker of PCD.'

'Oh, Mr Weicker, Meg will be sorry she missed your call. She's out of town today.'

Bernie frowned. He wanted to know where she was. 'Can I reach her?'

'I'm afraid not. But I'll be hearing from her late this afternoon. May I have her phone you?'

Bernie thought swiftly. It would sound wrong if he didn't say yes. But he wanted to know when she'd be back. 'Yes, have her call. Do you expect her to be home this evening?'

'If not tonight, surely tomorrow.'

'Thank you.' Bernie hung up, angry that he couldn't reach Meghan, but glad he hadn't wasted a trip to Connecticut. He got back in the car and headed for Kennedy Airport. He might just as well get some fares today, but they'd better not tell him how to drive.

This time the special investigators of Helene Petrovic's death did not go to Phillip Carter. Instead, late Tuesday morning they phoned and asked if it would be convenient for him to stop in for an informal chat at the assistant state attorney's office in the Danbury courthouse.

'When would you like me to come?' Carter asked.

'As soon as possible,' Investigator Arlene Weiss told him.

Phillip glanced at his calendar. There was nothing on it that he couldn't change. 'I can make it around one,' he suggested.

'That will be fine.'

After he replaced the receiver he tried to concentrate on the morning mail. There were a number of references in on candidates whom they were considering offering to two of their major clients. At least so far those clients hadn't pulled back.

Could Collins and Carter Executive Search weather the storm? He hoped so. One thing he would do in the very near future would be to change the name to Phillip Carter Associates.

In the next room he could hear the sounds of Orsini moving into Ed Collins' office. Don't get too settled, Phillip thought. It was too soon to get rid of Orsini. He needed him for now, but Phillip had several replacements in mind.

He wondered if the police had been questioning Catherine and Meghan again.

221

He dialed Catherine at home. When she answered, he said, cheerfully, 'It's me. Just checking to see how it's going.'

'That's nice of you, Phillip.' Her voice was subdued.

'Anything wrong, Catherine?' he asked quickly. 'The police haven't been bothering you, have they?'

'No, not really. I'm going through Edwin's files, the copies of his expense accounts, that sort of thing. You know what Meg pointed out?' She did not wait for an answer. 'There are times when even though Edwin was billed for four or five days in a hotel, after the first day or two there were absolutely no additional charges on his bill. Not even for a drink or a bottle of wine at the end of the day. Did you ever notice that?'

'No. I wouldn't be the one to look at Edwin's expense accounts, Catherine.'

'All the files I have seem to go back seven years. Is there a reason for that?'

'That would be right. That's as long as you're supposed to retain records for possible audit. Of course the IRS will go back much further if they suspect deliberate fraud.'

'What I'm seeing is that whenever Edwin was in California that pattern of noncharges showed up in the hotel bills. He seemed to go to California a great deal.'

'California was where it was at, Catherine. We used to make a lot of placements there. It's just changed in the last few years.'

'Then you never wondered about his frequent trips to California?'

'Catherine, Edwin was my senior partner. We both always went where we thought we'd find business.'

'I'm sorry, Phillip. I don't mean to suggest that you should have seen something that I as Edwin's wife of thirty years never even suspected.'

'Another woman?'

'Possibly.'

'It's such a rotten time for you,' Phillip said vehemently. 'How's Meg doing? Is she with you?'

'Meg's fine. She's away today. It would be the one day her boss phoned her.'

'Are you free for dinner tonight?'

'No, I'm sorry. I'm meeting Mac and Kyle at the inn.' Catherine hesitated. 'Do you want to join us?'

'I don't think so, thanks. How about tomorrow night?'

'It depends on when Meg gets back. May I call you?'

'Of course. Take care of yourself. Remember, I'm here for you.'

Two hours later Phillip was being interrogated in Assistant State Attorney John Dwyer's office. Special investigators Bob Marron and Arlene Weiss were present with Dwyer, who was asking the questions. Some of them were the same ones Catherine had raised.

'Didn't you at any time suspect your partner might be leading a double life?'

'No.'

'Do you think so now?'

'With that dead girl in the morgue in New York who looks like Meghan? With Meghan herself requesting DNA tests? Of course I think so.'

'From the pattern of Edwin Collins' travels, can you suggest where he might have been involved in an intimate relationship?'

'No, I can't.'

The assistant state attorney looked exasperated. 'Mr Carter, I get the feeling that everyone who was close to Edwin Collins is trying in one way or another to protect him. Let me put it this way. We believe he is alive. If he had another situation, particularly a long-term one, he may be there now. Just off the top of your head, where do you think that could be?'

'I simply don't know,' Phillip repeated.

'All right, Mr Carter,' Dwyer said brusquely. 'Will

you give us permission to go through all the Collins and Carter files if we deem it necessary, or will it be necessary to subpoena them?'

'I wish you *would* go through the files!' Phillip snapped. 'Do anything you can to bring this dreadful business to a conclusion and let decent people get on with their lives.'

On his way back to the office, Phillip Carter realized he had no desire for a solitary evening. From his car phone he again dialed Catherine's number. When she answered, he said, 'Catherine, I've changed my mind. If you and Mac and Kyle can put up with me, I'd very much like to have dinner with you tonight.'

At three o'clock, from her hotel room, Meghan phoned home. It would be five o'clock in Connecticut, and she wanted to be able to talk to her mother before the dinner hour at the inn.

It was a painful conversation. Unable to find words to soften the impact, she told about the grueling meeting with Frances Grolier. 'It was pretty awful,' she concluded. 'She's devastated, of course. Annie was her only child.'

'How old was Annie, Meg?' her mother asked quietly.

'I don't know. A little younger than I am, I think.'

'I see. That means they were together for many years.'

'Yes, it does,' Meghan agreed, thinking of the photographs she had just seen. 'Mom, there's something else. Frances seems to think that Dad is still alive.'

'She *can't* think he's still alive!'

'She does. I don't know more than that. I'm going to stay in this hotel until I hear from her. She said she wants to talk to me.'

'What more could she have to say to you, Meg?'

'She still doesn't know very much about Annie's death.' Meghan realized she was too emotionally drained to talk any more. 'Mom, I'm going to get off

224

the phone now. If you get a chance to tell Mac about this without Kyle hearing, go ahead.'

Meghan had been sitting on the edge of the bed. When she said goodbye to her mother, she leaned back against the pillows and closed her eyes.

She was awakened by the ringing of the telephone. She sat up, aware that the room was dark and chilly. The lighted face of the clock radio showed that it was five-past eight. She leaned over and picked up the phone. To her own ears, her voice sounded strained and husky when she murmured, 'Hello.'

'Meghan, this is Frances Grolier. Will you come and see me tomorrow morning as early as possible?'

'Yes.' It seemed insulting to ask her how she was. How could any woman in her situation be? Instead, Meghan asked, 'Would nine o'clock be all right?'

'Yes, and thank you.'

Although grief was etched deeply in her face, Frances Grolier seemed composed the next morning when she opened the door for Meghan. 'I've made coffee,' she said.

They sat on the couch, holding the cups, their bodies angled stiffly toward each other. Grolier did not waste words. 'Tell me how Annie died,' she commanded. 'Tell me everything. I need to know.'

Meghan began, 'I was on assignment in Roosevelt-St Luke's Hospital in New York . . .' As in the conversation with her mother, she did not attempt to be gentle. She told about the fax message she had gotten, *Mistake. Annie was a mistake.*

Grolier leaned forward, her eyes blazing. 'What do you think that means?'

'I don't know.' She continued, omitting nothing, beginning with the note found in Annie's pocket, including Helene Petrovic's false credentials and death and finishing with the warrant issued for her father's arrest. 'His car was found. You may or may not know that

225

Dad had a gun permit. His gun was in the car and was the weapon that killed Helene Petrovic. I do not and cannot believe that he could take anyone's life.'

'Nor do I.'

'Last night you told me you thought my father might be alive.'

'I think it's possible.' Frances Grolier said, 'Meghan, after today I hope we never meet again. It would be too difficult for me and, I suppose, for you as well. But you and your mother are owed an explanation.

'I met your father twenty-seven years ago in the Palomino Leather Shop. He was buying a purse for your mother and debating between two of them. He asked me to help make the choice, then invited me to lunch. That's how it began.'

'He'd only been married three years at that time,' Meghan said quietly. 'I know my father and mother were happy together. I don't understand why he needed a relationship with you.' She felt she sounded accusing and pitiless, but she couldn't help it.

'I knew he was married,' Grolier said. 'He showed me your picture, your mother's picture. On the surface, Edwin had it all: charm, looks, wit, intelligence. Inwardly he was, or is, a desperately insecure man. Meghan, try to understand and forgive him. In so many ways your father was still that hurt child who feared he might be abandoned again. He needed to know he had another place to go, a place where someone would take him in.'

Her eyes welled with tears. 'It suited us both. I was in love with him but didn't want the responsibility of marriage. I wanted only to be free to become the best sculptor that I was capable of being. For me the relationship worked, open-ended and without demands.'

'Wasn't a child a demand, a responsibility?' Meghan asked.

'Annie wasn't part of the plan. When I was expecting her, we bought this place and told people that we were

226

married. After that, your father was desperately torn, always trying to be a good father to both of you, always feeling he was failing both of you.'

'Didn't he worry about being discovered?' Meghan asked. 'About someone bumping into him here the way his stepbrother did?'

'He was haunted by that fear. As she grew up, Annie asked more and more questions about his job. She wasn't buying the story that he had a top-secret government job. She was becoming known as a travel writer. You were being seen on television. When Edwin had terrible chest pains last November he wouldn't let himself be admitted to the hospital for observation. He wanted to get back to Connecticut. He said, "If I die, you can tell Annie I was on some kind of government assignment." The next time he came he gave me a bearer bond for two hundred thousand dollars.'

The insurance loan, Meghan thought.

'He said that if anything happened to him, you and your mother were well taken care of, but I was not.'

Meghan did not contradict Frances Grolier. She knew it had not occurred to Grolier that because his body had not been found a death certificate had not been issued for her father. And she knew with certainty that her mother would lose everything rather than take the money back that her father had given this woman.

'When was the last time you saw my father?' she asked.

'He left here on January twenty-seventh. He was going to San Diego to see Annie, then take a flight home on the morning of the twenty-eighth.'

'Why do you believe he's still alive?' Meghan had to ask before she left. More than anything, she wanted to get away from this woman whom she realized she both deeply pitied and bitterly resented.

'Because when he left he was terribly upset. He'd learned something about his assistant that horrified him.'

227

'Victor Orsini?'

'That's the name.'

'What did he learn?'

'I don't know. But business had not been good for several years. Then there was a write-up in the local paper about a seventieth birthday party that had been given for Dr George Manning by his daughter, who lives about thirty miles from here. The article quoted Dr Manning as saying that he planned to work one more year, then retire. Your father said that the Manning Clinic was a client, and he called Dr Manning. He wanted to suggest that he be commissioned to start the search for Manning's replacement. That conversation upset him terribly.'

'Why?' Meghan asked urgently. 'Why?'

'I don't know.'

'Try to remember. Please. It's very important.'

Grolier shook her head. 'When Edwin was leaving, his last words were, "It's becoming too much for me . . ." All the papers carried the story of the bridge accident. I believed he was dead and told people he had been killed in a light-plane accident abroad. Annie wasn't satisfied with that explanation.

'When he visited her at her apartment that last day, Edwin gave Annie money to buy some clothes. Six one-hundred-dollar bills. He obviously didn't realize that the slip of Drumdoe Inn notepaper with your name and number fell out of his wallet. She found it after he left and kept it.'

Frances Grolier's lip quivered. Her voice broke as she said, 'Two weeks ago, Annie came here for what you'd call a showdown. She had phoned your number. You'd answered "Meghan Collins", and she hung up. She wanted to see her father's death certificate. She called me a liar and demanded to know where he was. I finally told her the truth and begged her not to contact you or your mother. She knocked over that bust I'd sculpted

228

of Edwin and stormed out of here. I never saw her again.'

Grolier stood up, placed her hand on the mantel and leaned her forehead against it. 'I spoke to my lawyer last night. He's going to accompany me to New York tomorrow afternoon to identify Annie's body and arrange to have it brought back here. I'm sorry for the embarrassment this will cause you and your mother.'

Meghan had only one more question she needed to ask. 'Why did you leave that message for Dad the other night?'

'Because I thought if he were still alive, if that line were still connected, he might check it out of habit. It was my way of contacting him in case of emergency. He used to beep in to that answering machine early every morning.' She faced Meghan again.

'Let no one tell you that Edwin Collins is capable of killing anyone, because he isn't.' She paused. 'But he *is* capable of beginning a new life that does not include you and your mother. Or Annie and me.'

Frances Grolier turned away again. There was nothing left to say. Meghan took a last look at the bronze bust of her father and left, closing the door quietly behind her.

49

On Wednesday morning, as soon as Kyle was on the school bus, Mac left for Valley Memorial Hospital in Trenton, New Jersey.

At dinner the night before, when Kyle had left the table for a moment, Catherine had quickly told Mac

229

and Phillip about Meghan's call. 'I don't know very much except that this woman has had a long-term relationship with Edwin; she thinks he's still alive, and the dead girl who looks like Meg was her daughter.'

'You seem to be taking it very well,' Phillip had commented, 'or are you still in denial?'

'I don't know what I feel anymore,' Catherine had answered, 'and I'm worried about Meg. You know how she felt about her father. I never heard anyone sound so hurt as she did when she called earlier.' Then Kyle was back and they changed the subject.

Driving south on Route 684 through Westchester, Mac tried to tear his thoughts away from Meghan. She had been crazy about Edwin Collins, a real Daddy's girl. He knew that these past months since she'd thought her father was dead had been hell for her. How many times Mac had wanted to ask her to talk it out with him, not to hold everything inside. Maybe he should have insisted on breaking through her reserve. God, how much time he had wasted nursing his wounded pride over Ginger's dumping him.

At last we're getting honest, he told himself. Everybody knew you were making a mistake tying up with Ginger. You could feel the reaction when the engagement was announced. Meg had the guts to say it straight out, and she was only nineteen. In her letter she'd written that she loved him and that he ought to have the sense to know she was the only girl for him. 'Wait for me, Mac', was the way she'd ended it.

He hadn't thought about that letter for a long time. Now he found that he was thinking about it a lot.

It was inevitable that as soon as Annie's body was claimed, it would be public knowledge that Edwin had led a double life. Would Catherine decide she didn't want to live in the same area where everyone had known Ed, that she would rather start afresh somewhere else? It could happen, especially if she lost the inn. That

230

would mean Meg wouldn't be around either. The thought made Mac's blood run cold.

You can't change the past, Mac thought, but you can do something about the future. Finding Edwin Collins if he's still alive, or learning what happened to him if he's not, would release Meg and Catherine from the misery of uncertainty. Finding the doctor Helene Petrovic might have dated when she was a secretary at the Dowling Center in Trenton could be the first step to solving her murder.

Mac normally enjoyed driving. It was a good time for thinking. Today, however, his thoughts were in a jumble, filled with unsettled issues. The trip across Westchester to the Tappan Zee Bridge seemed longer than usual. The Tappan Zee Bridge – where it all began almost ten months ago, he thought.

It was another hour-and-a-half drive from there to Trenton. Mac arrived at Valley Memorial Hospital at ten-thirty and asked for the director. 'I called yesterday and was told he could see me.'

Frederick Schuller was a compact man of about forty-five whose thoughtful demeanor was belied by his quick, warm smile. 'I've heard of you, Dr MacIntyre. Your work in human gene therapy is becoming pretty exciting, I gather.'

'It is exciting,' Mac agreed. 'We're on the cutting edge of finding the way to prevent an awful lot of diseases. The hardest job is to have the patience for trial and error when there are so many people waiting for answers.'

'I agree. I don't have that kind of patience, which is why I'd never have been a good researcher. Which means that since you're giving up a day to drive down here, you must have a very good reason. My secretary said that it's urgent.'

Mac nodded. He was glad to get to the point. 'I'm here because of the Manning Clinic scandal.'

Schuller frowned. 'That really is a terrible situation.

231

I can't believe that any woman who worked in our Dowling facility as a secretary was able to get away with passing herself off as an embryologist. Somebody dropped the ball on that one.'

'Or somebody trained a very capable student, although trained her not well enough, obviously. They're finding a lot of problems in that lab, and we're talking about major problems like possibly mislabeling test tubes containing cryopreserved embryos or even deliberately destroying them.'

'If any field is calling for national legislation, assisted reproduction is first on the list. The potential for mistakes is enormous. Fertilize an egg with the wrong semen, and if the embryo is successfully transferred, an infant is born whose genetic structure is fifty percent different from what the parents had the right to expect. The child may have genetically inherited medical problems that can't be foreseen. It—' He stopped abruptly. 'Sorry, I know I'm preaching to the converted. How can I help?'

'Meghan Collins is the daughter of Edwin Collins, the man who is accused of placing Helene Petrovic at the Manning Clinic with false credentials. Meg's a reporter for PCD Channel 3 in New York. Last week she spoke to the head of the Dowling Center about Helene Petrovic. Apparently, some of Petrovic's coworkers thought she might be seeing a doctor from this hospital, but no one knows who he is. I'm trying to help Meg find him.'

'Didn't Petrovic leave Dowling more than six years ago?'

'Nearly seven years ago.'

'Do you realize how large our medical staff is here, Doctor?'

'Yes, I do,' Mac said. 'And I know you have consultants who are not on staff but are called in regularly. It's a shot in the dark, but at this stage, when the investigators are convinced Edwin Collins is Petrovic's murderer, you can imagine how desperately his daughter wants to know if there was someone in her life with a reason to kill her.'

'Yes, I can.' Schuller began to make notes on a pad. 'Have you any idea how long Petrovic might have been seeing this doctor?'

'From what I understand, a year or two before she went up to Connecticut. But that's only a guess.'

'It's a start. Let's go back into the records for the three years she worked at Dowling. You think this person may have been the one who helped her to acquire enough skill to pass herself off as thoroughly trained?'

'Again, a guess.'

'All right. I'll see that a list is compiled. We won't leave out people who worked in the fetal research or DNA labs either. Not all the technicians are MDs, but they know their business.' He stood up. 'What are you going to do with this list? It will be a long one.'

'Meg is going to dig into Helene Petrovic's personal life. She's going to collect names of Petrovic's friends and acquaintances from the Rumanian Society. We'll compare names from the personal list with the one you send us.'

Mac reached into his pocket. 'This is a copy of a roster I compiled of everyone on the medical staff at the Manning Clinic while Helene was there. For what's it worth, I'd like to leave it with you. I'd be glad if you would run these names through your computer first.'

He got up to go. 'It's a big fishnet, but we do appreciate your help.'

'It may take a few days, but I'll get the information you want,' Schuller said. 'Shall I send it to you?'

'I think directly to Meghan. I'll leave her address and phone number.'

Schuller walked him to the door of his office. Mac took the elevator down to the lobby. As he stepped into the corridor, he passed a boy about Kyle's age in a wheelchair. Cerebral palsy, Mac thought. One of the diseases they were starting to get a handle on through gene therapy. The boy gave him a big smile. 'Hi. Are you a doctor?'

'The kind who doesn't treat patients.'

'My kind.'

'Bobby!' his mother protested.

'I have a son your age who'd get alone fine with you.' Mac tousled the boy's hair.

The clock over the receptionist's desk showed that it was quarter-past eleven. Mac decided that if he picked up a sandwich and Coke in the coffee shop off the lobby he could eat it later in the car and drive right through. That way he'd be back in the lab by two o'clock at the latest and get in an afternoon of work.

He reflected that when you passed a kid in a wheelchair, you didn't want to lose any more time than necessary if your job was trying to unlock the secrets of genetic healing.

At least he'd made a couple hundred bucks driving yesterday. That was the only consolation Bernie could find when he awakened Wednesday morning. He'd gone to bed at midnight and slept right through because he was really tired, but now he felt good. This was sure to be a better day; he might even see Meg.

His mother, unfortunately, was in a terrible mood. 'BerNARD, I was awake half the night with a sinus headache. I was sneezing a lot. I want you to fix those steps and tighten the railing so I can get down to that basement again. I'm sure you're not keeping it clean. I'm sure there's dust filtering up from there.'

'Mama, I'm not good at fixing things. That whole staircase is weak. I can feel another step getting loose. You wanna really hurt yourself?'

'I can't afford to hurt myself. Who'd keep this place nice? Who'd cook meals for you? Who'd make sure you don't get in trouble?'

'I need you, Mama.'

234

'People need to eat in the morning. I always fix you a nice breakfast.'

'I know you do, Mama.'

Today the cereal was lukewarm oatmeal that reminded him of prison food. Nonetheless, Bernie dutifully scraped every spoonful from the bowl and drained his glass of apple juice.

He felt relaxed as he backed out of the driveway and waved goodbye to Mama. He was glad that he'd lied and told her another basement step was loose. One night, ten years ago, she'd said that she was going to inspect the basement the next day to see if he was keeping it nice.

He'd known he couldn't let that happen. He'd just bought his first police scanner radio. Mama would have realized it was expensive. She thought he just had an old television set down there and watched it after she went to bed so she wouldn't be disturbed.

Mama never opened his credit card bill. She said he had to learn to take care of it himself. She handed him the phone bill unopened too, because, she said, 'I never call anybody.' She had no idea how much he spent on equipment.

That night when he could hear her deep snores and knew she was in a sound sleep, he'd loosened the top steps. She'd had some fall. Her hip really had been smashed. He'd had to wait on her hand and foot for months, but it had been worth it. Mama go downstairs again? Not after that.

Bernie reluctantly decided to work at least for the morning. Meghan's mother had said she would be back today. That could mean *anytime* today. He couldn't phone and say he was Tom Weicker again. Meghan might have already called the station and found out that Tom hadn't tried to get her.

It was not a good day for fares. He stood near the baggage claim area with the other gypsy drivers and

235

those fancy-limousine chauffeurs who were holding cards with the names of the people they were meeting.

He approached arriving passengers as they came down the escalator. 'Clean car, cheaper than a cab, great driver.' His lips felt stuck in a permanent smile.

The trouble was, the Port Authority had put so many signs around, warning travelers against taking a chance on getting into cars not licensed by the Taxi and Limousine Commission. A number of people started to say yes to him, then changed their minds.

One old woman let him carry her suitcases to the curb, then said she'd wait for him, that he should go for his car. He tried to take the bags with him, but she yelled at him to put them down.

People turned their heads to look at him.

If he had her alone! Trying to get him in trouble when all he wanted to do was be nice. But of course he didn't want to attract attention, so he said, 'Sure, ma'am. I'll get the car real quick.'

When he drove back five minutes later, she was gone.

That was enough to set him off. He wasn't going to drive any jerks today. Ignoring a couple who called out to him to ask his rate to Manhattan, he pulled away, got on the Grand Central Parkway and, paying the toll on the Triborough Bridge, chose the Bronx exit, the one that led to New England.

By noon he was having lunch, a hamburger and beer, at the bar of the Drumdoe Inn, where Joe the bartender welcomed him back as a regular patron.

50

Catherine went to the inn on Wednesday morning and worked in her office until eleven-thirty. There were twenty reservations for lunch. Even allowing for drop-ins, she knew that Tony could handle the kitchen perfectly well. She would go home and continue to go through Edwin's files.

When she passed the reception area, she glanced into the bar. There were ten or twelve people already seated there, a couple of them with menus. Not bad for a weekday. No question business in general was picking up. The dinner hour especially was almost back to where it had been before the recession.

But that still didn't mean that she could hang onto this place.

She got in her car, reflecting that it was crazy that she didn't make herself walk the short distance between the house and the inn. I'm always in a hurry, she thought, but unfortunately that might not be necessary much longer.

The jewelry she'd hocked on Monday hadn't brought in anything like what she'd expected. A jeweler had offered to take everything on consignment but warned that the market was down. 'These are lovely pieces,' he'd said, 'and the market will be improving. Unless you absolutely need the money now, I urge you not to sell.'

She hadn't sold. By pawning them all at Provident Loan, at least she got enough to pay the quarterly tax on the inn. But in three months it would be due again.

There was a message from an aggressive commercial real estate agent on her desk. 'Would you be interested in selling the inn? We may have a buyer.'

A distress sale is what that vulture wants, Catherine told herself as she drove along the macadam to the parking lot exit. And I may have to accept it. For a moment she stopped and looked back at the inn. Her father had fashioned it after a fieldstone manor in Drumdoe, which as a boy he had thought so grand that only the gentry would dare set foot in it.

'I'd welcome the errand that would send me to the place,' he'd told Catherine. 'And from the kitchen I'd peek in to see the more of it. One day, the family was out and the cook took pity on me. "Would you like to see the rest?" she asked, taking me by the hand. Catherine, that good woman showed me the entire house. And now we have one just like it.'

Catherine felt a lump form in her throat as she studied the graceful Georgian-style mansion with its lovely casement windows and sturdy carved oak door. It always seemed to her that Pop was lurking inside, a benevolent ghost still strutting around, still taking his rest in front of the fire in the sitting room.

He'd really haunt me if I sold it, she thought as she pressed down on the accelerator.

The phone was ringing when she unlocked the door to the house. She rushed to pick it up. It was Meghan.

'Mom, I have to hurry. The plane is starting to board. I saw Annie's mother again this morning. She and her lawyer are flying into New York tonight to identify Annie's body. I'll tell you about it when I get home. That should be around ten o'clock.'

'I'll be here. Oh, Meg, I'm sorry. Your boss, Tom Weicker, wanted you to call him. I didn't think to tell you when we talked yesterday.'

'It would have been too late to get him at the office anyhow. Why don't you call him now and explain that

238

I'll get back to him tomorrow. I'm sure he isn't offering me an assignment. I'd better rush. Love you.'

That job is so important to Meg, Catherine berated herself. How could I have forgotten to tell her about Mr Weicker's call? She flipped through her memo book, looking for the number of Channel 3.

Funny he didn't give me his direct line, she reflected as she waited for the operator to put her through to Weicker's secretary. Then she reasoned that of course Meg would know it.

'I'm sure he'll want to speak to you, Mrs Collins,' the secretary said when she gave her name.

Catherine had met Weicker about a year ago when Meg had showed her around the station. She'd liked him, although as she'd observed afterwards, 'I wouldn't want to have to face Tom Weicker if I'd caused some kind of major foul-up.'

'How are you, Mrs Collins, and how is Meg?' Weicker said as he picked up.

'We're all right, thanks.' She explained why she was calling.

'I didn't speak to you yesterday,' he said.

My God, Catherine thought, I'm not going crazy as well as everything else, am I? 'Mr Weicker, somebody called and used your name. Did you authorize anyone to phone?'

'No. Specifically, what did this person say to you?'

Catherine's hands went clammy. 'He wanted to know where Meg was and when she'd be home.' Still holding the receiver, she sank down onto a chair. 'Mr Weicker, somebody was photographing Meg from behind our house the other night.'

'Do the police know about that?'

'Yes.'

'Then let them know about this call too. And please keep me posted if you get any more of them. Tell Meg we miss her.'

He meant it. She knew he did, and he sounded genu-

239

inely concerned. Catherine realized that Meg would have given Weicker the exclusive story of what she had learned in Scottsdale about the dead girl who resembled her.

There's no hiding it from the media, Catherine thought. Meg said that Frances Grolier is coming to New York tomorrow to claim her daughter's body.

'Mrs Collins, are you all right?'

Catherine made up her mind. 'Yes, and there's something you should know before anyone else. Meg went to Scottsdale, Arizona, yesterday because . . .'

She told him what she knew, then answered his questions. The final one was the hardest.

'As a newsman, I have to ask you this, Mrs Collins. How do you feel about your husband now?'

'I don't know how I feel about my husband,' Catherine answered. 'I do know I'm very, very sorry for Frances Grolier. Her daughter is dead. My daughter is alive and will be with me tonight.'

When she was finally able to replace the receiver, Catherine went into the dining room and sat at the table where the files were still spread out as she had left them. With her fingertips, she rubbed her temples. Her head was beginning to ache, a dull, steady pain.

The door chimes pealed softly. Pray God it isn't the state attorney's people or reporters, she thought as she wearily got up.

Through the living room window she could see that a tall man was standing on the porch. Who? She caught a glimpse of his face. Surprised, she hurried to open the door.

'Hello, Mrs Collins,' Victor Orsini said. 'I apologize. I should have called but I was nearby and thought I'd take a chance and stop in. I'm hoping that some papers I need might have been put in Edwin's files. Would you mind if I go through them?'

Meghan took America West flight 292 leaving Phoenix

at one-twenty-five and due to arrive in New York at eight-oh-five p.m. She was grateful she'd been given a window seat. The middle one was not occupied, but the fortyish woman on the aisle seemed to be a talker.

To avoid her, Meg reclined the seat and closed her eyes. In her mind she replayed every detail of her meeting with Frances Grolier. As she reviewed it, her emotions seemed to be on a roller-coaster ride, going from one extreme to another.

Anger at her father. Anger at Frances.

Jealousy that there had been another daughter whom her father loved.

Curiosity about Annie. She was a travel writer. She must have been intelligent. She looked like me. She was my half-sister, Meghan thought. She was still breathing when they put her in the ambulance. I was with her when she died and I'd never known that she existed.

Pity for everyone: for Frances Grolier and Annie, for her mother and herself. And for Dad, Meghan thought. Maybe someday I'll see him the way Frances does. A hurt little boy who couldn't be secure unless he was sure there was a place for him to go, a place where he was wanted.

Still, her father had known two homes where he was loved, she thought. Did he need both of them to make up for the two he'd known as a child, places where he was neither wanted nor loved?

The plane's bar service began. Meghan ordered a glass of red wine and sipped it slowly, glad for the warmth that began to seep through her system. She glanced to one side. Happily, the woman on the aisle was engrossed in a book.

Lunch was served. Meghan wasn't hungry but did have the salad and roll and coffee. Her head began to clear. She took a pad from her shoulder bag and over a second cup of coffee began to jot down notes.

That scrap of paper with her name and phone number had triggered Annie's confrontation with Frances, her

241

demand to know the truth. Frances said that Annie called me and hung up when I answered, Meghan thought. *If only she'd spoken to me then.* She might never have come to New York. She might still be alive.

Kyle had obviously seen Annie when she'd been driving around Newtown. Had anyone else seen her there?

I wonder if Frances told her where Dad worked? Meghan thought, and jotted down the question.

Dr Manning. According to Frances, Dad was upset after speaking to him the day before Dad disappeared. According to the papers, Dr Manning said the conversation was cordial. Then what got Dad upset?

Victor Orsini. Was he the key to all this? Frances said that Dad was horrified by something he'd learned about him.

Orsini. Meghan underlined his name three times. He had come to work around the time Helene Petrovic was presented as a candidate to the Manning Clinic. Was there a connection?

The last notation Meghan made consisted of three words. *Is Dad alive?*

The plane landed at eight o'clock, exactly on time. As Meghan unsnapped her seat belt, the woman on the aisle closed her book and turned to her. 'I've just figured it out,' she said happily. 'I'm a travel agent and I understand that when you don't want to talk, you shouldn't be bothered. But I knew I'd met you somewhere. It was at an ASTA meeting in San Francisco last year. You're Annie Collins, the travel writer, aren't you?'

Bernie was at the bar when Catherine looked in as she was leaving the hotel. He watched her reflection in the mirror but immediately averted his eyes and picked up the menu when she looked in his direction.

He didn't want her to notice him. It was never a good idea for people to pay special attention to you. They might start asking questions. Just from that glance in the mirror, he could tell that Meghan's mother looked like a smart lady. You couldn't put too much over on her.

Where was Meghan? Bernie ordered another beer, then wondered if the bartender, Joe, wasn't starting to look at him with the kind of expression the cops had when they'd stop him and ask what he was up to.

All you had to do was say, 'I'm just hanging around,' and they were all over you with questions. 'Why?' 'Who do you know around here?' 'Do you come here much?'

Those were the questions he didn't want people around here to even start thinking.

The big thing was to have people used to seeing him. When you're used to seeing someone all the time, you never really see him. He and the prison psychiatrist had talked about that.

Something inside him was warning that it would be dangerous to go into the woods behind Meghan's house again. With the way that kid had been screaming, someone had probably called the cops. They might be keeping a watch on the place now.

But if he never ran into Meghan on a job because she was on leave from Channel 3, and he couldn't get near her house, how would he get to see her?

While he sipped his second beer, the answer came to him, so easy, so simple.

This wasn't just a restaurant, it was an *inn*. People stayed here. There was a sign outside that announced VACANCY. From the windows on the south side you should have a clear view of Meghan's house. If he rented a room he could come and go and no one would think anything of it. They'd *expect* his car to be there all night. He could say that his mother was in a hospital but would be getting out in a few days and needed a quiet place where she could take it easy and not have to cook.

'Are these rooms expensive?' he asked the bartender. 'I need to find a place for my mother, so she can get her strength back, if you know what I mean. She's not

243

sick anymore, but kind of weak and can't be fussing for herself.'

'The guest rooms are great,' Tony told him. 'They were renovated only two years ago. They're not expensive right now. It's between seasons. In about three weeks, around Thanksgiving, they go up and stay up through the skiing season. Then they get discounted again until April or May.'

'My mother likes a lot of sun.'

'I know half the rooms are empty. Talk to Virginia Murphy. She's Mrs Collins' assistant and handles everything.'

The room Bernie chose was more than satisfactory. On the south side of the inn, it directly faced the Collins house. Even with all the electronic equipment he'd bought lately he wasn't near the limit on his credit card. He could stay here a long time.

Murphy accepted it with a pleasant smile. 'What time will your mother check in, Mr Heffernan?' she asked.

'She won't be here for a few days,' Bernie explained. 'I want to be able to use the room till she's out of hospital. It's too long a trek to drive back and forth from Long Island every day.'

'It certainly is and the traffic can be bad too. Do you have luggage?'

'I'll come back with it later.'

Bernie went home. After dinner with Mama he told her the boss wanted him to drive a customer's car to Chicago. 'I'll be gone three or four days, Mama. It's an expensive new car, and they don't want me to speed. They'll send me back on the bus.'

'How much are they paying you?'

Bernie picked a figure out of the air. 'Two hundred dollars a day, Mama.'

She snorted. 'I get sick when I think of the way I worked to support you and got paid next to nothing

244

and you get two hundred dollars a day to drive a fancy car.'

'He wants me to start tonight.' Bernie went into the bedroom and threw some clothes in the black nylon suitcase that Mama had bought at a garage sale years ago. It didn't look bad. Mama had cleaned it up.

He made sure to bring plenty of tape cassettes for his video camera, all his lenses and his cellular telephone.

He told Mama goodbye, but didn't kiss her. They never kissed. Mama didn't believe in kissing. As usual, she stood at the door to watch him drive away.

Her last words to him were, 'Don't get in any trouble, Bernard.'

Meghan reached home shortly before ten-thirty. Her mother had cheese and crackers and grapes on the coffee table in the living room and wine chilling in the decanter. 'I thought you might need a little sustenance.'

'I need something. I'll be right down. I'm going to get comfortable.'

She carried her bag upstairs, changed into pajamas, a robe and slippers, washed her face, brushed her hair and anchored it back with a band.

'That feels better,' she said when she returned to the living room. 'Do you mind if we don't talk about everything tonight? You know the essentials. Dad and Annie's mother have had a relationship for twenty-seven years. The last time she saw him was when he left to come home to us and never arrived. She and her lawyer are taking the eleven-twenty-five red-eye tonight from Phoenix. They'll get to New York around six tomorrow morning.'

'Why didn't she wait until tomorrow? Why would anyone want to fly all night?'

'I suspect she wants to be in and out of New York as fast as possible. I warned her that the police would certainly want to see her and there'd probably be extensive media coverage.'

245

'Meg, I hope I did the right thing.' Catherine hesitated. 'I told Tom Weicker about your trip to Scottsdale. PCD carried the story about Annie on the six o'clock news and I'm sure they'll repeat it at eleven. I think they were as kind to you and me as possible, but it isn't a pretty story. I might add I turned the ringer off on the phone and turned on the answering machine. A couple of reporters have come to the door, but I could see their vans outside and didn't answer. They showed up at the inn, and Virginia said I was out of town.'

'I'm glad you gave the story to Tom,' Meg said. 'I enjoyed working for him. I want him to have the exclusive.' She tried to smile at her mother. 'You're gutsy.'

'We might as well be. And, Meg, he *didn't* call you yesterday. I realize now that whoever did call was trying to find out where you were. I called the police. They're going to keep an eye on the house and check the woods regularly.' Catherine's control snapped. 'Meg, I'm frightened for you.'

Meg thought, who on earth would have known to use Tom Weicker's name?

She said, 'Mom, I don't know what's going on. But for now, the alarm is set, isn't it?'

'Yes.'

'Then we might as well watch the news. It's time.'

It's one thing to be gutsy, Meg thought, it's another to know that a few hundred thousand people are watching a story that makes mincemeat of your private life.

She watched and listened as, with appropriately serious demeanor, Joel Edison, the PCD eleven o'clock anchor, opened the program. 'As reported exclusively on our six o'clock newscast, Edwin Collins, missing since January 28th and a suspect in the Manning Clinic murder case, is the father of the young victim, stabbed to death in mid-Manhattan twelve days ago. Mr Collins . . .

'Also the father of Meghan Collins of this news

246

team . . . warrant for arrest . . . had two families . . . known in Arizona as husband of the prominent sculptor, Frances Grolier . . .'

'They've obviously been doing their own investigation,' Catherine said. 'I didn't tell them that.'

Finally a commercial came.

Meg pushed the Off button on the remote, and the television went dark. 'One thing Annie's mother told me is that the last time he was in Arizona, Dad was horrified by something he'd learned about Victor Orsini.'

'Victor Orsini!'

The shock in her mother's voice startled Meg. 'Yes. Why? Has something come up about him?'

'He was here today. He asked to go through Edwin's files. He claimed that papers he needed were in them.'

'Did he take anything? Did you leave him alone with them?'

'No. Or maybe just for a minute. He was here about an hour. When he left he seemed disappointed. He asked if I was sure that these were all the files we'd brought home. Meg, he begged me for the present not to say anything to Phillip about being here. I promised, but I didn't know what to make of it.'

'What I make of it is that there's something in those files that he doesn't want us to find.' Meg stood up. 'I suggest we both get some sleep. I can assure you that tomorrow the media will be all over the place again, but you and I are spending the day going through those files.'

She paused, then added, 'I only wish to God we knew what we're looking for.'

Bernie was at the window of his room in the Drumdoe Inn when Meg arrived home. He had his camera with the telescopic lens ready and began taping when she turned on the light in her bedroom. He sighed with pleasure as she took off her jacket and unbuttoned her blouse.

Then she came over and tilted the blinds but didn't completely close them, and he was able to get glimpses of her moving back and forth as she undressed. He waited impatiently when she went downstairs. He couldn't see whatever part of the house she was in.

What he did see made him realize how clever he'd been. A squad car drove slowly past the Collins house every twenty minutes or so. Besides that he saw the beams of flashlights in the woods. The cops had been told about him. They were looking for him.

What would they think if they knew he was right here watching them, laughing at them? But he had to be careful. He wanted a chance to be with Meghan, but he realized now it couldn't be around her house. He'd have to wait until she drove away alone in her car. When he saw her going toward the garage, all he had to do was get downstairs quickly, get into his own car and be ready to pull out behind her when she passed the inn.

He needed to be alone with her, talk to her like a real friend. He wanted to watch the way her lips went up in a curve when she smiled, the way her body moved like just now when she took off her jacket and opened her blouse.

Meghan would understand that he'd never hurt her. He just wanted to be her friend.

Bernie didn't get much sleep that night. It was too interesting to watch the cops driving back and forth.

Back and forth.

Back and forth.

51

Phillip was the first one to call on Thursday morning. 'I heard the newscast last night and it's all over the papers this morning. May I come by for a few minutes?'

'Of course,' Catherine told him. 'If you can pick your way through the press. They're camped outside the house.'

'I'll go around to the back.'

It was nine o'clock. Meg and Catherine were having breakfast. 'I wonder if anything new has developed?' Catherine said. 'Phillip sounds upset.'

'Remember you promised you wouldn't say anything about Victor Orsini being here yesterday,' Meg cautioned. 'Anyhow I'd like to do my own checking on him.'

When Phillip arrived it was clear that he was very concerned.

'The dam has burst, if that's the proper metaphor,' he told them. 'The first lawsuit was filed yesterday. A couple who have been paying for storage of ten cryopreserved embryos at the Manning Clinic have been notified there are only seven in the lab. Clearly, Petrovic was making a lot of mistakes along the line and falsifying records to cover them. Collins and Carter have been named as codefendants with the clinic.'

'I don't know what to say anymore except that I'm so sorry,' Catherine told him.

'I shouldn't have told you. It isn't even the reason I'm here. Did you see Frances Grolier being interviewed when she arrived at Kennedy this morning?'

'Yes, we did.' It was Meg who answered.

'Then what do you think of her statement that she believes Edwin is alive and may have started a totally new life?'

'We don't believe that for a minute,' Meghan said.

'I have to warn you that John Dwyer is so sure Ed is hiding somewhere that he's going to grill you on that. Meg, when I saw Dwyer Tuesday, he practically accused me of obstructing justice. He asked a hypothetical question: Assuming Ed had a relationship somewhere, where did I think it would be? Clearly you knew where to look for it.'

'Phillip,' Meghan asked, 'you're not suggesting that my father is alive and I know where he is, are you?'

There was no evidence of Carter's usually cheerful and assured manner. 'Meg,' he said, 'I certainly don't believe you know where to reach Edwin. But that Grolier woman knew him so well.' He stopped, aware of the impact of his words. 'Forgive me.'

Meghan knew Phillip Carter was right, that the assistant state attorney would be sure to ask how she knew to go to Scottsdale.

When he left, Catherine said, 'This is dragging Phillip down too.'

An hour later, Meghan tried calling Stephanie Petrovic. There was still no answer. She called Mac at his office to see if he had managed to reach her.

When Mac told her about the note Stephanie had left, Meghan said flatly, 'Mac, that note is a fraud. Stephanie never went with that man willingly. I saw her reaction when I suggested going after him for child support. She's mortally afraid of him. I think Helene Petrovic's lawyer had better report her as a missing person.'

Another mysterious disappearance, Meghan thought. It was too late to drive to southern New Jersey today. She would go tomorrow, starting out before daylight. That way she might evade the press.

She wanted to see Charles Potters and ask him to take her through the Petrovic house. She wanted to see the priest who had conducted the service for Helene. He obviously knew the Rumanian women who had attended it.

The terrible possibility was that Stephanie, a young woman about to give birth, might have known something about her aunt that was dangerous to Helene Petrovic's killer.

52

Special investigators Bob Marron and Arlene Weiss requested and received permission from the Manhattan district attorney to question Frances Grolier late Thursday morning.

Martin Fox, her attorney, a silver-haired retired judge in his late sixties, was by her side in a suite in the Doral Hotel, a dozen blocks from the medical examiner's office. Fox was quick to reject questions he felt inappropriate.

Frances had been to the morgue and identified Annie's body. It would be flown to Phoenix and met by a funeral director from Scottsdale. Grief was carved on her face as implacably as it would be in one of her sculptures, but she was composed.

She answered for Marron and Weiss the same questions she had answered for the New York homicidal detectives. She knew of no one who might have accompanied Annie to New York. Annie had no enemies. She would not discuss Edwin Collins except to say that, yes, she did think there was a possibility he chose to disappear.

'Did he ever express any desire to be in a rural setting?' Arlene Weiss asked.

The question seemed to penetrate Grolier's lethargy. 'Why do you want to know that?'

'Because even though his car had been recently washed when it was found in front of Meghan Collins' apartment building, there were traces of mud and bits of straw embedded in the tread on the tires. Ms Grolier, do you think that's the kind of place he might choose to hide?'

'It's possible. Sometimes he interviewed staff members at rural colleges. When he talked about those trips, he always said that life seemed so much less complicated in the country.'

Weiss and Marron went from New York directly to Newtown to talk to Catherine and Meghan again. They asked them the same question.

'The last place in the world I could see my husband is on a farm,' Catherine told them.

Meghan agreed. 'There's something that keeps bothering me. Doesn't it seem odd that if my father were driving his car, he'd not only leave it where it was sure to be noticed and ticketed but would also leave a murder weapon in it?'

'We haven't closed the door to any possibilities,' Marron told her.

'But you're concentrating on *him*. Maybe if you take him out of the picture completely, a different pattern will start to emerge.'

'Let's talk about why you made that sudden trip to Arizona, Miss Collins. We had to hear about it on television. Tell us yourself. When did you learn that your father had a residence there?'

When they left an hour later, they took the tape containing the Palomino message with them.

252

'Do you believe anyone in that office is looking beyond Dad for answers?' Meghan asked her mother.

'No, and they don't intend to,' Catherine said bitterly.

They went back into the dining room where they'd been studying the files. Analysis of the California hotel charges pinpointed year by year the times Edwin Collins had probably stayed in Scottsdale.

'But that isn't the kind of information that Victor Orsini would care about,' Meg said. 'There's got to be something else.'

On Thursday at the Collins and Carter office, Jackie, the secretary, and Milly, the bookkeeper, conferred in whispers about the tension between Phillip Carter and Victor Orsini. They agreed that it was caused by all the terrible publicity about Mr Collins and the law suits being filed.

Things had never been right since Mr Collins died. 'Or at least since we thought he died,' Jackie said. 'It's hard to believe that with a nice, pretty wife like Mrs Collins, he'd have someone on the side all these years.

'I'm so worried,' she went on. 'Every penny of my salary is saved for college for the boys. This job is so convenient. I'd hate to lose it.'

Milly was sixty-three and wanted to work for two more years until she could collect a bigger social security check. 'If they go under, who's going to hire me?' It was a rhetorical question that she frequently asked these days.

'One of them is coming in here at night,' Jackie whispered. 'You know you can tell when someone's been going through the files.'

'Why would anyone do that? They can have us dig for anything they want,' Milly protested. 'That's what we're paid for.'

'The only thing I can figure is that one of them is trying to find the file copy of the letter to the Manning

253

Clinic recommending Helene Petrovic,' Jackie said. 'I've looked and looked and I can't put my hands on it.'

'You'd only been here a few weeks when you typed it. You were just getting used to the filing system,' Milly reminded her. 'Anyhow, what difference does it make? The police have the original and that's what counts.'

'Maybe it makes a lot of difference,' Jackie said. 'The truth is, I don't remember typing that letter, but then it was seven years ago and I don't remember half the letters that go out of here. And my initials *are* on it.'

'So?'

Jackie pulled out her desk drawer, removed her purse and plucked from it a folded newspaper clipping. 'Ever since I saw the letter to the Manning Clinic about Petrovic reprinted in the paper, something's been bothering me. Look at this.'

She handed the clipping to Milly. 'See the way the first line of each paragraph is indented? That's the way I type letters for Mr Carter and Mr Orsini. Mr Collins always had his letters typed in block form, no indentation at all.'

'That's right,' Milly agreed, 'but that certainly looks like Mr Collins' signature.'

'The experts say it's his signature, but I say it's awfully funny a letter he signed went out typed like that.'

At three o'clock, Tom Weicker phoned. 'Meg, I just wanted you to know that we're going to run the story you did on the Franklin Clinic in Philadelphia, the one we were going to use with the identical twin special. We'll schedule it on both news broadcasts tonight. It's a good, succinct piece on in vitro fertilization and ties in with what's happened at the Manning Clinic.'

'I'm glad you're running it, Tom.'

'I wanted to be sure you saw it,' he said, his voice surprisingly kind.

'Thanks for letting me know,' Meg replied.

Mac phoned at five-thirty. 'How about you and Catherine coming over here for dinner for a change? I'm sure you won't want to go to the inn tonight.'

'No, we don't,' Meg agreed. 'And we could use the company. Is six-thirty all right? I want to watch the Channel 3 news. A feature I did is being run.'

'Come over now and watch it here. Kyle can show off that he's learned to tape.'

'All right.'

It was a good story. A nice moment was the segment taped in Dr Williams' office, when he pointed to the walls filled with pictures of young children. 'Can you imagine how much happiness these kids are bringing into people's lives?'

Meg had instructed the cameraman to pan slowly over the photographs as Dr Williams continued to speak. 'These children were born only because of the methods of assisted reproduction available here.'

'Plug for the center,' Meg commented. 'But it wasn't too heavy.'

'It was a good feature, Meg,' Mac said.

'Yes, I think so. Suppose we skip the rest of the news. We all know what it's going to be.'

Bernie stayed in the room all day. He told the maid that he wasn't feeling well. He told her that he guessed all the nights he'd spent at the hospital when his mother was so sick were catching up with him.

Virginia Murphy called a few minutes later. 'We usually only have continental breakfast room service, but we'll be glad to send up a tray whenever you're ready.'

They sent up lunch, then later Bernie ordered dinner. He had the pillows propped up so it looked like he'd been in bed resting. The minute the waiter left, Bernie was back at the window, sitting at an angle so nobody who happened to look up would notice him.

255

He watched as Meghan and her mother left the house a little before six. It was dark, but the porch light was on. He debated following them, then decided that as long as the mother was along, he would be wasting his time. He was glad he hadn't bothered when the car went right instead of left. He figured they must be going to the house where that kid lived. That was the only one in the cul-de-sac.

The squad cars came regularly through the day, but not every twenty minutes any more. During the evening, he noticed flashlights in the woods only once. The cops were easing up. That was good.

Meghan and her mother got back home around ten. An hour later, Meghan undressed and got into bed. She sat up for about twenty minutes, writing something in a notebook.

Long after she turned off the light, Bernie stayed at the window thinking about her, imagining being in the room with her.

53

Donald Anderson had taken two weeks off from work to help with the new baby. Neither he nor Dina wanted outside assistance. 'You relax,' he told his wife. 'Jonathan and I are in charge.'

The doctor had signed the release the night before. He wholeheartedly agreed that it was better if they could avoid the media. 'Ten to one some of the photographers will be in the lobby between nine and eleven,' he'd predicted. That was the time new mothers and babies usually were discharged.

The phone had been ringing all week with requests for interviews. Don screened them with the answering machine and did not return any of them. On Thursday their lawyer phoned. There was definite proof of malfeasance at the Manning Clinic. He warned them that they'd be urged to join the class action suit that was being proposed.

'Absolutely not,' Anderson said. 'You can tell that to anyone who calls you.'

Dina was propped up on the couch, reading to Jonathan. Stories about Big Bird were his new favorites. She glanced up at her husband. 'Why not just turn off that phone?' she suggested. 'Bad enough I wouldn't even look at Nicky for hours after he was born. All he'd need to know when he grows up is that I sued someone because he's here instead of another baby.'

They'd named him Nicholas after Dina's grandfather, the one her mother swore he resembled. From the nearby bassinet, they heard a stirring, a faint cry, then a wholehearted wail as their infant woke up.

'He heard us talking about him,' Jonathan said.

'Maybe he did, love,' Dina agreed as she kissed the top of Jonathan's silky blond head.

'He's just plain hungry again,' Don announced. He bent down, picked up the squirming bundle and handed it to Dina.

'Are you sure he's not my twin?' Jonathan asked.

'Yes, I'm sure,' Dina said. 'But he's your brother, and that's every bit as good.'

She put the baby to her breast. 'You have my olive skin,' she said as she gently stroked his cheek to start him nursing. 'My little paisano.'

She smiled at her husband. 'You know something, Don. It's really only fair that one of our kids looks like me.'

Meghan's early start on Friday morning meant that she

257

was able to be in the rectory of St Dominic's church on the outskirts of Trenton at ten-thirty.

She had called the young pastor immediately after dinner the night before and set up the appointment.

The rectory was a narrow, three-story frame house typical of the Victorian era, with a wraparound porch and gingerbread trim. The sitting room was shabby but comfortable with heavy, overstuffed chairs, a carved library table, old-fashioned standing lamps and a faded Oriental carpet. The fireplace glowed with burning logs and breaking embers, dispelling the chill of the minuscule foyer.

Father Radzin had opened the door for her, apologized that he was on the phone, ushered her into this room and vanished up the stairs. As Meghan waited, she mused that this was the kind of room where troubled people could unburden themselves without fear of condemnation or reproach.

She wasn't sure exactly what she would ask the priest. She did know from the brief eulogy he'd delivered at the memorial mass that he'd known and liked Helene Petrovic.

She heard his footsteps on the stairs. Then he was in the room, apologizing again for keeping her waiting. He chose a chair opposite hers and asked, 'How can I help you, Meghan?'

Not 'What can I do for you?' but 'How can I help you?' A subtle difference that was oddly consoling. 'I have to find out who Helene Petrovic really was. You're aware of the situation at the Manning Clinic?'

'Yes, of course. I've been following the story. I also saw in this morning's paper a picture of you and that poor girl who was stabbed. The resemblance is quite remarkable.'

'I haven't seen the paper, but I know what you mean. Actually, that's what started all this.' Meghan leaned forward, locking her fingers, pressing her palms together. 'The assistant state attorney investigating

Helene Petrovic's murder believes that my father is responsible for Helene being hired at Manning and for her death too. I don't. Too many things don't make sense. Why would he want to see the clinic hire someone who wasn't qualified for the job? What did he have to gain by placing Helene in the lab in the first place?'

'There's always a reason, Meghan, sometimes several, for every action any human being makes.'

'That's what I mean. I can't find one, never mind several. It just makes no sense. Why would my father have even become involved with Helene if he knew she was a fraud? I know he was conscientious about his job. He took pride in matching the right people to his clients. We used to talk about it often.

'It's reprehensible to put an unqualified person in a sensitive medical situation. The more they investigate the lab at the Manning Clinic, the more errors they're finding. I can't understand why my father would deliberately cause all that. And what about Helene? Didn't she have any conscience in the matter? Didn't she worry about preembryos being damaged or destroyed because of her sloppiness, carelessness or ignorance? At least some stored embryos were intended to be transferred in the hope that they'd be born.'

'Transferred and born,' Father Radzin repeated. 'An interesting ethical question. Helene was not a regular churchgoer, but when she did come to mass, it was always the last one on Sunday and she would stay for coffee hour. I had the feeling there was something on her mind that she couldn't bring herself to talk about. But I must tell you that if I were applying adjectives to her, the last three that would come to mind are "sloppy, careless and ignorant." '

'What about her friends? Who was she close to?'

'No one I know of. Some of her acquaintances have been in touch with me this week. They've commented on how little they really knew Helene.'

'I'm afraid something may have happened to her

259

niece, Stephanie. Did you ever meet the young man who is her baby's father?'

'No. And neither did anyone else from what I understand.'

'What did you think of Stephanie?'

'She's nothing like Helene. Of course she's very young and in this country less than a year. Now she's alone. It may just be that the baby's father showed up again and she decided to take a chance on him.'

He wrinkled his forehead. Mac does that, Meghan thought. Father Radzin looked to be in his late thirties, a little older than Mac. Why was she comparing them? It was because there was something so wholesome and good about them, she decided.

She stood up. 'I've taken enough of your time, Father Radzin.'

'Stay another minute or two, Meghan. Sit down, please. You've raised the question of your father's motivation in placing Helene at the clinic. If you can't get information about Helene, my advice is to keep searching until you find the reason for *his* participation in the situation. Do you think he was romantically involved with her?'

'I very much doubt it.' She shrugged. 'He seems to have been sufficiently troubled trying to balance his time between my mother and Annie's mother.'

'Money?'

'That doesn't make sense either. The Manning Clinic paid the usual fee to Collins and Carter for the placement of Helene and Dr Williams. My experience in studying law and human nature has taught me that love or money are the reasons most crimes are committed. Yet I can't make either fit here.' She stood up. 'Now I really must go. I'm meeting Helene's lawyer at her Lawrenceville house.'

Charles Potters was waiting when Meghan arrived. She had met him briefly at Helene's memorial service. Now, as she had a chance to focus on him, she realized that he looked like the kind of family lawyer portrayed in old movies.

His dark blue suit was ultraconservative, his shirt crisp white, his narrow blue tie subdued, his skin tone pink, his sparse gray hair neatly combed. Rimless glasses enhanced surprisingly vivid hazel eyes.

Whatever items from the house Stephanie had taken with her, the appearance of this room, the first they entered, was unchanged. It looked exactly as Meghan had seen it less than a week ago. Powers of observation, she thought. Concentrate. Then she noticed that the lovely Dresden figures she'd admired were missing from the mantel.

'Your friend Dr MacIntyre dissuaded me from immediately reporting Stephanie's theft of Helene's property, Miss Collins, but I'm afraid I cannot wait any longer. As trustee I'm responsible for all of Helene's possessions.'

'I understand that. I simply wish that some effort could be made to find Stephanie and persuade her to return them. If a warrant is sworn out for her arrest, she might be deported.

'Mr Potters,' she continued, 'my concern is much more serious than worrying about the things Stephanie took with her. Do you have the note she left?'

'Yes. Here it is.'

Meghan read it through.

'Did you ever meet this Jan?'

'No.'

'What did Helene think about her niece's pregnancy?'

'Helene was a kind woman, reserved but kind. Her only comments to me about the pregnancy were quite sympathetic.'

'How long have you handled her affairs?'

'For about three years.'

'You believed she was a medical doctor?'

'I had no reason not to believe her.'

261

'Didn't she build up a rather considerable estate? She had a very good salary at Manning of course. She was paid there as an embryologist. But she certainly couldn't have made very much money as a medical secretary for the three years before that.'

'I understood she'd been a cosmetologist. Cosmetology can be lucrative, and Helene was a shrewd investor. Miss Collins, I don't have much time. I believe you said you would like to walk through the house with me? I want to be sure it's properly secured before I leave.'

'Yes, I would.'

Meghan went upstairs with him. Here too nothing seemed to be out of order. Stephanie's packing had clearly not been rushed.

The master bedroom was luxurious. Helene Petrovic had not denied herself creature comforts. The coordinated wall hanging, spread and draperies looked very expensive.

French doors opened into a small sitting room. One wall was covered with pictures of children. 'These are duplicates of the ones at the Manning Clinic,' she said.

'Helene showed them to me,' Potters told her. 'She was very proud of the successful births achieved through the clinic.'

Meg studied the pictures. 'I saw some of these kids at the reunion less than two weeks ago.' She picked out Jonathan. 'This is the Anderson child whose family you've been reading about. That's the case that started the state investigation of the lab at Manning.' She paused, studying the photograph on the top corner. It was of two children, a boy and girl, in matching sweaters with their arms around each other. What was it about them that she should be noticing?

'I really have to lock up now, Miss Collins.'

There was an edge in the attorney's voice. She couldn't delay him any longer. Meg took another long look at the picture of the children in matching sweaters, committing it to memory.

262

Bernie's mother was not feeling well. It was her allergies. She'd been sneezing a lot, and her eyes were itchy. She thought she felt a draft in the house too. She wondered if Bernard had forgotten and left a window open downstairs.

She knew she shouldn't have let Bernard drive that car to Chicago, even for two hundred dollars a day. Sometimes when he was off by himself too long, he got fanciful. He started to daydream and to want things that could get him in trouble.

Then his temper started. That's when she needed to be there; she could control an outburst when she saw it coming. She kept him on the straight and narrow. Kept him nice and clean, well fed, saw that he got to his job and then stayed in with her watching television at night.

He'd been doing well for such a long time now. But he'd been acting kind of funny lately.

He was supposed to call. Why didn't he? When he got to Chicago he wouldn't start following a girl and try to touch her, would he? Not that he'd mean to harm her, but there'd been too many times when Bernard got nervous if a girl screamed. A couple of girls he'd hurt real bad.

They said that if it happened again, they wouldn't let him come home. They'd keep him locked up. He knew it too.

The only thing I have really established in all these hours is the number of times my husband was cheating on me, Catherine thought as she pushed the files away late Friday afternoon. She no longer had any desire to go through them. What good would knowing all this serve her now? It hurts so much, she thought.

She stood up. Outside it was a blustery November afternoon. In three weeks it would be Thanksgiving. That was always a busy time at the inn.

263

Virginia had phoned. The real estate company was being persistent. Was the inn for sale? They must be serious, she reported. They'd even named the price at which they'd start negotiating. They had another place in mind if Drumdoe wasn't available, or so they said. But it might be true.

Catherine wondered how long she and Meg could twist in the wind like this.

Meg. Would she close in on herself because of her father's betrayal as she had when Mac married Ginger? Catherine had never let on that she knew how heartbroken Meg had been over Mac. Edwin was always the one their daughter had turned to for comfort. Natural enough. Daddy's girl. It ran in the family. I was Daddy's girl too, Catherine thought.

Catherine could see the way Mac looked at Meg these days. She hoped it wasn't too late. Edwin had never forgiven his mother for rejecting him. Meg had built up a wall around herself where Mac was concerned. And great as she was with Kyle in her own way, she chose not to see how hopefully he was always reaching out to her.

Catherine caught a glimpse of a figure in the woods. She froze, then relaxed. It was a policeman. At least they were keeping an eye on the place.

She heard the click of a key in the lock.

Catherine breathed a prayer of gratitude. The daughter who made everything else bearable was safe.

Now maybe for the moment she could stop being haunted by the pictures that had run side by side in the newspapers today, the official publicity head shot of Meg from Channel 3 and the professional head shot Annie had used for her travel articles.

At Catherine's insistence, Virginia had sent over all the papers delivered to the inn, including the tabloids. The *Daily News*, besides using the pictures, had printed a photocopy of the fax Meg had received the night Annie was stabbed.

The headline of their article read: DID THE WRONG SISTER DIE?

'Hi, Mom. I'm home.'

For reassurance, Catherine took one more glance at the policeman at the edge of the woods, then turned to greet her daughter.

Virginia Murphy was the semiofficial second in command of the Drumdoe Inn. Technically hostess at the restaurant, and reservation clerk as needed, she was in fact Catherine's eyes and ears when Catherine was not around or when she was busy in the kitchen. Ten years younger than Catherine, six inches taller and handsomely rounded, she was a good friend as well as a faithful employee.

Knowing the financial situation at the inn, Virginia worked diligently to cut corners where it wouldn't show. She passionately wanted Catherine to be able to keep the inn. She knew that when all this terrible publicity died down, Catherine's best chance to get on with her life began here.

It galled Virginia that she'd aided and abetted Catherine when that crazy interior designer came in with her violently expensive swatches and tile samples and plumbing-supply books. And that after the expense of the much-needed renovation!

The place looked lovely, Virginia admitted, and it certainly had needed a face-lift, but the irony would be to go through the inconvenience and financial drain of renovating and redecorating only to have someone else come in and buy Drumdoe at a fire-sale price.

The last thing Virginia wanted to do was to cause Catherine any more concern, but now she was getting worried about the man who had checked into room 3A. He'd been in bed since he arrived, claiming he was exhausted from running back and forth from Long Island to New Haven, where his mother was in the hospital.

It wasn't a big deal to send a tray up to his room. They could certainly handle that. The problem was that he might be seriously sick. How would it look if something happened to him while he was here?

Virginia thought, I'm not going to bother Catherine yet. I'm going to let it go at least for another day. If he's still in bed tomorrow night, I'll go up and have a talk with him myself. I'll insist that he allow a doctor to see him.

Frederick Schuller from Valley Memorial Hospital in Trenton called Mac late Friday afternoon. 'I've sent the roster of medical staff to Miss Collins by overnight mail. She'll have a lot of reading to do unless she knows what name she's looking for.'

'That was very quick,' Mac said sincerely. 'I'm grateful.'

'Let's see if it's helpful. There is one thing that might interest you. I was looking over the Manning Clinic list and saw Dr Henry Williams' name on it. I'm acquainted with him. He's head of Franklin Clinic in Philadelphia now.'

'Yes, I know,' Mac said.

'This may not be relevant. Williams was never on staff here, but I remembered that his wife was in our long-term care facility for two of the three years Helene Petrovic worked at Dowling. I used to run into him here occasionally.'

'Do you think there's any chance he's the doctor Petrovic may have been seeing when she was at Dowling?' Mac asked quickly.

There was a hesitation, then Schuller said, 'This borders on gossip, but I did make a few inquiries in the long-term unit. The head nurse has been there twenty years. She remembers Dr Williams and his wife very well.'

Mac waited. Let this be the connection we're looking for, he prayed.

266

It was clear that Frederick Schuller was reluctant to continue. After another brief pause he said, 'Mrs Williams had a brain tumor. She had been born and raised in Rumania. As her condition worsened, she lost her ability to communicate in English. Dr Williams spoke only a few words of Rumanian, and a woman friend came regularly to Mrs Williams' room to translate for him.'

'Was it Helene Petrovic?' Mac asked.

'The nurse never was introduced to her. She described her as a dark-haired, brown-eyed woman in her early to mid-forties, quite attractive.' Schuller added, 'As you can see, this is very tenuous.'

No it isn't, Mac thought. He tried to sound calm when he thanked Frederick Schuller, but when he hung up the phone, he said a silent prayer of gratitude.

This was the first break! Meg had told him that Dr Williams denied having known Petrovic before she joined the staff of the Manning Clinic. Williams was the expert who could have taught Petrovic the skills she needed to pass herself off as an embryologist.

54

'Kyle, shouldn't you be starting your homework?' Marie Dileo, the sixty-year-old housekeeper gently prodded.

Kyle was watching the tape he'd made of Meg's interview at the Franklin Clinic. He looked up. 'In a minute, Mrs Dileo, honest.'

'You know what your Dad says about too much television.'

'This is an educational tape. That's different.'

267

Dileo shook her head. 'You have an answer for everything.' She studied him affectionately. Kyle was such a nice child, smart as a whip, funny and little-boy appealing.

The segment with Meg was ending, and he turned off the set. 'Meg is really a good reporter, isn't she?'

'Yes, she is.'

Trailed by Jake, Kyle followed Marie into the kitchen. She could tell something was wrong. 'Didn't you come home from Danny's a little early?' she asked.

'Uh-huh.' He spun the fruit bowl.

'Don't do that. You'll knock it over. Anything happen at Danny's?'

'His mother got a little mad at us.'

'Oh?' Marie looked up from the meat loaf she was preparing. 'I'm sure there was a reason.'

'They put in a new laundry chute in his house. We thought we'd try it out.'

'Kyle, you two wouldn't fit in a laundry chute.'

'No, but Penny fits.'

'You put Penny in the chute!'

'It was Danny's idea. He put her in and I caught her at the bottom and we put a big quilt and pillows down in case I missed, but I didn't, not once. Penny didn't want to stop, but Danny's mother's real mad. We can't play together all week.'

'Kyle, if I were you, I'd have my homework done when your father gets home. He is not going to be happy about this.'

'I know.' With a deep sigh Kyle went for his backpack and dumped his books on the kitchen table. Jake curled up on the floor at his feet.

That desk he got for his birthday was a waste of money, Marie thought. She'd been about to set the table. Well, that could wait. It was only ten-past five. The routine was that she prepared dinner and then left when Mac got home around six. He didn't like to eat the

268

minute he walked in, so he always served the meal himself, after Marie had left.

The phone rang. Kyle jumped up. 'I'll get it.' He answered, listened, then handed the receiver to Marie. 'It's for you, Mrs Dileo.'

It was her husband saying that her father had been taken to the hospital from the nursing home.

'Is something the matter?' Kyle asked when she replaced the receiver.

'Yes. My Dad's been sick for a long time. He's very old. I have to get right to the hospital. I'll drop you at Danny's and leave a note for your father.'

'Not Danny's,' Kyle said, alarmed. 'His mother wouldn't like that. Leave me at Meg's. I'll call her.' He pressed the automatic dial button on the phone. Meg's number was directly under those of the police and fire departments. A moment later he announced, beaming, 'She said come right over.'

Mrs Dileo scribbled a note to Mac. 'Take your homework, Kyle.'

'Okay.' He ran into the living room and grabbed the tape he'd made of Meg's interview. 'Maybe she'll want to watch it with me.'

There was a briskness about Meg that Catherine did not understand. In the two hours since she'd come back from Trenton, Meg had been through Edwin's files, extracted some papers and made several phone calls from the study. Then she sat at Edwin's desk, writing furiously. It reminded Catherine of when Meg was in law school. Whenever she came home for a weekend, she spent most of it at that desk, totally preoccupied with her case studies.

At five o'clock, Catherine looked in on her. 'I thought I'd fix chicken and mushrooms for dinner. How does that grab you?'

'Fine. Sit down for a minute, Mom.'

Catherine chose the small armchair near the desk.

269

Her eyes slid past Edwin's maroon leather chair and ottoman. Meg had told her that they were duplicated in Arizona. Once an endearing reminder of her husband, they were now a mockery.

Meg put her elbows on the desk, clasped her hands and rested her chin on them. 'I had a nice talk with Father Radzin this morning. He offered the memorial mass for Helene Petrovic. I told him I couldn't find any reason why Dad would have placed Petrovic at the Manning Clinic. He said words to the effect that there was always a reason for someone's actions, and if I couldn't find it, maybe I should reexamine the whole premise.'

'What do you mean?'

'Mom, I mean that several traumatic things happened to us at once. I saw Annie's body when she was brought to the hospital. We learned that Dad almost certainly had not died in the bridge accident and we began to suspect that he had been leading a double life. On the heels of that, Dad was blamed for Helene Petrovic's false credentials and now for her murder.'

Meg leaned forward. 'Mom, if it hadn't been for the shock of the double life and Petrovic's death, when the insurers refused to pay, we would have taken a much longer look at the reason we thought Dad was on that bridge when the accident happened. Think about it.'

'What do you mean?' Catherine was bewildered. 'Victor Orsini was talking to Dad just as he was driving onto the ramp. Someone on the bridge saw his car go over the edge.'

'That someone on the bridge obviously was mistaken. And Mom, we only have Victor Orsini's word that Dad was calling him from that spot. Suppose, just suppose, Dad had already crossed the bridge when he called Victor. He might have seen the accident happening behind him. Frances Grolier remembered that Dad had been angry about something Victor had done, and that

270

when Dad called Dr Manning from Scottsdale, he had seemed really distraught. I was in New York. You were away overnight. It would be just like Dad to tell Victor he wanted to see him immediately, instead of next morning, as Victor said. Dad may have been insecure in his personal life, but I don't think he ever had any doubts professionally.'

'You're saying that Victor's a liar?' Catherine looked astounded.

'It would be a safe lie, wouldn't it? The time of the call from Dad's car phone was exactly right and could be verified. Mom, Victor had been at the office a month or so when the recommendation for Petrovic went to Manning. He could have sent it. He was working directly under Dad.'

'Phillip never has liked him,' Catherine murmured. 'But, Meg, there's no way to prove this. And you come up with the same question: Why? Why would Victor, any more than Dad, put Petrovic in that lab? What would he have to gain?'

'I don't know yet. But don't you see that as long as the police think Dad is alive, they're not going to seriously examine any alternative answers in Helene Petrovic's murder?'

The phone rang. 'Ten to one it's Phillip for you,' Meg said as she picked it up. It was Kyle.

'We've got company for dinner,' she told Catherine when she replaced the receiver. 'Hope you can stretch the chicken and mushrooms.'

'Mac and Kyle?'

'Yes.'

'Good.' Catherine got up. 'Meg, I wish I could be as enthusiastic as you about all these possibilities. You have a theory and it's a good defense argument for your father. But maybe it's just that.'

Meg held up a sheet of paper. 'This is the January bill for Dad's car phone. Look at how much that last call cost. He and Victor were on for eight minutes. It doesn't take eight minutes to set up a meeting, does it?'

'Meg, Dad's signature was on the letter to the Manning Clinic. That's been verified by experts.'

After dinner, Mac suggested that Kyle help Catherine with clearing the table. Alone with Meghan in the living room he told her about Dr Williams' connection to Dowling and possibly to Helene.

'Dr Williams!' Meghan stared at him. 'Mac, he absolutely denied knowing Petrovic before the Manning Clinic. The receptionist at Manning saw them having dinner together. When I asked Dr Williams about it, he claimed that he always took a new staff member out for dinner as a friendly gesture.'

'Meg, I think we're onto something, but we still can't be *sure* it was Helene Petrovic who accompanied Williams when he visited his wife,' Mac cautioned.

'Mac, it fits. Williams and Helene must have been involved with each other. We know she had a tremendous interest in lab work. He's the perfect one to have helped her falsify her curriculum vitae and to have guided her when she arrived at Manning.'

'But Williams left the Manning Clinic six months after Petrovic started to work there. Why would he do that if he was involved with her?'

'Her home is in New Jersey, not far from Philadelphia. Her niece said that she was often away for hours on Saturday and Sunday. Much of that time may have been spent with him.'

'Then where does your father's letter of recommendation come in? He placed Williams at Manning, but why would he have helped Petrovic get her job there?'

'I have a theory about that, and it involves Victor Orsini. It's starting to fit, all of it.'

She smiled up at him, the closest he'd seen to a genuine smile on her lips for a long time.

They were standing in front of the fireplace. Mac put

his arms around her. Meghan immediately stiffened and shifted to move out of his embrace, but he would have none of it. He turned her to face him.

'Get it straight, Meghan,' Mac said. 'You were right nine years ago. I only wish I had seen it then.' He paused. 'You're the only one for me. I know it now, and you do too. We can't keep wasting time.'

He kissed her fiercely, then released her, stepping back. 'I won't let you keep pushing me away. Once your life settles down again, we're going to have a long talk about *us*.'

Kyle begged to show the tape of Meg's interview. 'It's only three minutes, Dad. I want to show Meg how I can tape programs now.'

'I think you're stalling,' Mac told him. 'Incidentally, Danny's mother caught me at home when I was reading Mrs Dileo's note. You're grounded. Show Meg the tape, but then don't even *think* television for a week.'

'What'd you do?' Meg asked in a whisper when Kyle sat beside her.

'I'll tell you in a minute. See, here you are.'

The tape ran. 'You did a good job with that,' Meg assured him.

That night Meghan lay in bed for a long time, unable to sleep. Her mind was in turmoil, going over all the new developments, the connection of Dr Williams to Petrovic, her suspicions about Victor Orsini. Mac. I told the police if they'd stop concentrating on Dad they'd find the real answers, she thought. But Mac? She wouldn't let herself think about him now.

All this, yet there was something else, she realized, something that was eluding her, something terribly, terribly important. What was it? It had something to do with the tape of her interview at the Franklin Center. I'll ask Kyle to bring it over tomorrow, she thought. I have to see it again.

273

Friday was a long day for Bernie. He had slept until seven-thirty, real late for him. He suspected right away that he had missed Meghan, that she'd left very early. Her blinds were up, and he could see her bed was made.

He knew he should call Mama. She'd told him to call, but he was afraid. If she had any idea he wasn't in Chicago, she'd be angry. She'd make him come home.

He sat by the window all day, watching Meghan's house, waiting for Meghan to return. He pulled the phone as far as the cord would stretch so he didn't lose sight of the house when he phoned for breakfast and lunch.

He'd unlock the door, then when the waiter knocked, Bernie would leap into bed and call, 'Come in.' It drove him crazy that he might miss Meghan again while the waiter was fussing with the tray.

When the maid knocked and tried to open the door with her master key she was stopped by the chain. He knew she couldn't see in.

'May I just change the towels?' she asked.

He figured he'd better let her do that at least. Didn't want her to get suspicious.

Yet as she passed him, he noticed that she looked at him funny, the way people do when they're sizing you up. Bernie tried hard to smile at her, tried to sound sincere when he thanked her.

It was late afternoon when Meghan's white Mustang turned into her driveway. Bernie pressed his nose against the window, straining to catch a glimpse of her walking up the path to the house. Seeing her made him happy again.

Around five-thirty, he saw the kid dropped off at Meghan's house. If it wasn't for the kid, Bernie could be hiding in the woods. He could be closer to Meg. He'd be taping her so that he could keep her. Could watch her and be with her whenever he wanted. Except for that stupid kid. He hated that kid.

He didn't think to order dinner. He wasn't hungry.

274

Finally at ten-thirty his wait was over. Meghan turned on the light in her bedroom and undressed.

She was so beautiful!

At four o'clock Friday afternoon, Phillip asked Jackie, 'Where's Orsini?'

'He had an appointment outside the office, Mr Carter. He said he'd be back around four-thirty.'

Jackie stood in Phillip Carter's office, trying to decide what to do. When Mr Carter was upset he was a little scary. Mr Collins never used to get upset.

But Mr Carter was the boss now, and last night her husband, Bob, told her that she owed it to him to tell him that Victor Orsini was going through all the files at night.

'But maybe it's Mr Carter doing it,' she had suggested.

'If it is Carter, he'll appreciate your concern. Don't forget, if there's any trouble between them, Orsini is the one who'll leave, not Carter.'

Bob was right. Now Jackie said firmly, 'Mr Carter, it may be none of my business, but I'm pretty sure Mr Orsini is coming in here at night and going through all the files.'

Phillip Carter was very quiet for a long minute, then his face hardened and he said, 'Thank you, Jackie. Have Mr Orsini see me when he comes in.'

I wouldn't want to be in Mr Orsini's boots, she thought.

Twenty minutes later she and Milly dropped all pretense of not listening as through the closed door of Phillip Carter's office, they could hear his raised voice castigating Victor Orsini.

'For a long time I have suspected you of working hand-in-glove with Downes and Rosen,' he told him. 'This place is in trouble now, and you're preparing to land on your feet by going with them. But you seem to forget that you have a contract that specifically pro-

275

hibits you from soliciting our accounts. Now get out and don't bother to pack. You've probably taken plenty of our files already. We'll send your personal items on to you.'

'So that's what he was doing,' Jackie whispered. 'That is really bad.' Neither she nor Milly looked up at Orsini when he passed their desks on his way out.

If they had, they would have seen that his face was white with fury.

On Saturday morning, Catherine went to the inn for the breakfast hour. She checked her mail and phone calls, then had a long talk with Virginia. Deciding not to stay for the lunch serving, she returned to the house at eleven o'clock. She found that Meg had been taking the files to her father's study and analyzing them, one by one.

'The dining room is such a mess that I can't concentrate,' Meg explained. 'Victor was looking for something important, and we're not seeing the forest for the trees.'

Catherine studied her daughter. Meg was wearing a plaid silk shirt and chinos. Her chestnut hair was almost shoulder length now, and brushed back. That's what it is, Catherine thought. Her hair is just that little bit longer. The picture of Annie Collins in yesterday's newspapers came to mind.

'Meg, I've thought it through. I'm going to accept that offer on Drumdoe.'

'You're *what*?'

'Virginia agrees with me. The overhead is simply too high. I don't want the inn to end up on the auction block.'

'Mom, Dad founded Collins and Carter, and even under these circumstances, there must be some way you can take some money out of it.'

'Meg, if there were a death certificate, there would

276

be partnership insurance. With lawsuits pending there won't be a business before long.'

'What does Phillip say? By the way, he's been around a lot lately,' Meg said, 'more than in all the years he worked with Dad.'

'He's trying to be kind, and I appreciate that.'

'Is it more than kindness?'

'I hope not. He'd be making a mistake. I have too much to deal with before I even think in that direction with anyone.' She added quietly, 'But you don't.'

'What's that supposed to mean?'

'It means that Kyle isn't the greatest busboy. He was keeping an eye on you two and reported with great satisfaction that Mac was kissing you.'

'I am not interested—'

'Stop it, Meg.' Catherine commanded. She stepped around the desk, yanked open the bottom drawer, pulled out a half-dozen letters and threw them on the desk. 'Don't be like your father, an emotional cripple because he couldn't forgive rejection.'

'He had every reason not to forgive his mother!'

'As a child, yes. As an adult with a family who deeply loved him, no. Maybe he wouldn't have needed Scottsdale if he'd gone to Philadelphia and made peace with her.'

Meg raised her eyebrows. 'You can play rough, can't you?'

'You bet I can. Meg, you love Mac. You always have. Kyle needs you. Now for God's sake, put yourself on the line and quit being afraid that Mac would be imbecile enough to want Ginger if she ever showed up in his life again.'

'Dad always called you Mighty Mouse.' Meg felt tears burning behind her eyes.

'Yes, he did. When I go back to the inn, I'm going to call the real estate people. One thing I can promise. I'll raise their ante till they beg for mercy.'

*

277

At one-thirty, just before she returned to the inn, Catherine poked her head into the study. 'Meg, remember I said Palomino Leather Goods sounded familiar? I think Annie's mother may have left the same message on our home phone for Dad. It would have been mid-March seven years ago. The reason I can pinpoint it is that I was so furious when Dad missed your twenty-first birthday party that when he finally got home with a leather purse for you, I told him I'd like to hit him over the head with it.'

On Saturday, Bernie's mother could not stop sneezing. Her sinuses were beginning to ache, her throat was scratchy. She had to do something about it.

Bernard had let dust pile up in the basement, she just knew it. No question about it, that had to be it. Now the dust was filtering through the house.

She became angrier and more agitated by the minute. Finally, at two o'clock, she couldn't stand it any more. She had to get down there and clean.

First she heaved the broom and shovel and mop into the basement. Then she filled a plastic bag with rags and cleanser and threw it down the stairs. It landed on the mop.

Finally Mama tied on her apron. She felt the bannister. It wasn't that loose. It would hold her. She'd go slowly, a step at a time, and test each stair before she put her weight on it. She still didn't know how she'd managed to fall so hard ten years ago. One minute she'd been starting down the stairs, the next she was in an ambulance.

Step by step, with infinite care, she descended. Well, I did it, she thought as she stepped on the basement floor. The toe of her shoe caught in the bag of rags and she fell heavily to the side, her left foot bending beneath her.

The sound of Mama's ankle bone breaking resounded through the clammy basement.

278

55

After her mother went back to the inn, Meghan phoned Phillip at home. When he answered, she said, 'I'm glad to get you. I thought you might be in New York or at one of your auctions today.'

'It's been a rough week. I had to fire Victor yesterday afternoon.'

'Why?' Meg asked, distressed at this sudden twist of events. She needed Victor available while she was trying to tie him to the Petrovic recommendation. Suppose he left town? So far she didn't have any proof, couldn't go to the police with her suspicions about him. That would take time.

'He's a slippery one, Meg. Been stealing our clients. Frankly, from one or two remarks your dad made just before he disappeared, I think he suspected Victor was up to something.'

'So do I,' Meg said. 'That's why I'm calling. I think he might have sent out the Petrovic letter when Dad was away. Phillip, we don't have any of Dad's Daily Reminders with his business appointments. Are they in the office?'

'They should have been with the files you took home.'

'I would think so, but they're not. Phillip, I'm trying to reach Annie's mother. Like a fool I didn't get her private number when I was out there. The Palomino Leather Goods Shop contacted her and then gave me directions to her house. I have an idea that Dad may not have been in the office when that letter about Petrovic went to Manning. It's dated March 21st, isn't it?'

'I believe so.'

'Then I'm onto something. Annie's mother can verify it. I did reach the lawyer who came out here with her. He wouldn't give me the number but said he'd contact her for me.'

She paused, then said, 'Phillip, there's something else. I think Dr Williams and Helene Petrovic were involved, certainly while they worked together and maybe even before then. And if so, it's possible he's the man Petrovic's neighbor saw visiting her apartment.'

'Meg, that's incredible. Do you have any proof?'

'Not yet, but I don't think it will be hard to get.'

'Just be careful,' Phillip Carter warned her. 'Williams is very well respected in medical circles. Don't even mention his name until you can back up what you say.'

Frances Grolier phoned at quarter-to three. 'You wanted to talk to me, Meghan.'

'Yes. You told me the other day that you only used the Palomino code a couple of other times in all those years. Did you ever phone our house with that message?'

Grolier did not ask why Meg wanted to know. 'Yes, I did. It was nearly seven years ago, on March 10th. Annie had been in a head-on collision and wasn't expected to live. I'd tried the machine in the office, but as it turned out, it had been accidentally unplugged. I knew Edwin was in Connecticut and I *had* to reach him. He flew out that night and was here two weeks until Annie was out of danger.'

Meg thought of March 18th seven years ago, her twenty-first birthday. A black-tie dinner dance at Drumdoe. Her father's phone call that afternoon. He had a virus and was too sick to get on the plane. Two hundred guests. Mac with Ginger, showing pictures of Kyle.

She'd spent the night trying to smile, trying not to show how bitterly disappointed she was that her father was not with her on this special night.

'Meghan?' Frances Grolier's controlled voice at the other end of the phone was questioning.

'I'm sorry. Sorry about everything. What you've just told me is terribly important. It's tied to so much of what's happened.'

Meghan returned the receiver to its cradle, but held onto it for several minutes. Then she dialed Phillip. 'Confirmation.' Quickly she explained what Frances Grolier had just told her.

'Meg, you're a whiz,' Phillip told her.

'Phillip, there's the bell. It must be Kyle. Mac is dropping him off. I asked him to bring something over for me.'

'Go ahead. And Meg, don't talk about this until we get a complete picture to present to Dwyer's office.'

'I won't. Our assistant state attorney and his people don't trust me anyhow. I'll talk to you.'

Kyle came in smiling broadly.

Meghan bent down to kiss him.

'Never do that in front of my friends,' he warned.

'Why not?'

'Jimmy's mother waits at the road and kisses him when he gets off the bus. Isn't that disgusting?'

'Why did you let me kiss you?'

'It's okay in private. Nobody saw us. You were kissing Dad last night.'

'He kissed me.'

'Did you like it?'

Meg considered. 'Let's just say that it wasn't disgusting. Want some cookies and milk?'

'Yes, please. I brought the tape for you to watch. Why do you want to see it again?'

'I'm not sure.'

'Okay. Dad said he'll be about an hour. He had to pick up some stuff at the store.'

Meghan brought the plate of cookies and the glasses of milk into the den. Kyle sat on the floor at her feet;

281

using the remote control, he once again started the tape of the Franklin Center interview. Meg's heart started to pound. She asked herself, What is it I saw in this tape?

In the last scene in Dr Williams' office, when the camera panned over the pictures of the children born through in vitro fertilization, she found what she was looking for. She grabbed the remote from Kyle and snapped the Pause button.

'Meg, it's almost over,' Kyle protested.

Meg stared at the picture of the little boy and girl with identical sweaters. She had seen the same picture on the wall of Helene Petrovic's sitting room in Lawrenceville. 'It *is* over, Kyle. I know the reason.'

The phone rang. 'I'll be right back,' she told him.

'I'll rewind. I know how.'

It was Phillip Carter. 'Meg, are you alone?' he asked quickly.

'Phillip! I just found confirmation that Helene Petrovic knew Dr Williams. I think I know what she was doing at the Manning Clinic.'

It was as though he hadn't heard her. 'Are you alone?' he repeated.

'Kyle is in the den.'

'Can you drop him off at his house?' His voice was low, agitated.

'Mac's out. I can leave him at the inn. Mother's there. Phillip, what is it?'

Now Carter sounded unbelieving, near hysteria. 'I just heard from Edwin! He wants to see both of us. He's trying to decide if he should turn himself in. Meg, he's desperate. Don't let anyone know about this until we have a chance to see him.'

'Dad? Phoned you?' Meg gasped. Stunned, she grasped the corner of the desk for support. In a voice so shocked it was barely a whisper, she demanded, 'Where is he? I've got to go to him.'

282

56

When Bernie's mother regained consciousness, she tried to shout for help, but she knew none of the neighbors could hear her. She'd never make it up the stairs. She'd have to drag herself into Bernard's TV area where there was a phone. It was all his fault for not keeping the place clean. Her ankle hurt so much. The pains were shooting up her leg. She opened her mouth and took big gulps of air. It was agony to drag herself along the dirty, rough concrete floor.

Finally she made her way into the alcove her son had fashioned for himself. Even with all the pain she was in, Mama's eyes widened in amazed fury. That big television! Those radios! Those machines! What was Bernard doing, throwing away money on all these things?

The phone was on the old kitchen table that he'd carried in when one of their neighbors put it at the curb. She couldn't reach it, so she pulled it down by the cord. It clattered on the floor.

Hoping she hadn't broken it, Bernie's mother dialed 911. At the welcome sound of a dispatcher's voice, she said, 'Send an ambulance.'

She was able to give her name and address and tell what had happened before she fainted again.

'Kyle,' Meg said hurriedly, 'I'm going to have to leave you at the inn. I'll put a note on the door for your dad. Just tell my mother that something came up, that I had to leave right away. You stay with her. No going outside, okay?'

'Why are you so worried, Meg?'

'I'm not. It's a big story. I have to cover it.'

'Oh, that's great.'

At the inn, Meg watched until Kyle had reached the front door. He waved and she waved back, forcing a smile. Then she put her foot on the accelerator.

She was meeting Phillip at a crossroads in West Redding, about twenty miles from Newtown. 'You can follow me from there,' he had hurriedly told her. 'It's not far after that, but it would be impossible for you to find it alone.'

Meg did not know what to think. Her mind was a jumble of confused thoughts and confused emotions. Her mouth was so dry. Her throat simply would not swallow. *Dad was alive and he was desperate!* Why? Surely not because he was Helene Petrovic's murderer. Please, dear God, anything but that.

When Meg found the intersection of the narrow country roads, Phillip's black Cadillac was waiting. It was easy to spot him. There was no other car in sight.

He did not take the time to speak to her but held up his hand and motioned for her to follow him. Half a mile later he turned sharply onto a narrow hard-packed dirt road. Fifty yards after that the road twisted through a wooded area and Meghan's car vanished from the view of anyone driving past.

Victor Orsini had not been surprised by the showdown with Phillip Carter Friday afternoon. It had never been a question of *if* it would happen. The question for months had been *when*.

At least he had found what he needed before he lost access to the office. When he left Carter, he had driven directly to his house at Candlewood Lake, fixed himself a martini and sat where he could look over the water and consider what he ought to do.

284

The evidence he had was not enough alone and without corroboration, would not stand up in court. And in addition, how much could he tell them and still not reveal things that could hurt him?

He'd been with Collins and Carter nearly seven years, yet suddenly all that mattered was that first month. It was the linchpin connecting everything that had happened recently.

Victor had spent Friday evening weighing the pros and cons of going to the assistant state attorney and laying out what he thought had happened.

The next morning he jogged along the lake for an hour, a long healthy run that cleared his head and strengthened his resolve.

Finally, at two-thirty Saturday afternoon, he dialed the number Special Investigator Marron had given him. He half-expected that Marron might not be in his office on Saturday, but he answered on the first ring.

Victor identified himself. In the calm, reasoned voice that inspired confidence in clients and job candidates, he asked, 'Would it be convenient if I stopped by in half an hour? I think I know who murdered Helene Petrovic . . .'

From the front door of the Drumdoe Inn, Kyle looked back and watched Meghan drive away. She was on a story. Cool. He wished he was going with her. He used to think he'd be a doctor like Dad when he grew up but had decided being a reporter was more fun.

A moment later a car zoomed out of the parking lot, a green Chevy. That's the guy who didn't run over Jake, Kyle thought. He was sorry he didn't get a chance to talk to him and thank him. He watched as the Chevy turned down the road in the direction Meg had gone.

Kyle went into the lobby and spotted Meg's mother and Mrs Murphy at the desk. They both looked serious. He went over to them. 'Hi.'

'Kyle, what are you doing here?' That's a heck of a

way to greet a kid, Catherine thought. She ruffled his hair. 'I mean, did you and Meg come over for some ice cream or something?'

'Meg dropped me off. She said to stay with you. She's working on a story.'

'Oh, did she get a call from her boss?'

'Somebody called her and she said she had to leave right away.'

'Wouldn't that be great if she's being reinstated?' Catherine said to Virginia. 'It would be such a morale booster for her.'

'It sure would,' Murphy agreed. 'Now what do you think we should do about that guy in 3A? Frankly, Catherine, I think there's something a little wrong with him.'

'Just what we need.'

'How many people would stay in a room for nearly three days and then go charging out so fast he almost knocked people down? You just missed him, but I can tell you there appeared to be nothing sick about Mr Heffernan. He tore down the stairs and ran through the lobby, carrying a video camera.'

'Let's take a look at the room,' Catherine said. 'Come with us, Kyle.'

The air in 3A was stale. 'Has this room been cleaned since he checked in?' Catherine asked.

'No,' Murphy said. 'Betty said he would let her in just to change the towels, that he just about threw her out when she tried to clean up.'

'He must have been out of bed sometime. Look at the way that chair is pulled up to the window,' Catherine commented. 'Wait a minute!' She crossed the room, sat in the chair and looked out. 'Dear God,' she breathed.

'What is it?' Virginia asked.

'From here you can look directly into Meg's bedroom windows.' Catherine rushed to the phone, glanced at the emergency numbers listed on the receiver and dialed.

'State police. Officer Thorne speaking.'

286

'This is Catherine Collins at the Drumdoe Inn in Newtown,' she snapped. 'I think a man staying at the inn has been spying on our house. He's been locked in his room for days, and just now he drove away in a mad hurry.' Her hand flew to her mouth. 'Kyle, when Meg dropped you off did you see if a car followed her?'

Kyle sensed that something was very wrong, but surely it couldn't be because of the nice guy who was such a good driver. 'Don't worry. The guy in the green Chevy is okay. He saved Jake's life when he drove past our house last week.'

In near despair, Catherine cried, 'Officer, he's following my daughter now. She's driving a white Mustang. He's in a green Chevy. *Find her! You've got to find her!*'

57

The squad car pulled into the driveway of the shabby one-story frame house in Jackson Heights, and two policemen jumped out. The shrill ee-aww of an approaching EMS ambulance sounded over the screech of a braking elevated train at the station less than a block away.

The cops ran around the house to the back door, forced it open and pounded down the stairs to the basement. A loose step gave way under the weight of the rookie, but he grabbed the railing and managed to keep from falling. The sergeant stumbled over the mop at the foot of the stairs.

'No wonder she got hurt,' he muttered. 'This place is booby-trapped.'

Low moans from a crudely enclosed area drew them

287

to Bernie's alcove. The police officers found the elderly woman sprawled on the floor, the telephone beside her. She was lying near an unsteady table with an enameled-steel top heaped with phone books. A worn Naugahyde recliner was directly in front of a forty-inch television set. A shortwave radio, police scanner, typewriter and fax machine crowded the top of an old dresser.

The younger cop dropped down on one knee beside the injured woman. 'Police Officer David Guzman, Mrs Heffernan,' he said soothingly. 'They're bringing a stretcher to take you to the hospital.'

Bernie's mother tried to speak. 'My son doesn't mean any harm.' She could barely get the words out. She closed her eyes, unable to continue.

'Dave, look at this!'

Guzman jumped up. 'What is it, Sarge?'

The Queens telephone directory was spread open. On those pages nine or ten names were circled. The sergeant pointed to them. 'They look familiar? In the last few weeks all of these people reported threatening phone calls.'

They could hear the EMS team. Guzman ran to the foot of the stairs. 'Watch out or you'll break your necks coming down here,' he warned.

In less than five minutes, Bernie's semiconscious mother had been secured to a stretcher and carried to the ambulance.

The police officers did not leave. 'We've got enough probable cause to take a look around,' the sergeant commented. He picked up papers next to the fax machine and began to thumb through them.

Officer Guzman pulled open the knobless drawer of the table and spotted a handsome wallet. 'Looks as though Bernie might do a little mugging on the side,' he commented.

As Guzman stared at Annie Collins' picture on her driver's license, the sergeant found the original of the fax message. He read it aloud. ' "Mistake. Annie was a mistake." '

Guzman grabbed the phone from the floor. 'Sarge,' he said, 'you'd better let the chief know we found ourselves a murderer.'

Even for Bernie it was hard to keep far enough behind Meghan's car to avoid being seen. From the distance he watched her begin to follow the dark sedan. He almost lost both cars after the intersection, when they suddenly seemed to vanish. He knew they must have turned off somewhere, so he backed up. The dirt road through the woods was the only place they could have gone. He turned onto it cautiously.

Now he was coming to a clearing. Meghan's white car and the dark sedan were shaking up and down as they covered the uneven, rutted ground. Bernie waited until they were past the clearing and into another wooded area, then drove the Chevy through the clearing.

The second clump of woods wasn't nearly as deep as the first. Bernie had to jam on his brakes to avoid being seen when the narrow track abruptly turned into open fields again. Now the road led directly to a distant house and barn. The cars were heading there.

Bernie grabbed his camera. With his zoom lens it was possible to track them, until they drove behind the barn.

He sat quietly, considering what he should do. There was a cluster of evergreens near the house. Maybe he could hide the Chevy there. He had to try.

It was past four, and the fading sunlight was obscured by thickening clouds. Meg drove behind Phillip along the winding, bumpy road. They came out of the wooded area, crossed a field, went through another stretch of woods. The road straightened out. In the distance she saw buildings, a farmhouse and barn.

Is Dad here in this godforsaken place? Meg

wondered. She prayed that when she came face to face with him, she would find the right words to say.

I love you, Daddy, the child in her wanted to cry.

Dad, what happened to you? Dad, why? the hurt adult wanted to scream.

Dad, I've missed you. How can I help you? Was that the best way to start?

She followed Phillip's car around the dilapidated buildings. He parked, got out of his sedan, walked over and opened the door of Meg's car.

Meg looked up at him. 'Where's Dad?' she asked. She moistened lips that now felt cracked and dry.

'He's nearby.' Phillip's eyes locked with hers.

It was the abrupt way he answered that caught her attention. He's as nervous about this as I am, she thought as she got out of the car.

58

Victor Orsini had agreed to be at John Dwyer's office in the Danbury courthouse at three o'clock. Special investigators Weiss and Marron were there when he arrived. An hour later, from their impassive faces, he still did not know if they were putting any stock in what he was telling them.

'Let's go through this again,' Dwyer said.

'I've gone through it a dozen times,' Victor snapped.

'I want to hear it again,' Dwyer said.

'All right, all right. Edwin Collins called me on his car phone the night of January 28th. We spoke for about eight minutes until he disconnected because he

290

was on the ramp of the Tappan Zee Bridge and the driving was very slippery.'

'When do you tell us everything you talked about?' Weiss demanded. 'What took eight minutes to say?'

This part of the story was what Victor had hoped to gloss over, but he knew unless he told the complete truth he would not be believed. Reluctantly, he admitted, 'Ed had learned a day or two before that I'd been tipping off one of our competitors to positions our major clients would be looking to fill. He was outraged and ordered me to be in his office the next morning.'

'And that was your last contact with him?'

'On January 29th I was waiting in his office at eight o'clock. I knew Ed was going to fire me, but I didn't want him to think I'd cheated the firm out of money. He'd told me that if he found proof that I'd been pocketing commissions, he'd prosecute. At the time I thought he meant kickbacks. Now I think he was referring to Helene Petrovic. I don't think he knew anything about her, then must have found out and thought I was trying to pull a fast one.'

'We know the commission for placing her at the Manning Clinic went into the office account,' Marron said.

'He wouldn't have known that. I've checked and found that it was deliberately buried in the fee received for placing Dr Williams there. Obviously Edwin was never supposed to find out anything about Petrovic.'

'Then who recommended Petrovic to Manning?' Dwyer asked.

'Phillip Carter. It had to be. When the letter endorsing her credentials was sent to Manning on March 21st almost seven years ago, I'd only been at Collins and Carter a short time. I'd never even heard that woman's name until she was murdered less than two weeks ago. And I'd bet my life Ed didn't either. He was away from the office the end of March that year, including March 21st.'

He paused. 'As I've told you, when I saw the news-

291

paper with the reprint of the letter supposedly signed by him, I knew it was a phony.'

Orsini pointed to the sheet of paper he had given to Dwyer. 'With his old secretary, who was a gem, Ed had gotten in the habit of leaving a stack of signed letterheads she could use if he wanted to dictate over the phone. He trusted her completely. Then she'd retired, and Ed wasn't that impressed with her replacement, Jackie. I can remember him ripping up those signed letterheads and telling me that from then on he wanted to see everything that went out over his signature. On the blank letterheads he always signed in the same place, where his longtime secretary had left a light pencil mark; thirty-five lines down and beginning on the fiftieth character. You've got one in your hands now.

'I've been going through Ed's files, hoping that there might be other signed letterheads that he'd missed. I found the one you're holding in Phillip Carter's desk. A locksmith made a key for me. I imagine Carter was saving this in case he needed to produce something else signed by Edwin Collins.

'You can believe me or not,' Orsini continued, 'but thinking back to that morning of January 29th, when I waited in Ed's office, I had the distinct feeling he'd been there recently. The H through O drawer in the filing cabinet was open. I'd swear he had been looking at the Manning file for any record of Helene Petrovic.

'While I was waiting for him, Catherine Collins phoned, worried that Ed wasn't home. She'd been at a reunion in Hartford the night before and found the house empty when she returned. She tried the office, to see if we'd heard from him. I told her about speaking to him the night before when he was on the ramp of the Tappan Zee Bridge. At that time I didn't know anything about the accident. She was the one who suggested that Ed might have been one of the victims.

'I realized it was possible, of course,' Victor said. 'Ed's last words to me were about how slippery the

292

ramp was, and we know the accident took place less than a minute later. After talking to Catherine, I tried to call Phillip. His phone was busy, and since he lives only ten minutes from the office, I drove to his house. I had some idea we might want to drive down to the bridge and see if they were pulling victims out of the water.

'When I arrived, Phillip was in the garage, just getting in his car. His jeep was there as well. I remember he made a point of telling me he'd brought it down from the country to have it serviced. I knew he had a jeep that he used to get around his farm property. He'd drive the sedan up and then switch.

'At the time I thought nothing of it. But in this last week I reasoned that if Ed wasn't involved in that accident, went to the office and found something that sent him to Carter's home, whatever happened to him took place there. Carter could have driven Ed away in his own car and hidden it somewhere. Ed always said Phillip had a lot of rural property.'

Orsini looked at the inscrutable faces of his interrogators. I've done what I had to do, he thought. If they don't believe me, at least I tried.

Dwyer said in a noncommittal tone, 'This may be helpful. Thank you, Mr Orsini. You'll hear from us.'

When Orsini left, the assistant state attorney said to Weiss and Marron, 'It fits. And it explains the findings of the forensic lab.' They had just received word that analysis of Edwin Collins' car revealed traces of blood in the trunk.

59

It was nearly four o'clock when Mac completed his last errand and started home. The butcher, the baker, the candlestick maker, he thought. He'd gone to the barber, picked up the dry cleaning and stopped at the supermarket. Mrs Dileo might not be back from taking care of her father to do the usual shopping on Monday.

Mac felt good. Kyle had been thrilled to be visiting with Meg. There'd certainly be no problem for Kyle if Mac succeeded in rekindling the feelings Meg had once had for him. Meggie, you don't have a chance, Mac vowed. You're not getting away from me again.

It was a cold, overcast day, but Mac had no thought of weather as he turned onto Bayberry Road. He thought of the hope in Meg's face when they'd talked about Petrovic's connection to Dr Williams and the possibility that Victor Orsini had forged Edwin's name to Petrovic's letter of recommendation. She'd realized then that her father might be proven innocent of any connection to the Petrovic case and the Manning Clinic scandal.

Nothing can change the fact that Ed had a double life all those years, Mac thought. But if his name is cleared of murder and fraud, it will be a hell of a lot easier for Meg and Catherine.

The first warning that something was wrong came as Mac neared the inn. There were police cars in the driveway, and the parking lot was blocked. A police helicopter was landing. He could see another one with the

294

logo of a New Haven television station already on the ground.

He pulled his car onto the lawn and ran toward the inn.

The door of the inn was flung open, and Kyle rushed out. 'Dad, Meg's boss didn't call her to cover a story,' he sobbed. 'The man who didn't run over Jake is the guy who's been watching Meg. He's following her in his car.'

Meg! For a split second Mac's vision blurred. He was in the morgue looking down at the dead face of Annie Collins, Meg's half sister.

Kyle grabbed his father's arm. 'The cops are here. They're sending helicopters to look for Meg's car and the guy's green car. Mrs Collins is crying.' Kyle's voice broke. 'Dad, don't let anything happen to Meg.'

Tailing Meghan as she followed the Cadillac deeper into the countryside, Bernie felt slow, burning anger. He'd wanted to be alone with her with no one else around. Then she'd met up with that other car. Suppose the guy Meg was with tried to give him trouble? Bernie patted his pocket. It was there. He never could remember if he had it with him. He wasn't supposed to carry it, and he'd even tried to leave it in the basement. But when he met somebody he liked and started to think about her all the time, he got nervous and a lot of things started to be different.

Bernie left the car behind the clump of evergreens, took his camera and carefully approached the cluster of ramshackle buildings. Now that he was up close he could see that the farmhouse was smaller than it seemed from a distance. What he'd thought was an enclosed porch was actually a storage shed. Next to that was the barn. There was just enough space for him to slide in sideways between the house and the storage shed.

The passageway was dark and musty, but he knew it was a good hiding place. From behind the buildings he could hear their voices clearly. He knew that, like the window in the inn, this was a good place for him to watch and not be seen.

Reaching the end of the passageway, he peeked out just enough to see what was going on.

Meghan was with a man Bernie had never seen before, and they were standing near what appeared to be an old well, about twenty feet away. They were facing each other, talking. The sedan was parked between them and where Bernie was hiding, so he crouched down and crept forward, hidden from sight by the car. Then he stopped, lifted his camera and began to videotape them.

60

'Phillip, before Dad gets here, I think I know the reason for Helene Petrovic being at Manning.'

'What is it, Meg?'

She ignored the oddly detached tone in Phillip's voice. 'When I was in Helene Petrovic's house yesterday, I saw pictures of young children in her study. Some of them are the same pictures I'd seen on the walls of Dr Williams' office at the Franklin Center in Philadelphia.

'Phillip, those kids weren't born through the Manning Clinic, and I'm sure I understand Helene's connection to them. She wasn't losing embryos at Manning through carelessness. I believe she was stealing those embryos and giving them to Dr Williams for use in his donor program at Franklin.'

Why was Phillip looking at her like that? she wondered suddenly. Didn't he believe her? 'Think about

296

it, Phillip,' she urged. 'Helene worked under Dr Williams for six months at Manning. For three years before that, when she was a secretary at Dowling, she used to haunt the laboratory. Now we can connect her to Williams at that time as well.'

Now Phillip seemed at ease. 'Meg, it fits. And you think that Victor, not your father, sent the letter recommending Petrovic to Manning?'

'Absolutely. Dad was in Scottsdale. Annie had been in an accident and was close to death. We can prove Dad wasn't in the office when that letter was sent.'

'I'm sure you can.'

The call from Phillip Carter to Dr Henry Williams had come in at three-fifteen Saturday afternoon. Carter had demanded that Williams be summoned from examining a client. The conversation had been brief but chilling.

'Meghan Collins has tied you to Petrovic,' Carter told him, 'although she thinks Orsini sent the letter of recommendation. And I know that Orsini's been up to something, and may even suspect what happened. We could still be all right, but no matter what, keep your mouth shut. Refuse to answer questions.'

Somehow Henry Williams managed to get through the rest of his appointments. The last one was completed at four-thirty. That was when the Franklin Assisted Reproduction Center closed on Saturdays.

His secretary looked in on him. 'Dr Williams, is there anything else I can do for you?'

Nobody can do anything for me, he thought. He managed a smile. 'No, nothing, thank you, Eva.'

'Doctor, are you all right? You don't look well.'

'I'm fine. Just a bit weary.'

By four-forty-five everyone on the staff had left and he was alone. Williams reached for the picture of his deceased wife, leaned back in his chair and studied it. 'Marie,' he said softly, 'I didn't know what I was getting

297

into. I honestly thought that I was accomplishing some good. Helene believed that too.'

He replaced the picture, folded his hands under his chin and stared ahead. He did not notice that the shadows outside were deepening.

Carter had gone mad. He had to be stopped.

Williams thought of his son and daughter. Henry Jr was an obstetrician in Seattle. Barbara was an endocrinologist in San Francisco. What would this scandal do to them, especially if there was a long trial?

The truth was going to come out. It was inevitable. He knew that now.

He thought of Meghan Collins, the questions she had asked him. Had she suspected that he was lying to her?

And her father. Appalling enough to know without having to ask that Carter had murdered Helene to silence her. Had he anything to do with Edwin Collins' disappearance as well? And should Edwin Collins be blamed for what others had done?

Should Helene be blamed for mistakes she hadn't made?

Dr Henry Williams took a pad from his desk and began to write. He had to explain, to make it very clear, to try to undo the harm he had done.

When he was finished, he put the pages he had written in an envelope. Meghan Collins was the one who deserved to present this to the authorities. He had done her and her family a grave disservice.

Meghan had left her card. Williams found it, addressed the envelope to her at Channel 3 and carefully stamped it.

He stopped for a long minute to study the pictures of the children who had been born because their mothers had come to his clinic. For an instant the bleakness in his heart was relieved at the sight of their young faces.

Dr Henry Williams turned out the light as he left his office for the last time.

He carried the envelope to his car, stopped at a nearby mailbox and dropped it in. Meghan Collins would receive it by Tuesday.

By then it wouldn't matter to him any more.

The sun was getting lower. A wind was flattening the short blades of yellowed grass. Meghan shivered. She'd grabbed her Burberry when she'd rushed out of the house, forgetting she'd removed the lining for her trip to Scottsdale.

Phillip Carter was wearing jeans and a boxy winter jacket. His hands were in its roomy pockets. He was leaning against the open fieldstone well.

'Do you think Victor killed Helene Petrovic because she decided to quit?' he asked.

'Victor or Dr Williams. Williams might have panicked. Petrovic knew so much. She could have sent both of them to prison for years if she ever talked. Her parish priest told me he felt she had something on her mind that troubled her terribly.'

Meg began to tremble. Was it just nerves and the cold? 'I'm going to sit in the car till Dad gets here, Phillip. How far does he have to come?'

'Not far, Meg. In fact he's amazingly nearby.' Phillip took his hands out of his pockets. The right hand held a gun. He gestured toward the well. 'Your psychic was right, Meg. Your dad's under water. And he's been dead a long time.'

Don't let anything happen to Meg! It was the prayerful plea Mac whispered as he and Kyle entered the inn. Inside, the reception area was teeming with police and media. Employees and guests watched from doorways. In the adjacent sitting room, Catherine was perched at the edge of the small sofa, Virginia Murphy beside her. Catherine's face was ashen.

When Mac approached her, she reached up and clasped his hands. 'Mac, Victor Orsini's talked to the police.

Phillip was behind all this. Can you believe it? I trusted him so completely. We think he's the one who called Meg, pretending to be Edwin. And there's a man who's following her, a dangerous man with a history of obsessive attachments to unsuspecting women. He's probably the one who scared Kyle on Halloween. The New York police phoned John Dwyer about him. And now Meghan is gone, and we don't know why she left or where she is. I'm so afraid I don't know what to do. I can't lose her, Mac. I couldn't stand that.'

Arlene Weiss rushed into the sitting room. Mac recognized her. 'Mrs Collins, a traffic helicopter crew thinks they spotted the green car on an old farm near West Redding. We told them to stay out of the area. We'll be there in less than ten minutes.'

Mac gave Catherine what he hoped was a reassuring embrace. 'I'll find Meg,' he promised. 'She'll be all right.'

Then he ran outside. The reporter and cameraman from New Haven were rushing toward their helicopter. Mac followed them, scrambling behind them into the chopper. 'Hey, you can't get on here,' the burly reporter shouted over the roar of the engine revving up for takeoff.

'Yes, I can,' Mac said. 'I'm a doctor. I may be needed.'

'Shut the door,' the reporter yelled to the pilot. 'Get this thing in the air.'

Meghan stared in confusion. 'Phillip, I . . . I don't understand,' she stammered. 'My father's body is in that well?' Meg stepped forward, placing her hands on the rough, rounded surface. Her fingertips curled over the edge, feeling the clammy dampness of the stone. She was no longer aware of Phillip or the gun he was pointing at her or the barren fields behind him or the cold, biting wind.

She stared down into the yawning hole with numbing horror, imagining her father's body lying at the bottom.

300

'You won't be able to see him, Meg. There isn't much water down there, hasn't been for years, but enough to cover him. He was dead when I pushed him in, if that's any consolation. I shot him the night of the bridge accident.'

Meg whirled on him. 'How could you have done that to him? He was your friend, your partner. How could you have done that to Helene and Annie?'

'You give me too much credit. I had nothing to do with Annie's death.'

'You meant to kill me. You sent me the fax saying Annie's death was a mistake.' Meg's eyes darted around. Was there any way she could get to her car? No, he'd shoot her before she'd taken a step.

'Meghan, *you* told me about the fax. It was like a gift. I needed people to believe that Ed was still alive, and you delivered the way I could do it.'

'What did you do to my father?'

'Ed called me from the office the night of the accident. He was in shock. Talked about how close he'd come to being caught in the bridge explosion. Told me he knew Orsini was cheating on us. Told me that Manning had talked about us placing an embryologist named Petrovic Ed had never heard of. He'd gone directly to the office and had been through the Manning file and couldn't find any reference to her. Blamed it on Orsini.

'Meghan, try to understand. It would have been all over. I told him to come to my house, that we'd figure it out, confront Orsini together in the morning. By the time he walked in my door he was ready to accuse me. He'd pieced it all together. Your father was very smart. He left me no choice. I knew what I had to do.'

I'm so cold, Meghan thought, so cold.

'Everything was fine for a while,' Phillip continued. 'Then Petrovic quit, telling Manning she'd made a mistake that was going to cause a lot of trouble. I couldn't take a chance that she'd give everything away, could I? The day you came to the office and talked about

301

the girl who'd been stabbed, how much she looked like you, that was when you told me about the fax. I knew your father had something going out West somewhere. It wasn't hard to figure he might have had a daughter there. This seemed the perfect time to bring him back to life.'

'You may not have sent the fax, but you made the phone call that sent Mother to the hospital. You ordered those roses and sat next to her when they were delivered. How could you have done that to her?'

Only yesterday, Meghan thought, Father Radzin told me to look for the reason.

'Meghan, I lost a lot of money in my divorce. I spent top dollar for property I'm trying to hold on to. I had a miserable childhood. I was one of ten kids living in a three-bedroom house. I'm not going back to being poor again. Williams and I found a way to make money with nobody hurt. And Petrovic cashed in, too.'

'Stealing embryos for the Franklin Center donor program?'

'You're not as smart as I thought, Meghan. There's so much more to it than that. Donor embryos are small time.'

He raised the pistol. She could see the muzzle aimed at her heart. She watched his finger tighten on the trigger, heard him say, 'I kept Edwin's car in the barn till last week. I'll keep yours in its place. And you can join him.'

In a reflex action, Meghan threw herself to the side.

His first bullet went over her head. His second hit her shoulder.

Before he could fire again, a figure came hurtling from nowhere. A heavy figure with a rigid outstretched arm. The fingers that grasped the knife and the shimmering blade itself were one, an avenging sword that sought out Phillip and found his throat.

Meghan felt blinding pain in her left shoulder. Blackness enveloped her.

302

61

When Meghan regained consciousness she was lying on the ground, her head in someone's lap. She forced her eyelids open, looked up and saw Bernie Heffernan's cherubic smile, then felt his moist kisses on her face and lips and neck.

From somewhere in the distance she heard a whirring sound. A plane? A helicopter. Then it faded and was gone.

'I'm glad I saved you, Meghan. It's all right to use a knife to save someone, isn't it?' Bernie asked. 'I never want to hurt anybody. I didn't want to hurt Annie that night. It was a mistake.' He repeated it softly, like a child. 'Annie was a mistake.'

Mac listened to the radio exchange between the police helicopter and the squad cars that were rushing to the area. They were coordinating strategy.

Meg is with two killers, he realized suddenly – that nut who was in the woods Sunday night and Phillip Carter.

Phillip Carter, who betrayed and murdered his partner, then posed as protector to Catherine and Meghan, privy to every step of Meg's search for truth.

Meghan. Meghan.

They were in a rural area. The helicopters were beginning to descend. Vainly Mac searched the ground below. It was going to be dark in fifteen minutes. How could they pick out a car when it was dark?

'We're at the outskirts of West Redding,' the pilot

303

said, pointing ahead. 'We're a couple of minutes from where they spotted the green Chevy.'

He's crazy, Meg thought. This was Bernie, the cheerful parking attendant who often told her about his mother. How did he get here? Why was he following her? And he said he had killed Annie. Dear God, he killed Annie!

She tried to sit up.

'Don't you want me to hold you, Meg? I'd never hurt you.'

'Of course you wouldn't.' She knew she had to soothe him, keep him calm. 'It's just that the ground is so cold.'

'I'm sorry. I should have known that. I'll help you.' He kept his arm around her, hugging her as they awkwardly struggled together to their feet.

The pressure of his arm around her shoulder intensified the pain from the bullet wound. She mustn't antagonize him. 'Bernie, would you try not to . . .' She was going to pass out again. 'Bernie,' she pleaded, 'my shoulder hurts so much.'

She could see the knife he had used to kill Phillip lying on the ground. Was this the knife that had taken Annie's life?

Phillip's gun was still clutched in his hand.

'Oh, I'm sorry. If you want I'll carry you.' His lips were on her hair. 'But, stand here for just a minute. I want to take your picture. See my camera?'

His camera. Of course. He must have been the cameraman in the woods who had almost strangled Kyle. She leaned against the well as he videotaped her and watched as he walked around Phillip's body, taping him.

Then Bernie laid the camera down and came over to her. 'Meghan, I'm a hero,' he bragged. His eyes were like shiny blue buttons.

'Yes, you are.'

'I saved your life.'

'Yes, you did.'

304

'But I'm not allowed to carry a weapon. A knife is a weapon. They'll put me away again, in the prison hospital. I hate it there.'

'I'll talk to them.'

'No, Meghan. That's why I had to kill Annie. She started to scream. All I did when I saw her that night was to walk up behind her and say, "This is a dangerous block. I'll take care of you."'

'You said that?'

'I thought it was you, Meghan. You'd have been glad to have me take care of you, wouldn't you?'

'Yes, of course I would.'

'I didn't have time to explain. There was a police car coming. I didn't mean to hurt her. I didn't even know I was carrying the knife that night. Sometimes I don't remember I have it.'

'I'm glad you were carrying it now.' The car, Meg thought. My keys are in it. It's my only chance. 'But Bernie, I don't think you should leave your knife here for the police to find.' She pointed to it.

He looked back over his shoulder. 'Oh, thank you, Meghan.'

'And don't forget your camera.'

If she wasn't fast enough, he'd know that she was trying to get away. And he'd have the knife in his hand. But when he turned and started to walk the half-dozen steps to Phillip's body, Meghan whirled, stumbling in her weakness and haste, yanked open her car door and slid behind the wheel.

'Meghan, what are you doing?' Bernie shrieked.

His hands grabbed the handle of the car door as she clicked the lock. He hung onto the handle as she threw the car into gear and plunged her foot down on the gas pedal.

The car leaped forward. Bernie kept his grip on the handle for ten feet, shouting at her, then let go and fell. She careened around the buildings. He was emerging

305

from the passageway between the house and shed when she headed down the dirt road through the open fields.

She had not reached the wooded area when in the rearview mirror she saw his car lurch forward in pursuit.

They were passing over a wooded area. The police helicopter was in front of them. The photographer and cameraman were straining their eyes.

'Look!' the pilot shouted. 'There's the farmhouse.'

Mac never knew what made him look back. 'Turn around,' he shouted. 'Turn around.'

Meg's white Mustang shot out of the woods, a green car inches behind it, repeatedly smashing into it. As Mac watched, the Chevy pulled alongside the Mustang and began sideswiping it, trying to run it off the road.

'Go down,' Mac shouted to the pilot. 'That's Meghan in the white car. Can't you see he's trying to kill her.'

Meghan's car was faster, but Bernie was a better driver. She had managed to stay ahead of him for a short time, but now could not escape him. He was slamming into the driver's side door. Meghan's body whipped back and forth as the air bag ballooned from the center of the wheel. For an instant she could not see, but she kept her foot on the accelerator, and the car zigzagged wildly through the field as Bernie kept attacking it.

The driver's side door smashed into her shoulder as the Mustang teetered and flipped over on its side. An instant later flames burst through the hood of the engine.

Bernie wanted to watch Meghan's car burn, but the police were coming. He could hear the scream of approaching sirens. Overhead he heard the din of a helicopter coming closer. He had to get away.

Someday you'll hurt someone, Bernie. That's what worries us. That's what the psychiatrist had told him.

306

But if he got home to Mama, she'd take care of him. He'd get another job parking cars where he could be home every night with her. From now on he'd only make phone calls to women. Nobody would find out about that.

Meghan's face was fading from his mind. He'd forget her the way he forgot all the others he had liked. I never really hurt anyone before and I didn't mean to hurt Annie, he reminded himself as he drove through the hastening darkness. Maybe they'll believe me if they find me.

He drove through the second patch of woods and reached the intersection where they'd turned off onto the dirt road. Headlights snapped on. A loudspeaker said, 'Police, Bernie. You know what to do. Get out of the car with your hands in the air.'

Bernie began to cry. 'Mama, Mama,' he sobbed as he opened the door and lifted his arms.

The car was on its side, the driver's door was pressing against her. Meghan felt for the button to release the seat belt but could not find it. She was disoriented.

She smelled smoke. It began pouring through the vent. Oh God, Meghan thought. I'm trapped. The car was resting on the passenger door.

Waves of heat began to attack her. Smoke filled her lungs. She tried to scream but no sound came.

Mac led the frantic race from the helicopter to Meg's car. Flames from the engine shot up higher just as they reached it. He could see Meg inside, struggling to free herself, her body illuminated by the flames that were spreading across the hood. 'We've got to get her out through the passenger door,' he shouted.

As one, he, the pilot, the reporter and cameraman put their hands on the superheated roof of the Mustang. As one they pushed, rocked, pushed again.

'Now,' Mac shouted. With a groan they threw their

307

weight against the car, held while tortured palms blistered.

And then the car began to move, slowly, resistantly, then finally in rapid surrender it slammed onto its tires, once more upright.

The heat was becoming unbearable. As in a dream, Meghan saw Mac's face and somehow managed to reach over and release the door lock before she passed out.

62

The helicopter landed at the Danbury Medical Center. Dazed and blinded with pain, Meghan was aware of being taken from Mac's arms, lifted onto a stretcher.

Another stretcher. Annie being rushed into Emergency. No, she thought, no. 'Mac.'

'I'm here, Meggie.'

Blinding lights. An operating room. A mask over her face. *The mask being removed from Annie's face in Roosevelt Hospital.* 'Mac.'

A hand over hers. 'I'm here, Meggie.'

She awoke in the recovery room, aware of a thick bandage on her shoulder, a nurse looking down at her. 'You're fine.'

Later they wheeled her to a room. Her mother. Mac. Kyle. Waiting for her.

Her mother's face, miraculously peaceful when their eyes met. Seeming to read her thoughts. 'Meg, they recovered Dad's body.'

Mac's arm around her mother. His bandaged hands. Mac, her tower of strength. Mac, her love.

Kyle's tearstained face next to hers. 'It's all right if you want to kiss me in front of people, Meg.'

On Sunday night, the body of Dr Henry Williams was found in his car on the outskirts of Pittsburgh, Pennsylvania, in the quiet neighborhood where he and his wife had grown up and met as teenagers. He had taken a lethal dose of sleeping pills. Letters to his son and daughter contained messages of love and pleas for forgiveness.

Meghan was able to leave the hospital on Monday morning. Her arm was in a sling, her shoulder a vague, constant ache. Otherwise she was recovering rapidly.

When she arrived home, she went upstairs to her room to change to a comfortable robe. As she started to undress, she hesitated, then went to the windows and closed the blinds firmly. I hope I get over doing that, she thought. She knew it would be a long time before she would be able to banish the image of Bernie shadowing her.

Catherine was getting off the phone. 'I've just cancelled the sale of the inn,' she said. 'The death certificate has been issued, and that means all the joint assets Dad and I held are unfrozen. The insurance adjustors are processing payment of all Dad's personal policies as well as the one from the business. It's a lot of money, Meg. Remember, the personal policies have a double indemnity clause.'

Meg kissed her mother. 'I'm so glad about the inn. You'd be lost without Drumdoe.' Over coffee and juice she scanned the morning papers. In the hospital, she'd seen the early morning television news reports about the Williams suicide. 'They're combing the Franklin Center records to try to find out who received the embryos Petrovic stole from Manning.'

309

'Meg, what a terrible thing it must be for people who had cryopreserved embryos there to wonder if their biological child was born to a stranger,' Catherine Collins said. 'Is there enough money in the world for anyone to do something like that?'

'Apparently there is. Phillip Carter told me he needed money. But Mom, when I asked him if that was what Petrovic was doing, stealing embryos for the donor program, he told me I wasn't as smart as he'd thought. There was more to it. I only hope they find out what in the records at the center.'

Meghan sipped the coffee. 'What could he have meant by that? And what happened to Stephanie Petrovic? Did Phillip kill that poor girl? Mom, her baby was due around this time.'

That night when Mac came, she said, 'Dad will be buried day after tomorrow. Frances Grolier should be notified about that and told the circumstances of Dad's death, but I dread calling her.'

Mac's arms around her. All the years she'd waited for them.

'Why not let me take care of it, Meggie?' Mac asked.

And then they'd talked. 'Mac, we don't know everything yet. Dr Williams was the last hope for understanding what Phillip meant.'

On Tuesday morning, at nine o'clock, Tom Weicker phoned. This time he did not ask the teasing-but-serious question he'd asked yesterday: 'Ready to come back to work, Meg?'

Nor did he ask how she was feeling. Even before he said, 'Meg, we've got a breaking story,' she sensed the difference in his tone.

'What is it, Tom?'

'There's an envelope marked "Personal and Confidential" for you from Dr Williams.'

'Dr Williams! Open it. Read it to me.'

310

'You're sure?'

'Tom, open it.'

There was a pause. She visualized him slitting the envelope, pulling out the contents.

'Tom?'

'Meg, this is Williams' confession.'

'Read it to me.'

'No. You have the fax machine you took home from the office?'

'Yes.'

'Give me the number again. I'll fax it to you. We'll read it together.'

Meghan gave the number to him and rushed downstairs. She got to the study in time to hear the high-pitched squeal of the fax. The first page of the statement from Dr Henry Williams slowly began to emerge on the thin, slick paper.

It was five pages long. Meghan read and reread it. Finally the reporter in her began to pick out specific paragraphs and isolated sentences.

The phone rang. She knew it was Tom Weicker. 'What do you think, Meghan?'

'It's all there. He needed money because of the bills from his wife's long illness. Petrovic was a naturally gifted person who should have been a doctor. She hated seeing cryopreserved embryos destroyed. She saw them as children who could fill the lives of childless couples. Williams saw them as children people would pay a fortune to adopt. He sounded out Carter, who was more than willing to place Petrovic at Manning, using my father's signature.'

'They had everything covered,' Weicker said, 'a secluded house where they brought illegal aliens willing to be host mothers in exchange for ten thousand dollars and a bogus green card. Not a high price when you think Williams and Carter were selling the babies for a minimum of one hundred thousand dollars each.

'In the past six years,' Weicker went on, 'they've

311

placed more than two hundred babies and were planning to open other facilities.'

'And then Helene quit,' Meghan said, 'claiming she'd made a mistake that was going to become public.

'The first thing Dr Manning did after Petrovic quit was to call Dr Williams and tell him about it. Manning trusted Williams and needed to talk to someone. He was horrified at the prospect of the clinic losing its reputation. He told Williams how upset Petrovic was and that she thought she'd lost the Anderson baby's identical twin when she slipped in the lab.

'Williams called Carter, who immediately panicked. Carter had a key to Helene's apartment in Connecticut. They weren't romantically involved. Sometimes he'd need to transport embryos she'd brought from the clinic immediately after they were fertilized and before they were cryopreserved. He'd rushed them to Pennsylvania to be transferred to a host womb.'

'Carter panicked and killed her,' Weicker agreed. 'Meg, Dr Williams gave you the address of the place where he and Carter kept those pregnant girls. We're obliged to give that information to the authorities, but we want to be there when they arrive. Are you up to it?'

'You bet I am. Tom, can you send a helicopter for me? Make it one of the big ones. You're missing something important in the Williams statement. He was the person Stephanie Petrovic contacted when she needed help. He was the one who had transferred an embryo into her womb. She's due to give birth now. If there's one redeeming feature about Henry Williams, it's that he didn't tell Phillip Carter that he'd hidden Stephanie Petrovic. If he had, her life wouldn't have been worth a plugged nickel.'

Tom promised to have a helicopter at the Drumdoe Inn within the hour. Meghan made two phone calls. One to Mac. 'Can you get away, Mac? I want you with me for this.' The second call was to a new mother. 'Can you and your husband meet me in an hour?'

The residence of Dr Williams described in his confession was forty miles from Philadelphia. Tom Weicker and the crew from Channel 3 were waiting when the helicopter carrying Meghan, Mac and the Andersons touched down in a nearby field.

A half-dozen official cars were parked nearby.

'I struck a deal that we'll go in with the authorities,' Tom told them.

'Why are we here, Meghan?' Dina Anderson asked as they got into a waiting Channel 3 car.

'If I was sure, I would tell you,' Meghan said. Every instinct told her she was right. In his confession, Williams had written, 'I had no idea when Helene brought Stephanie to me and asked me to transfer an embryo into her womb that if a pregnancy resulted, Helene intended to raise the baby as her own.'

The young women in the old house were in various stages of pregnancy. Meghan saw the heartsick fear on their faces when they were confronted by the authorities. 'You will not send me home, please?' a teenager begged. 'I did just what I promised. When the baby is born, you will pay me, please?'

'Host mothers,' Mac whispered to Meghan. 'Did Williams indicate if they kept any records of whose babies these girls are carrying?'

'His confession said they're all the babies of women who have embryos cryopreserved at Manning,' Meghan said. 'Helene Petrovic came here regularly to be sure these girls were well cared for. She wanted all the cryopreserved embryos to have a chance to be born.'

Stephanie Petrovic was not there. A weeping practical nurse said, 'She's at the local hospital. That's where all our girls give birth. She's in labor.'

313

'Why are we here?' Dina Anderson asked again an hour later, when Meghan returned to the hospital lobby.

Meghan had been allowed to be with Stephanie in the last moments of her labor.

'We're going to see Stephanie's baby in a few minutes,' she said. 'She had it for Helene. That was their bargain.'

Mac pulled Meghan aside. 'Is it what I think?'

She did not answer. Twenty minutes later the obstetrician who had delivered Stephanie's baby stepped off the elevator and beckoned to them. 'You can come up now,' he said.

Dina Anderson reached for her husband's hand. Too overwhelmed to speak, she wondered, Is it possible?

Tom Weicker and the cameraman accompanied them and began taping as a smiling nurse brought the blanket-wrapped infant to the window of the nursery and held it up.

'It's Ryan!' Dina Anderson shrieked. 'It's Ryan!'

The next day, at a private funeral mass at St. Paul's, the mortal remains of Edwin Richard Collins were consigned to the earth. Mac was at the grave with Catherine and Meg.

I've shed so many tears for you, Dad, Meg thought. I don't think I have any left in me. And then she whispered so silently that no one could hear, 'I love you, Daddy.'

Catherine thought of the day when her door bell had rung and there stood Edwin Collins, handsome, with the quick smile she'd so loved, a dozen roses in his hands. *I'm courting you, Catherine.*

After a while I'll remember only the good times, she promised herself.

Hand in hand the three walked to the waiting car.

An Exclusive Interview With

MARY HIGGINS CLARK

The "Queen of Suspense" Talks About Her Life and Work

What inspired All Around the Town?

I became intrigued by a psychological problem due to childhood trauma, a major element of *All Around the Town*.

Laurie Kenyon, 21 years old, is a senior at a New Jersey college. Obsessed with her English professor, Allan Grant, a married man, she had been hiding outside his home, watching him through the sliding glass doors of his study and writing him passionate love letters. When he is found stabbed to death, Laurie's fingerprints are everywhere – on the door, on his desk, on the knife. Laurie is arraigned on a murder charge, but has no memory of the crime.

Attorney Sarah Kenyon, Laurie's older sister, believes that the key to Laurie's defense lies in the trauma caused by her abduction at age four, an experience she cannot recall. Sarah brings in Dr. Justin Donnelly, a prominent psychiatrist, to help Laurie break through to these two lost years.

What Sarah does not know is that Bic Hawkins, a fundamentalist preacher and his wife Opal, Laurie's abductors, are now famous television evangelists. Before releasing her, Bic had threatened Laurie with death if she ever talked about him and Opal. If Laurie does remember what transpired during the two years she was with them, Bic and Opal will be ruined. They have too much at stake to take that chance.

In controversial court cases, similar psychology factors have influenced judgments of defendants' culpability.

How did you become interested in multiple personality disorder?

I have always been fascinated by the condition of multiple personality disorder. I remember as a small child hearing about a woman who would lose whole blocks of time, who would one day awaken and be a totally different personality. The woman's doctor thought it was a thyroid problem.

Then, nearly twenty years ago, I read *Sybil* and really began to understand and sympathize with all the ramifications of the causes and effects of this disorder. A fictional story concerning it began in my subconscious.

Two years ago, a friend who is an art therapist at the National Center for the Treatment of Dissociative Disorders visited me and asked me to sign a book for one of her patients, an M.P.D. When I asked the name, she hesitated and said, "Let's see, which personality reads your books?" At that moment, I knew the time had come to tell that story.

You write convincingly of the processes of law. Have you ever worked in a law firm?

No. I have no formal legal experience, but my two oldest children are lawyers. One of them, my daughter, a former prosecutor, is now a Superior Court Judge. I have always listened to discussions of law, always attended trials around the country and studied newspapers for intriguing cases. I never take a case and fictionalize it, but an aspect of a case may provide the basis for an idea.

For the last several years, a new legal defense has been presented in courts in the United States – the multiple personality defense. For example: "I am not a drug user. My alter personality, Grace, takes drugs." Using this defense in cases where the accused person's host personality was not aware of committing a crime seemed to me to be a potentially powerful subject.

What prompted you to choose the world of personal ads as a background for Loves Music, Loves to Dance?

People in all walks of life are turning to personal ads to find romance or companionship. Personal ads, however, are risky. In the search for that "someone," people are throwing caution to the winds. Meeting strangers on an anonymous basis is dangerous, especially for women. Women can fall prey to sexual harrassment, rape, even murder. Yet personal ads are a growing trend. With the pace of modern living, there is less and less opportunity to meet others through traditional channels – family, friends, community. That is why personal ads are an integral part of newspapers and magazines in the largest city or the smallest hamlet. They have become big business in America. The scary aspect is that you are taking on faith what a stranger tells you – his name, his job, his marital status, his background.

Three years ago, I was Chairman of the International Crime Writers Congress, I was dashing from panel to panel to make sure that all was going well. When I stopped in the auditorium where an FBI agent was speaking, I stayed for the whole lecture. He was talking about a serial killer who had enticed his victims through personal ads. The words "loves music, loves to dance" walked through my mind and I knew the seed for another book had been planted.

How did you come into contact with the FBI for your research?

The speaker that day was Robert Ressler, Director of Behavioral Forensic Services, who has since retired from the FBI. As the FBI's top criminologist and Serial Murder and Violent Crime expert, he had conducted original research in violent criminal behavior and interviewed some of the most notorious criminals such as David Berkowitz, the "Son of Sam Killer"; Ted Bundy, killer of over 35 women; Richard T. Chase, the "Vampire Killer"; John Wayne Gacy, Chicago killer of 33 boys; and Charles Manson. Robert Ressler acted as my consultant on *Loves Music, Loves to Dance*.

What are some cases of women murdered through personal ads?

The first serial killer to be recognized in criminology to use the technique of personal ads to lure his victims was Harvey Glatman, who placed ads for both dates and models. Glatman killed seven young women. In each case, he performed a ritual. Before strangling them, he would photograph them, with their hands and mouths taped. I saw the photographs he had taken of these terrified young women. Harvey Glatman, who was executed for his murders, is considered a classic case. Since then, the FBI has become aware of other cases of homicide which have occurred as a result of women answering personal ads. Men who perpetrated such murders have managed to go unsuspected for years. They are often extremely intelligent and personable – just the kind of guy a mother would like her daughter to bring home.

Where do you get the inspiration for your plots?

From real life. I attend criminal trials regularly. The amount of coincidence in crime is staggering. For example, a young nurse in New Jersey was on her way to work and someone got into her car at a red light. A few minutes later she was dead. She was going to work. She wasn't doing anything foolish. She is typical of characters in my books – people to whom things happen, who are not looking for trouble.

What kind of people do you write about?

Nice people whose lives are invaded by evil. They are people with whom we can identify – leading ordinary lives and going about their business. My heroines are strong women who take a major role in solving their own problems. A man may come in to help at the end, but the woman herself basically copes with the menacing situation.

You introduce us to widely differing worlds in your writings. How do you achieve the sense of authenticity that characterizes your novels?

New settings provide a springboard for fresh and different characters. Backgrounds for my novels include medicine, law, government, fashion, social trends such as the personal ads phenomenon in *Loves Music, Loves to Dance*. For all my books, I do substantial research to give them a flavor of authenticity.

What is the basis of your first bestseller, Where Are the Children?

In New York, there was a sensational case in which a beautiful young mother was on trial for murdering her two small children. I didn't write about that case but imagined: Suppose your children disappear and you are accused of killing them – and then it happens again.

Where Are the Children? is about a woman whose past holds a terrible secret. Nancy Harmon had been found guilty of murdering her two children but was released from prison on a legal technicality. She abandons her old life, changes her appearance and leaves San Francisco to seek tranquillity in Cape Cod. Now she has married again, has two more lovely children and a life filled with happiness . . . until the morning when she looks for her children, finds only a tattered mitten and knows that the nightmare is beginning again.

The theme of a missing child struck a personal chord in me. Once when we moved to a new home, my youngest daughter, Patty, was briefly missing. That's when I experienced the panic any mother feels under these circumstances.

Weep No More, My Lady *takes place in a luxurious spa. Why did you choose this setting for a suspense novel?*

It used to be only the rich who could afford to go to spas. Today, with widespread interest in health and beauty, spas are accessible to everyone. An intriguing thought crossed my mind: Suppose a killer in a wet suit is stalking the grounds of one of these spas . . .

The story revolves around the mysterious death of stage and screen star Leila LaSalle. Was her fall from her penthouse terrace suicide or murder? This is the question plaguing her sister, beautiful Elizabeth Lange. Min, an old friend of Leila's, is the owner of luxurious Cypress Point Spa. She invites Elizabeth to the spa, where she encounters a cast of characters each of whom had a motive for killing her sister – and one who is now trying to murder her.

I thoroughly enjoyed my research on this novel. I went to luxurious spas in this country and in Europe and then created my own. In the character of Leila, I envisioned Rita Hayworth, one of the most beautiful women who ever graced the screen. This book is not about her or her personality, but I saw her physical appearance when I created Leila.

How did you get the intimate knowledge of the fashion world, the setting of While My Pretty One Sleeps?

I grew up hearing about the world of fashion from my mother, who had been the bridal buyer at B. Altman's. I also wrote a syndicated radio show, "Women Today," for which I regularly interviewed designers and fashion editors and attended fashion events. It gave me the chance to see both the glamour and the agony of the fashion industry.

Ethel Lambston, prominent gossip writer, is about to rock the fashion industry with an exposé revealing the secrets of top fashion designers. The story opens with Ethel's killer driving, in a blinding snowstorm, to a state park in Rockland County, N.Y., to bury Ethel's body. The first to notice Ethel's disappearance is Neeve Kearney, beautiful young owner of an exclusive Madison Avenue boutique where Ethel bought all her clothes. She lives with her father, Myles Kearney. A retired police commissioner, he has never forgiven himself because his wife was murdered after he ignored a threat to her life. Neeve becomes deeply involved in the investigation of Ethel's murder. She also becomes a target for the killer.

In this novel, I have included themes based on my view of family relations. I created a strong father-daughter relationship because I am tired of books about parents and children at each other's throats. I got along well with my parents and I get along fine with my children. The book also has a strong love story reflecting my belief that some people are meant for each other.

The Anastasia Syndrome and Other Stories, *a novella and short stories, covers such themes as parapsychology and supernatural phenomena. Have you delved into these subjects?*

Yes, I took a course in parapsychology at New York's New School of Social Research, during which I observed people being regressed to former lifetimes. I don't believe in reincarnation, but I am fascinated by its dramatic possibilities.

The novella, *The Anastasia Syndrome*, was inspired by the true story of Anna Anderson, the woman who claimed to be the Grand Duchess Anastasia. The issue of Anna Anderson's claim has been debated and tried in court for over fifty years and remains, to this day, an enigma. In *The Anastasia Syndrome*, Judith Chase, a prominent historical writer, is living in London and becoming traumatized by early childhood memories of bombing raids during World War II, in which she was orphaned. She goes to a prominent psychiatrist for help and becomes the victim of his experiments in regression. She is regressed not only to her childhood tragedy, but to 1660, the era of the Civil War in England. In this regression process, she absorbs the persona of murderous Lady Margaret Carew, a woman with a mission of vengeance. In her persona of Lady Carew, Judith becomes the subject of a massive hunt by Scotland Yard.

The four stories in *The Anastasia Syndrome and Other Stories* deal with such themes as obsession and supernatural phenomena. Obsessive love is the theme of "Terror Stalks the Class Reunion." A supernatural phenomenon occurs in "Double Vision." "Lucky Day" begins with a premonition of imminent danger. "The Lost Angel" is a Christmas story in which a mother's intuition becomes the overpowering force in the search for a lost child.

The book reflects an intense personal interest on my part in such phenomena as sixth sense and thought transference.